Praise for
Bitter in the Mouth

"A moving investigation of invented families and small town subterfuge . . . Reminiscent of *The Heart is a Lonely Hunter,* with its hurt souls nursing private truths and yearning for love."
—*The New York Times Book Review*

"In *The Writing Life,* Annie Dillard advises would-be writers to find their bone, the thing that drives them to write. . . . Monique Truong's bone is the outsider's plight, and her pen is a scalpel, laying perfect words down along that nerve until even the happiest reader understands what it means to forever stand apart from your family and the larger society you inhabit." —*Los Angeles Times*

"Fast-moving and beautifully strange . . . [Linda's] tasting words . . . quickly becomes second nature and eventually, metaphorical poetry. It has a poignancy that sneaks up on you, just like Truong's entire clever tale." —*Time Out New York*

"A deeply compassionate and artfully crafted novel."
—*O: The Oprah Magazine*

"Truong is amply aware of the power of [words]. . . . [She] wields her narrative like a quarterstaff, knocking readers' expectations right out from under them." —*The Washington Post*

"A fascinating conceit and a bright riff on the power of language."
—*San Francisco Chronicle*

"A flavorful, haunting journey . . . Truong is a powerful writer."
—*The Oregonian*

"Truong's work begins to take on its own distinctive flavor, a fusion of the palpable and the intangible. . . . A rare, refreshing palate—one to savor."
—*The Miami Herald*

"Linda's extraordinary tale is the coming-of-age story of 'smart girls' everywhere."
—*Ms. Magazine*

"A book that offers up a taste of something many of us search all our lives to find—that unique flavor we hope to finally recognize as our own authentic selves."
—*Atlanta Journal-Constitution*

"Devour this novel."
—*Ladies' Home Journal*

"A uniquely creative and captivating account of a young woman discovering herself."
—*Lambda Literary*

"Truong's mesmerizing prose beautifully captures [the heroine's] taste-saturated world, and her portrait of a broken family's secretive pockets and genuine moments of connection is affecting."
—*Publishers Weekly* (starred review)

"Absorbing . . . Truong is a gifted storyteller, and in this quietly powerful novel she has created a compelling and unique character."
—*Booklist* (starred review)

"Be prepared for a full range of tastes of life in *Bitter in the Mouth*: friendship, loyalty, love, family, and, above all, the mysteries at every corner of one's history that make us who we are. Monique Truong is a great observer and a beautiful writer."

—Yiyun Li, author of *Gold Boy, Emerald Girl*

"Monique Truong creates a world so subtle, mysterious, moving, and sensory that it heightens our consciousness of those qualities in our own lives. *Bitter in the Mouth* is the rare novel that makes one life story unique and universal at the same time."

—Gloria Steinem

Also by Monique Truong

The Book of Salt

Watermark: Vietnamese American Poetry and Prose
(co-editor)

Bitter in the Mouth

- immigrant
- Vietnamese-American
- has won multiple awards
- B.I.T.M (2010)
- The Sweetest Fruits (2020)
- moved to U.S. in the 70s

Bitter in the Mouth

A Novel

Monique Truong

Random House Trade Paperbacks  New York

2011 Random House Trade Paperback Edition

Published in the United States by Random House Trade Paperbacks, an imprint of The Random House Publishing Group, a division of Random House, Inc., New York.

RANDOM HOUSE TRADE PAPERBACKS and colophon are trademarks of Random House, Inc.
RANDOM HOUSE READER'S CIRCLE & Design is a registered trademark of Random House, Inc.

Originally published in hardcover in the United States by Random House, an imprint of The Random House Publishing Group, a division of Random House, Inc., in 2010.

Grateful acknowledgment is made to the following for permission to reprint previously published material:
Hal Leonard Corporation: Excerpt from "He Called Me Baby," words and music by Harlan Howard, copyright © 1961 (renewed 1989) by Beechwood Music Corp.; excerpt from "Coat of Many Colors," words and music by Dolly Parton, copyright © 1969 (renewed 1997) by Velvet Apple Music; excerpt from "Reunited," words and music by Dino Fekaris and Freddie Perren, copyright © 1978, 1979 by Universal-Polygram International Publishing, Inc. and Perren-Vibes Music, Inc. All rights controlled and administered by Universal-Polygram International Publishing, Inc.; excerpt from "You Belong to Me," words and music by Pee Wee King, Redd Stewart and Chilton Price, copyright © 1952 (renewed) by Ridgeway Music Company, Inc. All rights reserved. International copyright secured. Reprinted by permission of Hal Leonard Corporation.
Hal Leonard Corporation and Cherry Lane Music Corporation: Excerpt from "Come Fly With Me," words by Sammy Cahn, music by James Van Heusen, copyright © 1958 by Cahn Music Co., WB Music Corp. and Maraville Music Corp. Copyright renewed. All rights for Cahn Music Co. administered by WB Music Corp. International copyright secured. All rights reserved. Reprinted by permission of Hal Leonard Corporation and Cherry Lane Music Corporation..

Library of Congress Cataloging-in-Publication Data
Truong, Monique T. D.
Bitter in the mouth: a novel / by Monique Truong.
p. cm
ISBN 978-0-8129-8132-2
eBook ISBN 978-0-6796-0342-9
I. Title.
PS3620.R86B57 2010
813'6—dc22
2009051674

Printed in the United States of America

www.randomhousereaderscircle.com

Book design by Elizabeth A. D. Eno

For my mother

"An' they chased him 'n' never could catch him 'cause they didn't know what he looked like, an' Atticus, when they finally saw him . . . he was real nice. . . ."

His hands were under my chin, pulling up the cover, tucking it around me.

"Most people are, Scout, when you finally see them."

—To Kill a Mockingbird

six narrative elements of fiction:
theme, plot, point of view, setting,
characters, style

CONFESSION

. . . August 3, 1998

Chapter 1

I fell in love with my great-uncle Harper because he taught me how to dance. He said that rhythm was allowing yourself to feel your blood coursing through you. He told me to close my eyes and forget the rest of my body. I did, and we bopped our nonexistent selves up and down and side to side. He liked me because I was a quiet child. He showed me photographs of himself as a boy. He referred to himself in the third person. This here is Harper Evan Burch, he would say. The boy in those photographs was also a quiet child. I could tell from the way that his arms were always flat by his side, never akimbo or raised high to the North Carolina sky. We were both compact, always folding ourselves into smaller pieces. We both liked music because it was a river where we stripped down, jumped in, and flailed our arms around. It was 1975 then, and the water everywhere around us was glittery with disco lights. My great-uncle Harper and I, though, danced to Elvis Presley, Jerry Lee Lewis, and Fats Domino. We twisted, mashed-potatoed, and winked at each other whenever we opened our eyes. My great-uncle Harper was my first love. I was seven years old. In his company, I laughed out loud.

I'm not ashamed to admit that I have tried to find him in the male bodies that I lie next to and that I see him now only when I turn off the lights. His bow tie undone, hanging around his shirt collar—modest isosceles triangles, considering the fashion at the time, his pants cuffed and creased, his graying hair cut the same as when he was a boy, a wedge of it hanging over one eye, the other one a blue lake dappled by the sun.

My great-uncle Harper wasn't where I thought I would begin, but a family narrative should begin with love. Because he was my first love I was spared the saddest experience in most people's lives. My first love and my first heartbreak were dealt by different pairs of hands. I was lucky. My memories of the two sensations, one of my heart filling and one of it emptying, were divided and lodged in separate bodies. I can still recall the feeling that came over me when my great-uncle Harper first placed the record needle onto a spinning 45. It happened right away. I felt that everything deep within my body was rising to the surface, that my skin was growing thin, that I would come apart. If this sounds painful, it wasn't. It was what love did to my body, which was to transform it. I would come apart like a fireworks display, a burst of light that would grow larger and glow, and make the person below me say, "Ah!" I remembered saying my great-uncle's name aloud. This memory of my first love was then safe from all that was to come.

I'll tell you the easy things first. I'll use simple sentences. So factual and flat, these statements will land in between us like playing cards on a table: My name is Linda Hammerick. I grew up in Boiling Springs, North Carolina. My parents were Thomas and DeAnne. My best friend was named Kelly. I was my father's tomboy. I was my mother's baton twirler. I was my high school's valedictorian. I went far away for college and law school. I live now in New York City. I miss my great-uncle Harper.

But once these cards have been thrown down, there are bound to be distorting overlaps, the head of the Queen of Spades on the body of the King of Clubs, the Joker's bowed legs beneath a field of hearts: I grew up in (Thomas and Kelly). My parents were (valedictorian and baton twirler). My best friend was named (Harper). I was my father's (New York City). I was my mother's (college and law school). I was my high school's (tomboy). I went far away for (Thomas and DeAnne). I live now in (Boiling Springs). I miss (Linda Hammerick). The only way to sort out the truth is to pick up the cards again, slowly, examining each one.

My grandmother Iris Burch Whatley died on February 14, 1987. She had never told a lie, and the fear of that had kept our family, a shrinking brood, together. As her health began to fail, we began to show our true colors. When she passed away, we bloomed like the petals of an heirloom rose, which then faded and fell to pieces. Iris was my mother's mother and my great-uncle Harper's older sister.

For a woman on her deathbed, my grandmother Iris looked remarkably pulled together. Her eyebrows had been freshly drawn in. Her lips were a frosted coral. Her gray hair had just been done in a modified, somewhat modernized bouffant. She had a visiting nurse and a visiting beautician. They were some of the perks of dying at home.

What I know about you, little girl, would break you in two. Those were the last words that my grandmother ever said to me.

Bitch, I said back to her in a voice as calm as if she had asked me for the time and I, standing by her bedside, had replied, Noon.

My great-uncle Harper let out a single hiccup, which was his way of suppressing a laugh. My grandmother's milky blue eyes closed and didn't open up again, according to my great-uncle, until a full minute later. DeAnne (that was what I called my mother by then) took that time to whisper, Hush your mouth, Linda. Then she pointed an outraged finger at the door, which I slammed shut on my way out.

For DeAnne, that exchange was a final excruciating example of what her seventy-four-year-old mother and her nineteen-year-old daughter had in common. My grandmother Iris and I were both speaking the truth, and DeAnne couldn't stand to hear it.

DeAnne had called me home from college to say my goodbyes:

Take a plane, Linda. For God's sake, don't take the bus again.

Are you sure this time? I've three exams next week—

I'll pay for the ticket.

Fine.

That was the longest conversation DeAnne and I had had in months. I loved my mother from the age of seven to eleven. That was four good years we had together, which was longer than most marriages. I would learn that bit of statistics in my sophomore psychology class, The American Family at the End of the 20th Century: Dysfunction, Dysfunction, What's Your Function? During my four years at Yale, I would gravitate toward classes with the word "dysfunction" featured prominently in the title or repeated at least several times in the course descriptions. I also would wish with every bone in my body that my father was still alive so that I could share with him what I had learned.

When my father died (he preceded Iris, to my great regret), he and DeAnne had been married for almost twenty-five years, many of them happy. The "happy" part was also according to my great-uncle Harper. I saw only the other parts. There was no physical violence or sobs or expletives. There was only unhappiness. I had no older brothers and sisters to report to me of better times: Mom and Dad used to give each other a kiss between saying "good" and "morning"; Dad tied on an apron every Sunday night and made grilled cheese sandwiches and tomato soup from a can; Mom stayed in the kitchen with him and flipped through a magazine. All of that, if it took place, was lost to me.

I don't know why but I knew that my father was going to leave me too soon. So I missed him even when he was alive. Every time he left town on business, usually just an overnight trip to Raleigh, I would catch a cold. When he came back home, I would get well.

For his part, my father never thought about missing me. Of course, he would be there to see me graduate from high school, attend his alma maters, enter the profession that nourished him, live in the city that he shared with me at bedtime in lieu of a fairy tale.

My grandmother Iris's funeral was delayed by a week because of the flowers. After her second heart attack, Iris had told us that she wanted magnolias on her coffin. Boughs and boughs of them, a cascading river of glossy green leaves with brown suede undersides, creamy blossoms the size of soup bowls floating among them. Iris didn't go into such details, but that was how my great-uncle Harper had envisioned the flowers when his sister told him what she expected. But in the middle of February, there weren't any magnolias to be had in Boiling Springs or anywhere else in the state of North Carolina. The florist in nearby Shelby had to special-order them from a wholesaler in New York City, who had to wait for a midweek shipment from somewhere in South America before the branches could be overnighted to Boiling Springs in a box almost as large as my grandmother's coffin. Baby Harper (*that* was what my grandmother had called her little brother since the day he was born, and that was sixty-three years ago by then) made all the funeral arrangements, and he would be the first to say that the flowers were the most complex and challenging part of it all. He took copious notes. Do's and don'ts for when his day came:

- ✳ Do have the wake at the Cecil T. Brandon Home of Eternal Rest; ask for the "Dignified Departure" package.
- ✳ Don't waste money on real flowers; one dead thing is enough.
- ✳ Do use a caterer from Asheville; see folder labeled "Victuals" for phone numbers and addresses.
- ✳ Don't place an order for the deviled eggs; they are delicious, but the old people will pass gas.

My great-uncle made a folder for his notes, showed it to me, and then alphabetized it in his personal files under *T* for "The End."

Before his retirement my great-uncle Harper was a librarian at Gardner-Webb Baptist College, the intellectual hub of Boiling Springs. At work his methodology was conventional and efficient, but that wasn't the case in his own home. His books were shelved in alphabetical order but not by titles. *A* for "Acerbic," *B* for "Buy Another Copy as Gift," *C* for "Cow Dung, as in This Stinks," *D* for "Devastating," *E* for "Explore Further," *F* for "Foreign" (foreign meant that my great-uncle couldn't relate to the characters in the book, not that the author was from another country), and so on. He would explain the system to me and give me typewritten pages identifying all twenty-six categories. This and his "The End" folder would be the closest documents to a will that Baby Harper (he had admitted to me long ago that he liked being called *that,* even when his sister, Iris, wasn't around) would ever prepare. When Iris passed away, my great-uncle had never left the continental United States, and the acquisition of the magnolias for her coffin made him think about places in the world even more southern than where he was born and raised. That thought sent him to the bookstore, where he bought a couple of travel guides and a novel, *One Hundred Years of Solitude.* Baby Harper filed these books under *E.*

My grandmother Iris was what her doctor called a "brittle" diabetic. During the course of a given day, her blood sugar levels would spike and then plunge precipitously. This roller-coastering exerted a tremendous amount of stress on her internal organs, especially her heart. She was lucky to have lived so long after the onset of the disease. The diagnosis of her diabetes had coincided with the fifth anniversary of the death of her husband, Walter Wendell Whatley. I have no memories of my grandfather, or Judge Whatley, as the rest of the county called him. Fifteen years my grandmother Iris lived on in Boiling Springs without him. After the first ten on her own, she told me that she wasn't lucky to have lived so long. She knew that I was the only one in her family who wasn't unnerved by her honesty.

Sadness attacked my grandmother at the weakest point of her body—her mouth. She loved her husband, but she had always lusted for sugar. While Walter Wendell was still alive, she stayed away from sweets, particularly the doughy and fried variety, in order to keep his eyes on her figure. Her dress size, a respectable eight, and her hairdo, a shoulder-length froth that required twice-weekly visits to Miss Cora's Beauty Emporium, had remained unchanged from the day that she had met Walter Wendell. Once he passed on, there was no good reason for her to stay the same. She cut several inches off her hair, setting her short locks in hot rollers by herself unless it was a special occasion. She also crammed herself with jelly doughnuts, apple fritters, cinnamon twists, and chocolate-covered crullers. The closest Krispy Kreme—she liked the one-stop shopping—was across the state line in Spartanburg, South Carolina. My great-uncle Harper told me that during the first year of Iris's solitary life in the green-shuttered colonial on Piedmont Street, she drove the thirty-eight miles between Boiling Springs and Spartanburg so often that she could do it in the darkness of the predawn with her eyes closed, dreaming of Walter Wendell.

As with most addicts, my grandmother Iris liked to share the experience. She was the one who gave me my first full bottle of Dr Pepper, straight from the fridge, not even bothering with a glass. I was seven at the time (already dancing with my great-uncle Harper), and I thought it was the beginning of something great between my grandmother and me. Iris took out a bottle for herself, and with three swigs she emptied every drop of its molasses-colored liquid.

Don't tell anyone, she said as she dabbed the corners of her mouth with a paper napkin.

About the Dr Pepper? I asked.

No, you little canary, she replied. About how I let you drink it straight from the bottle.

I remembered looking down at what was cold in my hands. There were sweat beads rolling down the glass bottle, just like in a television commercial. The bottle was still almost full. The initial rush of carbonation had burned my tongue, so I was trying to sip it slowly. Thanks to my grandmother Iris I had learned an important lesson: The difference between a fact and a secret was the slithery phrase "Don't tell anyone." I felt like pouring my Dr Pepper into the sink. I went out to the backyard of my grandmother's house and soaked the roots of her dogwood tree with it instead.

My grandmother's doctor had told her to stay away from the soft drinks. They will kill you even faster than those doughnuts, he had warned her. Presented with her options, she often joked that she chose Dr Pepper over Dr. Peterman. She had known Dr. Peterman from the time that he was little Artie Peterman in grade school with her daughter, DeAnne. He was smart and a know-it-all back then too, Iris told me, but also a nose picker and a bed wetter. No fancy medical degree could change those facts, my grandmother declared. Another important life lesson had been imparted and learned: The past was an affliction for which there was no cure.

I was fourteen when my grandmother Iris had her first heart attack. The second one occurred a week into my freshman year of college. That was when I had caught the Greyhound bus home. I had packed an overnight bag and headed to the bus station, but I couldn't get my body to board the bus. I returned to the station every day until I could hand the driver my ticket. DeAnne couldn't believe it when I showed up in the hospital room a full week after we had spoken on the phone. I walked into that fluorescent-lit room humming with monitors, and I too was in a state of disbelief. My grandmother Iris was still alive.

You might as well have walked home, DeAnne said to me, her voice muffled. She had dropped her head into her hands—the left one held her relief, the right one her despair—after I had greeted her with a casual lifting of my chin.

Next time, I said.

A quick glance at the hospital bed had told me that there would be another chance to disappoint DeAnne. My grandmother Iris was still about a size fourteen, and I knew that she wasn't going to Heaven while she was still a plus size. Her husband, Walter Wendell, wouldn't recognize her, and all the fuss of dying would be for naught.

My grandmother had reached her apex at size twenty (or an eighteen at the Dress Barn in Belwood), but she had been losing weight steadily over that past year. Dr. Peterman thought he was finally getting his message across to his patient, but I knew she wasn't dropping the pounds to get better control of her diabetes and to put less strain on her heart. She had told me that she didn't need little Artie Peterman to tell her that more than a decade of consuming the equivalent of a pound of sugar a day had damaged her body beyond repair. My grandmother Iris was simply getting ready for the next stage of her life, in the same way that most brides would prepare for their wedding day.

Five months later, what was left of our family gathered in my grandmother's dining room, which had become her bedroom ever since walking upstairs became impossible for her. This time it wasn't after a heart attack but before one. Iris could feel that a third and final one was coming. She didn't consult with Dr. Peterman. She just told her daughter, DeAnne.

DeAnne had been reading a self-help book entitled *Mothers Who Don't Know How to Mother,* and she was pages away from the last chapter, "Aging and the Inevitability of Kindness." Upon hearing her mother's self-diagnosis, DeAnne must have gone up to the second-floor bathroom of her childhood home, turned on the faucets, and cried. (I was very familiar with DeAnne's belief that the sound of running water could hide grief.) After that was when DeAnne had called me and told me to take an airplane home.

I found DeAnne's book—a dog-eared page told me where she had stopped reading—in the kitchen garbage. (I was also familiar with DeAnne's belief that the trash could make things disappear.) The book was waterlogged, as if DeAnne had tried to drown it. She might have. Or she might have just dropped it, her hands clumsy from grief, into the overflowing tub. I knew that she was ashamed that she had bought the book in the first place. My father would have told her it was rubbish. No one can tell you how to live *your* life, DeAnne! Personal accountability was my father's religion. Southern Baptist was just his social circle. When my father had passed away, my great-uncle Harper and I thought that DeAnne would turn into another Iris. But so far, there had been no change in hairstyle, no weight gain. On the outside, DeAnne had stayed exactly the same.

On a bright February morning, I stood with DeAnne and Baby Harper by Iris's bedside. Is this all, my grandmother must have asked God as she looked up at our three faces. DeAnne, widowed. Alone. Baby Harper, never married. Alone. Linda . . . and that was when my grandmother said the last thing that she would say to me, her only grandchild. Iris's words—*What I know about you, little girl, would break you in two*—slipped out of her mouth, uncontrollable and unstoppable, like how all those fried pieces of glazed dough had slipped into that same hole.

My grandmother died the following morning. Valentine's Day would never be the same for us, the two Hammericks and the one Burch who remained. The red puffy hearts that decorated the shop windows and the Hallmark cards would remind us of the seventy-four-year-old one that had constricted and failed. For us, the fourteenth of February was from then on Iris's Day, and she wasn't even a saint.

About a month after my grandmother's funeral, I was in the middle of a freshman literature seminar, Dysfunctionalia: Novels of Misspent Southern Youths and Their Social Context, 1945 to the Present, and I was trying to focus on the discussion of the lesbian subtext in Carson McCullers's *The Member of the Wedding*, when the tears began to fall. I was crying not out of regret for what I had said to my grandmother but for not staying longer by that old dying woman's bedside. Another minute and her lids would have opened and her lips might have followed. Another minute and a little skeleton key might have fallen out of her mouth, rejected at last by a body ridding itself of what it didn't want to take to the grave. But now several feet of Carolina dirt and an air-locked coffin had turned that minute into something immeasurable.

I excused myself and walked out of the seminar room. The room was an aviary-like space in a Gothic Revival tower, one of many architectural pretensions that lent a sense of history to the Yale campus. The other eleven students and the visiting professor all saw the wet streaks on my face, and I knew each of them wondered who had brought me to tears. Making another student cry, while in a class, that is, with a particularly brilliant or cutting comment was a badge of honor on that campus. One of the rules of the game was that one couldn't self-congratulate. Credit for the act had to be bestowed and acknowledged by those who were present in the classroom, usually with a casual lifting of the chin.

As I walked down the spiral of stone steps that led from the crenellated tower to the vaulted main floor of the building, I thought about my father and how he had wound his body up and down those same stairs. Two generations of Hammerick men had preceded Thomas at Yale, and now there I was, a modern, slightly modified representative of the family.

I pushed open a set of heavy wooden doors and faced the month of March in New Haven, Connecticut. My head dropped and my neck retracted into my coat and scarf. My grandmother Iris had told me that the weather up North was going to break my spirit. She said that it would feel like wearing a wet wool coat during the winter months and the rest of time like sitting in a Turkish bath. I knew that she had never been to New Haven, never worn a wet wool coat, and never even seen a Turkish bath. But, of course, what Iris Burch Whatley had said was no lie. My grandmother also told me that I couldn't leave my family behind like a pair of shoes that no longer fit. What's wrong with going to Gardner-Webb Baptist College, she had asked. I remembered hearing a single hiccup after she said this to me, but I didn't remember my great-uncle Harper being in the room.

I walked to my room on Old Campus and climbed into bed. When I pulled the sheet and blanket over my head, it was only half past three in the afternoon. In that artificial darkness, I said a word softly to myself. I drew out the "Ham," lingered on the "me," and softened the clip of the "rick." I repeated the word, and with every slow joining of its three syllables, the fizzy taste of sweet licorice with a mild chaser of wood smoke flooded my mouth. A phantom swig of Dr Pepper. This one's for you, Iris. I closed my eyes and said goodbye to my grandmother, who seemed for a moment not so far away.

the name holds conflicting feelings + memories with it

-what secret was Iris talking about? the fact that Linda can taste words?

Chapter 2

My first memory was a taste. For most of my life I have carried this fact with me not as a mystery, which it still is, but as a secret. The mystery had two halves. The halves had within them other chambers and cells. There was something bitter in the mouth, and there was the word that triggered it.

I'll begin on the side of taste:

It was bitter in the way that greens that were good for us were often bitter. Or in the way that simmering resentment was bitter.

I have not yet found a corresponding flavor in food or in metaphor. But such a "match," even if identified, would only allow me the illusion of communication and you the illusion of understanding. I could claim, for example, that my first memory was the taste of an unripe banana, and many in the world would nod their heads, familiar with this unpleasantness. But we all haven't tasted the same unripe fruit. In order to feel not so alone in the world, we blur the lines of our subjective memories, and we say to one another, "I know exactly what you mean!"

The other side of the mystery is the word:

For me, the few words that *didn't* bring with them a taste were sanctuaries, a cloister in which I could hear their meanings as clear as my own heart beating. The rest of my vocabulary was populated by an order of monks who had broken their vows of silence and in this act had revealed themselves to me. Not their innermost feelings of sadness or ecstasy. Not the colors that they wore underneath their robes. But what they last placed in their mouths.

When I first moved to New York City, I wrote to Kelly that I had made a mistake. That I should have gone back to North Carolina for law school, that I missed her, missed Baby Harper, even missed Boiling Springs, our emphatically named hometown. That was in the fall of 1990, when email was just beginning its takeover of personal communication, starting with university campuses nationwide. The e. e. cummings of the written word was only months away, but Kelly and I hadn't and wouldn't succumb to the lowercase, the off and on punctuation, nor the flights of fancy spelling and syntax. From the earliest days of our friendship, we have relied on carefully written letters to keep each other informed of our inner lives. We behaved like characters in a Jane Austen novel long before either one of us knew what that meant. Kelly sent the first one, dated July 11, 1975.

"My name is Kelly. I am seven years old. I live in the red brick house. Welcome to Boiling Springs!"

The letter wasn't particularly elegant or inviting of a response, and at the time I didn't understand what she meant by the last sentence. But I admired her use of the exclamation mark. Worse letters of introduction have been written by hands much older than Kelly's and on stationery not nearly as pink. A red strawberry at the four corners of the sheet.

Kelly was advanced for her age in many ways. She took to grammar, capitalization, and punctuation early on. Her mother, Beth Anne, told her kindergarten teacher that no one taught Kelly these rules and regulations and that her daughter had picked them up from reading the newspapers. When asked who taught Kelly how to read the Shelby *Star* at such an early age, Beth Anne had replied that Kelly was born knowing how. In the first grade, Kelly memorized the contents of Strunk and White's *The Elements of Style.* She also committed to memory the "Forms of Address" chart at the back of Webster's New Collegiate Dictionary, handy for anyone planning to write a letter to a foreign ambassador or to a chancellor of a university, for instance.

At age seven, Kelly was also awkward, fat, and shy. These traits, as much as her intellectual precociousness, accounted for her chosen form of communication. I, also seven years old, showed her letter, which I had found on our hallway table, to my father. I had nominal reading and writing skills for my age, so I needed an older pair of eyes to guide me. My father asked me if I wanted to write back. If yes, he would deliver my letter. The omission of a last name and "the red brick house" being the closest thing to a mailing address would have stumped some fathers, but not mine.

Kelly's father, Carson Powell, Jr., worked for my father, Thomas Hammerick. I didn't know this back then. Nor did I know that these two men, lawyers by day, had just begun their second jobs as postmaster general and mailman for a very small country. The only other address in this land was "the gray and blue ranch house." The colors I provided, and my father contributed the architectural classification. For the first dozen or so letters, the correspondents were Kelly, my father, and me. I listened and nodded as he spelled the words out for me so that I could slowly print them—my vowels three times as large as my consonants—onto the sheet of paper. Pale yellow with a red and black ladybug at the upper right corner. Restrained design choice for a girl of seven, my father must have thought. He had taken me to Hudson's department store in Shelby so that I could choose my own box of stationery. His was plain and white, watermarked to show its quality, and DeAnne's had pink spray roses on it. Neither was suitable for a girl of seven.

That summer of letter writing—Kelly and I wrote to each other every day—made an impression on my father. He told my great-uncle Harper that he would never forget how I had answered the first question that Kelly sent to me. In letter #3, Kelly asked, "What is your favorite color?"

Fire, I told my father, was my answer.

He asked me if I understood the question.

Yes, she asked what color I liked—

And your answer is "fire"? Do you mean the color red?

I like red and yellow and orange and blue. . . .

I listed for him all the colors that I had seen in a flame and that I knew the names for. My father understood then the response as I had meant it. Another child, with similar preferences, might have said a "rainbow," but I had never seen a rainbow in real life.

According to my great-uncle Harper, my father also never forgot that I showed to him the first letter that I had ever received. That the receipt of something sealed, meant only for my eyes, was shared with him, unsolicited and unprovoked.

At the end of that summer, my father suggested that we invite this "Kelly Powell" girl over to the house for a sleepover. The look in my eyes made him stop talking in midsentence. I hadn't told him about my secret sense. When I heard or said the word "Kelly," I tasted canned peaches, delicious and candy-sweet. This, however, was the first time I had heard anyone say "Powell." The word was a raw onion, a playground bully with sharp elbows shoving all other flavors aside. Luckily for our friendship, little girls didn't often call each other by their full names.

"I'm the one still here in Boiling Springs," Kelly began her letter back to me. "You didn't make a mistake. I did. At the risk of sounding like a DP song, I've made so many mistakes in the past few years that it's now a habit I can't kick," she continued. Kelly wrote that she had even thought about overnighting her letter to New York City, given the forlorn tone of my five pages to her. But she didn't. The main reason we both loved this ritual of pen, paper, and stamps (the philatelic design announced the writer's mood: My letter had been posted with two Grand Canyons, and Kelly's response featured a Niagara Falls) was the waiting and the eventual receipt. It was one of the few examples in our young lives of patience rewarded.

The "DP" in the fourth sentence of Kelly's letter was a reference to our mutual childhood obsession, one that we now laugh and swear never to tell another living soul about. From the time we were eight, Dolly Parton has been our Madonna (the original one, not the "Like a Virgin" one who would be made famous in our teens by MTV), but being Southern Baptists, we didn't fully understand the role that Dolly was playing in our lives. She was a beautiful mystery to us. Her voice. Her hourglass figure. Her white-blond tresses. Her glossy teeth, ringed by her glossier lips. Each of her outfits was a rhinestone miracle to us. We wrote fan letters to her and sent them to each other to read. We thought that if we ever met her in person she would recognize our inherent goodness and take us home with her. We weren't sure where she lived, but we thought it was probably near the Grand Ole Opry. We cut her pictures out of *TV Guide* and cried when her specials came on past our bedtimes. When my mother found the hagiography (all three of us thought of it then as merely a scrapbook) that Kelly and I had made out of construction paper and masking tape, she told us that Dolly Parton had a beautiful voice but that she was trashy. My mother didn't have a knack for speaking with children. The first question that tumbled out of our small mouths was always "What does that mean?" DeAnne, unsure most of the time of what she meant, never stayed around long enough to answer. She was an actor with one line to deliver and then exited stage left. Such a performance left Kelly and me to make up our own meaning for *trashy:* a thing that is thrown away for no good reason, as in undervalued. Kelly and I vowed to be trashy, which to us also held the promise of a Cinderella-like redemption, when we grew up.

Kelly kept her promise. She lost weight during the summer before high school and never looked back at those thirty pounds or her first thirteen years of life. Even in a town as small as Boiling Springs, where the same kids tormented one another from kindergarten to grave, one summer could change everything. In how many backyards lay the molted skins of girls who vowed to no longer be fat, awkward, and shy? In Boiling Springs, during the summer of '82, there was only one. America wide, that figure was being closely monitored by the ad sales department of *Seventeen* magazine. There was money to be made from such tenderness and desperation. I stayed the same that summer, except for the cigarettes and my bra size, which came into existence at a 32-A. Kelly had been a 36-C since the seventh grade, but none of the boys had noticed because the rest of her was also large. A summer of Weight Watchers frozen dinners supplemented with frequent doses of Ex-Lax would carve away the adolescent fat and make those breasts pop. A high school girl's social life could be made with perfect skin, nice hair, and a pretty smile *or* with so-so versions of all the above and an impressive set of knockers. No one taught Kelly these rules and regulations either. She followed the example set by our Madonna. Kelly and I had already started to refer to Dolly Parton as "DP" by then, just in case anyone got hold of our letters. Ever since DP's co-starring role—Kelly and I didn't like to call it a "comeback performance"—in the movie *9 to 5*, we were very protective of our longtime association with her. That summer I was beyond DP's benevolent guidance, and Kelly knew it.

"I'm totally freaked out about us," Kelly wrote. "You've got to choose *before* you walk into the halls of Boiling Springs High School what sort of girl you want to be. So far, I think you've got only one option: smart. But I'm not sure how you're going to pull that off!"

Together Kelly and I would achieve her goal for my classification. Throughout grade school and middle school, I had been a C student. Standardized test scores, however, showed that my reading comprehension skills were well above average. My math scores were also consistently high. The problem was my inability to concentrate in class.

When my teacher asked, "Linda, where did the English first settle in North Carolina?" the question would come to me as "Lin-da*mint,* where did the English*maraschinocherry* first*Pepto-Bismol* settle*mustard* in North*cheddarcheese* Carolina*cannedpeas*?"

My response, when I could finally say it, I experienced as "Roanoke Island*bacon.*"

Many of the words that I heard or had to say aloud brought with them a taste—unique, consistent, and most often unrelated to the meaning of the word that had sent the taste rolling into my mouth. On my report cards, my teachers conveyed this undetected fact to my parents as "your daughter's unwillingness to pay attention in class."

I had shared my secret sense with Kelly in letter #26. After she read that her name tasted of canned peaches, she wrote back and asked, "Packed in heavy syrup or in its own juice?"

"Heavy syrup," I replied in letter #28.

The tiny miracle of our friendship was the question—What does that mean?—that was never asked.

That summer of transformation had us thinking about the suppression of taste. Kelly and I knew that I would never become an A student unless I could stop, or at least minimize, what I called the "incomings." We considered Big Red chewing gum, Tic Tacs, Lemonheads, and wintergreen Lifesavers. None was strong enough. We then experimented with Skoal. Kelly stole a tin of the dipping tobacco from her father's car. I threw up. My second try was more successful. I was sick to my stomach and light-headed, but I was able to keep the little pouch of tobacco between my cheek and gum long enough for the tobacco to do its work. To test out its effectiveness, Kelly recited for me the words of our favorite DP song, like it was a poem.

Back through the years
I go wonderin' once again
Back to the seasons of my youth
I recall a box of rags that someone gave to us.

The taste of the tobacco—a mouthful of earth, damp and just plowed; dried leaves and apple peels; the kick of turpentine; and the surprise ending of honey—was overpowering every one of the incomings.

As Kelly reached the words of the refrain, I joined the recitation.

My coat of many colors
That my momma made for me
Made only from rags
But I wore it so proudly.

We laughed out loud. At DP's hard-luck lyrics, at the English accent that Kelly and I faked as we spoke these words from memory, at the drool running down my chin. The brown saliva flooding my mouth made it clear that dipping tobacco, though highly effective, was unsuitable for classroom use. (In college, when I first heard the word "heterogeneity," I recognized the taste of Skoal, like a heavyweight boxer pummeling the inside of my mouth. In the middle of the lecture hall, a lone female voice was heard profaning, "Shit!" which I, the speaker, experienced as Shit*margarine*!)

After a couple more days of candy trials and some impulsive shoplifting of mouth sprays, Kelly and I decided on cigarettes for both of our transformative needs. We remembered from our eighth grade study packet "Alcohol, Tobacco, and Firearms: With Rights Come Responsibilities" that cigarettes had a dampening effect on the taste buds. From the Virginia Slims magazine ads, we also understood that cigarettes were ideal for losing weight. We knew, of course, that cigarettes could cause cancer. The "could" was because North Carolina led the country in tobacco production, and our civic studies teacher, Mrs. Duke, was a distant but loyal relation of *the* Duke family, whose tobacco fortune gilded the Old North State.

I sneaked six cigarettes from DeAnne's purse for the experiment. DeAnne smoked half a pack of Winston Reds every time my father went out of town. She chain-smoked them inside the bathroom of the master bedroom with the fan on. The circulation of air, like the sound of running water, hid nothing in our house. I, sniffling from a runny nose or woozy from the mild fever that always accompanied my father's absences, would find the water-soaked butts carefully wrapped up and thrown into the kitchen garbage. Kelly and I smoked three cigarettes apiece. We coughed out all the smoke from our first ones, but, as with the Skoal, the second try did the trick. All of a sudden we were inhaling like our mothers and fathers. The third cigarettes of our young lives, we smoked in front of the full-length mirror in Kelly's bedroom. We practiced holding the smoldering wand in between our fingers until we could dangle it just so. We ashed into an empty Pepsi can.

Cigarettes were even better than the dipping tobacco for suppressing the incomings. We decided that I would smoke in between my classes and that the lingering taste of the smoke would easily get me through the hour-and-fifteen-minute-long class periods. The unresolved question was where would I smoke. In the girls' bathroom hiding in a stall, or out in the open, by the back entrance of the gym?

Kelly and I had the longest conversations that we had ever had in the history of our friendship that afternoon. What we said to each other didn't really matter. What we enjoyed most was the rare sound of our voices commingling. After the taste of the cigarette smoke faded, we put on a recording of "Coat of Many Colors" and lay on the floor of Kelly's bedroom. When strapped to music, words fired blanks. This was one of the mystery's earliest revelations. So as Dolly sang, I experienced no incomings, nothing but a slight lifting sensation in my head, the residual nicotine high, which was taking me up and into the music. "I've never felt closer to DP's voice," I wrote to Kelly later that night. What I meant was that I have never felt closer to Kelly's.

Our letter-writing habit would serve us well in high school, as open displays of cross-clique interactions weren't understood or condoned among the 162 students of Boiling Springs High School. Like most other high schools in America, BSHS was a Byzantine court ruled by a football player and a cheerleader, but because of its diminutive size, its social machination was even more rarefied. There were limited spaces within the top ranks, and a fall from grace could happen at any moment with the speed and force of a knife in the dark. As Kelly soared into the stratosphere of tow-headed popularity, she was careful to court the upper-class girls in the inner circle, while their boyfriends circled her like she was a wounded animal. Beth Anne, amazed by her daughter's relocation from the bottom to the top of the heap, rewarded Kelly with the uniform of popular high school girls circa 1982. Gloria Vanderbilt jeans, Izod polo shirts, and Bass penny loafers—ubiquitously available "designer" labels, more aspiring than elite, form-fitting but never tight, and expensive but affordable at 25 percent off. This was middle-class America's version of *bon chic bon genre*, and Kelly wore it well.

I smoked my way into an attention span that matched my academic potential. For most of my freshman year at BSHS, I hid in the girls' bathroom with my packet of Winston Reds until one day I realized that I was behaving like my mother, DeAnne. I then smoked brazenly and with great skill out by the back entrance of the gym—French inhaling, releasing the occasional smoke rings, all with a studied indifference, as though the cigarette were just another finger on my hand. My appearance in the school's designated "Smoking Area" muddled my social classification. Heretofore I wasn't just a smart girl, but the Smartest Girl, which meant I wasn't a girl at all. The walls of my pigeonhole were further weakened by my easy acquaintanceship with three other students who called the Smoking Area their home base. The two guys, both sophomores, and the one girl, a two-time junior, looked me over and nodded at one another. Look at what the nicotine dragged here, was what that gesture meant. I liked them immediately because they made no effort to talk to me. I recognized them as Chris Johnson, Tommy Miller, and Susan Taylor, three kids who had decided to remove themselves from the ass kissing, shameless power grabbing, and half-hidden hypocrisies that walked the halls of BSHS like special-ed students whom everyone saw but no one acknowledged. The stoners, as they were called (though I never saw them smoking anything but cigarettes), wore black concert T-shirts (Rush, Iron Maiden, AC/DC), Wrangler jeans, and Converse high-tops. They were the closest things to a counterculture that BSHS had to offer.

"I know you think you're happy," I wrote to Kelly in letter #742, at the end of our freshman year. "But as your best friend I must tell you that you're not. There are times in the lunchroom when I want to get up and slap you. I hear you laughing, and I know those guys you sit with aren't funny. Not even close. You know what's worse? When I hear you laugh, it makes me feel lonely."

Our friendship was by then the fourth secret that I had to keep inside of me. Kelly was the only person whom I had shared my secret sense with, and that was secret number one. Secrets two and three (and Bobby, the name of the winged monster who had brought them into our lives) were already so deep within us that Kelly never even counted them. Only I did. When Kelly got pregnant during our junior year in high school, that would be the fifth secret.

Kelly went to live with her aunt in Rock Hill, South Carolina. A year and eight months later, Kelly returned to Boiling Springs with a GED and no baby, a bundle of pink flesh that she left over the state line for her aunt to raise. Kelly then enrolled in Gardner-Webb Baptist College, where all the young men were future deacons of their congregations and all the young women were virgins with a lowercase *v.* I had graduated valedictorian of the BSHS class of 1986 and was already a world away in New Haven.

Our letters have never stopped. Anger, disappointment, and shame at times have slowed their comings and goings, but we understood, without really fully understanding, that the words that we wrote to each other couldn't have existed in speech. The white paper—we both had switched to thin airmail paper by the age of fourteen—was for us the cover of night. We wished, without knowing it, that we loved each other, that we wanted to touch each other's bodies. That way we could write to each other all the sweet things that we wanted whispered in our ears by the boys, dumb and cruel, who had so suddenly replaced DP as our beautiful mystery.

Chapter 3

My father's unhappiness was a piece of fine mesh in his throat which all of his words had to push past with some care. Because Thomas Hammerick had lived in the South for most of his life, no one around him took notice of the slightly slowed rhythm of his speech. When he was older, people thought of the pauses between his words as evidence of his sound judgment.

What I wanted to know was who placed the scrim there. My father wouldn't have acknowledged this as a question. He believed that he alone was responsible for the hills and vales of his emotions. That was in part the reason for his unhappiness. The other parts came from his firm belief in the existence of the Reasonable Man. I was introduced to the Reasonable Man (and recognized him immediately as my father) during my first year of law school. The Reasonable Man was a legal standard that was once evoked with much frequency by the courts to weigh the actions or inactions of the rest of us. Would the Reasonable Man sign a contract without ever reading a word of it? Would the Reasonable Man leave a young child at home unsupervised? Would the Reasonable Man kill his wife in the rage of seeing her naked in another man's arms?

In many ways, the Reasonable Man standard was the juristic analog to the question posed today on billboards and bumper stickers by fundamentalist Christians: What would Jesus do?

Jesus and the Reasonable Man often had the same response. But there were points of divergence, which were dutifully respected, thanks to the constitutional firewall between Church and State. The Reasonable Man, for instance, would have answered, "Hell, yes!" to the third question. Thus, his love-scorned, emasculated rage was at one time acknowledged by many courts as a mediating factor, which would lessen his culpability and his jail time for blowing his wife's brains to bits. The Reasonable Man, of course, wouldn't witness a scene of marital betrayal, walk away, and return a couple of hours later with a loaded gun. That would imply premeditation, which would cancel out the value (to him) of a mediating circumstance. A truly Reasonable Man apparently always packed heat, which would be immediately available to him should he be spurned and, in that unthinking instance, commit his crime of passion. When I was first introduced to him, I immediately understood that the Reasonable Man wasn't an ideal husband.

When I was eight years old, I thought my father was one of the men on TV who met with prisoners in windowless rooms and advised them to "cut a deal," which I thought was a procedure involving a very large knife. Justice, a small bronze statue on my father's desk, held a scale. I thought she could have other utensils as well. When I was eleven and reading *To Kill a Mockingbird,* I thought my father was Atticus Finch. That meant I was Scout. That meant my mother was beautiful but dead, and my great-uncle Harper could be my older brother, Jem. When Kelly heard about my new family, she asked me who would be Boo Radley. I shrugged and said he wasn't kin. That was true, but it didn't answer her question. Kelly never asked me who would be Dill because we told each other that we didn't think about boys. Kelly knew that I liked saying this character's name aloud, though. "Dill" was one of the rare words that was faithful to itself. "Dill" tasted of fresh dill, a bright grassy entryway leading into a room where something faintly medicinal had recently been stored. This happy coincidence of meaning and flavor, however, didn't leave the word neutralized and without power. The word could still disrupt, dismay, or delight. In this instance, "Dill" was a promise ring. Inside its one syllable was a summer that would bring, along with the fireflies and the scuppernongs, a boy who would kiss me when my brother, Jem, wasn't looking.

As with the other milestones in our lives, Kelly was the first to know that we had reached one in the summer of '79. In letter #394, written during this summer before the sixth grade, when we were both freshly eleven, Kelly told me that I had a crush on Dill, which was OK by her, because she had a crush on Wade Harris, whom she pointed out was a "real" boy. This letter was significant for reasons related and unrelated to the idea of physical attraction. It was the first time that Kelly would use the attack-retreat-attack instinct against me. That instinct (as well as the recognition of it) lay dormant in a girl's body until hormones gave it a good, permanent kick in the ass.

attack: weaken opponent
by identifying an
embarassing truth;

retreat: profess in a casual
way that the truth
wasn't really an issue
after all; and

attack: deliver in the fewest
possible words the

real reason for putting
the sentence on paper.

Kelly, in other words, had called dibs on Wade Harris.

The real boy lived in the house one over from mine, identical except for the color, his a faded-T-shirt red. The real boy chipped a front tooth in my backyard, going headfirst down the slide. The real boy held my hands from second to fourth grade during the weekly square dances (held during gym class and considered by Boiling Springs Elementary to be both physical education and music appreciation). Before the caller's voice on the scratchy, banjo-laden record could tell us to do-si-do, shoot the star, and daisy chain, there was Coach Dewey's voice taking attendance.

"Hammerick*DrPepper*, Linda*mint*."

"Here*hardboiledegg*."

"Harris*pecan*, Wade*orangesherbet*."

"Here*hardboiledegg*."

Alphabetical order was the same as fate at Boiling Springs Elementary. Within its static student body, Harris always followed Hammerick, and Harris always danced with Hammerick (at least until fifth grade, when the principal no longer thought it was a good idea to provide boys and girls with weekly opportunities to touch one another).

Wade, the orange sherbet boy, was now off limits to me.

This too was a function of hormones. This understanding between two best friends who had allowed boys into their lives and into their letters. Wade was now Kelly's, a part of her sentimental property, a *W* to add to her *K*. I was left with Dill, a boy whose full fictional name was Charles Baker Harris. According to his creator, he was from the Mississippi branch of the Harris family. Kelly suggested that we think of Dill and Wade as cousins.

"No," I wrote back in letter #395. "They're twins."

If writing the letter now, I would add that all eleven-year-old boys are imagined. Or at least their souls are. Eleven-year-old girls construct them out of grinning school photos, Popsicle sticks, and a couple of fallen eyelashes (longer than our own lashes because the males of every species are showoffs).

But back then "they're twins" only meant that I wanted Kelly to share. One set of fraternal twins for two best friends. Kelly wrote back and agreed. Why wouldn't she? She got the boy with the hands, warm with matching calluses where his palms had folded over the handlebars of his green Schwinn Sting-Ray, his grip strong and tight. I got the boy who, though fully formed on the page, would never be born.

The introduction of Dill and Wade into our letters marked the beginning of doubt. Before this, Kelly and I had experienced fear. Of the dark. Of being alone. Of monsters (imaginary and real). Doubt, however, scared us in an entirely different way. Kelly and I saw a future (otherwise known as the sixth grade) in which we would remain invisible and unchanged while around us other girls suddenly bloomed. In Kelly's version, the girls burst, blousy peonies after the first hot summer night. In mine, after seven days and seven nights of rain, these girls became dandelions while we remained green clumps of crabgrass. Kelly and I knew what we needed. Lips that looked pink, wet, and just licked. Sally Campbell's lips had started to look that way at the beginning of fifth grade. Sally was pretty, and pretty girls were always ahead of the rest of us. Sally's lips and also her mouth smelled of strawberry bubblegum. Kelly and I were jealous of both the shine and the scent. In order to make us feel better, I told Kelly that the word "Sally" tasted of pumpkin, without the brown sugar or the cinnamon. Just a squash.

Sally, nonetheless, set the example for us. Lips that could be seen from across the classroom we understood were desirable, and gloss for them had to be our first acquisition. Kelly begged her mother, Beth Anne, and then resorted to a promise of future weight loss for a shade of pink called Flamingo Paradise, which Beth Anne picked out for her. Beth Anne, at the time, didn't pay attention to Kelly. Beth Anne completely ignored the fact that her only daughter had asked her for lip gloss, strawberry-bubblegum-flavored. Flamingo Paradise was lipstick, the kind that my grandmother Iris wore. It went on creamy but soon became cracked and dry. The only flavor it gave to our lips was something that also belonged to Iris: talcum powder mixed with a crushed vanilla cream wafer. Kelly and I hated everything about Flamingo Paradise. We even hated the name. Paradise better have something else in it besides a flamingo, we thought.

By mistake or as an extra incentive, Beth Anne threw in a case of blue eye shadow, Ocean Lite, which Kelly and I immediately tried. The way it sparkled and became almost silver on our lids made us feel trashy. We were old enough by then to know what that word meant, and we didn't want to be trashy. We were also old enough to know that our idol Dolly Parton had a heavy hand with the makeup brush and shouldn't be used as a template for our own efforts. We still secretly loved the way she looked in all her photos. She shone. She would become more and more otherworldly with each passing year. She would no longer walk beside us, though (because we were embarrassed by her), a good mother who could help us cross the street or sing us to sleep at night. She hovered above us now, out of sight.

From the start, Kelly and I pooled all of the little tubes and cases of makeup and kept them in her bedroom. Her canopy bed, the yellow eyelet bedspread, the daffodils painted on the white dresser drawers and matching mirror, all said "GIRL!" and they provided the perfect laboratory space for me to become more like one. Kelly had always been a girl. She might have been Beth Anne's fat daughter in waiting, but from the day she was born she was her father's princess.

I was my father's tomboy.

From as far back as I could remember, my room was done up in a plaid of green and blue (Yale blue, as it turned out). The furniture (American Colonial) was dark oak, and the pictures on the walls were of tall ships (whaling vessels). I loved these framed prints, a triptych of the same vessel during three different voyages at sea. I woke up every morning to the waves curling up their hulls, to a lone seagull skimming the water, to clouds pink with the beginning or the end of a day. Until I saw Kelly's bedroom, it hadn't occurred to me that other little girls woke up to posters of daisy-sniffing clowns, puppies in wooden crates, or, in Kelly's case, kittens with unraveling balls of yarn. I never asked my father why tall ships, but I'm sure his answer would have been that ships got you places. He was right. Those ships made me consider the oceans of the world, made me want to learn their names, live on the very edge of them. Planes and cars and trains could get you places as well. So maybe the answer, the less logical one, had something to do with the bodies of water themselves, those difficult-to-navigate expanses in between lands.

Other than the maritime prints, my bedroom was a room with a bed, a desk, a chair, and no toys. My father said that play was something children should do outside in the sunshine. He said play was also about strengthening the body. All the toys he gave me fulfilled both tenets. Bicycle, jungle gym, swing set, Nerf balls, and a trampoline. My hair was cut short to keep it out of my eyes when I jumped up and down. My jeans were Toughskins to keep the knees from ripping when I fell. My skin deepened into a warm brown from all the afternoons of growing strong and tall underneath the North Carolina sun.

During the summer when Kelly and I were only eleven and already painting our faces with Paradise and Ocean hues, my father must have sensed that there was change in the air. His response was preemptive in nature. He began to tell me that my cheeks were pink like apple blossoms. That my eyes were the shape of hickory nuts. That the color of my hair was that of a river at nighttime. He didn't know that my great-uncle Harper had been telling me things like this for years.

The appearances of Dill and Wade in our letters also marked the beginning of reticence. That word wasn't part of my vocabulary yet. So, instead, I thought I was being selfish. The result was the same, a withholding.

In America, a country of abundance, in North Carolina, a state of plenty, children were expected to share. Most childhood misbehaviors could be traced to a refusal to do so, and parents and teachers hurled reprimands accordingly. *Stop being selfish! Why are you so selfish? Selfish children don't go to Heaven! No dessert for the selfish!* This last one was a favorite of my mother. She had learned from her mother that food was both reward and punishment. Considering what came into and out of my mother's kitchen—the unnecessarily canned vegetables, the shaken and baked, the hamburger helpmeets, and so on—the food at our table was always punishment. The last word of my mother's mealtime threat, though, was for me an antidote. The word "selfish" brought with it the taste of end-of-the-summer corn on the cob. Not the kernels but the juice at the honeycombed core after everything has been gnawed away. Poor DeAnne—she had no way of knowing why her rebukes always brought a smile to my face.

This was my silent mealtime prayer:

Say it again.
Tell me I'm selfish.
Please, help me get the taste of your dinner out of my mouth.

The nightly cross that I had to bear was dependably one of the following casseroles: chicken à la king, tuna noodle, beefy macaroni.

Consistency was the strongpoint of my mother's kitchen. Variety meant never having the same casserole two nights in a row. Variety also meant that the casserole's crispy topping was a rotation of bread crumbs, crushed saltine crackers, broken potato chips, or Durkee's fried onions (the last only on Thanksgiving, Christmas, and other special occasions). For a brief time in the mid-eighties, right before my father passed away, when DeAnne was experimenting with "exotic" flavors, her weekly menu also included a three-layer taco casserole (one of the layers was the contents of a small bag of corn chips) and a chow mein surprise casserole (the surprise was several hot dogs cut into matchstick-size strips, which, when cooked, would curl up into little pink rubber bands). No matter the recipe, a can of condensed cream of mushroom soup, the all-American binding agent of disparate foodstuff, was mixed in. The Great Assimilator, as I call it now, was responsible for the uniform taste of all of DeAnne's casseroles. Whether à la king, tuna, or beefy (different from beef itself), these casseroles also shared the same texture, as if all their ingredients had been made to wear a sweater. I have since learned that foods named for the pot or pan that they were cooked in probably had little else going for them. Meat loaf or a Bundt cake, for example.

As I grew older and as my affection for DeAnne didn't, I began to throw her words back at her in the form of a question. "No-*grapejelly* dessert for the selfish*cornonthecob*?" I would ask her, as if she had admonished me in a foreign language that I couldn't quite understand. The act of repeating her words, of course, served multiple purposes.

According to DeAnne, I was being selfish because I hadn't finished my dinner; there were starving children in Africa (which she thought of as one big country); and my serving of casserole could have been sent to feed them. At the dinner table, I was being selfish to save my life and, though they didn't know it, also the lives of my African counterparts, and it felt good.

In letter #395, I was being selfish and it felt bad. A wasp sting, a blow to the face, a skinned knee. In the four years that Kelly and I had been writing to each other, I had never kept a thought from her. We were the twins, conjoined at the foreheads, our thoughts silently traveling back and forth through hidden circuitries. Until Kelly claimed Wade in letter #394, he had never made an appearance in my letters because he was a part of my life in the way that a neighbor's dog or a mailman was. Wade was a constant, dependable, and not-unpleasant presence. He first came around to the blue and gray ranch house because of the slide in the backyard, but after he chipped his tooth he kept to the swing set. He then came around for the newly installed jungle gym. If I was playing on it, he would join me with no more than a "Hi" spoken to the lawn. If I was inside the blue and gray ranch house, he would climb onto the bars and hang upside down by his knees from the highest rung, his hair a suspended crown of hay. He was unremarkable, except for the taste of his name. In letter #395, I could have told Kelly that "Wade" was orange sherbet in my mouth. I didn't. I wanted that part of him for myself. I was the wasp, the fist, the gravel road.

Before the summer of Dill and Wade, Kelly and I had traded letters about another boy, her cousin Bobby, but he didn't count. Bobby was older than us. He was in high school when we were still in the fifth grade. His hair was parted down the middle, and the feathered sides were held in place with hairspray. He had a permanent shadow above his upper lip. It looked to us like he hadn't washed his face properly.

In letter #329, Kelly wrote that Bobby had made her touch his privates. Kelly and her cousin were in the basement of the red brick house. He sat down next to her on the couch. He picked up her hand and placed it in between his legs. She wrote that it felt warm and then hard. Bobby closed his eyes, and his head fell backward, an invisible pair of hands pulling on the wings in his hair. Bobby told her not to tell anyone. I began letter #330 with "Gross!" written over and over again. Each time the word meant something different. I should have just written, "Tell your father!"

Bobby continued to cut the grass for the Powells all through that spring and summer of '79. Kelly's mother, Beth Anne, disliked the sound of the riding mower and made her appointments at Miss Cora's Beauty Emporium on the afternoons when her nephew came to the house. When she had hired Bobby, Beth Anne had told him that he was always welcome to come inside for a soft drink and to wash his hands once he was done. Kelly learned not to go into the basement when Bobby was circling the house. Next she learned that she needed but didn't have a way to lock her bedroom door. Kelly then told her mother that the sound of the riding mower hurt her ears too and asked to be dropped off at my house when Bobby came around. The problem was solved until my mother hired Bobby to cut our lawn. That was when she became DeAnne to me. A mother would have known better. The summer of Dill and Wade would end for me with Bobby. Kelly's cousin was no longer a boy. He was a monster. He was a menace. He was the half-hidden blade of the lawn mower. He wasn't how we had imagined the boys in our lives to be. Forced hands, eyes shut, blood.

CHAPTER 4

THE TRUTH ABOUT MY FAMILY WAS THAT WE DISAPPOINTED ONE another. When I heard the word "disappoint," I tasted toast, slightly burned. But when I saw the word written, I thought of it first and foremost as the combining or the collapsing together of the words "disappear" and "point," as in how something in us ceased to exist the moment someone let us down.

Small children understood this better than adults, this irreparable diminution of the self that occurred at each instance, large and small, of someone forgetting a promise, arriving late, losing interest, leaving too soon, and otherwise making us feel like a fool. That was why children, in the face of disappointments, large and small, were so quick to cry and scream, often throwing their bodies to the ground as if their tiny limbs were on fire. That was a good instinct. We, the adults or the survivors of our youth, traded in instinct for a societal norm. We stayed calm. We swallowed the hurt. We forgave the infraction. We ignored that our skin was on fire. We became our own fools. Sometimes, when we were very successful, we forgot entirely the memory of the disappointment. The loss that resulted, of course, could not be undone. What was gone was gone. We just could no longer remember how we ended up with so much less of our selves. Why we expected nothing, why we deserved so little, and why we brought strangers into our lives to fill the void.

On the eve of a departure, confessions and revelations were bound to occur. On August 23, 1986, my great-uncle and I engaged in both. I was leaving the next day to go to Yale—a plane flight to New York City and then a bus ride to New Haven. I thought that I was leaving Boiling Springs for good. I had failed to factor in the magnetic pull of funerals. I was eighteen years old and full of rage. DeAnne, no longer my mother, was the reason. That was what I wanted my great-uncle Harper to know that night.

Baby Harper and I were having dinner together, as we had done every Saturday night for close to a year by then. We went into Shelby and sat in our usual booth at Bridges Barbecue Lodge. We each ordered a pulled pork sandwich, a side of coleslaw, fries with an extra order of barbecue sauce for dipping, peach cobbler (only available on Saturdays), and a bottle of Cheerwine, a cherry-flavored cola bottled in nearby Salisbury, which my great-uncle said brought out the "fruit" in Bridges's sauce. Bridges Barbecue Lodge had two things going for it, which was more than I could say for the other dining options in town, Pizza Inn, Waffle House, Arby's, Roy Rogers, and Hardee's. In the mid-eighties the greater Boiling Springs–Shelby area attracted only the B-list fast-food chains. Bridges was in a league of its own. The first thing that made Bridges special was that, even by the standards of North Carolina barbecue, Bridges's sauce was extraordinarily vinegary, which meant it was extraordinarily good. (I have a fantasy that someday I'll hear *the* word that makes me taste Bridges's sauce. In this fantasy, I die happy, knowing what my last word on earth will be.) The merit of sauce was often debated in this part of the state, with some folks coming down on the side of Slo Smoking Steakhouse & Bar-

B-Que on E. Dixon Boulevard. "Fools," my great-uncle always said under his breath whenever we would drive past Slo's parking lot. He would check out the parked cars, making a mental note of their license plates, their makes. The same way that a minister would drive by a strip club, if there had been one in Cleveland County. Second, Bridges had a great sign. Four pink neon pigs all in a row. Baby Harper and I liked it when the sign flickered on and off, sending a pig in and out of the void of the night sky. Often a pig would go unseen for a couple of months before the sign could be fixed. When I was younger, my great-uncle Harper would say that the unlit pig was the one that went to market. That night, he said that the unlit pig was the one we were eating, and then he hiccupped. My great-uncle was a charming man even with sauce on his chin.

Baby Harper, bless his heart and the rest of him as well, was the family photographer. His albums—there are one hundred of them if you don't count the ones that he sent to me in New York City in a box marked HANDLE WITH CARE—were a testament to his lifelong need to be present and not present. He received his first camera, a Kodak Baby Brownie Special, in 1940, when he was sixteen years old. At the start, he was a bad photographer or an accidental artist. The first album was mostly of the backs of heads, blurred torsos, and shoes in mid-stride. He called them "candidgraphs," but after his sister, Iris, saw what she looked like with a fork in her mouth and a lock of hair in her eyes, she told him to quit taking bad photographs of good-looking people. I wouldn't have imagined that my grandmother Iris was ever good-looking, but, thanks to my great-uncle, I didn't have to.

H.E.B. Two (a typed label with my great-uncle's initials and a number was taped on to every album's spine) showed an Iris—twenty-seven years old, married, and mother to an eight-year-old named DeAnne—with the face of a Hollywood starlet. Eyebrows plucked and shaped, lips dark with lipstick, Iris was from this album on always ready for Baby Harper. Or rather, Baby Harper was from this album on always made to wait for Iris. He still managed now and then to take an unposed photograph of her. There was a series of them at the end of H.E.B. Four. Each one was a close-up of some detail of Iris's attire. A glove with three pearl buttons, the last one freed from its loop. A silk organza hibiscus, complete with quivering (thus blurry) stamens, perched atop a hat. A high-heeled shoe with a shiny oval buckle. When Baby Harper first showed these candidgraphs to me, I felt like looking the other way. I didn't understand why I didn't want to see them; why the images made me feel so sad. How could I have known then that what I was feeling had little to do with what was being photographed and everything to do with the photographer and the longing of his gaze?

Baby Harper was always there to document us, but because he never allowed anyone to take his place behind the camera nor bothered with a tripod, he was never documented. (The few photographs of him from his childhood were the exceptions. He couldn't exercise his will back then.) In this clever way, my great-uncle hid from the official history of our family. By excluding himself, he ensured that our history was a false one. Or, at the least, an incomplete one. He never hid that fact from me. My great-uncle always suggested that his photographs weren't to be trusted, that the real points of interest were elsewhere. When we looked through the "before you were with us" albums, he would stop at each photograph and tell me about the occasion and the faces present (mostly the same ones, except some no longer looked the same, were no longer alive, or for other reasons were no longer a part of our lives), and then he would tell me what I couldn't see. He would say, "Well, Linda Vista, you know how your grandma Iris gets at Christmastime. Right before this one here was taken, she was doing that whisper-yelling thing that makes me break into a sweat. The girl working for us at the time—here, see, that's the corner of her apron. The rest of her was hurrying as fast as she could to get back to the kitchen, but I caught her. Well, part of her. Poor thing had been passing around a tray of those little biscuits and Virginia ham things that no one makes anymore. Well, she dropped some. Just slid right off the tray. Girl might as well have dropped a crystal vase. Who knew biscuits could explode like that? Poor girl picked up what she could, but those biscuits were made right, and by that I mean they were made by someone *other* than your grandma. Well, Iris crossed the room, leaned into that girl, and whisper-yelled something that scared her white, which was saying something. It's a shame that the trusty Kodak wasn't fast enough to get the girl's face. But if you look real close, you can see the crumbs still on the carpet there by Iris's pumps. That girl didn't last long. Gone by the New Year, I think. But, the notable thing here, Linda Vista, is that smile on your grandma's face."

Baby Harper liked to talk, and he liked to call me Linda Vista. The first of these inclinations would suggest that he was an unsuitable companion for me. But when he got started, it was like a claim that you would hear in a car commercial: "from zero to sixty miles per hour in ten seconds." As his words gained velocity, they acquired a rhythm. As his words acquired a rhythm, they took on a melody. In that way, Baby Harper sang to me, a cappella. In that way, I was able to hear his words without the usual incomings. We were each other's ideal companion in other ways as well.

Why he called me Linda Vista wasn't as easy to explain. Every time I asked him, he gave me a different answer. Because names are like socks—they should be changed now and then. Because without you, there would be no other vistas in Cleveland County. Because, on its own, "Linda" is a name for a forty-year-old woman who smokes a pack a day. Because no one calls you Linda Vista but me. My great-uncle Harper was full of reasons, which I now know made him the antithesis of the Reasonable Man, he who never has more than one reason (that being the right one) for his actions. I think that was why Baby Harper loved my father so much. We loved our opposites so that we could free ourselves from our selves. And sometimes we loved our opposites because rejection was better than a void.

Our attraction was mutual and immediate. Even within our own family, we chose. I was the only grandchild in the family. Baby Harper was the only singing-talker. There were worse reasons to fall in love. What was it like for a person like me to be with a singing-talker like him? Kelly had asked me. I had no way to explain it to her until I was in New Haven and had experienced the first heavy snowfall of my life:

You are walking on the snow-covered ground. There is a crunching that accompanies your steps. If you walk for long enough you forget that there is a sound that accompanies your every footfall. You forget until you walk onto a patch where the snow has melted away. That first silent step startles you and reminds you that there isn't always snow.

No one called him Baby Harper—not to his face, that is—but Iris and me. Even I loved my grandmother when she said his name aloud.

"Baby*honey* Harper*celery.*"

The honey, a percolating bubble full of flowers and citrus, bursts wide open when the sea of celery—the only vegetable I know that comes pre-salted—washes in. An unexpectedly pleasurable combination of flavors that made me wobbly in the knees.

It wouldn't be the last time that I would fall for a name. Canned peaches. Dill. Orange sherbet. Parsnip (to my great regret). None of those whom I have loved since Baby Harper have ever given me more.

Baby Harper asked me where DeAnne was tonight. In between bites of Bridges's pulled pork, I said that DeAnne was a witch. Baby Harper let out another little hiccup. He always enjoyed it when my responses didn't answer his questions. He liked it when they came close but then would swerve and miss. What I wanted my great-uncle to know was that I held DeAnne responsible for Bobby, but under the fluorescent lights, amid the drone of nuclear families dining, awash in the vinegary miasma of Bridges, I couldn't say his name aloud.

Monster. Menace. Blade.

Later that night, when I finally told my great-uncle Harper, he cried. He held my hands and cried. His own hands were trembling. I told him that it would be all right, that it had been all right for years now, seven, in fact, which did little to console him. We were sitting side by side by then, on the green velvet divan that was the centerpiece of his living room. My great-uncle was a sixty-two-year-old, never-married male librarian with a velvet divan, which he pointed out to me was the same color as the curtains that Scarlett O'Hara had made into a gown. These weren't clues; they were flashing signs. I loved him more because of them. The good folks of the greater Boiling Springs–Shelby area looked at my great-uncle and looked right past him. They are the unlit pigs, I remembered thinking that night.

Revelation is when God tells us the truth. Confession is when we tell it to Him. *Or* when we tell it to the person in our lives who makes us feel closest to Him. Kelly and I had come up with the "*Or*" and what followed it. Before Bobby, before the summer of Dill and Wade, Kelly and I were amateur theologians who supplemented our Sunday-school education with our own addition to the Scriptures. We drafted a new book of the New Testament, and we entitled it *Illumination*. Kelly came up with the name. She had a sophisticated vocabulary for a ten-year-old. She said the title aloud to me and asked, "So?"

"Prunes*scallion,*" I replied, making a face.

Kelly laughed. She understood that there was something unpleasant hidden within the word "prune" as well as the word "illumination," so she repeated both words until I begged her to stop.

"Or what*grahamcracker*?" Kelly asked.

"I'll never*bubblegum* speak*lemonade* to you*cannedgreenbeans* again*pancakenosyrup*!"

"You*cannedgreenbeans* never*bubblegum* say any*rice*thing*tomato* to me now," Kelly said, rolling her eyes.

If you charted our friendship, 1978 was a peak year for us. Our world was small and intimate and complete. We were ten years old. We were in the fourth grade. We had no pets, no siblings, and no crushes. We had our devotion to each other, to Dolly Parton, and, with *Illumination*, our devotion to Jesus. In letter #253, I asked Kelly what that word meant.

"Light," she wrote back. "Also what happens when we have light. We can see more and better things." Kelly dotted the *i* in the two *light*s and the one *things* with a heart, an anatomically correct one, complete with left and right ventricles.

Illumination began with how we felt about Jesus. We started with a list of the things that we loved about Him.

- ✝ *We love you Jesus! because you were a real cute baby.*
- ✝ *We love you Jesus! because your arms are always wide open, and you want to hug us.*
- ✝ *We love you Jesus! because people follow you around like sheep.*
- ✝ *We love you Jesus! because your hair is long and shiny. (We think you use Breck shampoo.)*
- ✝ *We love you Jesus! because wherever you go you bring your own illumination.*

At the end of the writing of *Illumination*, when we were almost eleven and felt very confident about our faith (which was good, as we were about to stop believing in ourselves), we listed the Ten Commandments and then the ways out of them. Kelly said they were called "Exemptions," and then she asked, "So?"

"Nothing*tomato*," I replied.

Kelly took out a small spiral notebook that she kept in her

purse—I didn't have one yet because my father said that everything that I needed should fit in my back pockets—and she wrote down "exemption." She was keeping a list of words that fired blanks. She thought eventually we would see a pattern. None emerged because she lost interest and then she lost the notebook.

- ✗ *Thou shall not kill, unless thou is killing to save Jesus.*
- ✗ *Thou shall not steal, unless it is to take back what was stolen from thou, which meant it was yours in the first place.*
- ✗ *Thou shall not covet thy neighbor's wife, unless thy own wife is dead and thou are very lonely.*

Kelly kept our only copy of *Illumination* because she was the scribe. She was the scribe because her handwriting was better than mine. Her handwriting was better than mine because she had written letters even before I came into her life. She told me that the letters had been addressed to Nobody and signed Somebody. Or maybe it was the other way around.

My great-uncle Harper and I were both the confessors that night. My hands, in fact, had been the first to tremble. After our dinner at Bridges, we drove back to Boiling Springs and to his house, a Greek Revival with a pristine exterior painted in "Clotted Cream," which he proudly noted was a color that he had researched for period authenticity and then had had custom-mixed. Baby Harper began as he usually did: "Linda Vista, come sit by me." We arranged ourselves on the divan, and he returned to the subject that I had introduced earlier at Bridges. "Now you know your momma is *not* a witch, Vista Girl," he said. "But when we were both young, I thought she was one too."

DeAnne and her uncle Harper were only eight years apart in age. That I knew. What I didn't know was that from the moment Iris and Walter Wendell brought DeAnne down the stairs of the green-shuttered colonial on Piedmont Street, wrapped in the same baby blanket that had covered Baby Harper during his first hours of life, he decided that he didn't care for his niece, and he told her so every time he was left alone with her. He whispered, "You're a bag of bones," into her infant ears. He handed her "Your name is Mud" notes when she began to walk but long before she could read. As his vocabulary developed and hers was still limited to "momma" and "papa," Baby Harper's scribbling became more direct and to the point: "Incubus, Succubus, wish you weren't with us." When Iris pried these slips of paper from DeAnne's moist little hands, the ink was already smudged and the messages were beyond reproach. As my great-uncle told this to me, he flipped through the pages of H.E.B. Nine and stopped at a photograph of DeAnne standing beside a cake with eight lit candles. He pointed to her right hand balled into a fist and to what looked like the corners of a handkerchief poking through it. He said *that* was the last note that he ever gave to her. I asked him what the note said. Then I asked him why he stopped.

"I forgive you," the note said.

When DeAnne turned eight, the age that Baby Harper was when she came into the world, he realized something very important about her, something that was probably inborn and fixed. His niece would never write a note back to him. Not even to ask, "Why?" Baby Harper knew that if he continued to despise DeAnne for simply being (in the way, in between him and Iris, in the center of every family gathering enjoying the grace that belongs only to the youngest of the flock) and, more important, if he continued to let her know it, he would be committing an even greater sin than he had bargained for. The meek shall inherit the earth. Baby Harper wasn't sure he understood why they would, but he sure wasn't going to bet against God. His niece, DeAnne, was a Whatley in name and in blood. She hadn't inherited a drop of the Burch battery acid that flowed through Iris's veins (and to a lesser extent his own). My great-uncle Harper, and this was the revelation, said that maybe skipping a generation was God's way of balancing out the world.

What Harper Evan Burch didn't say, but that everyone else in Boiling Springs knew, was that, in the case of the Burch family, God had already balanced out the world by destroying a whole generation. The "smiting" had taken place two weeks after Iris's wedding to Walter Wendell. Her mother and father had escorted her father's two spinster sisters back to the ladies' hometown of Macon, North Carolina, where the Burch family's streak of mean had earned these two women a new last name. There they were known as the "Burr Sisters." There a fire swept through the family's former plantation house and killed them all in their sleep. Iris and Baby Harper were left with the green-shuttered colonial in Boiling Springs, but the land in Macon, according to the sisters' will, went to a local society of cat lovers, a member of which had traveled to Venice, Italy, and reported back that there were entire islands there set aside as cemeteries for their friends the noble felines. The charred remains of the house and the surrounding fifty-five acres became just that kind of island right there in Macon. After the will had gone through probate and the deed to the land was transferred, an allegation surfaced that the Burr Sisters hadn't even liked cats. They just liked their niece and nephew less.

I never saw even a hint of my great-uncle's early feelings toward DeAnne. When I was growing up, he spent a lot of time over at the blue and gray ranch house, though he avoided dinnertime whenever possible. My great-uncle would show up right as dessert was being served. DeAnne never had any pretensions that she could produce edible baked goods, so store-bought cakes and pies or wobbly cubes of Jell-O ("homemade") were what we all looked forward to at the end of our meals.

Baby Harper usually brought with him a couple of shirts along with an envelope containing the buttons that had fallen off them. DeAnne would take out her sewing basket, and my great-uncle would sit down next to her on the couch, leaning his head in to hers as if he were the one guiding the needle up and down. DeAnne never seemed to mind. I thought there was real affection between them.

I asked him that August night if that was true.

He nodded and said, "Linda Vista, I fell in love with your momma the day she married Thomas."

Chapter 5

There was a ghost who haunted North Carolina. Her name was Virginia Dare, and there was no historical record of her after the ninth day of her life. Her father's name was Ananias, and her mother's was Eleanor. She was born on August 18, 1587, which was a Monday, and she was baptized that following Sunday. Because of that drop of water, whatever became of her body, her soul was welcomed into the Kingdom of Heaven. This fact kept John White, her grandfather and the man who failed her, from drowning himself at high tide. Virginia—or should I call her by her last name, because from the first day of her life she had earned it—was born on Roanoke Island off the coast of what would be called North Carolina, where no English child's umbilical cord had ever been cut and tied. Dare was brave and foolish and defiant to have survived the circumstances of her birth. It was undeniable that her arrival gave hope to the adults in the colony, a hope so pure and unreasonable that it lasted for only a couple of hours. Then her arrival reminded these adults that they were low on food and supplies and that their first winter in the New World was nearing. Dare reminded them that they could die. A small bundle of pink flesh triggered these emotions in them. The adults met and debated and decided that some among them would have to return to England for provisions and for additional men and women, who, and this part was left unsaid, would have a stronger resolve than they. When it came time for the roll call for volunteers for the journey, the three who didn't say "aye" were Ananias, Eleanor, and Eleanor's father, John White. A small bundle of pink flesh had made these three foolish and defiant and brave. John White, though, was destined to leave his grandchild behind. He was the governor of the colony, and without his presence on the returning ship there would have been the strong suspicion of desertion or mutiny. On August 27, he looked back at Roanoke Island and saw his daughter, Eleanor, standing on the sandy shore with Dare in her arms. Where was Ananias, John White wanted to know. The question grew in importance in John White's mind as the ship crossed the Atlantic. He knew that he would have to wait many months before he could learn the answer, and that made him angry with his son-in-law for prompting the question in the first place.

The Atlantic was too cooperative, John White also found himself thinking during the journey away from his new home. The ocean he knew was always brutal but in different ways. John White was right. The Atlantic safely returned him and his crew to a country at war. England's ships, sailors, supplies, and every available maritime resource for the next three years were devoted to the sinking of the Spanish fleet. John White, during those years, developed a hatred for his son-in-law that bordered on a kind of obsession. The vein in John White's temple throbbed and threatened to explode. He needed to focus on that anger because otherwise his breaking heart would have caused him to let out a sound like that of a sheep bleating. His Eleanor and his Dare standing alone on the shores of Roanoke Island for who knows how long? That was the question that was driving John White mad.

My father believed in the Old North State. When I was eight years old, a significant age in our family, my father gave me a book entitled *North Carolina Parade: Stories of History and People.* The book was published in 1966, two years before I was born. It had the look and feel of a book written in a much less complicated decade than the sixties. The illustrations were inky black and white, gestural and naïve. The text, co-written by a man who, per his photo on the dust jacket, looked like a 1940s movie star, and a woman who took her photo with her cat, had much of the same qualities. Thirty-two short chapters all with the tone and depth of a sixth-grade book report. I was immediately pulled in. There was something reassuring about having the history and people of your world reduced to 209 pages and a handful of drawings. True to his nature, my father wanted me to have a book that would foster a sense of security and belonging. *North Carolina* contained easy-to-read histories, and he thought that they would do the trick. They did. But the trick was a different one from what he had intended. *North Carolina* was a bait and switch.

As with all fairy tales, a crime was committed. In "Snow White," there was a poisoning. A hostage situation was at the heart of "Beauty and the Beast." "Hansel and Gretel" featured attempted cannibalism. "Cinderella" involved the lesser offense of party crashing. *North Carolina* began with a trespassing. Not a "Goldilocks and the Three Bears" domestic breaking and entering but an act of large-scale land grabbing. But at first I thought *North Carolina*'s opening chapter about the baby Virginia Dare and the Lost Colony of Roanoke Island was about the crime of kidnapping or mass murder. Of course I did. I was being shown the world through Dare's barely opened eyes. History always had a point of view. That was a trick worth learning.

Another was that history was what you wanted to remember. In *North Carolina* there was only one mention of a slave, George Moses Horton, who had earned extra money for his master by writing love poems for the young men of the University of North

Carolina at Chapel Hill. George Moses composed these poems while he worked the land on his master's farm. Little Virginia Dare would have asked how terrible could this "peculiar institution" have been if there was poetry in the fields?

North Carolina had yet another trick up its sleeve. History was in the missing details. The Wright brothers' first flight on December 17, 1903, from Kitty Hawk, North Carolina, was witnessed by a small group of people, including "a boy from Kitty Hawk village." Why did the co-authors of *North Carolina*—the movie star look-alike and the cat lover—separate this boy from the group, and then leave him standing on the sand of Kitty Hawk, nameless and without a word to contribute? Another forgotten child on the coast of North Carolina was, perhaps, their theme. *North Carolina* was chock-full of children, well loved and well remembered. Buck Duke, Andrew Johnson, Daniel Boone, who all grew up to be somebody. Yet, it was this anonymous boy and the baby Virginia Dare, one without a name and the other without a future, who drew me in again and again. *North Carolina*'s final trick was this. It was neither a history nor a fairy tale, but a mystery.

When I left Boiling Springs for the optimistically named New Haven, I took *North Carolina* with me to remind me of my father's face when I thanked him for the book and to remind me of the place where he was born and where he died. His afterbirth and his body were buried in the same land that had received his father's and forefathers' bodies. Ashes to ashes, dust to dust, Carolina to Carolina. In that way, my father belonged to an ancient order of men. In all other ways, my father was a modern man. He had traveled far from his home to educate himself among the race of men known as Yankees. He was never afraid, because his father and grandfather had commingled with these same folks and returned home to Charlotte, North Carolina, more or less unchanged. Within the Hammerick clan, a change of any kind was one more than was necessary. My great-grandfather Graven Hammerick, upon his return from New Haven, was said to have refused the cornbreads served to him by his mother because they weren't sweet enough for his northern-influenced palate. Because she couldn't stand the sight of him not eating, his mother always had a batch made just for him with heaping spoonfuls of sugar added to the batter, but she also made it a point to wrap these squares in a black cloth before bringing them to the table. She wanted to remind her son that something inside of him had died. My grandfather Spartan Hammerick caught the travel bug after his graduation from Yale and spent two years crisscrossing Europe. During this time abroad, he sent home only two postcards, each written and postmarked on the date of his mother's birthday. Spartan returned to Charlotte with a stack of letters scented by the hands of an Italian baronessa, which his mother found and made him burn. For the Hammericks, the important thing was that their men came home again. When my great-uncle Harper told me this, I thought, Of course they came home. Where else in the world could they live with those first names?

I have never met anyone on my father's side of the family. All that I know about them is courtesy of my great-uncle Harper. Unlike the Burch branch of our family, no tragic event had wiped the Hammericks from the face of the earth. The tragedy here was my father. Thomas had come home to North Carolina, but he had brought too much of the world back with him. From where they stood, scattered about the four corners of Mecklenburg County in the towns of Charlotte, Cornelius, Pineville, and Mint Hill, the Hammerick clan closed ranks, leaving Thomas and the family that he had formed standing on the outside.

The first sign that Thomas Hammerick differed from his forefathers was his decision not to attend the law school at UNC Chapel Hill. For that part of his education, he not only stayed north of the Mason-Dixon line, but he went to Columbia, a school in the Yankee epicenter, that wasps' nest known as New York City. The fear was that Thomas would bring a girl home with him. One of the Lawson brothers had gone to New York City to study law, and he came home with a "Jewess" for a wife. That event provided for many years' worth of chatter and gossip. The young Mrs. Lawson, née Feldmann, insisted that her husband furnish her with two of everything for the kitchen. The young Mrs. Lawson made Mr. Lawson come home before sunset but only on Friday nights. The young Mrs. Lawson performed rituals with candles and foreign-language prayers. The now-much-older Mrs. Lawson was rumored to be haughty, lacking in social graces, and rarely seen outside of her own house.

When Thomas Hammerick returned to Charlotte alone, without altered taste in foods, scented letters, or any other visible signs of a foreign attachment, his family rewarded him with a brand-new 1956 Chevrolet Bel Air, which he uncharacteristically accepted. Except for the dining room full of wedding presents three and a half years later, which weren't his alone to refuse, Thomas never took another gift from his family. By the time I came along, his motto was "A gift means that you didn't earn it." Thankfully it didn't apply to his only child. As a father, he was generous. More or less. The "less" was because he never gave me what I wanted. He gave me only what he wanted me to have. I found this was often true with philanthropy and with love. The giver's desire and fulfillment played an important role.

As was the case with his father and grandfather, Thomas was an only child. The quasi one-child policy within this branch of the Hammerick clan was regarded with suspicion in Mecklenburg County. It was as if the Hammerick men had stood on a street corner and announced through a bullhorn that they had lost the will to touch their wives after the first couple of tries. It also smacked of stinginess. A not-so-subtle effort to consolidate wealth, most people thought.

The second sign that Thomas had strayed from a clearly marked path was his decision not to join the family's business. The Hammericks had made their money in cotton, which was another way of saying that they had made their money in slaves, but beginning with Graven's generation the family's income no longer had a direct connection to the land. Founded by Graven, the department store of Hammerick & Sons (the *s* showed that Graven was an optimist in his heart of hearts) was located in downtown Charlotte in a now-landmarked building, as it had been one of the first in the city to feature an electric elevator. Hammerick & Sons had to turn to a distant relation of the family to take over as the store's general manager. But even that didn't cause the family gates to shut on my father. Thomas was still in his family's good graces because he hadn't strayed very far. He had moved to Shelby in nearby Cleveland County and accepted a position with the law firm of Fletcher Burch, which weren't the last names of two people but the full name of one man.

When he was alive, "Fletch" Burch had a reputation. That was all that was ever said about Fletch in polite company, and, according to Baby Harper, my grandparents Spartan and Glory Hammerick were very polite. They were also very well informed. They knew that the law firm of Fletcher Burch had been in the capable hands of his son-in-law, Walter Wendell Whatley, ever since Burch's untimely death in a house fire. Through Spartan's cronies within the Mecklenburg County Democratic Party, he knew that Walter Wendell was going to run for a judgeship and that he was going to win. Through Glory's crones within the Charlotte Junior League, she knew that Walter Wendell and his wife, Iris, had an unmarried, pretty, blond daughter who was the same age as Thomas. Among the Hammericks, having a judge in the family was as good as having a minister. The Hammericks wanted to have an inside edge in both Heaven and Hell. The Hell that they feared was the one here on earth, a.k.a. any court of law. The Hammerick men, prior to Thomas, became lawyers not to practice law but to protect themselves from it. Unlike his father, Graven, Spartan was a pragmatist. If he had to choose between a judge and a minister, Spartan would rather have the judge on his side. Spartan knew that his odds, even without a minister, were better up in Heaven.

My father dated DeAnne Whatley for three years before they were married, and my great-uncle Harper's camera was on him from day one. Thomas walking up to the door of the green-shuttered colonial. Thomas standing in the backyard by the dogwood tree with a cigarette in his hand. Thomas sitting inside of his new Bel Air with the windows rolled up. This *here* was the confession. Because this wasn't how young men posed with their new cars. They stood next to them. They leaned their hips against the doors. They touched the hoods. The photograph of Thomas neatly tucked inside of that two-toned, red and white sedan made it look more like a flashy coffin than a car.

If he weren't my father, I would say that Thomas Hammerick was a calculating man for dating the boss's daughter. Though technically, he didn't ask DeAnne out until Walter Wendell had left the firm to become Judge Whatley. Six months after my father joined the firm of Fletcher Burch, Walter Wendell handed the managing partnership over to Carson Powell, the man who one day would have a granddaughter named Kelly. The courthouse in Shelby, visible from the front windows of Fletcher Burch's firm, had enough Corinthian columns and domes to strike awe and inspire trepidation in those who entered it. Located in the town's main square in order to remind us of the centrality of the Law in our everyday lives, the courthouse was surrounded by century-old water oak trees. On the afternoon that Walter Wendell strolled from one side of the street to the other for his swearing-in, he stopped by Thomas's office and invited him to the house on Piedmont Street for dinner. So, in fact, it was Walter Wendell who asked Thomas out on the first date.

Baby Harper was thirty-three years old when Thomas Hammerick pulled up to the green-shuttered colonial in his red and white Bel Air. My great-uncle already owned the Greek Revival by then, but he came over to Iris and Walter Wendell's house for dinner on most nights because Iris always had someone new cooking in the kitchen. Baby Harper liked the variety. He said it was like going to a different restaurant every couple of months. These cooks usually left once they had told Iris where she could shove their biscuits to keep them nice and warm.

My great-uncle told me that my father was handsome. That made me blush. I was twelve years old when I began to ask Baby Harper about the mysterious coupling of Thomas and DeAnne. I was just beginning to see my father as a person and a man. I stared hard at the photographs that my great-uncle was showing me, and I tried to imagine how that young man had become my father. That young man had dipped himself again and again into melted wax and was now unrecognizable underneath the accumulated layers. That young man had taken his eyes out and replaced them with a pair of thick glasses. That young man had lost his head of hair. I must have looked disappointed because Baby Harper said, "It's all right, Linda Vista. Your father, he had his moment in the sun."

There were three years' worth of photographs of Thomas Hammerick standing, sitting, and eating meals at the Whatleys'. There was also a set of candidgraphs from this period tucked into the back of one of the H.E.B.'s. Shoes were the recurring theme. Baby Harper had moved away from the blurry mid-strides of his youth. His taste had matured to close-ups of shoelaces untied. It was easy to recognize my father's shoes in these images. Leather wing tips, dark brown. When I was younger, the perforated pattern on the toe caps of my father's shoes made me think of the tops of Ritz crackers, and later those same tiny holes made me think of constellations in the night sky. Through the years, the only thing that had changed about my father's footwear was that he tied a more secure knot. When he passed away, in his closet were four pairs of shoes, exactly the same. The left heels were worn along the outside edge, and the right toes had a deep crease across them. DeAnne gave them to my great-uncle Harper because he wore the same size.

In the official photographs from "the courting years," as my great-uncle called them, DeAnne and Thomas never touched. *Here* was another confession. DeAnne always looked at Thomas and never at the camera. She was twenty-five years old, the same age as her beau, but she looked a decade older than he. Our family, my great-uncle told me, was afraid that DeAnne's "window" was about to close.

Now when I think about this euphemism, this aperture of feminine viability, I think of Rapunzel locked in her tall tower, staring down at the world, waiting for the plea that one day would change her life.

DeAnne had graduated from Gardner-Webb Baptist College and was working two days a week in the alumni office. Iris thought it would be a good way for her daughter to meet eligible men, but the only men DeAnne met there were those old enough to donate large sums of money to their alma mater. One by one, June after June, DeAnne's friends married the sons of these men and were now into their second pregnancies. On her days off, DeAnne went to visit these new mothers in their houses and hold their babies. When she looked at Thomas, that must have been what she saw. When Thomas looked straight ahead into the camera, he saw a small dark hole.

The other details of their courtship were lost to me because they were lost to my great-uncle Harper. When Thomas and DeAnne began driving off in the Bel Air right after dinner, not even waiting for the dessert, there was nothing that Baby Harper could do but have another cup of coffee. My great-uncle must have felt a lot of things sitting there nursing that second cup that he knew would keep him awake, pacing the halls of his Greek Revival. One of them was this. Baby Harper was anticipating the one-word epithet that Iris would spit at all of us before she died. As Thomas drove DeAnne along a moonlit road, never pushing past twenty-five miles per hour in a vehicle built for speed, DeAnne was thinking of the same two syllables. As Iris climbed into the four-poster bed that her parents had shared, like their fiery deaths, she said a prayer that she and Walter Wendell would never suffer its biting cold, alone.

When Thomas asked for DeAnne's hand in marriage, he and Walter Wendell were in the living room of the green-shuttered colonial. Baby Harper was in the dining room. Baby Harper overheard Walter Wendell say, "Counselor, I was going to have you disbarred if you'd waited a day longer!" There was laughter, and then there was a hush as Walter Wendell got right down to business. His daughter, DeAnne, was going to make it possible for him to keep the promise that he had made when he too had joined the family.

Like Thomas, Walter Wendell had joined the firm of Fletcher Burch first, though it didn't take him three years to marry the boss's daughter. He married Iris in three months. Fletch Burch had called him "Whirlwind Walter" while slapping him repeatedly on the back on the day of the wedding. Everyone knew that young Walter Wendell, bridegroom, was also now the firm's newest partner. Fletch's management philosophy was simple. Family first. No one had predicted that in a matter of days Whirlwind Walter would again earn his name.

Walter Wendell knew that Fletch understood ambition. Fletch, however, also believed in a man keeping his word. Walter Wendell handing over the law firm, if only temporarily, to a non-family steward wasn't part of the bargain that Fletch had made with his son-in-law. If only more than a cupful of his ashes had been found, Fletch would have turned over in his grave, knocked a hole through the side panel of his coffin, and headed straight for the courthouse to drag Walter Wendell off the bench. There were probably enough ashes to make a fist, though, and Walter Wendell had dreamed about that fist coming down on his head, a gavel demanding justice.

My father must have known what he was getting himself into. A partnership at Fletcher Burch was like a brand-new Bel Air. He hadn't earned it. Thomas must have known that DeAnne was the key, and, as was true of all keys, she could open doors and lock them shut.

Chapter 6

Orville Wright was the first American man to fly. His older brother Wilbur was the second. Together they entered history as "the Wright brothers," equal and two-headed. In the privacy of their sibling rivalry, alone and always one-sided, Wilbur never forgot that Orville was the first to raise himself off the ground and touch it down again with all his limbs intact. The brothers knew that their true achievement wasn't flight but flight accompanied by a safe landing. Icarus flew. It was how he descended that determined why his story was told and retold. *Icarus flew.* That was what the brothers said to each other by way of a prayer, and as a reminder that flying wasn't their only goal. Wilbur, till the day he died, would look into Orville's eyes, which reminded him of his own and of the North Carolina sky, and see there a speck of gray, a plane lifting into the clear blue. When Orville blinked, this reminded Wilbur that the first flight was only twelve seconds long. Between the two of them, there were four successful attempts that day. The last one and the longest in duration belonged to Wilbur: fifty-nine seconds. An appreciable difference that, once their identities became factually entwined, was often overlooked and forgotten. Wilbur flew. He wrote it on a piece of paper and placed it inside his shoe. He did it to assert his personhood and to document the singularity of his achievement. *Wilbur flew.*

I first read about the Wright brothers in the pages of *North Carolina,* and from that moment on I have liked Wilbur better. I cross-stitched his two-word declaration of independence onto a handkerchief that I made in my sixth-grade home economics class. I used periwinkle floss and dotted the *i* with a star. I received a C-minus for my efforts. My stitches were uneven, and the cursive *f* looked more like a *b.* I had intended the handkerchief as a Christmas gift for Kelly. I kept it instead.

From second to eighth grade, Wade and I shared the same school bus stop, located at the front of his house by a SLOW CHILDREN sign. We were the only kids who lived on Oak Street. Irony, thankfully, came late to us. We were lucky in that way. On cold fall mornings Wade's mom would send him out with two paper cups of hot cocoa, the kind with the very small marshmallows included in the mix, so tiny that they threw off our sense of perspective. Looking down at these floating white dots, we felt like giants. The first time Wade handed me a cup, he said, "My mom*chocolatemilk* says this is for you*cannedgreenbeans*." After that, the handoffs were silent. What more was there to say? Cup, cocoa, giants, wait, cold, bus, school. All the important things between us were already established and understood. I didn't need another word, and he, being a boy, didn't know that words were necessary. We left the empty cups at the base of the street sign and climbed aboard the bus, and by the time we were dropped off in the afternoon the cups were gone.

On colder winter mornings, Wade's mom drove us to school. DeAnne never offered, and my father would have disapproved if he had known. What was he paying taxes for if his daughter was being shuttled to school in a private vehicle? If he was in a joking mood (most people didn't know that my father had a sense of humor), he would have said, ". . . in a private Episcopalian vehicle?" Wade's mom would have laughed at that. She laughed a lot. She laughed a lot with Wade. In the mornings, when he opened the front door of the faded-red-T-shirt house, I would hear her. That was even better than the cocoa.

Wade's sense of humor, like my father's, was dry and difficult to detect. That was how I knew that his mom would have laughed at a line like "Episcopalian vehicle." There was an absurdist quality about it—that anyone would use "Episcopalian" to modify a car—that she would have appreciated. Also, in light of what became of her, I think she would have enjoyed the critique, tucked in between those two words, of a small town's proclivity for parceling differences, big and small.

The first time that her son and I had what could be called a conversation, I was the initiator. It was the first day of sixth grade, and Wade and I were, as usual, waiting for the school bus. Wade must have wanted to ride his new ten-speed bike to school instead. He was looking up at the familiar street sign. He looked amused and disgusted at the same time. Irony, an avenging angel, had visited him. Wade's hands were shoved into the front pockets of his jeans. His T-shirt said ASTEROIDS in yellow letters, edged in a ring of red, both colors primary and bold. I was thinking about how an additional *s* could really change the meaning of this word. I was thinking about Kelly writing K+W all over her new binders and notebooks. I looked down at the sidewalk, and then my words came out softly, barely audible. I knew because Wade asked, "Huh?"

I repeated my question, looking up not at his face but at the center of his T-shirt. I meant my question to be comprehensive. I wanted to know what his mom was laughing about that morning, and I wanted to know what she had been laughing about for the past five years.

Wade began with the past five years.

"I tell*brownsugar* her jokes*cornflakes*," he replied.

"What*grahamcracker*?" I asked, even though I had heard him. Every word. I just wanted him to say them again because of what they were doing to my mouth.

He did. This time he added, "Every*Ritzcracker* morning*Hardee'scheeseburger*."

"What*grahamcracker* was it today*oatmeal*?" I asked.

"Knock*peanutbrittle* knock*peanutbrittle*," he said.

"Oh," I said, moving my eyes from ASTEROIDS up to the street sign, in anticipation that our exchange was coming to an end. But Wade wasn't finished. He wanted to tell me about that morning.

"Say, 'Who's there*applejuice*?'" he said.

"Who's there*applejuice*?"

"Wade*orangesherbet*."

"Wade*orangesherbet* who?"

"Wade*orangesherbet* who? Wade*orangesherbet* who?! Mom*chocolatemilk*, I'm your son*cinnamon*. Jeez, don't you*cannedgreenbeans* remember*butterpecanicecream* me?"

I laughed out loud.

Wade looked amazed.

"That was dumb*cannedspinach*," I said.

"I know*grapejelly*," he said, grinning, as the school bus pulled up and opened its door.

I sat up front, and Wade went to the back, same as in previous years. When the bus pulled up to Kelly's stop (three after ours), I turned around and caught a glimpse of him. He was staring out of the window. There was a *W* written onto the pane. On the tip of his right index finger must have been an oval of dust.

Kelly squeezed in next to me and whispered, "Cute*mashedpotatoes*."

I thought she meant my new purse, a Bermuda bag like hers. My father had finally given in after DeAnne took him aside during a recent Sunday dinner and whisper-yelled to him that my MONTHLY CYCLE had started and that I would need something to carry my FEMININE HYGIENE PRODUCTS in.

DeAnne, just like her mother, Iris, had perfected the art. She yelled the embarrassing parts and whispered the rest. My grandmother, whose sense of humor was barbed like her tongue, leaned across the dinner table and asked if I knew why a woman's monthly cycle was called her "period." Iris smiled before quickly answering her own question: Because when a woman mentions it to a man, that's the end of their conversation. My great-uncle Harper lowered his eyes, picked up his fork, and pushed the food on his plate into four equal quadrants. My great-uncle called this move "the cross of avoidance."

When my father returned to the dinner table, his face was flushed. DeAnne's wasn't. Iris was right. My father never brought up the purse or its function again.

Kelly stole a quick glance over her shoulder, and I knew. She hadn't meant the green turtles stitched across the cover of my Bermuda bag but Wade, the orange sherbet boy.

If Kelly and I were a suspension bridge (and we were, or at least our friendship was), this was the moment when our steel cables began to snap. I had had the entire summer to prepare, and still the moment took my breath away.

Kelly had spent that summer—what I called the summer of Dill and Wade but for her it was mostly the summer of Wade—writing very long letters to me. I wrote to her too, but my missives became shorter and shorter. I had less and less to say. As she was the one who had declared a crush on a real boy, she became the heroine of our lives and our letters. I became a mirror or an echo. Every Saturday night, Kelly wrote her weekly *Wade Report.* Kelly and her parents had their weekly dinner out at Slo Smoking. Barbecue was as great a divider as religion, greater if you believed my great-uncle Harper. Slo Smoking and Bridges were parallel universes, where Southern Baptists, Episcopalians, and the small band of Catholics (this was what the adults in our lives always called them, which at first made me think that the Small Band of Catholics were a musical group, something along the lines of the Partridge Family), though never the former Miss Feldmann (who didn't eat pork, the only meat worth barbecuing in the Old North State), could bury their differences in paper napkins soaked with sauce and then separate again along two distinct lines. We were a Bridges family, and Kelly knew it. Where you consumed your pulled pork and coleslaw was another form of fate in the greater Boiling Springs–Shelby area.

Every Saturday, the Powells arrived at Slo Smoking at 5 P.M. sharp, and Wade and his folks came in fifteen minutes later. I had never been inside of Slo, so I didn't know if they had booths or tables. Kelly didn't provide me with such useful details. She was interested only in Wade. What he had on (always Levi's and a T-shirt); what soft drinks he ordered (7UP); what he may have been thinking (there's that nice girl from homeroom!) when she and her folks walked by his family on their way out. Kelly never gave up on the exclamation mark. She was very optimistic for a fat girl. Maybe she knew all along that fat wasn't an immutable characteristic. Fat wasn't fate.

My response to the *Wade Report* was not to submit one of my own. That summer, I saw the orange sherbet boy every day, except Sundays, riding his new ten-speed up and down our street. I missed the green Schwinn Sting-Ray. The new bike, with its multicolored metallic finish, looked fast, and he rode it fast. About a week before the beginning of school, Wade had stopped his bike in front of the blue and gray ranch house and watched as our jungle gym was being hauled onto the back of a pickup truck. I was standing in the front doorway of the house, also witnessing the final stage of its removal. DeAnne wanted the space in the backyard for a rose arbor, and she declared that I was too old now for that-jungle-thing anyway. She had called it that-jungle-thing from day one. Wade and I looked at each other as the pickup truck pulled away. He waved to me. Kelly, all summer long, was never able to include those four words in her reports.

The look of Kelly's letters changed that summer. She no longer dotted her *i*'s with an anatomical heart. The ventricles receded into the organ. The muscle puffed and took on the symmetrical shape of its most common misrepresentation. It was fitting that she signaled her abandonment of reality in this small way.

On the bus that first morning of sixth grade, I knew that nothing had changed between Kelly and Wade. She was still an invisible fat girl, and he was a beatific boy, a body that she had dragged into her life by the sheer force of her will. In the years that followed, Kelly would join the ranks of the beautiful and the popular, but nothing, I thought, had changed between the two of them. The orange sherbet boy and I, though, we were in for a transformation. As the school bus turned in to the short driveway that led to our middle school, I turned my head for another glimpse of Wade.

"Cute*mashedpotatoes*," Kelly whispered again into my ear.

The word that shot out of my mouth surprised her. I knew because she pulled her hand away from the row of turtles marching across my new purse. This time she wasn't talking about Wade, but I was.

"Mine*apple*," I said.

Chapter 7

On the tenth day of her life, Virginia Dare was taken from the arms of history and placed on legend's lap. Unfortunately for her, legend was a man. Legend wasn't dirty and old, but mean and probably love-scorned in light of his treatment of her. Dare's years as a sticky-faced toddler, a quiet adolescent, and an acne-prone teen were altogether ignored and forgotten. When Dare reemerged after her disappearance, she did so fully formed, Athena-like from the foreheads, or was it Diana-like from the groins, of the men who called North Carolina home. The women, on the same shores, wouldn't have imagined Dare's life in quite the same way. Around the campfires and by the hearths, a story of physical beauty, male envy, naïve love, and violence-as-antidote was born. This story was given Virginia Dare's name. As this was an American legend, it also included Indians and a brief and unsettling mention of Queen Elizabeth.

Legend had it (because he willed it and made it so) that Virginia Dare was raised by kindly Indians, who were charmed and perhaps civilized by her mere presence. Why and how Virgin—that was how the Indians had truncated her name, thus revealing her true narrative essence—became an orphan was never addressed. That sort of information would have given her character too much psychological depth and nuance. Virgin, as far as legend was concerned, was a young woman of startling beauty, and she attracted the attention of a handsome Indian brave named O-kis-ko. She called him "O!" for short. Virgin and O! were very happy together, as attractive couples often are in legends, and this enraged another Indian man named Wanchese, an evil magician whom we can assume was also lonely and ugly. Wanchese cast a spell and turned Virgin into the White Doe, which as a species was known for its attractive tail. The White Doe could be released from the evil spell only if shot through the heart by an arrow made from oyster pearl. O! possessed such an arrow. Unfortunately for O!, Wanchese possessed an arrow made of sterling silver, given to him by Queen Elizabeth. Legend unwisely left the connection between the Indian magician and Queen Elizabeth to our imagination. On the day of a big hunt, O! and Wanchese saw the White Doe, and they shot their arrows at the same time, if you know what I mean. They pierced the animal's heart at precisely the same moment. The White Doe was transformed back into a beautiful young woman by the oyster-pearl arrow, and she died, pierced through and through by the silver one.

I dare you. I double dare you. I Virginia Dare you. That was the progression, the upping of the ante that Kelly and I devised for ourselves. A Virginia Dare meant different things to us at different times in our girlhood, but it was always an invocation of a danger that mystified us.

We were both eight years old when we first read about Virginia Dare in the pages of *North Carolina.* Kelly and I thought that the story about the first child of our state was a warning about how being too beautiful could get us killed. It was already a common hazard in the other stories of our youth. Snow White, too beautiful and poisoned. Cinderella, too beautiful and condemned to domestic hard labor. Beauty, eponymously too beautiful and given up to a Beast. So when Kelly and I first evoked Virginia Dare's name, the challenge was this: to not brush our teeth for a week. We figured that neglecting our mouths and what was inside of them would be the easiest way to ensure that being too beautiful, a potentially deadly fate, wouldn't happen to us. From all the toothpaste and mouthwash commercials on TV, which always ended with the girl and the guy getting their mouths *too* close to each other, we knew that white teeth and fresh breath were essential for beauty. We didn't want any boy to get too close to us. It was a dare that we both thought up and accepted.

I gave up on not brushing after three days. The bits of food stuck in between my teeth made the incomings even worse, like being served food on an already dirty plate. Kelly lasted the whole week. She was a natural faker. For seven mornings and seven nights, she went into the bathroom and squeezed a bit of toothpaste into her hands, which she would then wash with warm water, leaving the bathroom and herself smelling minty fresh. She would also wet her toothbrush and smear a dot of toothpaste onto the basin of the sink, leaving it there as a false residue. Kelly wrote in letter #64 that it was also very important not to smile. How Beth Anne didn't notice that her only child hadn't brushed her teeth or smiled for a week were questions that we didn't think to ask back then.

When we were eleven and we Virginia Dared, the lurking fear was that the love of an ugly man would turn us into an animal. Being ugly, we understood by then, was the same as being evil. Jesus, for instance, was a very handsome man. That was why we adored Him. He was our first crush. Kelly had a poster of Him up in her room. I thought of Him before I went to bed every night. This was called worshipping and praying, and we were encouraged to do both. This time Kelly came up with the dare and it was this: to go to bed naked. No nightgown. No underwear. Kelly, already a

B-cup, had forgotten all about her cousin Bobby. I hadn't forgotten. He had asked her if she slept that way. He had whispered the question, and the words had tickled her ear. He then whispered nothing as he forced Kelly's hand. Bobby was only months away from riding in circles around the blue and gray ranch house. The winged monster hadn't found me yet, but he would.

I wrote to Kelly that sleeping without clothes on was a sin. Jesus, I was certain, was never naked.

"Then how did Jesus take a bath?" Kelly wrote back, double-daring me.

"Jesus didn't have to take a bath because he was always clean," I replied, Virginia Daring her.

Kelly accepted. We agreed that she would do it the next time I slept over. Even though "it" was a sin, I felt that I had to be present for verification purposes.

A week later, we climbed into Kelly's canopy bed and got under its yellow eyelet covers. It was a Saturday night, and we had spent most of it eating junk food and putting the final touches on our scrapbook devoted to Dolly Parton. By bedtime we were stuffed with potato chips and images of our idol, which made us greasy and glowing. Our soundtrack that day and every day of 1979 was Dolly's album *Heartbreaker.* We liked the title song best. "*Heartbreaker . . . sweet little love maker . . . couldn't you be just a little more kind to me.*" We really liked what Dolly wore on the album cover. A pink dress with a hemline that was higher in front than at the back and silver high-heeled shoes. Her hairdo looked to us like a swirl from the top of a lemon meringue pie. When we looked at her picture, we felt a vibration all around our bodies. This was the effect of experiencing pure joy. We would miss this sensation in the years to come.

Kelly wiggled out of her nightgown and then her undershirt and panties and handed them to me. I placed the bundle on the nightstand on my side of the bed. She whispered that the sheets felt "slippery*milk,*" and I gulped, breathless for a second. I reached up to turn off the bedside lamp, and the eyelet covers lifted up with me. A faint smell of sweat and baby shampoo rose up from the bed. I reached for Kelly's hand and we closed our eyes. We thought that holding hands would allow us to have the same dreams. It never happened that way, but it did give us the feeling of being closer.

We Virginia Dared for the last time when we were fourteen. Kelly flipped through my well-worn copy of *North Carolina* and gave it one final incisive read. She laughed that sharp, quick laugh that smart girls all had, until they found out that the sound of brilliance flashing made boys nervous. Most of these girls, Kelly included, then adopted that slow, bubbling giggle that put boys at ease. It was the kind of laughter that said, "I'm stupid. You can take off my shirt, if you want." Kelly, who had understood subtext long before she knew that there was a word for it, asked me if I understood what this Dare story was *really* about. Not waiting for my answer, Kelly told me that the White Doe was a warning about arrows. Be careful of a man's arrow, or maybe the warning was even more specific. You don't know if a man is good or evil until you see his arrow. Another quick, sharp laugh. I blushed. Kelly then proposed the last Virginia Dare of our youth. "Speaking of penetration" was how she indelicately began.

It was the summer before high school, and Kelly and I had just reached the watershed decisions to diet and to smoke. I understood the need for our transformation, but I didn't understand where our transformation was going to lead us. Kelly understood. Again, she called dibs. Wade was to be her arrow. I would be left to find mine among the other young males in Boiling Springs. According to the thesaurus, a book that would become increasingly invaluable to me for reasons that Roget couldn't have imagined, another word for "arrow" was "shaft." According to the dictionary, another meaning of "shaft" was to treat unfairly.

As Kelly spoke the words I dare you, I double-dare you, I Virginia Dare you (when she said "you," she usually meant "us") to lose your virginity before the end of the year, she knew that I had already lost mine, by force and not by choice. Yet she said the words anyway, banishing from my experience and hers all the hidden dangers of our shared girlhood. As far as Kelly was concerned, both of us could still choose who would approach us first with a bow and arrow.

My period began when I was eleven years old, three months after DeAnne thought it had. I woke up one morning to stickiness between my legs and the smell of raw meat in my bed. There was no one to tell. The news had preceded the occurrence. I practiced saying it anyway, "My period*blueberrymuffin* started*unsaltedbutter* today*oatmeal*." This was a comforting sentence for me. Or rather the words triggered a sequence of comforting flavors for me. I had just learned the trick of stringing together words to produce the tastes that I wanted. I was particularly fond of this thread: "walnut, elephant, candle, jogger." These words brought forth the following in this satisfying order: ham steak, sugar-cured and pan-fried; sweet potatoes baked with lots of butter; 7UP (though more of the lime than the lemon, like when it's icy cold); fresh strawberries, sweet and ripe.

Growing up with DeAnne for a mother, I could count on one hand the times that I have had a really good meal like that. Every once in a while an ingredient would slip past DeAnne's fingers unspoiled. Fresh strawberries, for example. During the summers, my great-uncle Harper and I would go to the pick-your-own farms in the nearby town of Kings Mountain, and the berries that we brought back were so red, perfect, and fragrant that even DeAnne left them alone. That was perhaps my favorite memory of my mother, her walking out of the kitchen with a cut-glass bowl full of strawberries. A bowl of Cool Whip would be waiting at the table for them, but I never touched the stuff, not after Baby Harper called it edible shaving cream.

I didn't understand until I had left Boiling Springs and specifically the sphere of influence of DeAnne's kitchen why so many of the incomings of my childhood were mildly unpleasant, bland, or unremarkable at best. The reason was disarmingly simple. The experiential flavors had to come first. Once the memories of them—of the canned, the frozen, the surprised, the à la king—had lodged themselves in my brain, then and only then could these tastes attach themselves to the words in my vocabulary, without cause or consideration for the meanings of the words.

I too had to disregard the meanings of the words if I wanted to enjoy what the words could offer me. At first, the letting go of meaning was a difficult step for me to take, like loosening my fingers from the side of a swimming pool for the very first time. The world suddenly became vast and fluid. Anything could happen to me as I drifted toward the deep end of the pool. But without words, resourceful and revealing, who would know of the dangers that I faced? I would be defenseless. I would drown. Maybe all children felt this way. We grabbed on to words because we thought they could save us. "Momma" got us a pair of hands, a bosom to hide our faces in. "Papa" got us a lift skyward, a perch on a shoulder. Maybe our first words all had the same meaning: Save me! A plea that, if answered, reinforced our desire to acquire more, to amass a vocabulary that could be our arsenal against the unknown terrors of life. To let go of meaning was to allow for the possibility that words didn't hold within them this promise of salvation. Or, because of my misuse of the words, I alone wouldn't be saved. Of course, I was afraid.

The first time it was out of necessity. I was hungry and the casserole du jour was chicken à la king, my least favorite in DeAnne's rotation. As she scooped it onto our plates, she announced its name, as if we had never seen this dish before. As usual, there were gray slices of canned mushrooms to which the thick, dun-colored sauce refused to adhere. A repulsion on a molecular level, perhaps. The sauce stuck to the egg noodles and the chicken pieces instead, lending its gluey, spongy texture to both the starch and the meat. I excused myself from the dinner table to go wash my hands, and then

I, a skinny eleven-year-old, sat on the edge of the bathtub and blurted out, "Not again*pancakenosyrup.*"

There it was. Sustenance. Simple. Without sauce.

Each repetition of "again" was a revelation. The faster I said it, the more intense and mouth-filling the taste became. Each repetition was a restitution for past meals suffered. Each repetition was an inoculation for future meals to be endured. I wanted to see how many times I would have to say the word in order to approximate the feeling of being full. I flipped on the bathroom fan so that no one would hear. Soon a knock on the bathroom door and my father's voice saying my name in the form of a question made me stop short.

Why hadn't I stumbled on this simple solution before? I had edged close to it. I had learned that the word could diminish and deflect. DeAnne's favorite dinnertime rebuke, "selfish*cornonthecob,*" had already taught me that lesson. I was slower to understand that the word could also fulfill and satisfy. But let me ask this question. How old were you when you first touched yourself for the sake of pleasure? Your body and its attendant parts were always there, were they not? But we all have to learn how to use what we were born with for something other than the functional and the obvious. All of our bodies hold within them secret chambers and cells.

When I was growing up, the taste of pancakes meant the kind that my great-uncle made for me from Bisquick. If condensed cream of mushroom soup was the Great Assimilator, then this "instant" baking mix was the American Dream. With it, we could do anything. Biscuits, waffles, coffee cakes, muffins, dumplings, and the list continues to grow even now in a brightly lit test kitchen full of optimism. My great-uncle used Bisquick for only one purpose, which was to make pancakes, but he liked knowing that the possibilities, the sweet and the savory, were all in that cheery yellow box. Baby Harper wasn't a fat man, but he ate like a fat man. His idea of an afternoon snack was a stack of pancakes, piled three high. After dancing together, Baby Harper and I would go into his kitchen, where he would make the Dream happen. He ate his pancakes with butter and Log Cabin syrup, and I ate my one pancake plain, each bite a fluffy amalgam of dried milk and vanillin. A chemical stand-in for vanilla extract, vanillin was the cheap perfume of all the instant, industrialized baked goods of my childhood. I recognized its signature note in all the cookies that DeAnne brought home from the supermarket: Nilla Wafers, Chips Ahoy!, Lorna Doones. I loved them all. They belonged, it seemed to me, to the same family, baked by the same faceless mother or grandmother in the back of our local Piggly Wiggly supermarket.

The first time that I tasted pancakes made from scratch was in 1990, when Leo, a.k.a. the parsnip, made them for me. We had just begun dating, and homemade pancakes was the ace up his sleeve. He shook buttermilk. He melted butter. He grated lemon zest. There was even a spoonful of pure vanilla extract. I couldn't bring myself to call what he had made for us "pancakes." There were no similarities between those delicate disks and what my great-uncle and I had shared so often in the middle of the afternoon. Leo told me that another word for pancakes was "flapjacks." I couldn't bring myself to call them that either, because "flapjacks" sounded to me like a euphemism for an uncircumcised penis (this objection I shared with Leo, which made him laugh and then, in typical male fashion, he asked me how many had I seen). I also didn't like the word "flapjacks" because it tasted of sauerkraut (this objection I didn't share with Leo, because how could I?). I settled on "griddle cakes," two words that had no taste whatsoever. Voids.

Over the course of our almost eight-year-long relationship, Leo would understand that I had a sensitivity to words. He just never would understand why. He thought that I was too attuned to their sounds. Yes and no. He thought that I made too many associations between the words and tangential, wholly subjective concepts (see *flapjacks*). Yes and no. He thought that I was clinically depressed. Leo thought everyone was clinically something. He was in his last year of medical school and had just finished his psych rotation when we first met. I had learned by then how to control my facial expressions. I no longer winced, for example, when I heard "prune" or "Powell" or "you" or any of the hundreds of words that I found literally distasteful. I couldn't control, however, the cumulative effect of having to experience their incomings. So on those days when I had encountered too many of them, Leo would find that I was subdued and in search of a dark, quiet room. The opposite, of course, was also true (see *walnut* or *elephant* or *candle* or *jogger*). My emotional lows and highs were therefore inexplicable and unpredictable to Leo.

Some people were smart like a diamond. Kelly, for example. Reflective, impressive clarity, beautiful to have around. When I was in college and especially in law school, I realized that the people around me were smart like a whip. Scarring, thought-clearing, exhilarating, and best to be avoided. Leo was a whip. He was hyperarticulate. His mouth was never quite able to keep pace with his brain. His gray cells pushed out his words, configured into perfectly constructed sentences, paragraphs, and pages. In this way, he was a variant on the singing-talker, a cappella. And like my great-uncle Harper, Leo chose me.

It was possible that I fell in love with Leo the moment he told me his first name, which tasted of parsnips, a peculiar vegetable, or rather a distinctive one:

A celery and a potato meet and have a love child. The celery departs soon thereafter, and the potato thinks of their fleeting time together with fondness and longing. Skating around the edges of their unlikely love affair is a McIntosh apple, contributing to the tableau all of its faint spiciness but none of its obvious sweet or sour.

Yes, it was very possible that I fell in love with his name first.

"Leo*parsnip,*" I remembered saying back to him and smiling.

The Amtrak train was pulling out of Penn Station. It was the Wednesday before Thanksgiving, and the train from New York to

Boston was packed. He was walking slowly through the crowded car trying to find an available seat. Before sitting down next to me, he said, "Hi*greenLifesavers,* my name*grapes* is Leo*parsnip.* Is this seat*rawcarrots* taken?" Unremarkable, except for the unnecessary volunteering of a first name. Quotidian. Banal. Except to me. My smile must have encouraged him to continue the conversation despite the headphones that I had over my ears. He mouthed, "What are you listening to?"

"Dolly Parton*Sweet'nLow,*" I replied.

He laughed.

I should have lied. I should have answered Bach or U2. I never told the truth about DP. Never. So, why had I without hesitation offered up the Madonna of my childhood to this stranger on a train? Thanksgiving, perhaps. Baby Harper was far away, and my body was moving even farther north. The slight rubbing of a stranger's coat sleeve against mine. The taste of his name in my mouth. All these things were also possible answers.

I turned off my Walkman, took off my headphones, and Virginia Dared myself to ask him, "What's*grahamcracker* so funny*cucumber,* Leo*parsnip?*"

Chapter 8

Wilbur Wright would remember the sound of the wind rushing into him at thirty-one miles per hour as a song written only for him. Even as he was experiencing the sensation of speed—the coldest day in December he could ever imagine, his internal organs lurching forward telling him to go *faster, faster*—he knew the song would soon end. The question was how.

Wilbur, as his younger brother Orville had done just minutes before, was lying flat on his stomach, and above and below him were two flat fabric "wings" stretched tight over a delicate framework of wood. To those in the village of Kitty Hawk who had seen it but didn't understand it, Wilbur was strapped inside of a giant box kite, a toy that these two well-mannered, well-dressed brothers had come to play with on the shores of the Atlantic, among the sand dunes and the wind gusts of the Outer Banks of the Old North State. This was the fourth time that the Wright brothers had come to Kitty Hawk, and each time they had kept to themselves except for the occasional trips into the village to buy food and supplies. The ladies of Kitty Hawk and their daughters had observed that neither Wilbur, the elder, with the balding, egg-shaped head, nor

Orville, the younger, with the dashing mustache, wore a wedding band. The brothers were both a bit slight of build for some tastes, but all of Kitty Hawk were in agreement that these two men must be of independent means to have the time and the money to amuse themselves as they did. The daughters of Kitty Hawk understood, though, that these men had eyes only for the heavens above them. Wilbur, especially, was always looking up. Blue skies with billowy white clouds would make his plain, serious face cavort. He and Orville would exchange a quick, knowing look, and like lovers they were off to the beach. There in a shack, or a "hangar," as the brothers called it, their true love waited for them. Wilbur and Orville gave every penny they made to her. They gave her their youth. She would make them immortal. She was 745 pounds, had a motor filled with fuel, and was ready for flight.

As Wilbur took in the village of Kitty Hawk from 852 feet up in the air, he thought for one second about the pact that he and Orville had entered into and for another second he felt fear. A third second was devoted to their father, Bishop Milton Wright of the Church of the United Brethren in Christ, and to his sermons about the Devil and the great and evil deeds that he allowed men to do in his name. This sequence of thoughts left Wilbur with fifty-six seconds remaining to fly unencumbered. He did. All the while, Wilbur was hearing his song.

From sixth to eighth grade, Wade the orange sherbet boy and I continued the conversation that I had started on the first day of sixth grade. We began the moment that we both got to the bus stop in the morning, and we ended five to seven minutes later, when the bus pulled up to the SLOW CHILDREN sign. What began with his repertoire of knock-knock jokes grew to include the pros and cons of his favorite arcade games, his thoughts on why basketball was better than football, and what small animals he had spotted while riding his bike around Boiling Springs. I told him about what I was reading, mostly Greek myths and about the constellations that went with them. I drew the stars for Wade on my notebook because when he and I talked they were hidden in the sky. I told Wade that if we had lived long ago we would have used these constellations to remember stories and to find our way home again when we sailed the seas. He said he had been to the Outer Banks and had seen the Atlantic Ocean and that he didn't like its choppy waters. I said I hadn't made up my mind, which really meant that I hadn't seen anything larger than Moss Lake, landlocked and nearby.

Because there was always a known and dependable endpoint to our talks, I was able to enjoy them. I was also fast learning the art of hiding what was happening to me inside. If the incomings were particularly unpleasant—mornings were, and still are, the most difficult time for me as I'm more sensitive after a night of sleep and silence—I would pretend to look at something past Wade's shoulders, behind me, or down at my shoes.

Later in life, I would find that this technique worked well for other reasons as well. Men would think that I was distracted, uninterested, or bored with them, and they would work even harder to get my attention. I had inadvertently tapped into the shallow recesses of the male psyche and into the instinct known as the Chase. The principles were simple, though many books have been written about them for consumption by lovelorn females. The first principle was that the most coveted Prey was the one that didn't want to be caught (see such classics as *Catch Me If You Can* and *Foxes & Bunnies*). The second principle was that the most coveted Prey was the one that was in someone else's mouth (see *I'll Have What He's Having* and *First, You Date His Best Friend*).

Wade and I were precariously close but not yet part of the full-blown pursuit. Our morning exchanges of jokes, declaratives, and minutiae were our way of running around each other and sniffing at each other's scent. Talking with Wade made me feel like I was dancing fast with my eyes closed. I was learning that I was willing to endure a lot of words to feel this way. My whole body was awake. I heard Wade's voice, as I heard my great-uncle's 45's, with my skin. How Wade felt talking to me wasn't a question that I had to ask myself or him because doubt, a toxin that entered my body at the onset of puberty, was miraculously absent. On these mornings, Wade and I were in the privacy of a small town with a dwindling population and a low birthrate. We had Oak Street to ourselves.

On the bus, during school hours, and among our classmates, Wade was a boy and I was a girl, indifferent to each other. We were all living through the last days of our gender segregation. Though pretty girls like Sally Campbell and fat ones like Kelly Powell had already divulged to their best friends that integration wasn't only inevitable it was exceedingly desirable. For now, Wade and I kept to our assigned worlds even as we exited the bus in the afternoons. We were careful, as eyes were on us. We were cautious not to look at each other or to wave goodbye because it would have been a signal to the others.

On the last morning of seventh grade, Wade told me that he and his mother were going to Florida for the summer. His grandmother lived in Tampa, and she was lonely for her daughter and grandson. That was what his mother told him at the time. Then Wade asked me whether my heart was beating fast.

I answered yes. It was true, and it didn't occur to me to lie.

He said that his was too.

I understood that in the coded language of late boyhood this meant that he was looking forward to seeing me in the fall, to resuming our morning talks, to feeling once again like he was riding his bike down a hill with his arms raised high above his head.

In law school, I would learn that translators, the ones who performed simultaneous translations for the United Nations, for instance, didn't translate word for word. Instead, the translators would see an image in their heads as they heard language A, and then they would describe that image back using language B. That was what was happening to me. Two years' worth of five to seven minutes a day, five days a week, had made me fluent in another language. I understood Boy or, at the least, I understood this boy. I smiled at him to let him know.

By the seventh grade, what had begun as the *Wade Report* had become the *Wade Daily News.* Kelly was the editor in chief, and I was the sole subscriber. It was a good and early lesson on why we shouldn't believe all that we read. Kelly also continued to write K+W on all of her notebooks, a constellation with an accompanying myth. I saw it every day but that didn't make it true. I understood then why the word "crush" was used to describe a one-sided bout of adoration. The object of her desire—her crush—was pressing down on a main artery, cutting off the blood flow to her brain. I was amazed by the degeneration. She was blessed with a lot of gray cells to begin with, so what was happening to her wasn't as crippling as it could have been. Her fantasy life with Wade was undeniably rich and full and sustaining her through the last years of her invisibility and isolation. Kelly's letters to me then were lit up with conjectures. He looked at her in the hallway. He dropped a pencil by her desk in math class. He looked happy yesterday on the bus; maybe he was thinking about her.

The flip side of Kelly's constructed reality was her complete and irreversible silence about her cousin Bobby. She never talked about him, and I in turn had to do the same because she was the only one who knew. Her willed amnesia didn't keep him from being present in my life. He was there every time I heard the whirr of a lawn mower or saw the wings of a bird spread for flight. Sometimes he was there when I looked at Kelly. That was the unexpected part, the haunting of one body by another body, the transference of culpability from the perpetrator to the one who had knowledge of the crime. Back then, all I understood was that sometimes when I looked at Kelly I felt a flash of hate. The saving grace—besides what Jesus did to Bobby—was that I never saw Bobby in Wade. When I looked at the orange sherbet boy, I never saw the same body. I never recognized the hands, the rise and fall of the chest, each intake quick and sharp.

I would recognize the monster, robber, blade, in plenty of other male bodies, though. My tenth grade algebra teacher, Pastor Reynold, Leo's older brother—they all would show themselves to me in different ways. Sometimes their confessions were fast and intense and then quickly disappeared. The pastor's eyes staring not into my soul but at my breasts, for example. More often their confessions were obvious and unrelenting. The algebra teacher's hand on the small of my back every time I stood at the blackboard had nothing to do with simplifying an equation. Leo's brother telling me stories from their childhood, ones that always ended with little Leo lying in a puddle of mud or crying, was another example.

When we reconvened at the SLOW CHILDREN sign, which was now not only insulting but also inaccurate, on the first morning of eighth grade, I looked at Wade and saw him through Kelly's eyes. Wade was beautiful. My heart was beating fast even before he smiled. Travel had changed him. The distance between North Carolina and Florida had elongated his body. He was a whole head taller. His hair was sun-bleached from spending every day of the summer at the beach. His tanned skin was the same color as mine. Miraculously, we resumed the rhythm of our morning conversations, with their easy exchanges of unrelated topics and un-prioritized asides.

Over the next few weeks, though, it would become clear to me that the subjects that interested Wade had now changed. He told me about skateboarding, about bands that I had never heard on the radio, and, like my father, he dreamed aloud about New York City. Travel had made Wade worldly. In the parlance of thirteen-year-olds circa 1981, he was cool. He had crossed several state lines and lived in a city with more than one traffic light. He had seen television channels you had to pay for and spent many hours watching one called MTV, where songs had short movies to accompany them. In other words, Wade had time-traveled into the near future.

I had remained the same. I had spent the summer of '81 reading the *Lord of the Rings* trilogy and *Seventeen* magazine. I understood that the former was a kind of mythology. It took me much longer to understand that the latter was one as well. The Beautiful American Girl was on every glossy page of *Seventeen.* I should have known that the magazine was a poisoned apple, seeing how it was my grandmother Iris who had given me the subscription. I was still the same girl. Kelly was the same girl too.

Kelly got on the bus, and as usual she could hardly breathe. She whispered in my ear, "Oh, my God*walnut*!" She squeezed my arm tighter and tighter as the bus got closer to school. She didn't dare to turn her head around for her usual glimpses of her intended, who had become so beautiful that he was almost otherworldly.

I experienced something new that morning too. It was both pleasurable and uncomfortable. There was a sensation at the back of my head as if someone were holding his hands close to my hair but never quite touching. I turned around and Wade smiled at me. He had handed me a note as the school bus had pulled up to our stop that morning. This act alone told me that the orange sherbet boy was no longer the same. What the note said confirmed it. The piece of notebook paper, folded into a triangle, sat inside my purse until third period, when I went to the bathroom and into a stall to read it. "I missed you," Wade had written.

Others in our eighth grade class had also time-traveled that summer. Some of the girls had even caught up with Sally Campbell. "Their bra sizes are now one half of their IQs," Kelly wrote in letter #594. Their lips were shiny and their golden hair was curled on their shoulders just so. They wore their newfound beauty as a right, never doubting that they deserved the attention that went with it. These girls and Sally instantly formed a clique and immediately began to exclude and oppress. This act was as natural as breathing to them. As Kelly and I watched these girls, we thought about the fish that climbed out of the primordial pool all those eons ago and how they never looked back. During the first few hours of a very long school year, Kelly and I already understood that we were the fish still swimming in circles. I was wondering when I would develop a nice set of lungs. Kelly was thinking about how to call attention to hers.

Among the boys in our class, four of them had had growth spurts and were equal to Wade in height, but they had achieved it in awkward ways. They flailed their spindly arms and ropey legs like some deep-sea cephalopod. Their heads were too small and out of proportion with their newly extended bodies. None were beautiful. They acknowledged their deficiencies in body and in grace by becoming even better friends with Wade. They punched him in the arm and grabbed him by the shoulders because they wanted to touch him. They talked football, basketball, and baseball with him to feel the vicarious surge of adrenaline that some of them would later realize was a stand-in for sex and war. But at the age of thirteen, they were expected not only to watch but to play these organized games, and they acted out their enthusiasm with a mixture of hope and bravado. Subconsciously, most of them were looking forward to the time when their aging bodies could no longer act on these expectations. As with sex and war, they would prefer to watch. The pressure of performance and the imperative for victory could then be transferred onto other men. For now they had Wade to project their desires and fears upon. Nature had elected him their king. They weren't equipped to dethrone him, and so they followed him. All of this took place on the first day of eighth grade. No wonder we were collectively tired and dazed on our bus ride home.

Travel also made Wade fearless. He grabbed my hand even before the bus had pulled away that afternoon.

"Did you*cannedgreenbeans* read*potatochips* it?" he asked.

"Yes."

"So?"

I turned away and I ran.

Wade stood there and watched me. I knew because I had that feeling again, the hands almost touching the back of my hair.

I ran because I didn't know what to say. I wanted to release all the pressure that had so suddenly built up in my limbs. I wanted to touch him, and if I had stayed I wouldn't know how.

The next morning I told my father that I had menstrual cramps, and I asked him to drive me to school. He did so without saying a word and with a worried look in his eyes. He had an early meeting that morning so I was at school a half hour before everyone else, but I was glad to be there and not at the SLOW CHILDREN sign. Before we left the house, my father had asked DeAnne to pick me up after school. She did. I told the same lie for the rest of the week. I saw Wade in our classes, but there he wore his new crown and was surrounded by his knights and supplicants. In this realm, I was a serf. Kelly, of course, was worried and wrote expanded editions of the *Wade Daily News* so that I wouldn't miss anything that happened. In letter #598, I told Kelly that all week long I felt like I had a toothache, except that it was in my entire body. That part was true.

The problem with a menstrual excuse was that it had a natural shelf life, viable for about five to seven days per month. To try to extend it beyond this would mean a visit to our family physician, Dr. Peterman. That following Monday I knew that I had to walk out of my front door and face the king. I was prepared. I had written Wade a note and handed it to him as soon I saw him that morning. The note was folded into a rhombus. He smiled without even reading it. He put it in the back pocket of his jeans, and then he told me the names of skateboarding tricks—Ollie, kickflip, Bert Slide—that he had been practicing all summer long. I told him that if I was a character in *The Lord of the Rings* I would be a hobbit, one of those who stayed at home in the Shire, unidentified by name or deeds but safe and warm.

When Wade unfolded the rhombus, it said, "I missed you too." The miracle of our courtship was that it was mutual, simultaneous, and had begun long before we were old enough to be self-aware.

That night I said goodbye to Dill. I opened up the pages of *To Kill a Mockingbird* and read again the sentences that made me adore him: "Summer was our best season: . . . it was a thousand colors in a parched landscape; but most of all, summer was Dill." Our summer had ended. We parted company cordially. Dill said to me that "he would love me forever and not to worry, he would come get me and marry me as soon as he got enough money together, so please write."

Inside my notebook I wrote, L+W. Then I erased it, knowing that it was better to use the name for Wade that I alone knew.

L+OSB.

CHAPTER 9

TOUCH WAS A SENSE NOT EXPLORED OR CELEBRATED IN MY FAMILY. That was why they favored big cars. Cadillac Eldorados, Chrysler LeBarons, Chevy Suburbans. All these models found their way into the garages of the blue and gray ranch house, the green-shuttered colonial, and the Greek Revival. These vehicles allowed the five of us to sit inside them without ever having to touch one another. Our thighs would never rub. Our shoulders would never press. We were buffered from one another by ample elbow and legroom. I believed that this desire to avoid touch was also behind their preference for long-sleeved shirts and modest clothing, their nonconsumption of alcohol, their disdain for dancing (except for Baby Harper, of course), their nondisplay of physical affection, and all the other particulars of our faith. Southern Baptists wanted to feel the Spirit and only the Spirit. A noncorporeal embrace was why we raised our arms up to the Lord every Sunday. I never saw my father kiss my mother. I never saw my mother kiss my grandmother. My grandmother's lips were used only to purse. My great-uncle's were used to whistle the greatest hits of Patsy Cline.

When we were eight, Kelly showed me how to blow a kiss. She

said that she had seen her aunt, who was visiting from Rock Hill, South Carolina, do it. There were two steps. The kissing of my own palm was a revelation. My lips were warm. They were soft. They could exert pressure. But it was the blowing of the invisible kiss into the air that was magic. In fact, I remembered thinking that I would rather do *this* than pull a rabbit out of a hat or pull a coin from behind someone's ear or saw a woman in half (how come men never get split in two?). Kelly and I had a good couple of weeks sending kisses to each other via the air until my mother told us that it was unnatural and to cease it. After DeAnne walked out of the room, Kelly and I shrugged our little shoulders. Kelly then asked if I wanted her to kiss me for real, so that I would know what it felt like. I shook my head no and ran away screaming. She ran after me screaming. We were full of joy, throwing kisses at each other and grabbing them from the air.

The orange sherbet boy's lips didn't taste like orange sherbet. I didn't think that they would, but I had hoped. I was somewhat disappointed. As we waited out the last year of our shared conveyance, Wade, beautiful at thirteen, leaned over one morning and kissed me on the lips. "Pressed" was probably the more accurate verb. Yes, he pressed me. Seconds before, we were a boy and a girl standing next to each other. The distance between our bodies was out of habit and not out of a lack of curiosity. His movement was swift and unexpected. I remembered the smell of his clothes—his mom, like mine, must have used Tide—as the first of the atmospheric changes. The second was the instant warming of the air temperature as his breath came near. The third was that it became suddenly dark. As Wade pulled away, he said my name aloud for no one but himself. I opened my eyes, and we were a boy and a girl who had kissed. He had broken an invisible seal around our bodies. A thin covering of skin had peeled away from us, and we were new underneath and tender as a bruise. Seconds later, my grandmother Iris's words came out of me swift and unexpected. "Don't tell*brownsugar* any*riceone**breadandbutterpickles,*" I said.

"Sure*cannedtuna,*" Wade replied, shrugging his shoulders. "It's no*grapejelly*body's*cannedmushrooms* business any*rice*way*cannedpears.*"

I didn't say anything, letting him think that *that* was the reason.

Our minutes were up, and the school bus turned the corner onto Oak Street. Three stops later, Kelly climbed aboard, sat down beside me, taking up three quarters of the vinyl-covered seat, and squeezed my hand to say hello. I squeezed her hand in response. Our thighs rubbed. Our shoulders pressed. We were in the eighth grade and riding toward the end of our years of physical and emotional intimacy. Kelly would soon find that being touched by a boy reinforced the ameliorative and addictive feeling of being desired, a sensation that would be so new to her at the age of fourteen that she could have screamed with delight every time she felt it. She would Virginia Dare one boy after another to kiss her. She would Virginia Dare them to do other things with her too.

From the day that I had received the first of her letters, Kelly was my world. She was my link to such concepts as girlhood, friendship, and intimacy. I loved her more than I loved Wade. I didn't want this boy to change the love that I had for my best friend. I knew that fact when Wade kissed me. I also knew that I would kiss him again, and that Kelly could never know. What this really meant was that I wasn't sure that Kelly loved *me* more. I had seen her puffy hearts with the K+W inside of them, and there was doubt in mine.

Wade, for his own reasons, kept his promise. He never kissed me again at the bus stop. He waited till we were inside his house. His mother was rarely home, though she didn't have a job. Wade and I were both blind to what these midafternoon absences could mean. When we walked into the faded-red-T-shirt house, we knew it was ours. We went to his bedroom, and he would shut the door, which had a lock. He would kiss me first. We would touch each other by way of exploration, not of land and river ways or the open seas but of space, the breathless frontier above our heads, of stars and planets, and the possibilities of flight. We were no longer children, but we were teenagers only in our age. When we touched each other, we felt on our skin the recent scars of skinned knees and scraped elbows. When Wade said that he had broken bones, he meant that he had broken bones. He didn't mean disappointments, heartbreaks, or failures of the spirit. "Euphemism" was a word for a concept that neither one of us was familiar enough with to use.

I soon learned that "touch" was a word that described two types of sensations. To touch was to press down with the skin on my fingertips, the soft soles of my feet. To be touched was to feel the weight of another person on that same skin. My afternoons with the orange sherbet boy taught me that I was fond of both. Wade became silent when either was occurring. His eyes widened and he stared at me as if I would at any moment shatter or run away. Then, when I didn't, he would reward me with that slow grin of his, the facial equivalent of our southern drawl.

The first time we lay down next to each other, Wade had that grin on his face. We lay on our backs, our hands clasped on top of our T-shirt-covered bellies. We stared up at the ceiling, plain and white (though I thought I saw stars) the way that the walls of his room had been before he covered them with posters of bands and one for an art exhibit that his mother had taken him to in Tampa. Glossy white paper with bold black text that read T(R)AMPA(RT). Below the words were two outlines of a circle, like the number eight lying on its side. Wade told me that this was the hobo sign for "Don't give up." He said that he and his mom had gone to the "opening" at a gallery, and the artist was there too. The artist, a young man, didn't look happy and was drinking a lot of the free wine, but all the people there tried to talk to him anyway. I wasn't sure I understood why, but from the tone of Wade's voice I knew that the artist had opened up his world. Then without pause or transition, Wade told me that last summer in Tampa he had kissed a girl.

Something in me froze. If I had to pinpoint what it was, I would say that it was my stomach. It was somewhere in that region, deep and large and vital. I should have asked Wade why he kissed her. Did she ask him to or did he volunteer? Instead, I asked a ridiculous question, one that was apparently hardwired into my female brain: What's her name? I would find myself asking this question again at other moments in my life. The name of the kissed-girl, the I-had-coffee-with-girl, or the fucked-girl was beside the point. The point was that there was another girl.

Hardwired as well, Wade responded that it didn't mean anything. He just wanted to see what it was like, you know, to kiss someone on the lips. My stomach relaxed, and I repeated the phrase again in my head. *It didn't mean anything.* This was also beside the point. The point remained the same. There was another girl.

My first kiss was Wade's second (or third or fourth). I stared up at the ceiling so white that it was hurting my eyes, making me tear up. Wade, without saying a word, reached for my hand and held it until I stopped. I should have asked him why he told me. I could have lived the rest of my life (or the rest of eighth grade) thinking that I was first, and what harm would that have done him or the kissed-girl, whatever her name was. But if I had asked Wade this question, his answer would have been "I don't know why I told you." It wouldn't have been a lie because he really didn't know.

In the past few months, we had triggered behaviors and responses within each other that we would recognize and repeat in the years to come. At the time, however, the behaviors and responses were new and puzzling. Often we felt as if we had someone else inside of us and that person did and said things that we hadn't agreed to and failed to understand the motives for. In this instance, the person inside of Wade was setting up a rivalry between the kissed-girl in Tampa and me, the girl lying next to him on a cold February afternoon in Boiling Springs. The kissed-girl's existence, now revealed, was a threat, a possibility, a likelihood that she could again be first. Her existence was useful to Wade, though he had only a vague idea why.

Wade and I spent the month of March taking off our clothes. Our sweaters, our T-shirts, our jeans, until a thin layer of cotton covered us from ourselves. We were no longer children, but we looked like children in our modest cotton underwear. His white briefs, my undershirt with a tiny yellow bow at the V-neckline, his socks with the three stripes, blue, red, blue, at the calves. We weren't afraid of each other, but we were sometimes shy, lying there on top of his bedspread shivering but not cold. I continued to touch. His body was becoming familiar territory to me. His hip bones were sharp. His collar bones formed the edges of two small ponds. His face was as smooth as mine. I closed my eyes and pretended to be blind, seeing with my fingers and hands. So did he. He slipped his hands underneath my undershirt and felt for the circles of skin where my breasts would be. His palms brushed my nipples, and I said his name aloud because I wanted to taste it. He shivered in response.

"April showers bring May flowers" was the first line of poetry I ever learned. It had an internal rhyme. It was prophetic. It was hopeful. It was true. At the end of April, Wade told me that he and his mom were going back to Tampa for the summer. He didn't even have to bring up the kissed-girl. She entered his bedroom and lay down in between us. I hated her, and I still didn't know her name. Wade, as if coming out of a fog and seeing her there too, understood why he had told me about her. Wade then asked me to be his first.

"Please*lemonjuice,* Linda*mint,*" he said.

To this day those two words heard in combination will make me see Wade's face. Teenage girls everywhere have seen that same expression of hope and desire. Simple as a teenage boy.

I wasn't, but I felt that I was, special. Simple as a teenage girl. Bobby walked into Wade's bedroom. The winged monster put a forefinger to his lips, and went, Shhhh. Or he could have been imitating the hiss of a snake. He stood by the window and stared at me. Outside, big droplets of rain were bouncing off the roof of the faded-red-T-shirt house. Inside, Wade and I heard what sounded like a pan of hot oil sizzling and popping all around us. Wade held his breath and I held mine. The only one in the room taking in air was Bobby, and he didn't even need it. The steadiness of Bobby's chest going up and down, so assured and so patient, convinced me that Wade would know. Wade would know that he wasn't first. I let out my breath and I lied.

"I'm not ready*orangejuice,*" I said to the orange sherbet boy.

"Oh," he replied.

One syllable with no incoming, a placeholder until a thought came to mind, a guttural sound made at moments of surprise, confusion, frustration, or disappointment, "oh" could also be an indicator of indifference, as in I care so little about what you've said to me that I can't be bothered to respond with a real word. In some instances, "oh" was the sound of a body absorbing rejection.

I sat up, pulled my sweater over my head, put on my jeans and sneakers, and looked around and saw that Bobby was no longer in the room.

"I'll see you*cannedgreenbeans* tomorrow*breakfastsausage,* Wade*orangesherbet,*" I said, before closing the door of his bedroom on my way out. I pressed my ear to his door and I didn't move. The person inside of me wouldn't let me go. She knew that a confession was forthcoming. The confession turned out to be the name of the kissed-girl.

"Please*lemonjuice,* Julie*caramelcandy.*"

Wade was no longer a child. He had a Plan B. The person inside of him had a line, and he was practicing it. The last word of the plea was apparently interchangeable.

The flowers that arrived in May were tiny, red, and frilly. In the mornings I would see them in the whites of my eyes. A splash of water made them bloom more. Eyedrops only made them pink. I hated them for giving me away. I was suffering from an ailment inaccurately known as heartbreak. (A glass breaks. A fever breaks. A ray of sunlight breaks through the clouds. A heart is a muscle and it hurts like one, aches and pulls.) By the end of that month, when the school year ended, I was exhausted, mostly from the inability to understand what had happened to me and Wade.

We had continued to spend our mornings and afternoons together in our usual way. But every time I saw him, I heard his voice in my head saying the kissed-girl's name. What I never heard again was "Please*lemonjuice,* Linda*mint.*"

Wade and I thought that we had till the end of the weekend to say our goodbyes. His mom had told him that they weren't leaving for Tampa until Monday morning, but sometime after the Harris family returned from their usual Saturday night 5:15 P.M. dinner at Slo Smoking and before the sunrise on Sunday, Wade's mom took one of the family cars, two suitcases, and left town without him. The orange sherbet boy woke up and found himself belonging to a broken family. (A family breaks.)

Mrs. Harris's hairdresser knew before anyone else did. It could be argued that her hairdresser knew even before she knew. There had been the recent change in her hair color, including blond highlights, and then the accessorizing with a headband, a twist of light blue rayon, considered fashionable in Hollywood in 1982 but somewhat slatternly in Boiling Springs. Once the first Monday-morning appointment arrived at Miss Cora's Beauty Emporium, the news about Wade's mom was set loose. By then, all the drapes were drawn shut at the faded-red-T-shirt house. The house was in mourning. Or its occupants were ashamed. I didn't know then that there was a one-word encapsulation for those two feelings: "mortification." Wade's dad, known to his congregation in Shelby as the Reverend Canon of the Episcopal Church of the Redeemer, didn't leave the house that Sunday. On Monday morning, he drove his son, Wade, to the airport to board a flight to Tampa, alone. Before leaving, Wade had knocked on the back door of the blue and gray ranch house. He handed me a note that promised me that he would call when he got to his grandmother's. He never called, all summer long. Nor was the written word again employed.

Wade's halo was a product of the sun, a dependent of its rays. The more time he spent outside, the more light his head of hair attracted and trapped, like fireflies in a jar. But during the summer of '82, his fireflies would all die, and everybody in Boiling Springs knew why. Wade, my orange sherbet boy, had lost his mom. She didn't pass away. She drove away. Miss Cora's Beauty Emporium buzzed with the news. Beth Anne came home and told it to her husband, Carson junior. Kelly overheard and pretended that she hadn't. According to Beth Anne, Mrs. Harris had always been too showy with her clingy shirts and above-the-knee skirts. The reverend's wife, according to her hairdresser, was now living in Myrtle Beach, South Carolina. She had found work as a cocktail waitress in an oceanside hotel. This was the same hotel where she and her husband had stayed just a year before, on their fifteenth wedding anniversary, and where she had met a bartender who gave her free drinks every night after her husband fell asleep at his usual bedtime of 10 P.M. Everybody knew that Episcopalians liked a cocktail now and then, and this part of the story only confirmed it.

As far as the Southern Baptists were concerned, Episcopalians were third on the list of local religious nonconformists. At the top was the former Miss Feldmann. Second was the small band of Catholics. The talk about them usually centered on how the small band, i.e. the congregation of St. Mary's, always managed to have enough funds for the upkeep of their church and most recently for the new stained-glass windows (all six depicted a dove emerging from a shatter of blue and yellow triangles, which intentionally or unintentionally created an "explosion of faith" effect when seen from the outside). Papal money was said to have been involved. Kelly wrote in letter #658 that she tuned out of her parents' conversation at this point because Catholics weren't half as interesting as her parents made them out to be. Sally Campbell, for example, was a Catholic and she was boring. Kelly also wrote that the lesson to be taken from Wade's mom's "escapade" was that we should be very careful what we say to our hairdressers when we have them. The lesson that I would take from it was that we changed when our mothers left us. Our fireflies died.

When I saw Wade on our first day of high school, I assumed from the subdued color of his hair that it must have rained every day while he was in Tampa with his grandmother. Then a vision of his mother basking in the rays of Myrtle Beach with her new hair color and her new life flashed in between us. Bleached and beached, the Reverend Harris's ex-wife–cum–cocktail waitress had become instantly legendary among the women of the greater Boiling Springs–Shelby area. She was even more legendary among the men. She was the community's cautionary tale against beachside hotels, blond highlights, clingy shirts, exposed knees, flirty headbands, and hard liquor. She was the fantasy for all these things as well. Wade returned home to Boiling Springs, a small town made even smaller by its infatuation with this vivid specter of his mother. Wade, as if anticipating this tightening focus, had transformed himself over the summer into the perfect specimen of the all-American teenage boy. He must have seen kissed-girl's copies of *Seventeen* magazine because he showed up at Boiling Springs High School looking like he had walked off one of its pages. His hair was cut short with a part to the side. He wore a pale blue polo shirt and a pair of khakis. On his feet were penny loafers, complete with pennies tucked into their slits. I walked right past him and didn't stop until he said my name. I turned around and looked from the linoleum floor up, taking in the copper coins, the neutral-colored pant legs, the pastel torso, the pale face, the brown hair, and saw someone whom I didn't recognize.

In my junior year of college, when I saw *Rebel Without a Cause* in my film studies class, Filmic Constructions of Masculinity: Boys Don't Cry But Sometimes They Dance, I realized that Wade, beautiful at thirteen, had looked like a disheveled James Dean. Wade, handsome at fourteen, was more of a Ken doll.

Wade recognized me because I was exactly the same, except that underneath my T-shirt I was wearing a training bra and in my purse I had a packet of Winston Reds. On the outside, though, I hadn't changed.

The bus stop was now at the YIELD sign at the corner of Laurel and Chestnut streets. I hadn't seen Wade there that morning. I would never see him there. During our freshman year, he got a ride to and from school from three other Ken dolls who were juniors and already had their driver's licenses. I don't know when Wade befriended them, how the distance between Tampa and Boiling Springs had been traversed by these boys that summer, but it had. Thanks to them, Wade had a ready-made coterie of friends, older boys who grabbed him by the skin on the back of his neck when they walked past him in the hall. Wade, the former king of eighth grade, was now their prince. In my letters to Kelly, I began referring to Wade as Cadmus, the prince of Phoenecia. Her brain, though, was already so obsessed with real boys that she was forgetting the life stories of the mythical ones. I had to remind her that Cadmus, while searching for a missing female member of his family, was told by an oracle to give up his search and become instead the founding father of the city of Thebes. Cadmus, impatient and resourceful, populated his new city by sowing its virgin soil with the teeth of a dragon, slain by his own hands. From each hard enameled seed sprang a man. Instant, easy, and no females required. Kelly wrote back in letter #661, "Whoa. You're way overthinking this one. Wade is a hunk, and he's popular. That's all."

Within the first few days of our freshman year, the world for Kelly flattened out and became a wide-open field. She could see straight across this expanse. There were no obstacles, natural or man-made. There was nothing lurking, dangerous, or ulterior. Some on this field were physically beautiful or handsome and would reap the bounty that would come with it. A few were smart and therefore would earn their good graces. The rest were losers who would work for minimum wage and amass nothing. We all deserved what was coming to us. High school was the beginning of our irreversible forced march. Kelly was thrilled with what she saw ahead of her. She was rushing toward it with her new body, her new clothes, and her new empty head.

I occupied my role as the Smartest Girl at BSHS with the intensity and fervor of the newly converted. I had no one to distract me. The orange sherbet boy was lost to me. This time it wasn't travel that had changed him. It was the coming home that did it. Kelly, my world, was wandering around a dense forest and mistaking it for a grassy meadow. To her great disappointment, though, Cadmus didn't ask her to be his second (the kissed-girl or some other girl must have been his first, explaining the immediate status bestowed upon him by the gaggle of older but still virginal Kens). Sally Campbell was born with a homecoming queen crown on her head. You can imagine the pain and joy that her mother felt. Sally laid eyes on Cadmus, and slipped her hands into his. By the end of the first week of our freshman year, the match was made public, the coterie celebrated with back slappings, and Sally got a ride home from the Kens.

For the remainder of my four years at BSHS, I disappeared into the walls. If it hadn't been for the smoke from my cigarettes or the smell of it in my hair, it would have been difficult to find me. In class, I took diligent notes with my head down, raising it only when I raised my hand to ask a question, to the mock groans of my fellow students. At lunchtime, I sat at the edge of the lunchroom until I decided that I would rather be outside smoking with the stoners: Chris Johnson, Tommy Miller, and Susan Taylor. They were always together, charmed by their shared exclusion. They, a Greek chorus, would have objected in unison to the characterization:

Exclusion? No fucking way, Linda!

These three had seen the same field that Kelly saw, and they turned around and walked the other way. Of the three of them, Chris Johnson, who shared the same first and last name as one of the Kens (it hadn't occurred to me then that it must have meant that they shared a forefather too), and I were the closest to being friends.

"There's a high*greenLifesavers*way*cannedpears* out of this hole*hushpuppies,* Linda*mint*." That was the first thing Chris said to me. I thought he was quoting a line from a movie. His non sequitur confused me until I looked into his eyes and understood that he was serious. The highway out of Boiling Springs was a fact that he held on to dearly, and he thought that I should be reminded of it too. I had been smoking with them for about a month by then. They had nodded at me but otherwise ignored me. They traded jokes with one another in the shorthand language of best friends: a couple of words and then convulsive laughter. I enjoyed the concision of their exchanges and didn't care that they were speaking a language I didn't understand. Chris was a sophomore, so he and I didn't have any classes in common. In the hallways, he always managed to see me first, and instead of saying hi he would repeat his favorite fact about our hometown to me. During his senior year, that greeting became downright exuberant. He meant it. He had been saving his money to buy a Greyhound ticket to Philadelphia to go live with his cousin. He said he was getting on that bus as soon as he got his diploma.

Tommy Miller was leaving town too. He was going with Susan Taylor to live in Richmond, Virginia. She had graduated the previous year but had stayed in town, working at the Super 8 motel outside of Shelby, in order to wait for him. I had no idea that they were a couple until one day I noticed that Tommy had placed a cigarette in his mouth, lit it with a couple of quick puffs, and handed it to Susan to smoke. I had to stifle a sigh. I was impressed by how natural Tommy's gesture was. He saw a need and he filled it, oblivious to the fact that he and Susan weren't alone. I was fourteen, and it was the most public act of intimacy that I had witnessed in real life. It was akin to the blowing of a kiss.

Chapter 10

I sometimes would crave a word. I would go to bed thinking about it, and in my dreams someone would say it. The next morning that word would be the first one in my head. I would go through my day hoping to hear it. For me there was, and still is, an appreciable distinction between hearing the word said and saying it for myself, though both would produce the same incomings. It was the difference between being served a good meal and having to cook one for myself. I would long for the word like it was a spoonful of peach cobbler, the kind that Bridges served only on Saturdays.

Food and taste metaphors were complicated for me. By complicated I mean that they were of no use to me. They shed their figurative qualities, their diaphanous layers of meaning, and became concrete and explicit. They left me literal and naked. The word that made me taste peach cobbler, for example, was "matricide."

The first time I heard this word said aloud was in a comp lit seminar, *The Oresteia:* It's a Family Affair. I was always unprepared for a new word's incoming. I was most startled when a new word had a very familiar taste. I would lose my ability to absorb what was happening to me. My body would respond to the taste, whether pleasant or unpleasant, with a twitch or a tremor, or an expletive would escape from my mouth. College was the most challenging time for me because my vocabulary was expanding by the minute. In my classes, I often had the shakes and exhibited what appeared to be a mild form of Tourette's syndrome. By the end of my freshman year at Yale, there were rumors circulating on campus that I was taking large quantities of speed, never slept, read every assigned page, and aced all my papers and exams, and was therefore responsible for skewing the delicate grading curve in all my classes. Only one of these accusations was true. I was often awake late into the night, but I wasn't poring over my assigned readings. I was reviewing the new words I had heard during the day. I whispered them to myself. I placed them in order, from sour to sweet. I organized them in descending gradation of saltiness. I saved the bitter ones for last, hoping as I always do to find a match for my first memory. Then there were the guilty pleasures, which I repeated out of gluttony or homesickness. "Matricide," for example.

❦

According to my great-uncle Harper, my mother was never young. He said DeAnne was born a thirty-five-year-old woman and remained that age until she turned thirty-six, and then she got older like the rest of us. If I was to believe my great-uncle, DeAnne's first smile gave her laugh lines. The first time she squinted at the sun her forehead wrinkled. When other little girls had freckles, she had age spots. My great-uncle swore that all this was true. I never had any problems believing in DeAnne's "prema" and "perma" maturity. As a mother, she had the rigidity and the timidity of an old woman. She had a couple of stock reprimands that she had learned from her mother, Iris. When DeAnne used these reprimands against me, she did so with a hesitancy that told me that she didn't really believe in them. Or she didn't understand them. *Put on a sweater or you'll get a cold!* DeAnne, armed with over forty years of real-life experience, knew that wearing a sweater wasn't a prophylactic against the common cold. Yet she said it anyway. *Don't be so selfish!* DeAnne, I was certain, didn't comprehend the differences among these three words: "selfish," "self-centered," and "self." I accused her of this in a letter written at the end of my sophomore year in college. Our sporadic communication ended with that missive.

From the age of seven to eleven, I loved DeAnne because that was what I thought was natural. On television (when no one was around I would watch it with the volume turned off), I saw children who cried when their mothers died. These same children would then have gauzy flashbacks of hugging their mothers, clinging to their necks or thighs. Because of my secret sense, I have always preferred the stories in the pages of books to those on the screen, but no matter the medium there seemed to be an overriding message: I was lucky to have a mother.

Rapunzel was taken away from her mother at birth. Her mother didn't even get to name her and probably wouldn't have chosen the name *Rapunzel.* Snow White and Gretel had stepmothers who plotted their violent deaths while Cinderella's own stepmother contemplated a slow death for her via the drudgery of housework and the crippling lack of a social life. Girls without their mothers were clearly at risk. Though in most of these stories, the girls eventually did find safety in marriage and lived happily ever after without bickering or marital strife.

Here were the high points of my relationship with my mother:

When I was seven, she brought me to Hudson's department store and bought me a year's worth of clothes. The girls' section was located on the second floor, which wasn't a full floor but more of very wide balcony with an ornate iron railing. I remembered sticking my head in between the iron curlicues and looking at the glass tops of the perfume and makeup counters down below.

When I was eight, she bought me a box of bright plastic hairpins in the shapes of various tropical fruits for my newly short hair. She had just given me a haircut, and I thought that she was concerned that people would think I was a boy. Bananas, pineapples, and oranges in my hair announced to the world that I was a girl.

When I was nine, she enrolled me in baton-twirling classes. (In letter #157, Kelly explained to me why she wasn't taking the class too: "I am fat. My mom says that no one wants to see a fat girl twirling a stick.") I went to baton class every Monday and Thursday after school, marched in the annual Shelby Thanksgiving Day parade, and then was asked not to come back to class after I threw my baton and it hit Sally Campbell in the face. I apologized but my teacher, Miss Wendy, didn't believe me. I couldn't help it. Saying, "I'm sorry*glazeddoughnut*" always brought a smile to my face.

When I was ten, she served fresh strawberries for dessert all summer long.

When I was eleven, I went with her to Miss Cora's Beauty Emporium and watched as she got a pretty new hairdo. Miss Cora looked at my hair, which had grown long again, and said to my mother that one of the other hairdressers could give me a China chop. My mother told Miss Cora that my hair was just fine the way it was.

The end.

When DeAnne let Bobby ride in circles around the blue and gray ranch house, I was eleven years old. Before she hired him to cut our lawn that summer, she had gotten her hair styled the same as his. They were both wearing the Dorothy Hamill wedge (though technically the male version should be called the Bruce Jenner). Dorothy wore it in 1976, Bobby and DeAnne wore it in 1979. Our town was the hospice for fads. Trends reached us in Boiling Springs only when they were about to peter out and die. If it had happened now, I would have understood that when a woman changed her hairdo, it was a signal that something else has altered inside. (See Joan of Arc before battle, Mia Farrow before marrying Frank Sinatra, my grandmother Iris after the passing of her husband, Walter

Wendell.) But it happened then, so I only thought that my mother looked pretty with her swingy new hairdo. From the way that Bobby smiled at her I thought that Bobby thought that my mother looked pretty too. I didn't understand that DeAnne was a forty-eight-year-old housewife, and that she would have to change a lot more than her hairstyle before Bobby would consider her worthy prey. All summer long, DeAnne and I would be mistaken about him.

The day before Bobby knocked on the door of the blue and gray ranch house and then pushed himself inside, I was in the car with DeAnne or, as I called her then, my mom. It was the end of the summer of '79. Kelly had claimed Wade, and I had clung to Dill. The sixth grade was looming. My mom and I were driving to meet Baby Harper at Bridges for dinner. My father was out of town for business, or that was what he told her at the time. My mom had the radio on and was shaking her hair to Peaches and Herb (a duo with a name that I have always thought would make a good and interesting salad).

Reunited and it feels so good
Reunited 'cuz we understood
There's one perfect fit and, sugar, this one is it.

I had noticed that since my mom got her new hairdo she had been listening to the radio a little louder. She also switched from station to station more often, as if trying to find a song that matched her mood. I have always equated listening to music with happiness. I assumed she did too.

For me, hearing a song was like watching that trick of a tablecloth being pulled away without disturbing any of its settings. Except in my case, everything on the table disappeared but the cloth, which was left behind, pristine as a blank sheet of paper. Glasses stained with whatever strong liquids they held last, plates and bowls full of bones, peels, seeds, and crumbs, all were cleared away and cleaned with one sweeping gesture. Songs performed that trick for me. Their words, docile and contented to convey meaning and nothing more, brought with them only what I allowed. My will was stronger than theirs. That was one definition of happiness.

I was humming along to the song on the radio. My mom was bobbing her head up and down, hands at ten and two on the steering wheel. We were getting nearer to Bridges, to seeing Baby Harper with his napkin already tucked into his shirt collar in anticipation of sauce. I must have felt as if none of that could ever change. In other words, I must have felt safe.

I blurted out as quickly as I could, "Mom*chocolatemilk*, you*cannedgreenbeans* know*grapejelly* what*grahamcracker* tastes like a walnut*hamsteaksugar-cured*? God*walnut* tastes like a walnut*hamsteaksugar-cured*. The word*licorice* God*walnut*, I mean*raisin*, and the word*licorice* tastes—"

"Linda*mint*, please*lemonjuice* don't talk*cornchips* like a crazy*heavycream* person*garlicpowder*," my mom said, cutting me off. She did this without taking her eyes off the road, her hands still on ten and two.

I'll give you all the love I have with all my might, hey-hey
Reunited and it feels so good
Reunited 'cuz we understood.

Peaches and Herb were still singing on the radio. My mom and I were still on our way to Bridges. My great-uncle Harper would be there waiting for us, his blue eyes gentle as landlocked lakes.

So, I tried again. I said this time slower, "Mom*chocolatemilk*, honest. I mean*raisin* it. Words*licorice*, they have a taste. Mom*chocolatemilk* tastes like chocolate*cannedbeefbroth* milk*Pringles* and—"

"Linda*mint*. Stop*cannedcorn* it! I can handle*FruitStripegum* a lot of things*tomato*. God*walnut* knows*grapejelly* I have had to with you*cannedgreenbeans*. But I won't handle*FruitStripegum* crazy*heavycream*. I won't have it in my family*cannedbeets*. Do you*canned-*

greenbeans understand*eggnoodles* me?" my mom asked without really asking.

The song ended and Rod Stewart's "Da Ya Think I'm Sexy?" came on. My mom switched to another station. I knew what she thought. Rod Stewart, like Dolly, was trashy. I don't remember what the other station was playing. It might have been a commercial for used cars. It might have been a news report. I looked over at my mom. Her lips were a straight line. She was done talking now.

But her words—*I won't have it in my family*—were reverberating inside the car, like the notes of a skipping record. They were getting more insistent with each repetition, drowning out the radio entirely. I knew what my mom meant. *If you want to be one of us, Linda, you hush your mouth.*

We pulled into the Bridges parking lot. I saw my great-uncle's car parked by the front doors. He was fond of saying that he and Bridges were meant to be because he always got the best parking space there, never fail. He was the first person I knew who thought that available parking was a way to divine one's fate. He wouldn't be the last. Parking spaces, tea leaves, playing cards, the lines on our palms. We all want a way to know where we should be in the world.

Before my mom got out of the car, she looked at herself in the rearview mirror and she fixed her perfect hair.

I never loved DeAnne the way I loved my father. His entrance into a room comforted me. I trusted that he would protect me from the animal noises in the night, the common cold, the deep end of the pool. He wasn't a physically demonstrative father—his favored gesture of affection was rubbing the top of my head and gently tousling my hair—but I didn't need him to be that. I only needed him to be physically near.

Girls without their fathers were also at risk. I didn't learn this from the fairy tales of my youth, because in those stories the fathers were present in the castles and in the cottages. The fairy-tale fathers, however, were unforgivably weak and always thinking with their groins. These men would rather sacrifice their daughters than risk harm to themselves. Rapunzel's father loved her mother so much that he stole for the woman. When he was caught, he was a coward, and instead of paying with his own life he promised away their unborn child. Gretel was very much alive, as was her brother, Hansel, when their father tried to do away with them. Three times he tried. ("Abandonment in the forest" was a bloodless euphemism for attempted murder.) Of course, there was Beauty. Was she not the poster child for daughters of men who dodged their responsibilities and used their female offspring as human shields?

Fairy-tale fathers were also criminally negligent. Where was Cinderella's father when she was being verbally abused and physically demeaned by her stepmother and stepsisters? Perhaps he was so besotted, his wits so dulled by his nightly copulation with his new wife, that he failed to notice the degraded condition of his daughter. Snow White's father, a king no less, was equally negligent and plainly without any power within his own domestic realm. Under his very roof, his new wife plotted the murder of his child, coerced one of his own huntsmen to carry out the deed, then ate what she thought was the girl's heart. This king was no king. He was a fool who left his daughter woefully unprotected.

When I first heard these stories, I assigned to these men no blame because they wore the solemn and adored mantle of "father." I understood them to be, like my own father, men who went to work every day, who returned home exhausted and taciturn, and who fell asleep in their easy chairs while reading the newspaper. I assumed that they, like my father, would have protected their daughters if only they had known of the dangers their girls faced during those dark hours after school and before dinner.

Under my father's own roof, his wife hired a predator, lusted after him, trusted him to be alone with her daughter, and when the evidence of the predator's crime emerged, sought solace and explanation in the body of the victim. Menstrual blood was normal, a byproduct of a girl's body coming of age. Buy the girl a box of protection and a purse to hide it in. Blood from the torn hymen of an eleven-year-old would have been a crime, the subject of tragedies from the time of the ancient Greeks to the American South. Wash clean the undergarments with Tide and rest assured that there will be no stain.

When I had questions about our family, my great-uncle Harper had the answers. He had the evidence that we existed. He would pull out the appropriate H.E.B.'s and the stories would begin. I remembered asking him why my father had married DeAnne. I was fifteen years old at the time, and what I really wanted to know was why DeAnne's heart hadn't been smashed to bits like mine. My great-uncle didn't know about Wade and me. He did know that my first year of high school hadn't been my finest or happiest. Baby Harper, by way of a greeting, had taken to asking me, "Where's the funeral today, Vista Girl?"

His sister may have been the one named Iris, but my great-uncle was the seer in the family. I had been in mourning for most of the school year. Kelly. Wade. All those damn fireflies. Now that the summer—dull, restorative, and hopefully transformative—was finally here, I decided that I might as well make my grief public. Finding black clothing in the young-miss section at Hudson's department store was impossible. It was always Easter Sunday in the South. Peach-blossom pink, forsythia yellow, spearmint green were always in style and readily available. So instead, I bought a box of black Rit dye and threw every item of clothing I owned into the washing machine. With one rinse cycle, I became a widow. My father thought it was a catastrophic laundry mistake and asked me if I needed money to buy some new clothes. I told him that black was my favorite color.

With his usual unflappability, my father said, "Dear*fishsticks* Heart, I thought that fire*sweetenedcondensedmilk* was your favorite-*HawaiianPunch* color."

I knew what he meant, and I couldn't help but smile. I was pleased that my father had remembered the first question that Kelly had ever sent to me and the answer that I had given. DeAnne didn't have a clue of what her husband meant and asked him, "What on earth are you talking about, Thomas?"

DeAnne then stared at me, and I stared back at her.

When my father employed sarcasm, which was 84 percent of the time, a known hazard of the legal profession, he called me "Dear Heart." When I first heard that term of endearment, I thought my father was saying "deer" heart. I had just read the legend of Virginia Dare, and the image that came into my eight-year-old head was that of a dying animal with its heart split in half. Homonyms always had the same incomings. So whether it was "dear" or "deer," I experienced the same taste: fish sticks, complete with the metallic aftertaste of freezer burn. "Heart" had no incoming. Maybe my father did mean "Deer Heart." Now that he is gone, everything about him has become so unclear to me. Not like an image that has been smudged or blurred. But one that may have never existed.

That summer when I was fifteen, the question I had wasn't whether my father loved DeAnne but *why* he loved her. That was when Baby Harper told me about DeAnne being born thirty-five years old. I laughed until he showed me proof. We looked at photographs of her as a baby, and she looked like all other babies. In other words, DeAnne looked like an old man. Then, at about the age of four, DeAnne Whatley began to resemble a female dwarf, approximately thirty-five years of age. Baby Harper pointed out that it had little to do with her face but, rather, it was the way that she carried her little body, the set of her shoulders, the bend of her neck, and the slight hunching of her upper body, as if someone had just pushed her into a corner. We looked at these photographs of her as a young child, and we marveled at how her blond curls, her pinafores, her Mary Janes all had lost their ability to connote youth. On her, these Shirley Temple affectations were inappropriate and verging on the grotesque. When DeAnne was sixteen, she looked like Joan Crawford in *Mildred Pierce,* a curtain of bangs drawn tightly shut across her forehead, the rest of her hair pulled back into bundles of curls on either side of the nape of her neck. That look actually suited DeAnne. Baby Harper pointed out that *Mildred Pierce* had come out in 1945, and these photographs of DeAnne were taken in 1948. A lag time of three years was what he wanted to impress upon me, and that DeAnne, even back then, wasn't "oh current." In her mid-twenties when she began dating Thomas, she tried out Audrey Hepburn's look in *Funny Face,* but the wispy bangs and the loose ponytail—so fresh and insouciant on Audrey—made DeAnne look like she was wearing a wig. This was the DeAnne whom Thomas met when he first went to dinner at the green-shuttered colonial.

"Linda Vista, you're trying to understand what Thomas *could* have seen in DeAnne," Baby Harper said. "The answer is more obvious than that, Vista Girl. You should look at these courting-days photographs and see what is there. An age-appropriate female, blond, medium build, all limbs present and accounted for, *and* she couldn't take her eyes off him. Linda Vista, that's all you need to know," he concluded, closing the cover of H.E.B. Twenty.

My great-uncle didn't hiccup after he said this, but I was certain he was joking. At the age of fifteen, I couldn't imagine that the decision to marry someone could be based on such shallow things. I opened up H.E.B. Twenty again, and I looked at my father and DeAnne's wedding photographs. On December 10, 1960, the day she became DeAnne Hammerick, she was au courant, wearing her hair in a First Lady–Elect Jacqueline Kennedy bouffant. The top of DeAnne's head looked like a day-old balloon, soft and about to deflate. She should have stuck with the Mildred Pierce. According to Baby Harper's photographs, DeAnne didn't smile once on her wedding day. She looked straight at the camera, and her expression was one of concentration, as if she were trying to stay awake or walk a very thin line. Standing beside her, Thomas wasn't wearing the thick, black-framed eyeglasses that he soon would wear until the day he died.

My great-uncle Harper didn't have to point it out to me. Not in one of these photographs was DeAnne looking at Thomas. Their gold bands, her grandmother's silverware, a complete set of new china, including a soup tureen, a cut-glass punch bowl encircled by matching cups, and a church full of people were all present and accounted for. She had them and Thomas by her side. This man wasn't going anywhere, was what she must have thought.

"Doesn't Thomas look handsome in his tuxedo?" Baby Harper asked. "He and DeAnne were both twenty-eight. Well, he was twenty-eight. DeAnne was her usual age of thirty-five. Miss Vista, you know what the saddest thing about that day was? Your grandma Iris looked more beautiful than DeAnne. It wasn't right. I told Iris to let DeAnne have her day. To try to wear something, you know, matronly. Iris couldn't and wouldn't do it. Iris wore a pale pink gown and looked like a June bride at her daughter's December wedding. Iris could never be kind to that girl. Now you know what they say, Linda Vista. Beautiful women never love their daughters. Either too pretty and competition or too ugly and an embarrassment. Now, I don't know about that. Most things attributed to what 'they say' are usually wrongheaded. But this one, I must say, Linda Vista, there seems to be some truth in it."

I continued to flip through the pages of the H.E.B., hoping to find something else, something that was definitive, surprising, or exceptional about this man and this woman. I asked Baby Harper where they honeymooned. Moss Lake, he replied. Moss Lake, I repeated. That's not a honeymoon; that's a day trip. My great-uncle knew that was what I was thinking, and he nodded his head in agreement. Then he got up from the divan and went into the kitchen. I knew he would return with two glasses of iced sweet tea garnished with fresh mint sprigs that grew by the back door of his house. It was as if he knew, and those aromatic leaves, tucked among the ice cubes, were a coy reference. But my great-uncle, the singing-talker, never knew the taste of my name. I never told him because my secret sense wasn't an issue when I was with him. As he would say, I was right as rain when I was with him. When we were together, he was right as rain too. That was a better definition of happiness.

Chapter II

Memory is a curse. I wasn't the first to say this, but I was proof of it. My memory was sharp. A thorn, a broken water glass, a jellyfish in a wave that crashed into me and reached back for more. My secret sense, which I have come to understand as my condition, gave me a way to encode information that was immediate and long-lasting, an inborn mnemonic device.

The ancient Greeks had a mnemonic device that called for thinking of a path, say through the streets of a familiar city, and depositing along the way the information that they wished to retain. At the corner of the Street of Wine Merchants, they would place fact number one; continuing ahead twenty paces to the Fountain of Bacchus, they would place fact number two; turning right onto the Street of Pleasure Houses by the front door of the Pavilion of Virgins (the name was ironic because even back then virgins were rare and mythical beings), they would place facts number three through ten (because it was there among the rare and mythical beings that they wanted to linger); and in that way their journey would continue on. To retrace this path in their mind was to gather up the facts again, easy and showy as red roadside poppies.

My own mnemonic device worked in similar fashion, but instead of a path there was a multicourse meal prepared by a mad scientist who knew and cared nothing about food. To revisit the dishes and their chaotic juxtaposition of flavors was to recall with precision those facts, from the trivial to the significant, that I have acquired, via the spoken word, during the course of my life.

I recited in the fourth grade that the "Wright*Frenchfries* brothers' first*Pepto-Bismol* flight*cantaloupe* was on December*vanillaicecream* seventeenth*ketchup,* 19*whitebread*03," and I would never forget this date that is—forgive me, Wilbur and Orville—not all that useful to me in my day-to-day life. During my first year of law school, I met a young man on a train from New York to Boston, and the moment he sat down next to me and said, "Hi*greenLifesavers,* my name*grapes* is Leo*parsnip,*" I could never forget this man's name, even after I wanted to. When I was seven, I heard a word that made me taste an unidentifiable bitter, and I never forgot flames cutting through the seams of a trailer home, the sound of footsteps on gravel, then darkness. Not of nighttime, which it must have been, but of closed eyelids or a hand held tight over them.

But the example of the trailer home was out of order. It should have been listed first. Also, the example of the trailer home wasn't the same as the previous two. The difference was fact versus the absence of fact.

The Wright brothers existed in history. A man named Leo existed in my personal history. All three were documented by words and photographs and, in the case of Leo, also by a pair of his shoes, which emerged from the back of the bedroom closet after he had gone. Leather, the color of a cube of caramel, slip-ons, and brand new. They were pieces of his carefully constructed exoskeleton that he must have regretted leaving behind. A benign household shadow, maybe that of a puffy winter coat, had hid them for weeks, and then one day they were pushed into the light. I had seen the backyard of the blue and gray ranch house behave in the same way. Underneath a pin oak tree there was a patch of earth where no grass would grow. That skirt of soil would periodically offer up pieces of blue and white pottery and shards of dark-colored glass, as proof that others had been there before.

The trailer on fire might not have existed. There were no photographs and no history, official or anecdotal. There was only my memory: coffee left too long on the burner, an uncoated aspirin caught in the throat, how a drop of mercury might taste on the tip of the tongue. I have come close to identifying that taste of bitter, but close isn't good enough for a mnemonic device. As for the word that triggered it, the usual trailhead of my memories, it remains lost to me.

My great-uncle Harper, a sixty-two-year-old man, and I, an eighteen-year-old girl, sat holding each other's hands. On a late-August night in Boiling Springs, we confessed and we revealed. Spinning around us was more than one circle of grief. Like the rings of Saturn, the circles weren't solid and were composed of many shattered things. Baby Harper told me of his affection for my father, Thomas, and how it had allowed him, belatedly, to love my mother, DeAnne. I told Baby Harper the facts of a rape. I didn't understand then that facts were sharp and should be wrapped in asides or separated by deep breaths. I thought that the best way to deliver bad news was to deliver bad news.

This was what I told him. It was the end of the summer of '79. I was eleven. I didn't scream. I didn't struggle. I was motionless. When it was over, I stood in the shower for a long time. The water went from hot to lukewarm to cold. I didn't see the bruises on my thighs until the next morning. That was when I cried.

This was what I didn't tell my great-uncle Harper. There were also bruises around my neck. Bobby had pushed himself into my vagina and into my mouth, in that order.

I asked Kelly in letter #427 why her cousin Bobby had done

at the time it satisfied him but over time that perversion grew to where sexual battery was not enough for him so he did more

these things to me. What I meant was why had he treated me so differently. When Kelly was ten, Bobby had held her hand, forced it into the crotch of his pants. Why was that not enough for him when he found me?

When Bobby knocked on the front door of the blue and gray ranch house and asked me if he could use the bathroom, I should have slammed the door shut and locked it. DeAnne had gone to pick up a cake for my father's forty-seventh birthday, which we would celebrate later that night. Before she had gotten into the car, she had stopped to talk to Bobby. She smiled and flipped her hair. He smiled and flipped his hair. He sat on the riding mower, and she touched its steering wheel. All summer long I had seen these movements. I thought these movements meant that I was invisible and that I was safe. *it spoke to Bobby that he was welcome + that no one would stop him*

Knock, knock.

Who's there?

Bobby.

Bobby who?

Bobby, monster, menace, blade. *She should have but no one would have believed her because it was 1979 + she was an eleven year old kid*

Kelly in letter #428 wrote only three words: "Don't tell anyone." She was including herself. That was when I first understood that *anyone* was a big movie theater of a word with the lights turned down low. You never knew who was sitting inside.

I didn't tell.

For my father's birthday dinner, I wore a brown plaid skirt and a white turtleneck with pink roses appliquéd around the neck. I helped my father blow out the candles on his cake. I puckered my lips and pretended that I was pushing air past them. I smiled for my great-uncle Harper's camera. My grandmother Iris said I should have another piece of cake. A second helping offered by a fat person was a foreshadowing of what your own body would become *if* you accept. My grandmother was the one who taught this to me.

it was a test and a cruel one to

I smiled and declined. My grandmother Iris smiled and ate the last piece for me. *force onto a child — pretty much body-shamed her*

All night long I watched DeAnne to see if she would flip her hair. She didn't.

The following morning DeAnne placed a new purse—a Bermuda bag with a cover embroidered with green turtles—on my bed and a box of maxi pads. Next to these two items was a pair of my underwear, washed and neatly folded into a square. I had twisted them, crotch stiff with blood, inside a sheet of newspaper and thrown them away. This and other moments in my life have taught me that the trash was where you placed what you wanted to be found, whether you knew it or not. If you wanted a thing to disappear entirely, you burned it.

The thing about grass was that it grew back.

The thing about rapists was that they would do it again.

The thing about fate was that it often looked like the handiwork of a vengeful God.

Before Bobby was scheduled to return to the blue and gray ranch house, his car hit a telephone pole along Highway 150. He wasn't wearing his seat belt. He died on impact. The Shelby *Star* ran a front-page article along with a yearbook photo of the deceased, smiling. The tire marks, according to the reporter, showed that the driver had swerved abruptly. To avoid a small animal, perhaps a rabbit, suggested the reporter. (The dead are too often imbued with good intentions.)

Kelly, being family, went to the funeral. DeAnne, being careless, was also there. The funeral was closed-casket because Bobby's head had gone through the windshield.

✝ *I love you Jesus! because you took away his face, his hands, his hips, the warm breath from his body.*

✝ *I forgive you Jesus! for not doing it sooner. I know you must have tried.*

By the time I left Boiling Springs for New Haven, I understood that my great-uncle, Harper Evan Burch, if he could have chosen, would have inhabited a body different from the one that God had given him. His body wasn't his temple. It was his shroud. He would rather not be a witness to it. Even on the muggiest of summer days, he never wore shorts and never rolled up his sleeves. If he had lived in an earlier era, he would have worn gloves and a hat every day. If he had lived in a big city, he would have worn dark sunglasses. As far as I knew, he had only one mirror in his Greek Revival. The mirror, the size of a small envelope, hung above the bathroom sink. His house had been built during a time when one bathroom, large and spacious with two windows and a claw-foot tub, was thought suitable for a household of means. No master baths, no his and her baths, no half-baths, and no guest baths. Somewhere along the way, between the Greek Revival and the blue and gray ranch house, these additional toilets and sinks came to signify a kind of necessary plenty, a promise of never having to relieve yourself in the same room as another member of your household, and an emblem that declared to the world that we had freed ourselves from such unwanted intimacies.

When I was young, I could stand on a chair and see most of my face in this mirror. When I was older and had grown almost as tall as Baby Harper, I realized that the placement of the mirror allowed him to see only his mouth and his chin, probably for the purpose of shaving. The rest of his face was a white wall. This shunning of his own reflection coupled with his penchant for picture taking and never picture-taken led me to the simple conclusion: My great-uncle was a book that found itself inside the wrong cover. What this meant I thought I understood. I was wrong. Baby Harper was just beginning to reveal himself to me. He threw down the first of his cards after he heard about Bobby.

My great-uncle said that there was no shame worse than silence. He wanted to know why I hadn't told anyone about Bobby. What he meant was why hadn't I told him. He mourned for what had been stolen from me. The crime for him (and me) wasn't the loss of my virginity. The use of "loss" here suggested, inappropriately, a button on a shirt that could be found or replaced. The crime was the taking away of my right to choose. Included in this grief was Baby Harper's right to choose. He lived through my body in many ways. He had wanted for me (and him) a moonlit night, a crushed prom corsage, a slow dance, the backseat of a car. I never had these experiences. Nor did Baby Harper. I had other experiences. As did Baby Harper. He mourned that there was a part of my life that I had kept from him. He realized for the first time that there might be others. Included in this grief were the hidden rooms of his life. He told me that hurt was bad enough and that I should never add loneliness to it. That's why we get together and dance, he said. I didn't understand until then what my great-uncle had been teaching me since our earliest days together. We got together and moved our bodies because it exorcised our pain.

In a voice that I had never heard coming out of him, my great-uncle then said in a slow, precise cadence that God. may. have. taken. Bobby's. life. but. God. can't. give. you. your. life. back.

He told me to follow him into the garage. There, on a set of shelves along the back wall, he picked up a can of house paint. PEONY RED, the label said. Then he grabbed a flashlight and two paintbrushes and placed them inside of a plastic shopping bag. We climbed into his car and he drove to the Sunset Cemetery. Why Baby Harper had Peony Red house paint when all the walls of his house were eggshell white and why he knew exactly where Bobby was buried among the cemetery's 152 trees was how I knew that I had only a wallet-size photo of my great-uncle's life.

The headstone was pale granite, and it glowed in the light of a partial moon. We didn't need the flashlight to see what was carved into it. BELOVED. For the third time that night, my great-uncle reached out for my hands. Crickets chirped at our feet, the who-who of an owl was above us, and whiffs of honeysuckle played hide-and-seek with the summer night air. Baby Harper told me to take the front, and he would take care of the back. I couldn't move. I understood what he was saying to me, but I didn't understand the man. He dipped a brush into the paint and let the excess drip back into the can. He painted the word RAPIST down the length of the headstone. We stood there and looked at it. Then I did the same to its back. A summer night, honeysuckles, crickets, an owl, a moon. All stunned witnesses to what we had done. We got back into the car, and we left them all behind. My great-uncle's hands on the steering wheel. The broken line dividing the two-lane road. The trailer homes in the side-view mirrors. The water tower, a mushroom cloud over a pinprick of a town. Everything glowed that night. Less like stars and more like bleached bones.

After my father had passed away, I spent every weekend with Baby Harper. That Saturday night was no different, except that we cleaned our hands and underneath our fingernails with turpentine before saying good night. Baby Harper's guest room (he said that I was his one and only, and I believed him) held an antique sleigh bed and his collection of mourning embroideries. I preferred the whaling vessels on my bedroom walls to these faded, silk-flossed scenes of weeping-willow trees, Grecian urns, and young ladies draped upon them in grief, but the sleigh bed more than made up for their presence. Baby Harper had bought the bed from a widower, down in Greenville, South Carolina. Baby Harper said that widowers were the best sources for reasonably priced antiques. Men, in grief, discarded the trappings of their past. Women, in grief, hoarded. Or they embroidered, Baby Harper said, hiccupping. In spite of the bed's provenance, I liked it. The curved cherrywood frame lifted me high off the floor. A matching step stool sat beside the bed and allowed me to ascend onto it as if to a stage or a cloud. As I drifted off to sleep that night, I had no idea what my great-uncle was thinking as he lay in his own bed, his eyes closed, his breathing steady and slow. He had become a beautiful mystery to me.

Early the next morning Baby Harper drove me to the blue and gray ranch house. I had had my suitcases, both new because I had never needed suitcases before, packed a week ago. They were waiting for me in the living room. DeAnne, dressed for church, was drinking coffee at the kitchen table. She and Baby Harper exchanged good-mornings. I poured myself a glass of juice and sat down across from DeAnne. Baby Harper pulled out a chair, looked at us both, slid the chair back into its place, and said that he would be back at noon to take me to the airport. His voice lifted when he reached that last word. He pronounced it aiROport.

Baby Harper had never been on an airplane then, nor had I. The excitement he felt on my behalf was palpable. He had an image of air travel that belonged to the early days of commercial aviation, when passengers dressed in their best outfits, and everyone onboard, including the stewardesses, wore hats, as if they were all going to church. Maybe because in those days air travel did feel like being closer to God because it still felt like a miracle to them, albeit one that they could buy a ticket and be a witness to. Baby Harper weighed in a bit differently. He said that the passengers thought that they could die, and no one wanted to show up in Heaven in dungarees and a T-shirt. Both explanations, we decided, were true. Baby Harper promised me that he would give me something "special" to wear when the day came for my first flight.

We had spent the whole summer getting ourselves ready. For the most part, our preparations were the silent ones, the internal ones, the cataloging away of a moment or an act as we realized that it could be for the last time. Baby Harper took a lot of photographs of me that summer. He took them of my bare feet, my hands, my eyes. His favorite parts of me, he told me. If he had let me, I would have photographed his ears, his wrists, the thin band of skin between the cuff of his pants and his socks, visible only when he sat down and crossed his legs. My favorite parts of him that I could see.

The one-year anniversary of my father's death was that following month. I was relieved that I would be in New Haven by then. What would we have done together, DeAnne and I? Sung a hymn.

Held hands. Placed a bunch of carnations on my father's grave, then seen from the far corner of our eyes the white granite tombstone of BELOVED, the one whom she really mourned. She could do that on her own, I thought.

Since my father's passing, DeAnne and I had let ourselves be ourselves. We lived in a silent house. Conversations were no longer necessary, not because we understood each other's thoughts but because we didn't want to know what the other was thinking. Family meals were no longer obligatory. DeAnne ate in front of the television. I ate in my bedroom in front of a book. We ate the foodstuff of women living alone. Cans of tuna fish. Yogurt. Dried fruits. Salads splashed with bottled dressings. The smell of lit cigarettes, a habit that DeAnne no longer hid from me, was more pervasive now than the smell of her casseroles. A small blessing.

Baby Harper was the greatest blessing. He was a conduit and a haven. He had told DeAnne what colleges I was applying to and wrote the checks for my application fees when she forgot. He had told her that I had no intention of going to the prom and added that, in his opinion, no boy in Boiling Springs was good enough for me. He had offered his guest room to me on the weekends so that I wouldn't have to spend them with DeAnne *and* Iris, who had widowhood in common with her daughter now and liked her more because of it.

Every Saturday, DeAnne and Iris went to the movies, and then they went out for Iris's favorite dinner. Fried chicken, mashed potatoes, followed by a slice of coconut cream pie. Grease, carbohydrate, and sugar. Iris, the diabetic, really knew how not to live. Iris injected insulin to control her blood sugar, and the sight of her drawing up a syringe full, shooting herself in the thigh right through the fabric of her pant leg, and then reloading because one syringe wasn't enough, was the silent prayer that preceded all of our meals together.

Every Sunday, the two widows went to church with Baby Harper and prayed in the more usual way. On their feet, hands raised, palms tilted skyward, eyes closed, waiting for the Spirit to move them. Pastor Reynold demanded from his pulpit, Can you FEEL it? Can you FEEL it?

The last time I went to church with them I stood there and wondered if Can-you-feel-it? was the question that Mrs. Reynold heard when she and the pastor had sex. Which led to my follow-up question. Is Pastor Reynold fucking all of us right now? DeAnne and Iris, their eyes closed, swaying their bodies, waiting for IT. Baby Harper, eyes wide opened and body transported, waiting for IT.

No, Pastor Reynold, I don't feel a thing.

That was all it took. A question asked. A truthful response given. A decision made.

When I told DeAnne that I would no longer be going to church with them, she cried. My grandmother Iris accused me of never having been a true Christian in the first place. My great-uncle Harper sat at the dinner table speechless.

I said the first thing that came into my head, "I wish*BombPop* my father was still*sourcream* here*hardboiledegg*." We all knew what I meant. I meant that my grandmother would have never said those words to me if my father was still alive.

"Well, he isn't, and whose fault*boiledham* is that?" Iris snapped back. "It sure*cannedtuna* isn't God's*walnut* fault*boiledham*, little girl*salt*."

DeAnne sobbed into her napkin. My great-uncle Harper got up from the table and led her out of the room. After my father's passing, I had seen DeAnne treated like a blind person on more than one occasion.

My grandmother Iris and I remained seated at the dinner table. The casserole was still warm, a store-bought peach pie sat in its paper box on the sideboard, and my great-uncle's napkin was on the floor, where it had fallen.

I looked at the empty chair at the head of the table and thought about my father coming home again.

Chapter 12

My father was in love. I said this to his coffin as it was lowered into the ground. I was seventeen when he died. He was fifty-three. I thought my grandmother Iris would be the first to go. So did she. Once the news of his death had made the rounds of Boiling Springs and Shelby, and then Charlotte with one quick phone call to the Hammericks there, who acknowledged his death by sending a small jade plant in a wicker basket to the funeral home, I knew that Iris *wished* that she had been first. Iris saw the small potted plant sitting among the wreaths exploding with roses and lilies, and she saw it for what it was: an insult, anchored to rich soil and meant to grow with each passing day. After Iris read the names on the card, she asked Baby Harper to take the plant and its basket and put it inside his car. That night, after all the mourners had left the blue and gray ranch house, where they had gathered after the burial to deposit their offerings of casseroles and Bundt cakes (food for the dead, as I had always suspected), Iris took the plant out of the car and into the backyard, where she set fire to its basket.

For about a minute, an intense and unexpected light source threw Iris's shadow onto an exterior wall of the garage, where she appeared as a shapeless mountain. I wondered who these people in Charlotte were who thought that a jade plant could cause injury to a woman like Iris. I knew little about them, and it didn't occur to me then that they knew anything about me. The insult, like everything after a death, was intended for the living.

Iris was very much alive, and she made sure that the plant wasn't. Once the blaze died down, there was nothing left of the basket, and what was left of the jade plant had turned gray and mushy. Succulents didn't burn. They steamed. My great-uncle and I looked at each other, silently acknowledging that we learned something new every day. We were sitting at the kitchen table. DeAnne had already turned in for the night. When Baby Harper had seen Iris with the plant in her hands, he had reached for his camera. It was hanging around his neck as we sat there watching her. We had an unobstructed view through the screen door of Iris and her bonfire. He didn't touch the camera again, and he didn't say a word even after the flames had disappeared.

Baby Harper hadn't been saying much in those days right after my father's death. The singing-talker had given me that little prayer, written on a slip of paper. "Thomas was in love," the note said. Baby Harper and I were in the front seat of his car, and DeAnne and Iris were in the back. We were on our way to the funeral home. Baby Harper had meant it as a plea to God for mercy. That was how I had meant it as well when I said it to my father's coffin. A prayer should always have the word "love" in it. Or perhaps it was the other way around.

While Baby Harper was suffering from a loss of words, DeAnne and I were forgetting to do basic things for ourselves. Maybe that was why mourners brought food to the family of the deceased—if we didn't see it on our kitchen counters and in our refrigerator, we would forget to eat. DeAnne forgot to lock the doors of the house at night. I forgot to take out the trash. DeAnne forgot to turn on the lights. I forgot all about the mail. On the morning of the funeral, DeAnne forgot to zip up the back of her dress.

My grandmother Iris, Baby Harper, and I were sitting at the kitchen table waiting for her. When DeAnne walked into the room, Iris and I saw the *V* of skin on her back at the same time. Iris got up and, without saying a word, guided her daughter out of the room as if she were blind. I mouthed to my great-uncle, "Can you believe she forgot?" He shook his head no. At the time, I thought he meant no, he couldn't believe it. But he meant no, she hadn't forgotten. How could I have known then that twenty-five years of marriage meant twenty-five years of having someone to help you with the zipper that began at the small of your back?

The day of my father's funeral has become my familiar Greek city. Each hour was a street or a path. Each minute was a temple or a fountain. I revisited the city not to remember facts but to see them anew.

When I see that morning now, I see the faces around the kitchen table, and I see DeAnne's dress. Most clearly, I see the exposed skin, so pale against the black fabric of her dress, and I see there not a lapse in memory but the persistence of it. I feel anger, adult and reasoned, toward my lovesick father for squandering something valuable for something fleeting. I feel something nearing affection for DeAnne again.

At the end of his life, Thomas Hammerick wasn't a Reasonable Man. He was only a man, with a weak heart. He was in his car, parked in a driveway of a small A-frame house on Goforth Road. That was where the police officer and EMS workers had found him, slumped over the steering wheel like a drunk, his heart already a stone.

DeAnne and I had sat at the dinner table that night waiting for him, until the telephone rang. My father opened the front door of the blue and gray ranch house every weeknight at 5:30 P.M. We were seated around the table by 6 P.M. My father was always punctual. His schedule was firm, like his handshake. DeAnne and I had sat at the dinner table looking down at our place settings, thinking that we had both come to the table too early, that all the clocks in the house were running fast. The telephone rang and DeAnne went into the room to answer it. I heard her say hello. Then silence. I walked into the room just as she was hanging up the receiver. I followed her into the kitchen, where she turned off the oven. Inside a casserole had been drying up in the low heat. I followed her as she went back into the dining room. She turned around and looked at me, startled to see another person in the house. DeAnne thought of the casserole before she thought of me. My father had left me in this woman's care.

Goforth Road was where my father's twenty-two-year-old secretary lived. His car was parked in the driveway of her rented house. Long ago, when that road was named, it must have been someone's idea of a joke, as Goforth was a dead-end street. But the joke was now on us, the two Hammericks, the one Whatley, and the one Burch who remained.

News traveled fast in Boiling Springs, as there wasn't very far for it to go. The tight bundle of words, written up in a report at the police station, went home with the sergeant and was handed over to his wife. The next day the bundle, now an exaggerated whisper, arrived at the town's main switchboard, Miss Cora's Beauty Emporium, where it was distributed within the first fifteen minutes to two perms and one updo. The paths that the whisper, now a bona fide bit of juicy gossip, took to get to Iris and Baby Harper were different but of equal speed. Iris immediately telephoned DeAnne. Baby Harper kept it to himself. Three days later, I received a letter, #821, from Kelly, who was living in Rock Hill, South Carolina, by then. She didn't want me to hear about it from someone else. "Or knowing your family," Kelly wrote, "they'll try to keep it from you, which I know would be worse." In her hand, the news about my father again became a tight bundle of words:

At 7:42 P.M. on Wednesday, October 30, 1985, Thomas Hammerick was found dead in his car, parked in the driveway of 133 Goforth Road. Hammerick appeared to be fully clothed, with his head resting facedown on the steering wheel. The two EMS workers who examined him found that the deceased had on no underwear. After being questioned, Carrie Betts, the occupant of 133 Goforth Road, handed over the deceased's undershirt and boxers. Betts stated that Hammerick, in his rush to leave her house, must have forgotten to put them on. At which point, the EMS workers and the one police officer on the scene looked at one another and smiled.

On the day of my father's funeral, another letter from Kelly, #822, was waiting for me in the blue and gray ranch house. I didn't see the stack of mail on the hallway table until Baby Harper had left to drive Iris home that night. He or someone else must have taken in the contents of our overflowing mailbox for us. In lieu of attending the funeral, Kelly had sent me a long letter, posted with a folk-art duck decoy stamp.

Since leaving for Rock Hill to go live with her pregnancy and her aunt, Kelly's correspondence to me had consisted of a couple of lines scribbled on the backs of postcards, usually about how much weight she had gained. The subtext here was painfully clear, even to me. Her mistake was growing larger with every passing day, and she felt like a visitor within her own body. Some of her old self came back, both in substance and in style, in #822. Kelly wrote that she and her aunt had decided on the name Luke for the baby. Her aunt liked the name because of Luke and Laura from *General Hospital.* Kelly liked it because of Luke and Leia from *Star Wars.* "Just between us," Kelly wrote, " 'Skywalker' is the baby's middle name."

Kelly thought that the baby should have a secret name because he was a secret and because his father, like Skywalker's, wasn't going to be around much. I had avoided the topic of the baby's father because the one and only time that I had asked Kelly about him she wrote back that she didn't know who he was. Kelly knew everything. That was her way of saying she didn't want to tell me, and I didn't want to know why. A friendship, we were quickly learning, could be based on what we shared and on what we allowed each other to keep to ourselves.

My letters to Kelly during those same months had been about everything except the one topic that was consuming my thoughts. The crowning moment in the life of a high school overachiever, the college application season, was fast approaching. I was a Hammerick. We went to Yale. That much of the family history I knew. Grade point average? Check. A pack a day had very successfully kept the incomings away. Community service? Check. I volunteered five hours a week at Boiling Springs Elementary School, reshelving books in their library. My great-uncle said that I could call it "organizing and distributing reading materials to underprivileged southern youths." We both understood that the youths were underprivileged because they were living in Boiling Springs, not because they were economically down and out. Letters of recommendation? Check. Uncheck. Then check again. Shortly before my father passed away, he had arranged for a letter from William Hoyle, a member of the U.S. Congress from our district, who then bowed out of his promise in light of my father's "lack*applesauce* of moral*nutmeg* character*pickledwatermelonrind*." That elected bastard's secretary actually said this to me on the phone two weeks after my father's funeral. I hung up on her. When I told my great-uncle Harper about the phone call, he said that he would rather lack moral character than a heart, but that I was in luck because Congressman Hoyle lacked both.

I received another phone call from the congressman's secretary. This time she said that a recommendation letter was being sent on my behalf and that the congressman wished me continued success. My great-uncle Harper hiccupped when I told this to him. When I pushed him for his role in changing the congressman's mind, Baby Harper claimed that he had done nothing except mention to Iris what Wee Willie Hoyle thought of her deceased son-in-law. That was the first time I had heard anyone refer to the congressman as "Wee Willie." I was full of questions, but my great-uncle had nothing more that he wanted to say.

I turned to my grandmother Iris, who was more forthcoming. She told me that when Willie Hoyle and Baby Harper were young they were inseparable friends until she found them one day naked from the waist down trying on her girdles and stockings. Willie pointed a finger at Baby Harper and said that it was all his idea. That was when Iris began adding the editorialized "Wee" to the future congressman's first name. I was smiling at the thought of two mischievous little boys getting caught by an angry Iris, until she, the family truth teller, whisper-yelled at me that Baby Harper and Wee Willie were SIXTEEN years old when she found them half dressed in her clothes.

My grandmother, the plant arsonist, was also a petty extortionist. Just hearing her voice on the telephone must have made Congressman Hoyle change his mind and sign my recommendation letter. Wee Willie knew his constituents, and he knew that in their eyes his youthful indiscretion was worse than a lack of moral character. It was a sin that would render him unelectable. I assumed Iris burned and extorted for the same reason, to assuage her own wounded pride. Her little brother may have been a lacy-undergarment enthusiast, her son-in-law a philanderer who died without his boxers on, and her granddaughter a physical letdown in a training bra, but we all belonged to her. In her orbit, we were the pitted and scarred moons. Without us, she would have never needed to shine so brightly.

By the time I was in high school I had come to terms with the fact that my grandmother Iris and I were close in the way that

Maine and Hawaii were close. I believed that she was indifferent to me because I looked nothing like her.

I now know that it is no coincidence that the word "favor" is used to denote a physical resemblance. I favor you (your eyes, your chin). You favor me (with love and attention). Favor is a reciprocity based on a biological imperative; it is a primal vanity that has saved the lives of some babies and doomed others:

The floodwater is rising. You have only your two hands. Which child in your brood do you grab on to? The one who is your mirror image or the one who is unrecognizable? (Even though I have no siblings, I have always been thankful that Boiling Springs wasn't prone to high waters.)

During my sophomore year in college, I learned in my Alienation/Alien Nation seminar, cross-listed under sociology and literature, that a definition of "aberration" was a mirror that failed to produce an exact image. I understood long before this that the body, especially that of an offspring, was best when it was a reflective surface. DeAnne's, for example, came very close to Iris's, but there was something lacking in DeAnne's eyes and the shape of her lips. Iris was therefore looking forward to the next generation. Then I came along, and my grandmother's hopes died.

Iris tolerated me during my tomboy stage. There was even a mild spasm of interest when my mother made me take baton twirling lessons, a rite of Southern girlhood, which culminated with a march down Main Street in the Shelby Thanksgiving Day Parade. I was nine years old. Iris sat on a folding chair on the courthouse steps. My great-uncle was sitting beside her. When my troupe went by, he stood up and waved a sign: WE GIVE THANKS FOR LINDA! I chose to believe that my grandmother was waving at me too and not at Baby Harper to put down his sign.

Iris ignored me altogether when I started growing my hair long again, wearing gloss on my lips, and carrying a purse full of feminine protection. I had disappeared because I had disappointed. That was what I grew up believing.

What happened to Kelly only affirmed what I already knew about physical and emotional reciprocity. For the first thirteen years of her life, Kelly was to her mother, Beth Anne, no more than a disembodied voice. Kelly, who had reluctantly shown me her baby pictures, had been fat from day one. She came out of the womb with three chins and so many folds on her body that she was more Shar-Pei puppy than human baby. Fourteen years later, when Beth Anne finally recognized her pretty self in the being whom she had brought into the world, Kelly was, in essence, reborn. Kelly suddenly had a body, which was pleasing to the eyes and was therefore seen. During our freshman year at BSHS, I often imagined that my best friend had lost all of that weight but what was left of her wasn't physically attractive. What if inside the fat girl was a thin ugly girl? Or just a plain one? I had assumed a role in high school that came with only one required act. I had to earn straight A's. Kelly had assumed a role that called for her to be on display, to be chased like prey, to flirt and to tease, and to give in and be touched but never penetrated. Kelly was too smart to play her role successfully. She was too curious. *How does this feel?* She was too egalitarian. *Now you do it to me.* She was too truthful. *I don't want you to stop.*

Kelly left Boiling Springs in January of 1985. It was the last Saturday of the month. My bedroom was flooded with morning sunlight, but I was still in bed, eyes shut to the dust motes in the air and the whaling vessels at sea. I heard DeAnne calling my name. Then I heard, "Kelly*cannedpeaches* is on the phone*creamcheese*!" I opened my eyes, knowing something was wrong. Kelly and I rarely called each other, and when we did we exchanged verbal telegrams, short, clipped, efficient, and to the point.

"Hello," I said.

"Linda*mint*?"

"Yes."

"I have to go*boiledcarrots*."

"Where?"

"Rock*rawegg* Hill*driedapricot*."

"To your aunt's*cornbread*?"

"Yes."

"How long*grapeNehi*?"

"Nine months*saltinecracker*. Well, eight now."

"Oh, Jesus*friedchicken*."

"He had nothing*tomato* to do*grits* with it."

"You'll write*Frenchfries*?"

"Yes."

Click.

"Kelly*cannedpeaches*?"

Kelly wrote in letter #822 that she couldn't be away from Lil' Skywalker right now because she was breastfeeding him. Besides that, Beth Anne didn't want her coming back to Boiling Springs until all of her pregnancy weight had been lost. "Otherwise, people would know that I had been, well, you know . . . fat!" When I read this, I could almost hear Kelly's quick, sharp laugh in the room. Kelly added that she was getting the feeling that her aunt wanted her out of the house. Her aunt, a forty-year-old ex-hippie–cum–successful cat groomer, had read that breastfeeding for the first year of the baby's life was good for the baby's immune system, so Kelly knew that she wasn't going anywhere soon. In the meantime, the aunt was trying with little success to downplay her growing maternal yearnings and rivalry. Plopping down on the living room couch, her aunt would say, "Well, there you two are!" as if she had no idea that mother and child were just about to engage in the most primitive form of food service. Then her aunt would hold on to some part of Lil' Skywalker, usually one of his tiny feet, while Kelly breastfed him.

In her previous postcards and letters, Kelly hadn't shared with me many details about her pregnancy. In #822, she did. She recalled for me how her sense of smell had become hound-dog acute at the beginning of her second trimester. She wrote that she knew what food was cooking two houses away. She discovered that even boiled potatoes or heated-up milk gave off odors that left her nauseated and weak. She wrote that by the end of her fifth month her nose and her ankles ballooned with retained fluids. Her aunt cut all salt from her diet in an effort to relieve the swelling. This only made Kelly crave the taste of it more. She made do by discovering the hidden salt in foods. Tomato juice. Caramel candy. The filling of store-bought apple pie. Instant hot cocoa mix. By the start of her third trimester, Kelly thought that she could hear the sound of her skin stretching. She cried a lot then because she could no longer recognize her own body. She slept twelve to fourteen hours a day because it was the only tranquilizer allowed a pregnant girl. Her aunt, unmarried and anxious to become a single mother, spent her free time knitting a receiving blanket, a bonnet, and a pair of booties. Sometimes Kelly and her aunt would do mothers-to-be activities together, like when they chose the baby's name. As for the birth itself, Kelly wrote that she had no memory of it.

Kelly ended her letter to me with an ode to Lil' Skywalker's fingernails and toenails. They were the color of wax paper and almost as thin, she wrote. They were more insect wings than human body. They grew longer by the hour. They made her understand why we painted our nails with bright polish when we grew older. We were disappointed in what they had become. Thick and ridged, more carapace than human body. Kelly had bought a pair of small, round-tipped nail scissors for Lil' Skywalker, but her aunt had read that it was better to trim the nails by biting them off gently with your teeth. Kelly wouldn't do it, so her aunt did it for her. Kelly wrote that when she saw Lil' Skywalker's tiny fingers and then his tender toes in her aunt's mouth, she felt sick to her stomach. She wrote that he was so helpless. What Kelly meant was that she was so helpless.

After Lil' Skywalker's first birthday, Kelly was asked to leave the Rock Hill household. Her aunt promised that they would keep in regular contact, and they have. The arrangement was simple. The aunt telephoned Kelly every month. Kelly never telephoned the aunt. These calls, in addition to photographs of Luke on his birthdays and most holidays, except Mother's Day, were the extent of their interaction. The aunt proposed the following arrangement: If and when Luke asked about his birth mother, he would be told Kelly's name and contact information. As far as I know, Luke to this day has yet to ask. He doesn't know, then, that he has a secret middle name, Skywalker, or that for the first year of his life two seventeen-year-old girls exchanged letters referring to him by its diminutive. According to Kelly, he now looks exactly like his father. That was probably why she has never shown me a photograph of Luke. Her secret would be clearly written on his face.

After Kelly's aunt legally adopted Luke, the cat groomer left the lucrative world of feline fanciers behind to open the first yoga studio in Rock Hill, if not the very first one in the state of South Carolina. She learned hatha yoga through a video correspondence course offered by an enterprising commune in Northern California, located in an area now more commonly known as Silicon Valley. Yoga proved to be an inspired profit-generating enterprise for the commune and for Kelly's aunt. She and Luke moved into a larger house and took yearly trips to India, where she continued her studies with a yogi, and young Luke learned Hindi as a second language from his native nanny.

Kelly's aunt, who was Beth Anne's youngest sister, had never been close to their family. By the time Kelly was fourteen, her aunt was already limiting her appearances at their family gatherings to every other year. Her few visits with them were enough for Kelly to size her up. Her aunt was the only one on her mother's side of the family who had lived outside of the Bible Belt. Her aunt didn't have a college degree but did have a vocabulary of multisyllabic and sometimes foreign-sounding words. Kelly was smart enough to know that sometimes her aunt didn't really understand the meanings of these words but used them anyway. I remembered Kelly describing her aunt to me as "asspirational." I wrote back to Kelly that

I didn't think that was a word. Kelly responded that it should be one in order to emphasize the dumb ass lurking inside of such people. Nonetheless, when Kelly found herself pregnant, the first telephone call she made was to this woman.

When Kelly's aunt became Luke's legal mother, she ceased all contact with their extended family, who were frankly relieved, as the family embarrassment was now harboring another family embarrassment. Two disappearances for the price of one. A bargain, they thought. The family had long made it clear to Kelly's aunt that they were horrified by all of her life decisions, which they would list by the state followed by a brief description of what she "had gotten herself into" while there. California: commune. New Mexico: Indians. Arizona: cats. South Carolina: cats and yoga. In retrospect, the family realized that cat grooming was by far the most "normal" of the communities that this woman had thrown herself into.

Kelly's aunt had a name of course, but from the moment that Kelly went to live with her I never wanted to use it. Birth mothers were too often anonymous. I wanted the adoptive mother, for once, to be the nameless one.

As I read Kelly's letter with its full and detail-rich account of her baby's life to date, I remembered being infuriated. There wasn't another word about my father's passing. I couldn't believe how her maternity had changed her, dulled her regard for those around her except for the Breastfeeding One, and that she had thought it appropriate to share her lack of consideration with me. These sentiments were collapsed into one rhetorical question: What fucking world is she living in? The borders of my world were clear to me. My father was in an open coffin that was now closed and in the ground. DeAnne was in their bed, alone. My grandmother Iris was an overweight, vengeful diabetic with a taste for fire, and one of these traits would surely make her the next in our family to die. My great-uncle Harper, my dear singing-talker, was speechless with grief. What I needed from my best friend was sympathy, an acknowledgment of my loss, a shoulder to cry on. A baby named Lil' Skywalker was there instead.

At the farthest edge of the familiar city, there is a blue and gray ranch house. Kelly's letter waits for me there on the hallway table. Next to it is the ghost of the very first letter that she ever wrote to me. The postmaster general's sudden absence has left everything at risk of being undelivered and unread. I return there to examine and reexamine the body of letter #822. How many readings did it take before I found within it what Kelly, the new mother, already understood back then? I have lost count. After Iris passed away, I still didn't see it. Baby Harper, as his last gift to me, had made me see the sentence that Kelly never wrote but that informed her every word: Life trumps death.

The floodwater is rising. You have two hands and one heart (breaking, because you are witnessing your world disappearing). There is a crying baby and a corpse. Which do you embrace and take with you to higher ground? Whether the baby is your blood relation shouldn't change the answer.

Kelly, the new mother, understood that what had happened to me would happen to her baby much too soon. Because what difference was there between death and absence to the ones who were left behind?

Chapter 13

On a plantation located on the banks of the Roanoke River near the Virginia border but firmly on North Carolina soil, a baby boy was born into slavery. Someone, because we can't be certain that it was his father or mother, called him George, middle name Moses. The plantation owner who owned him was named William (undoubtedly chosen for him by his own father and mother), family name Horton. Therefore the baby's last name was also Horton, and it was the first of his shackles. George Moses Horton's earliest memory was of his mother's back bent over rows of tobacco as he clung to her, mesmerized by the up-and-down rhythm of hard labor. When George Moses was still a young child, William Horton moved his possessions—the china cabinet, the plantation desk, the silver candlesticks, the slaves, the horses, and the cows—to a parcel of land near the town of Chapel Hill. There, far from the sounds of the river, George Moses grew up and learned that his mother found comfort in the sounds of worship. She taught him the prayers, the hymns, all the words that could float out of their mouths in praise of God. George Moses took them all in, and one day he moved them around in his head and created something new, "Rise up, my soul, and let us go." He repeated these words to himself and rejoiced in the meaning, clear and stark, of what was to be the first line of a poem, a thing of his own creation that would belong only to him. More words sang themselves inside of his head and the poem was completed. The initial call-to-freedom thrust was by then disguised within a devotional message.

Rise up, my soul, and let us go
Up to the gospel feast;
Gird on the garment white as snow,
To join and be a guest.

George Moses's mother had taught him well. Words, he understood, were beautiful because they could reveal the truth and hide it at the same time. George Moses, when he was twenty years old, had a book's worth of his own poems hidden inside of him. He shared them with no one in order to keep them safe, especially from James Horton, son of William, who owned George Moses now and who would want to own his words too. A product of Horton's property was his property. Milk from his cows, tobacco from his land, child from his slave. George Moses knew the rules of the plantation. Within its confines he knew the boundaries, the invisible riverbanks, the state lines.

James Horton looked at George Moses one day and saw what he wanted to see, a tall young man with a calm, mild temperament who could be relied upon. George Moses was from then on sent to Chapel Hill on Sundays to sell the plantation's surplus fruits and vegetables. The Horton family couldn't possibly consume all those tomatoes and snap peas and strawberries and plums.

Chapel Hill was a sad new world for George Moses. All the same rules applied there, plus new ones that his mother couldn't have educated him about. The town was home to the University of North Carolina, and its streets were filled with young men George

Moses's age. When these students visited the market, they did so for entertainment and occasionally for the purchase of foodstuff. George Moses was commanded to perform a trick—*Come on now! Sing us a song. Dance a little. Your momma taught you a jig, didn't she?*—before they would buy from him. George Moses's pride gave him away. He opened up his mouth, and a poem poured out. The young men thought it was a fine trick. A slave who had memorized a poem! They slapped their knees and laughed. George Moses's pride was by now in full bloom. He told them in a low voice that the poem belonged to him. Of course, the moment those words were released into the open air the poem was no longer his.

❧

My great-uncle Harper was sixty-six years old, and he was about to take his first flight. To calm his nerves, he hummed Patsy Cline's "You Belong to Me" while waiting in the terminal of the Charlotte airport—*Fly the ocean in a silver plane. See the jungle when it's wet with rain*—until he remembered that Patsy had died in a plane crash. That and the fact that there was no ocean or jungle between the state of North Carolina and the state of Connecticut made him change his tune. Frank Sinatra's "Come Fly with Me" then kept him company until the boarding call. *Let's fly, let's fly away . . . Once I get you up there where the air is rarefied. We'll just glide, starry-eyed.* Baby Harper had thought about driving up to New Haven, but then he decided that he wanted to experience the journey as I had experienced it. He wanted to feel the ground beneath him slipping away, to see North Carolina getting smaller, its fields and towns becoming abstract, and finally disappearing below him. I told him it wasn't the sense of loss that dominated the experience of flight but the sense of momentum, a lifting up and away. That promise decided it for him.

It was May of 1990 and I was graduating from Yale. Baby Harper was my family, the only member who was there to see me receive my diploma. Baby Harper assured me that my father and my grandmother Iris would be watching from Heaven. He didn't mention my mother, DeAnne, who wasn't dead but whom I hadn't invited.

My great-uncle showed up to my graduation ceremony wearing a white linen suit with a cut that was slim and sharp, which he probably last wore when Eisenhower was first elected, an equally white oxford shirt, and a blue (for Yale) bow tie embroidered with cardinals (for the Old North State). He looked like a mix of Colonel Sanders, Tom Wolfe, and Pee Wee Herman. In other words, he looked like Baby Harper. I smiled widely and openly and without hesitation, something that I hadn't done during those past four years, when I saw him walking across the courtyard of Pierson, the residential college where I lived at Yale.

As a legacy, I had been assigned to the same residential college as my father and his forefathers. When I first saw Pierson, I had to laugh. Pierson was a green-shuttered colonial, albeit much grander in scale than Iris and Walter Wendell's house on Piedmont Street. There was often-repeated lore (both false and true, like the rest of the Yale campus) that before the Civil War Pierson was the sole residential college to provide living accommodations for those Southern gentlemen who had brought their property-valets up North with them. It was an apocryphal story. The residential college system at Yale didn't begin until 1933. That exculpatory fact, however, never explained another fact: why there was a wing of Pierson—whitewashed brick and festooned on the outside with decorative iron railings and stairs—known as the "Slave Quarters." Perhaps it was the inability to reconcile one true thing, the year of construction, with another true thing, the name of the wing, that made the antebellum myth necessary. A lie to create a more comprehensible truth, as it were. Actual slave quarters could be understood as the bones of history, reluctantly preserved. Fanciful, imagined slave quarters were, on the other hand, a pornography of history. I wondered what my father must have thought when he first saw the Slave Quarters of Pierson, how he must have felt traveling hundreds of miles due north only to be confronted with an ersatz South, and whether it had made him feel even farther away from home.

I glanced down from my great-uncle's face and suit and saw my father's shoes walking toward me. Wing tips, brown leather, handsome left heel worn on the outside edge, a deep crease across the charismatic right toe. I knew then that Baby Harper had tried to bring all that he could of Boiling Springs with him.

It had been almost five years since my father's passing and more than three since my grandmother's. DeAnne and I hadn't spoken since Iris's funeral. The last letter I had sent to DeAnne was at the end of my sophomore year. I assumed the next time I saw her would be at another funeral. I was hoping it wouldn't be Baby Harper's. That left us with only one other possibility. So be it, I thought.

Missing Baby Harper was the worst part of not going back to Boiling Springs. We spoke on the phone every week. He did most of the talking. I listened with the receiver pressed close to my ear. Every month, he sent me a check for "incidentals." That was what he wrote on the check's memo line. I used the money for cigarettes, which had become the opposite of that for me. "Integrals" were more like it. On my birthday and on every holiday that was printed on his wall calendar, he sent me a box of chocolates. He was partial to Whitman's Samplers. Me too. Since the fifth grade, I had begun the slow and methodical project of renaming the pieces inside of those trompe l'oeil cross-stitched boxes after the words that triggered their flavors. The Samplers proved to be an eclectic collection of words. I identified Cashew Cluster first, which was from then on "Russia." Dark Chocolate Molasses Chew turned out to be "Static." Cherry Cordial was "Neanderthal." Along with the chocolates, Baby Harper sent me photographs that he had taken in my absence, and they were of people I didn't know. He said that he had to branch out now, as there were so few of us left.

"Linda Vista!" My great-uncle Harper's voice reached me before his body did. "Now what have you gone and done?" There was a waver in his voice that I hadn't heard over the telephone lines.

I reached out and hugged him.

His embrace was awkward and sweet. His arms, as always, were unsure of where to make contact with my body. He smelled like the rooms of his Greek Revival. Witch hazel (his aftershave of choice), burned coffee, and lemon-scented Pledge. I felt a hand gingerly touching my hair. I lifted my face out of his lapel.

"I wanted*saltedbutter* to look more like you*cannedgreenbeans,*" I said. I meant it as a joke, but as soon as the sentence left my mouth I realized that it had sounded mocking, my default tone of voice at Yale.

Baby Harper took a couple of steps back. There was a look in his eyes—a cumulus cloud passing over a midday sun—that made me regret cutting off my hair.

When Baby Harper took me to the Charlotte airport for my first flight, he had with him one of his cameras, a simple point-and-shoot that he had gotten as a gift and rarely used. I remembered being surprised when he handed it to a young woman who was sitting next to us at the gate. He asked if she would take our photo. He then politely asked her to take two more. He knew that he had closed his eyes the first time the shutter closed. I thought that he wasn't used to the timing of the eyelids, the holding of a smile, the posing for posterity. Four years later, at my college graduation, I still hadn't seen these airport photographs. When I finally did, the one with his eyes shut made me cry.

As we stood there surrounded by Pierson's faded red bricks and its green shutters freshly painted for graduation, Baby Harper must have been thinking about the girl in those photographs, the girl who minutes later had turned around to wave goodbye to him before disappearing down a corridor that fed her into a swollen-bodied plane. He liked the way that there was a rhythm in her long hair as she walked away from him. He was looking at me and missing her.

"Well, Vista Girl, I'm deeply flattered by the gesture, then," Baby Harper said.

I beamed at him, relieved to see that his sense of humor was still the same.

I had cut my hair shorter than his ever was, but in an homage to him, I had my bangs cut asymmetrically so that they would hang over one eye. I had on a black suit that I had bought at the Salvation Army. The pants were full and wide-legged, and the little jacket was nipped at the waist, the narrow shoulders peaked. I had on a pair of crimson (for Harvard) pumps that made me a full three inches taller. My lipstick was a shade darker than my shoes. My eyeliner was liquid and its application was Cleopatra-like. In my four years at Yale I had learned many good and useful things. One was that there were different ways to hide. One way was to disappear into a crowd. Counterintuitively, another way was to stand out in a crowd. People saw only your costume and your mask, and they turned a blind eye to all that was underneath.

I had carefully cultivated, by the end of my freshman year, a look that Kelly had dubbed "the love child of Sid Vicious and Katharine Hepburn." I had sent Kelly an issue of the *Yale Daily News* in which there was a photograph of me smoking a cigarette in front of Sterling Memorial, the main library on campus. The photo accompanied an article about how smoking, despite the known health risks, was still "de rigueur" among the visual-arts and literature majors. It was a slice-of-campus-life piece, the kind of feature article assigned to a freshman to see if the cub reporter could wring some interest out of a banal subject. The reporter opined that perhaps the artsy majors all had a death wish because we knew that we would never find employment upon our graduation. I liked the photograph because I was scowling into the camera and giving the photographer the finger. Before sending the clipping to Kelly, I wrote over the body of the article: "Anti-Smoking Propaganda!!" In response, she sent me the descriptive phrase—love child of Sid Vicious and Katharine Hepburn—that I wasn't sure was accurate, but I liked the sound of it, the possibilities raised by that particular form of aesthetic miscegenation. I wrote back to Kelly that I would try my best to live up to it. By my senior year, I had succeeded and surpassed both of our expectations.

Another passing cumulus cloud.

I wanted to reassure Baby Harper that *we* hadn't changed. He and I were family, and nothing I could ever do to myself on the outside would alter that. I wanted him to stop examining me with those blue eyes of his, a bit faded from when I saw them last, and to look around him instead, to take in the other family groups that had gathered in the Pierson courtyard, each with a graduating son or daughter at their nucleus. I had experienced nothing in Boiling Springs that could have prepared me for these offspring. Their prep-school rivalries, their exclusive geographies, their rhythmless dancing, their indifference to the bitter cold, their L.L. Bean duck boots. I could have never disappeared into these people. If I had continued to try, I would have continued to fail.

Seeing my grandmother Iris in her coffin had made me understand that simple truth about myself. Even on the day of her funeral, my grandmother was the family's truth teller. Iris's face, too light with powder, wore a rueful expression, probably because the mortician had applied her lipstick a bit unevenly. Iris had prechosen, in addition to the magnolias and the caterer from Asheville, a carnation-pink dress, size eight, and ivory gloves with three pearl buttons at the wrists. Her satin pumps were dyed to match her dress. The shoes must have been purchased when she was still fat because her feet, now newly svelte, swam in them. A small clutch purse lay on its side by her gloved left hand. I remembered thinking, What do you need up in Heaven, Iris? A mirror, lipstick, and a twenty?

Iris was ready for Walter Wendell and God, in that order. True to herself to the very end, she had died as she had lived: self-satisfied, if not happy. She was the Queen of Hearts and the rest of us were her Jokers. She had occupied her baby brother's every thought. A full week after rigor mortis had set in, and wasn't she still telling him what to do? She had taken the occasion of her funeral to trump her daughter one last time. Lopsided lipstick aside, Iris was a stunner in carnation pink. Her daughter was eclipsed in mourning weeds. Iris was always the sun. In her final hours, she had flared and branded us with the Sallow A. We were all, in her eyes, alone in this world. What she meant was that we should follow her example and make the best of it.

With her lipstick smirk, my grandmother Iris looked amused by but not impressed with the magic trick that I had been attempting since leaving Boiling Springs. The disappearing girl could no longer disappear. The little canary, as she was fond of calling me, was therefore trying to transform herself into a white dove. In the process, I was becoming not invisible but nothing, and even with her eyes closed, Iris knew.

After my grandmother's funeral, I returned to New Haven and threw out my L.L. Bean and J. Crew catalogs, which from day one had shown up unsolicited in my Yale Station mailbox and promised me insouciant uniformity via a pair of khakis and a sweater set in aubergine. I discarded the string of fake pearls and the mock turtlenecks. I returned to the all-black wardrobe that had served me so well in high school, but this time I wasn't a blank slate. I constructed a persona out of thrift store clothes ripe with mothballs and disturbed dust. I made liberal use of high-octane drugstore cosmetics, with an eye toward classic Hollywood glamour and the other eye cocked toward London's Kings Road during its punk heyday. The effect that I achieved was that of a visual expletive, a sartorial expression of the bile, acid, and longing that would have otherwise stayed locked inside of me. I wanted to throw myself, bodily and with great élan, into a nonintersecting orbit, a parallel universe to that of my day-to-day world. I was, in other words, almost nineteen years old and finally forging myself.

"Now where's your hat, Vista Girl?" my great-uncle asked, after he had fully taken in my graduation day outfit. There was that waver again. Baby Harper sounded a bit hurt not to see the fedora, brown felt with a wide cream band, the "something special" that he had given to me for my first flight. He had handed the hat to me along with a wink, as the final boarding call was announced. At the time, I thought that both the hat and the wink were references to our previous conversations about my imminent, but hopefully not permanent, proximity to God, courtesy of American Airlines. I wouldn't understand that the wink and the hat meant something else entirely until I saw the album cover for "Come Fly with Me."

Leo would have the record in his collection, and, like all the objects in his life, it was in mint condition, this one kept free from household dust and oily fingertips by a plastic sleeve. The album art was an illustration in cool, breezy Mediterranean hues, featuring a young, lean Sinatra with a rakish smile on his face. Sinatra had one hand extended to a feminine one (the rest of her body was otherwise out of the picture); Sinatra's other hand was curled into a hitchhiker's thumbs up. In the background were white airplanes with jaunty red stripes ready and willing on the tarmac, and overhead there was a clear blue sky. It was a come-hither scene, a seduction involving travel, surely the precursor to the Mile-High Club. I would recognize the hat on Sinatra's head, a familiar thing that, in my mind, belonged first to my great-uncle Harper. When my great-uncle gave the fedora to me, he said he had bought it back in 1957 and had worn it exactly twice. When I saw Sinatra's album, I would make sure to check its release date: 1957. I was glad to know that at least on two occasions Baby Harper, at the age of thirty-three, was swank and wildly in style. I liked to imagine him as he must have been in those days. I never liked to imagine why he put the fedora away until he was sixty-two, when he gave it to me along with a wink, this long-held fantasy of flight, the promise of traveling fast and light, the romance that once you landed, you were somewhere.

Perhaps my great-uncle asked me about the fedora because he suddenly felt the distance between Boiling Springs and New Haven. He then leaned in and whispered in my ear, "Thomas would have been so proud of you, little girl." My great-uncle Harper never called me that. Only Iris called me "little girl," a term so painfully generic yet sweet and endearing all at once. Hearing it in combination with my father's given name made me drop my face back into my great-uncle's lapel. This time his arms quickly wrapped around me, and together we made Pierson, Yale, New Haven, the whole state of Connecticut, disappear.

Graduation was meant to impress upon us our special, lifelong status as Yalies. If the past four years hadn't accomplished it, then the four days' worth of university-organized events would certainly inculcate us with pride, a sense of privilege (very different from privilege itself, much like a whiff of scandal or a touch of class), and withering prejudice toward those who had spent their youth and tuition money elsewhere. At least that was what I thought at the time, and I wanted no part in this final indoctrination. A college graduation, like a wedding or a funeral, was a ceremony held in your honor but wasn't really meant for you. Yale understood this. I, being twenty-one and at the height of my self-centeredness, didn't. I had scanned the list of concerts, performances, nondenominational services, receptions, speeches, exercises, presentations, baccalaureates, and ceremonies, and then I had discarded the list. I had no intention of sending the schedule to my great-uncle Harper. I knew that he, if given the opportunity, would have wanted to attend them all. He was a man who adored the pomp and many of the circumstances. Though I knew that lately he had been availing himself of only one, a ceremony sad and unsettling to most, but not to Baby Harper.

The owner-director of the Cecil T. Brandon Home of Eternal Rest was so impressed, nay, "overwhelmed," after seeing photographs of Iris's funeral that he asked my great-uncle Harper to become the home's official bereavement photographer, part of an ongoing effort to provide a truly full-service funereal experience. When Baby Harper had telephoned me with the news, he spoke at an even faster pace than usual. His words were tumbling, doing somersaults and cartwheels, out of his mouth. His becoming a bereavement photographer was a fine example of how we sometimes didn't know what our dreams were until they came true. Baby Harper, retired from his job at the library, was already spending his days scanning the obituaries. He was immersing himself in his second favorite hobby, acquiring antiques from widowers. The offer that Cecil, or Mister T, as everyone else called him, made was irresistible to my great-uncle. To be paid to take photographs was, according to Baby Harper, like being paid to scratch an itch. And, of course, working for the Home of Eternal Rest also meant that my great-uncle would be notified, even before the Shelby *Star*'s obit writer, of Cleveland County's latest expiry. Mister T's was the funeral home of choice for the county for reasons that were unclear to me. Out of habit, perhaps. Mister T's was where my father was laid to Eternal Rest. Then Iris. Maybe the last thing that families and friends needed at a time of loss was to get lost on the way to the funeral home. I had told Baby Harper my theory, and he said it was a fine one. He said that he would suggest to Cecil that he use "You already know where we're located!" as the home's new slogan. I laughed out loud. On the other end of the telephone line, a single hiccup.

I knew that Baby Harper didn't need to be paid to attend funerals. He found them to be ideal social gatherings. His reasons were manifold. He liked it when folks got dressed up. Even on the hottest day in August no one would wear short sleeves or a miniskirt to a funeral. He also thought that most people looked more natural—"more like their everyday selves"—when they were photographed crying or on the verge of tears. He was, in addition, drawn to the inherent drama of funerals. They were occasions for solemnity but also fraught with the possibilities of fainting spells, exhortations to the Lord, and even the occasional bouts of coffin-clinging (a performance of love enacted only by widows, as men were socialized from birth to let go). I never thought it contradictory that the man who taught me how to do the Watusi, arms swinging, hips thrusting, hair flying, would find pleasure inside of a funeral home. Joy and grief were physical in nature, and Baby Harper was a man capable of appreciating both.

My great-uncle Harper found his new employer as attractive as his offer of employment. The clearest signal was "Cecil." From the first conversation that we had about him, Baby Harper never called him anything else. When I was growing up, I knew that Baby Harper liked men. That was never a mystery to me. My great-uncle always sat up a little straighter, sometimes touched the back of his neck, often let out a long breath whenever we saw a handsome man on television, but I didn't really notice until I began behaving the same way. I registered his desire for male members of the species at the same time that I registered my own desire for them.

I was thirteen when my great-uncle and I watched the film *Giant* together. It was a long and revealing Saturday afternoon in front of the television set. Elizabeth Taylor? We barely noticed. My great-uncle was slumped in a wingback chair, nursing an iced sweet tea. I was sprawled on the divan, picking at the frayed cuticles around my fingernails, trying to tune out the words coming from the television. Rock Hudson? Baby Harper put his iced sweet tea down on the coffee table. (Now *that* was a mystery to me: Why was this piece of furniture so beverage-specific?) I sat up, adjusting my T-shirt and shorts as if Rock Hudson could see that they were twisted and wrinkled. James Dean? My great-uncle was pitched forward in his chair. I slid off the divan and onto the floor in order to be closer to the television screen. Baby Harper and I were unified, dancing without moving a muscle, with our eyes wide open.

I was nine years old when I first heard the word "homosexual." My father was watching the evening news. "The Southern*hotdog* Baptist*tunacasserole* Convention*sweettea* has spoken out*strawberry-*

jam against*pancakenosyrup* ABC's new*peanutbutter* sitcom*eggnog* Soap*cloves,* which will feature*limabeans* a homosexual*tangerine* character*pickledwatermelonrind* played*baloney* by . . ."

I was sitting on the carpet by my father's easy chair, my head in reach of his hands in case he wanted to muss my hair, his version of a hug.

Delicious, I remembered thinking.

We didn't have tangerines very often, only once or twice a year, when Wade's grandparents drove up from Florida with a carload of citrus. Wade's mom would come by the blue and gray ranch house with a net bag full of them, which made me think that the fruits had been caught in the ocean, and my father would thank her for sharing a bit of the tropics with us. Wade's mom smiled and they engaged in what my great-uncle called "trading pleasantries." DeAnne quickly joined them at the doorway, eyeing Wade's mom and her offerings as if both were rotten. When my father first showed me how easy it was to peel a tangerine, I clapped. I was seven years old, and I thought it was a trick. I thought that he had rigged an orange to do *that*! When he gave me one to try, I felt the bliss of something so effortless. I would characterize it now as something so willing.

"They'll show*marshmallow* any*rice*thing*tomato* on TV these days*hardboiledeggyolk,*" DeAnne said, on her way to the dinner table with a casserole dish swaddled in her oven mitts. Exit stage left. I looked up at my father. His eyes focused on the anchorman's face, my father made no sign of acknowledging DeAnne.

Aside from the evening news with my father and the occasional old movies with my great-uncle, I avoided the television because of the nonstop incomings. There were rarely the natural pauses that occurred in everyday speech: the intake of breath, the reaching for a thought, and all the other golden moments of silence carved out by the tongue-tied, the lost for words, the dumbstruck, the inarticulate, and the shy. I found it exhausting to sit in front of a televised populace who always had something to say.

I wrote to Kelly that night and asked her what "homosessuel" meant and why Southern Baptists like us didn't like it. I couldn't use the dictionary because I rarely knew the correct spelling of a new word. Also, Kelly's definitions were better than those in the dictionary because hers were always grounded in the familiar. Her response to the first part of my question: "A homosexual is a queer. Like your great-uncle. My mom calls him a queer all the time. My father says your great-uncle is 'light in the loafers.' " Second part of the question: "I don't know."

Baby Harper had arrived in New Haven late on Sunday night, entirely missing that day's Baccalaureate in Woolsey Hall, Class Day on Old Campus, a Whiffenpoofs concert back at Woolsey Hall, and the Commencement Ball in the Payne Whitney Gymnasium, not to mention all the other self-congratulatory, circle-jerking (ah, there's my bilious vocabulary acquired while at Yale) events that had already taken place on Friday and Saturday. He checked himself into the Holiday Inn on Whalley Avenue, while a couple of streets away I was in my room in Pierson getting drunk with a boy whom I wanted to touch. We did. Until we were sore.

Here were two more useful things learned during my four years of higher education: Alcohol and sex made the incomings barely noticeable. Alcohol, like nicotine, gauzed the incomings. I could still taste them, but they were muted and manageable, like how the words of a heated argument coming from deep within a house would sound to a passerby on the sidewalk. Sex overrode the incomings entirely. The multiple and multiplying sensations of the body demanded all of my attention. But indifferent, lazy, annoying, is-it-over-yet? sex had the opposite effect. My brain, apparently as bored by the proceedings as my body, would intensify the tastes of the cliché words, cribbed from porn films and old issues of *Penthouse,* that served as the limited male vocabulary for these kinds of encounters. The truly perverse thing was that these stupid, uninspired words were often delicious. Cock*buttermilkbiscuit,* fuck-

limesherbet, pussy*toastedalmond,* baby*honey,* come*applebutter,* daddy*strawberryJell-O,* suck*cheesegrits.* I could go on, and I did.

When Kelly was younger and still reliant on food for her happiness, she suggested that I counter the effects of the incomings by eating more. She thought that I could supplant and overwhelm the phantom tastes with the "real" flavors on a very full plate. It was a reasonable hypothesis, especially coming from a fat girl, but a flawed one for reasons too complicated for me to understand back then. In the years since, I have pieced together the following:

While it is true that I experience every incoming as a taste in my mouth, it is my brain alone that is at work. The brain is a willful, dictatorial processor, and unless it is diverted (good sex) or chemically manipulated (nicotine or alcohol), the brain prevails over the tongue, that lesser, subservient organ, and easily trumps all of the sweets, salts, sours, and bitters that I could load onto it.

I didn't see Baby Harper until noon on Monday, when he came to Pierson for the final event of my graduation, the Presentation of the Diplomas. I knew that he had been on Old Campus earlier that morning waiting for a glimpse of me in my academic regalia, what other schools called cap and gown. At 9 A.M., graduates university-wide had gathered in the courtyards of their respective residential colleges and graduate schools and prepared to converge en masse in front of Sterling Memorial Library for a procession to Old Campus for the University Commencement Exercises. The graduates were led by our professors, their doctoral hoods lined with colorful velvets, while above them plane trees provided a canopy of spring green leaves. A professor at the head of the procession carried a mace and perhaps another carried a scepter, further gilding the mythology of a university with medieval bones. I had seen the Commencement Procession before, three times before, in fact. While my classmates had rushed off to begin their summers elsewhere, I had stayed in New Haven. While they had interned or traveled, I had worked at Sterling Memorial. It was my favorite building on campus, and as it was a library it was by its very function a quiet space.

Sterling Memorial, the main library at Yale, had been built to resemble a Gothic cathedral, replete with stained glass, carved stonework, and a crenellated tower. Completed in 1930, the structure was "as near to modern Gothic as we dared" according to its architect, James Gamble Rogers. The use of the word "dare" always intrigued me. It suggested boundaries and infractions. There was, as I had come to expect at Yale, a scandalous story attached to the library's design. The benefactress, an old woman with failing eyesight, wanted a place of worship, and Yale wanted a library. Flouting its own motto, *Lux et Veritas,* Yale presented her with a structural trompe l'oeil. A cathedral in its outlines, but in its details a pantheon to books, where King Lear was a demigod and Huckleberry Finn a mischievous angel. The visual world had already become a greasy smudge to the benefactress, so the old biddy died never knowing the difference.

Light and Truth, indeed.

Of course, the story wasn't true. The truth wasn't nearly as scandalous, or perhaps it was thought more so and had to be covered up with a falsehood. The money for the library came from John William Sterling, Class of 1864, a lawyer who left the majority of his vast fortune to Yale. When Sterling passed away, in 1918, he also left behind his live-in companion of almost fifty years, James Orville Bloss. If James had been a Jane, John would have married his beloved in a church or perhaps a Gothic cathedral. If James had been a Jane, John would have left his estate to his devoted spouse and not to his alma mater. James hadn't been a Jane, and Sterling Memorial, a Gothic folly in more ways than one, was constructed and became the heart of the Yale campus, holding within it silences of many kinds.

The individual wasn't the point of the Commencement Procession or the University Commencement Exercises. The Class of 1990 was the point. I knew that Baby Harper would never find me in the sea of black and blue caps and gowns, so I skipped it all—the parade and the spectacle—and slept in. When I saw him later that same day at Pierson, my great-uncle neither said nor did anything that indicated he had suspected my absence. We couldn't suspect what we couldn't imagine. My great-uncle Harper would never have thought of allowing me to stand alone in a crowd or to cheer for an empty seat. As I hugged him for the third time in three and a half years, it occurred to me that he might have even made a sign for me: LINDA, CLASSIEST IN THE CLASS OF '90!

Around us families were beginning to claim the rows of wooden folding chairs set up at one end of the Pierson courtyard. I took Baby Harper by the hand and led him to a seat that I had saved for him in the front row. I had left my cap and gown there, still stuffed inside of the plastic bag that they came in. I quickly put on my second costume of the day, smoothing out the wrinkles as best as I could, and I took my place with the other graduates. There were eighty-eight of us. After days of carefully orchestrated events in grand and soaring architectural spaces, the outdoor setup for the Presentation of the Diplomas had the feeling of a gospel revival in a small southern town. Handing out the diplomas within the respective residential colleges was an effort, an obvious ploy, I thought, to assure parents that their children had enjoyed a personalized, nay, "intimate," educational experience at Yale. The master and dean of each residential college could take the occasion to share heartwarming anecdotes and reveal something amusing or, at the very least, specific about their charges before bestowing upon us the most expensive pieces of paper that we would ever touch. In preparation for these final speeches, I had come with earplugs. For the next half hour, I watched Baby Harper's face as it registered and transmitted the pride that he felt. Then his hands came together, as did those around him, clapping out a rousing congratulatory one-two beat.

I could tell by the moving bodies around me that the roll call of names had begun. I waited till I saw Heather Garrison come forward to receive her diploma. Then I bowed my head slightly and removed the earplugs, and the cascade of incomings arrived, interrupted by spates of clapping, and the click-click of cameras. I was unaffected, or rather I was under-affected. Before leaving my room, I had smoked three cigarettes and drunk a shot of vodka for good measure. I was fixated now on Baby Harper's glowing face, taking in all that I had denied him on Friday, Saturday, and Sunday.

"Caleb*pear* Arthur*mayonnaise* Gruenfeld*maplesyrup*, cum laude, History*cherrypiefilling*.

Sascha*currypowder* Kay Haddley*driedbasil*, American*babyaspirin* Studies*Colgatetoothpaste*.

Linh-Dao Nguyen Hammerick*DrPepper*, summa cum laude, Literature*roastbeef*."

Not until I heard my name did I see that there was something different about Baby Harper. He had no camera with him. He just sat there smiling, his hands a beautiful blur.

because taking a picture would taint the importance of taking in the moment and memorizing every part of her achievement

REVELATION

August 4, 1998 . . .

Chapter 14

There were two kinds of absences: the void and the missing. The void was the person, place, or thing that was never there in the first place. The missing existed but was no longer present. One was theoretical loss. The other was actual. Which was worse? I never had a child. Or, I had a child but she was no longer mine. Either way, there was a hole. Only DeAnne was left to answer the question for me now. She still lived in the blue and gray ranch house. I knew this was true because in a fit of optimism, a form of mental illness in its own way, I had sent her a Christmas card, short and polite, along with a photograph of Leo and me. Leo was an example of both kinds of absences. He left me four months and three days after I posted that card in a red envelope with a Kwanzaa stamp. The stamp's design was my idea of a joke. I wondered if DeAnne would think that I had sent the card from some faraway country. DeAnne wrote back, short and polite, that we should come to Boiling Springs for a visit, as she would like to meet Leo.

When I first came to the blue and gray ranch house, I couldn't sleep. I was a seven-year-old with insomnia. Thomas and DeAnne must have been worried for me and for themselves. They had considered the question, and they—or at least Thomas—had answered that a void was worse. Thomas, whom I soon called Father, tried to soothe me with bedtime stories. For the first few weeks, he read fairy tales to me from a book so brand new that each page that he turned cracked its thick spine. I tried my best to hide my face. The only story that I could tolerate was "Goldilocks and the Three Bears." The rest contained too many sour words that made me agitated and kept me up long into the night. "Snow" was a dill pickle, a prolonged kind of tartness, like an endless amble down a long narrowing hallway. "Cinderella" was a shot of white distilled vinegar, the taste equivalent to the brightest, most direct incandescent light. Sour-tasting words were like caffeine to me. I don't know what Thomas must have thought, sitting there next to a child with her face underneath the covers but who was clearly wide awake. Thomas wasn't a very good storyteller. He never tried to read in different voices. Every character was a middle-aged man with a deep voice who read every sentence as a declarative, even when it was a question. After lightly touching the top of my head, the only part of me left uncovered, he would turn off the light, and the door to the room would click shut.

To pass my hours in the dark, I taught myself a game. I imagined not having different parts of my body. Left leg, right eye, both ears, a big toe. It was less macabre than it might sound. It was a cartoon version of dismemberment. There was no blood or pain, and I could reattach the parts again with a snap of my fingers, which meant that it was very important never to wish away the middle finger and thumb on my right hand. The point of the game, or perhaps it was more of an exercise, was to list the things that I could no longer do because of the missing part. Another point of the game was to rejoice in the things that I would again do, upon the reattachment. If it hadn't been 1975 or Boiling Springs, North Carolina, I would have been a seven-year-old in therapy.

Like Athena, I was born to my father, Thomas, fully formed. I had no writhing snakes but a ponytail of long black hair. Athena was born clad in full armor. I was born with the English language already in my mouth and a sixth sense but with no memory of my first six years of life. I was born to DeAnne this way too, but I always knew that I was more of my father's child. This was the story of my birth to Thomas, and to a lesser extent, DeAnne:

If the sky before a tornado could be bitten into and swallowed, then it might have the bitter taste that was my first memory. My second, third, fourth, and fifth memories following in quick succession were a flash of light, a trailer home with windows of flames, gravel crunching underneath feet, but they weren't my own, then darkness. What I remembered next was waking in a bed that didn't have my scent. There were too many blankets on top of me, and there were the faces of a man and a woman hovering above me. They tried to smile at me as if there was joy in their hearts. I saw their lips stretched and the whites of their teeth, but I didn't see joy. I began to cry. The woman tucked a strand of her blond hair behind her ear, and without saying a word she turned around and left the room. The man pushed his black-framed glasses higher up the bridge of his nose, leaned down, and softly stroked my hair.

"Linh-Dao, Linh-Dao," he said, almost whispering, as if he didn't want anyone but me to hear.

I didn't recognize the man or his words, so I closed my eyes again. My chest was heaving the spastic, irregular rhythm of grief. For what and whom, I didn't know.

"Linh-Dao," he repeated, this time louder.

I opened my eyes and looked up at him. He was a stranger to me, but I didn't feel fear toward him. Wasn't that the beginning of love?

"Can you*cannedgreenbeans* hear*hardboiledegg* me?" he asked.

I nodded my head.

"Linh-Dao, welcome to your new*peanutbutter* home*Pepsi*."

I shook my head because I understood his words, but his sentence made no sense to me.

"Linh-Dao, can you*cannedgreenbeans* tell*brownsugar* me what-*grahamcracker* happened last*blackpepper* night*banana*?"

I shook my head again.

"You*cannedgreenbeans* don't remember*butterpecanicecream,* Linh-Dao? Or you don't want*saltedbutter* to tell*brownsugar* me?"

It was, in retrospect, very lawyerly of Thomas to recognize that silence can hold within it different meanings and that he needed to identify which one I had in mind. His professional instinct was simply kicking in, but I thought that the shift in his tone of voice, from soothing to alert, meant that he was angry with me.

I was silent because I was scared. I was beginning to understand that this man was calling me by a name that he thought was mine. I began to cry again. This time I knew the source of my grief. I was lost, which was another way of saying that I had no memory of where I had been.

The man took off his eyeglasses and sat down on the floor, resting his back against the side of the bed. I could no longer see his face, but I could see his shoulders slowly rising and falling. He was taking the deliberate, steady breaths of a man attempting to calm himself. I didn't understand these movements back then, so I thought he was crying. I stopped my own tears because I thought it would stop his. Wasn't this the beginning of love?

Heal thyself! and Pray! were as close to mental health care as my family ever got. Thomas, my father, was partial to the first prescription. Self-reliance *and* reliance on God seemed like overkill to him. Another word for "pray" was "wish," and only children wished. Men accomplished. Women acted, with all the negative connotations that the word "act" could carry with it. My father never sat me down and shared these guiding principles with me, but I could discern them from everything that he did. He believed in analytical thinking. He didn't believe in analysis. In this case, the Reasonable Man and Jesus both commanded their flocks, "Don't look back!" Lot's wife was Exhibit A of the consequences of clinging to a catastrophic past and the dire repercussions of regret. I assumed that these were the reasons Thomas and everyone else in the family never spoke of how I came to be his daughter. In our small brood, no one wanted to be Lot's wife but for very different reasons.

Baby Harper's reasons were the easiest for me to understand. From our first moment together as great-uncle and grandniece, we were in love. About a week after I woke up in the blue and gray ranch house, he and Iris came to meet me. I was already answering to the name "Linda," which DeAnne told me was pretty when she gave it to me. What she meant was that it was prettier than the name that Thomas called me by. It didn't matter to me. Neither name was familiar to me. "Linda" was the void. "Linh-Dao" was the missing. "Linda," though, had a flavor that was so assertive that I almost spit when I first heard DeAnne say it. It wasn't the artificial, mellowed-out mints of toothpaste and chewing gum. I would soon identify the taste as mint leaves fresh from the garden, warmed by the sun, their aromatic oils primed and intensified. But when I first heard "Linda," I had no memory of having ever tasted a sprig of fresh mint, but I must have. I had no memory of tasting any of the other flavors that accompanied the English words that were already a part of my vocabulary, but I must have as well. Thomas never liked the name that his wife gave me, so he would often shorten it to "Lin," which, like "Linh-Dao," triggered no taste whatsoever. He also never legally changed my name, except to add his family name to it.

My great-uncle winked at me when Thomas brought "Linda" into the living room to meet the other half of the family. I hadn't mastered the wink yet, so I reciprocated with a slow blinking of both my eyes.

My great-uncle hiccupped.

I closed and opened my eyes again.

He laughed out loud.

To recount the days and the years before this moment would mean that Baby Harper would have to acknowledge that there was a time when his love for another human being wasn't fully reciprocated. Baby Harper would rather forget those years. By the time that he became my great-uncle, he was a man who had lived fifty-one years of life with a kind of imposed aphasia. The singing-talker could wax lyrical about everything except the impulses of his heart and those of his groin. That part of his vocabulary was lost to him in Boiling Springs. I wish I could say that my presence in his life gave these words back to him. But that would be a lie or a wish that hadn't come true.

Iris was sitting next to Baby Harper on the living room couch. When DeAnne's tentative hands scooted me in front of her, Iris extended her right hand to me. As always, Iris was telling her family the truth. In this instance, she didn't even need to use words—a handshake would do. Linda, the new addition to the family, was a business transaction. As with all contractual dealings—my grandmother had been married to a judge, after all—she understood that she was now under an obligation. As a grandmother, she had the duty to protect me from harm, to teach me right from wrong (or rather the acceptable from the unacceptable), and to endure, on her part, the questioning stares of her neighbors and friends without ever once opening up her mouth. Because if she did, she would have to admit that her family wasn't like theirs. As Iris had done with her own flesh and blood (a grown brother whom she still called Baby), she would see of me what she wanted, and she would ignore the rest. For Iris, "the rest" included most things about me, especially who I was before I became a Hammerick.

She never forgave DeAnne and Thomas for not giving her a grandchild in the usual way. I think Iris thought often of Walter Wendell and how if her husband had been alive none of this would have happened. Walter Wendell would have made certain that his son-in-law fathered a child like a real man and not via a piece of paper. When Iris looked at me, she was reminded of both the void and the missing. How she could stand to witness my face on a day-to-day basis for the next decade was in its own way a miracle. When I was fifteen (and recently bereft of Kelly and Wade), I accused my grandmother of never liking me. Our family had gone to Moss Lake to watch the Fourth of July fireworks. We had spread our blankets and lawn chairs on a rectangle of grass. My father and Baby Harper had gone back to the cars to get the coolers. DeAnne was saying hello to a friend whom she had spotted a couple of picnic blankets away. Iris and I were left alone with each other, which was when we usually laid our cards on the table. We sat and stared out at the lake ringed by children with water wings and inner tubes. Maybe it was the sight of them, these small beings saved from drowning, that brought forth my allegation.

"That doesn't stop*cannedcorn* me from being your grand*potatosalad*mother, Linda*mint*," was her response.

No, Iris, it never did.

DeAnne was playing a role. When I first became Linda, I wanted to tell her that "Mom" tasted of chocolate milk and that I loved chocolate milk. It quenched my thirst, made me feel full, and tasted like candy. I thought it was a magical potion for doing all three things at once. When I stopped calling her "Mom," I missed the word. DeAnne, though, was visibly relieved. I no longer caught her being startled by the sound of my voice calling her something that she tried to get used to, but never did.

DeAnne and Thomas were both forty-three years old when I became their only child. Why they never had children of their own was a topic that was also never discussed in my family. (When I think back to all the ellipses that we all nurtured like family pets, I'm amazed that my family had anything left to say to one another.) DeAnne must have thought that the question of children had been already decided by the time I came along.

Now that my own body has answered the question of children for me, I find myself wondering if it was his body or hers that failed them. I would guess it was Thomas. If DeAnne was the infertile one, he would have left her. Men do that. They replace broken women with whole ones. Women replace broken men too, but more often they try to fix them, mend their bones, lick clean their wounds. DeAnne probably agreed to my adoption in order to keep Thomas by her side so that she could continue to do those things for him with the hope that he would become whole again or become so broken that he would have no choice but to stay by her side.

After my surgery, I thought that Leo and I could still form a family. I said to him that we could adopt a child. He said to me that he wanted biological children. Leo said *this* to me. Those words, unthinking and unfeeling, shot from his mouth.

Kelly wrote that I should be thankful that Dr. Leo was an asshole. She was right. If Leo hadn't insisted that I have a full medical checkup before we announced our engagement—his physician version of a prenuptial—I would have died. I hadn't seen an OB/GYN since my freshman year of college, when I went to Planned Parenthood to get a prescription for birth control pills, which soon became an ill-advised method of contraception in the full-blown age of AIDS. In the twelve years since then, I hadn't gone for my annual exams. The men I had sex with wore condoms. I was young. I felt healthy. I had no family medical history to guide or warn me about the possible future of my body. Leo was visibly disturbed when he heard that I had been so remiss. As it turned out, he was equally disturbed by the fact that I was adopted. To Dr. Leo, I was a twenty-nine-year-old ticking time bomb with my deactivation wires not clearly color-coded. He was right. After my pelvic examination, the OB/GYN ordered a CT scan, which confirmed that there was a mass on one of my ovaries. I was checked into the hospital a week later for an oophorectomy. During the surgery both my ovaries were removed because the surgeon found an abnormality, which hadn't been visible in the CT scan, on the other ovary as well.

While I was in the hospital, Leo signed a lease for an apartment on the Upper West Side. Three weeks to the day that I came home to the brownstone that he and I shared in Chelsea, he sat down by the side of our bed and said that he was ending our relationship, that the movers were scheduled to come tomorrow from eight in the morning to three in the afternoon, and that I could keep the Nelson lamps but that he was taking the Eames lounge chair and ottoman, the Noguchi coffee table, and the Knoll love seat. All of the furniture that Leo had brought with him to the brownstone that we had lived in for the past three years had last names. He was a man fixated on provenance. This was a sign, a blinking neon pig of a sign, that I had ignored. Leo then asked me to give back the extra set of keys to his family's cabin in the Berkshires. I still thought that he was kidding, so I didn't even have the wherewithal to ask, "What's her name?"

I was a senior associate in a large law firm in New York City. I had full health benefits and a generous medical leave policy. I had a retirement fund and an investment portfolio. I owned the first two floors of a brownstone. Leo, before leaving the next day with the movers, listed these facts for me in that order. Then the diagnostician in him concluded, "Linda*mint,* I know*grapejelly* you'll be fine."

Kelly was right. Dr. Leo was an asshole. He saved my life and then he judged it useless to him.

Since leaving Boiling Springs, I was often asked by complete strangers what it was like to grow up being Asian in the South. You mean what was it like to grow up *looking* Asian in the South, I would say back to them with the southern accent that had revealed to them the particulars of my biography. My tweaking of their question often left them perplexed or annoyed, as if I were playing some irritating semantic game with them. For me, pointing out to them the difference between "being" and "looking" was the beginning, the middle, and the end of my answer. I would rarely offer them more.

I was still taken aback, startled, I suppose, that it was the outside of me that so readily defined me as not being from here (New Haven, New York, New World) nor there (the South). How could I explain to them that from the age of seven to eighteen, there was nothing Asian about me except my body, which I had willed away and few in Boiling Springs seemed to see anyway.

If Boiling Springs had been a larger town, it wouldn't have been possible. But Boiling Springs wasn't. The dwindling population there was small and insular enough to behave as one microorganism. These were the adults of Boiling Springs. (Their children, as children always do, had other ideas.) More specifically, these were the white men and women of Boiling Springs. My schoolteachers, until the time I was in high school, were white women. My schoolbus drivers from elementary school to middle school were old white men who had retired from some other job. My father's colleagues from his law firm were all middle-aged white men. DeAnne's friends were all middle-aged white women. Iris and Baby Harper seemed only to have each other.

There was, of course, a parallel adult world in my hometown that I came into contact with, but only in passing. These black men and women knew of me too, especially the women. When DeAnne would take me with her to the Piggly Wiggly or to Hudson's department store, the women who worked there looked at me with eyes that always made me uncomfortable. These women actually saw me, and what they wondered about me—why one of my own hadn't taken me in—made their hearts tender. The lunch ladies, with their hairnets and their plastic smocks, looked at me the same way. As did my father's secretary who lived on Goforth Road. The school janitors, the old men who pumped gas into my family's car, the middle-aged ones who cut our lawn before and after Bobby, the mailman. I learned early on not to meet their eyes, dark and deep as a river. If I saw them, I would have to see myself. I didn't want a mirror. I wanted a blank slate.

The word must have come down from the pulpits. The Southern Baptists, the Episcopalians, and the small band of Catholics were all in on the pact. They vowed to make themselves color-blind on my behalf. That didn't happen. What did happen was that I became a blind spot in their otherwise 20–20 field of vision. They heard my voice—it helped that I came to them already speaking English with a southern accent, which was the best and only clue that I had about my whereabouts before Boiling Springs—but they learned never to see me. It was an act of selective blindness that was meant to protect me from them, or perhaps it was the other way around. They knew that if they saw my face they would fixate on my eyes, which some would claim were almond-shaped and others would describe as mere slits. If they saw my hair, they would marvel at how straight and shiny it was or that it was limp and the color of tar. If they saw my skin, they would understand why they basked their bodies in the heat of the southern sun, though some would ask themselves how DeAnne could ever be sure that I was washed and clean. If they saw my unformed breasts, the twigs that were my arms and legs, the hands and feet small enough to fit inside their mouths, how many of the men would remember the young female bodies that they bought by the half hour while wearing their country's uniform in the Philippines, Thailand, South Korea, or South Vietnam? Complicit, because they would rather not know the answer to that question, the mothers and sisters and wives of these men looked right through me as well. Instead of invisibility, Boiling Springs made an open secret of me. I was the town's pariah, but no one was allowed to tell me so. In Boiling Springs, I was never Scout. I was Boo Radley, not hidden away but in plain sight.

The children of Boiling Springs had their own idea of how to welcome me to town. They were never fooled by my new name. "Linda Hammerick" was a mask only until I said, "Here." Then they would turn around and silently mouth "Chink" or "Jap" or "Gook" at me, so that our teacher wouldn't hear. Clever monsters, my classmates were, though not original. I had come to the blue and gray ranch house with those epithets already in me, yet another clue of where I had been before. As in the adult realm, the children's behavior toward me was dictated by some accord deep within them that I didn't understand until much later in our lives. The black girls in my class *never* called me a name other than "Linda."

They knew that the other names were meant to insult me, to punch holes into me, and make me fall down.

I understood, without really understanding, that "Chink" and "Jap" and "Gook" were intimately connected to how the children saw my body. I knew because of the gestures that accompanied these words. At recess, when fewer teachers were around, my classmates would pull up the outer corners of their eyes for "Chink" and pull down the corners for "Jap." Precise and systematic, these children were. There was also a rhyme that they recited that intertwined foreignness with an unclean and sexualized body.

Chinese, Japanese
Dirty knees,
Look at these!

Emily Dickinson, these monsters were not.

Their choreography, albeit communicative, was also pedestrian. They accompanied the second line of their rhyme with fingers pointed at their knees, and with the last line they used their small hands to pull out two tents from their shirts, at the loci of their own nonexistent breasts. Martha Graham, they were not either. But with what glee would they perform this for me.

Bravo, my little children. Who taught you these words? I had to figure it out for myself—because no one in my family ever told me—that your parents must have been your teachers. You, their darling little parrots, had become the mouthpieces for all that these men and women couldn't say aloud to me or to Thomas or DeAnne or Iris or Baby Harper but were free to say in front of their own children within the high walls of their own houses. If I hadn't come to Boiling Springs, whom would you have said these words to? You would have had to save up all the "Japs," "Chinks," and "Gooks" until another unsuspecting stranger came to town or when you grew up and ventured to metropolitan Raleigh or Charlotte or even farther afield for a job. When hard-pressed, you might have even used these words against a Cherokee, a Lumbee, or a Croatan. But there was no need to misapply the words in that way, because when I came to Boiling Springs the diversity drought was over. What joy I must have given you so early on in your lives. When you think back on your childhood, you must think fondly of me.

High school changed everything. What had begun as an untoward, heightened interest in my physical presence rapidly dissipated into a kind of non-seeing, the kind that their parents had professed to strive for but never achieved. I had no role to play within the romances, the dramas, and the tragedies that my classmates' hormones were writing for them. I was never considered a heroine, love interest, vixen, or villainess. Even Kelly assigned me the role of secret confidante and then audience member. To be the Smartest Girl in my high school was to be disembodied, which was what I thought I had wanted all along. I was the Brain. Everyone else around me became their bodies. The girls with the large breasts and long dancer legs became cheerleaders and Homecoming Queen. The boys with the throwing arms and the runner's calves became football players and Quarterback. It was a kind of fate that most of them embraced, including Kelly. I watched it all from a distance, which didn't give me objectivity or clarity. It just made me lonely.

When we first met, I tried to tell Leo about my childhood in Boiling Springs. He said that these experiences meant that I did know what it was like *being* Asian in the South. For a soon-to-be psychiatrist, he wasn't a very good listener. No, Leo, I knew what it was like *being* hated in the South. Leo would have me equate the two, equate my body with what others have projected onto it. I won't. (Like my great-grandfather Graven Hammerick, I'm an optimist at heart.) I believed, and still do, that this state of *being* that I was trying to understand had content and substance separate and apart from what Boiling Springs had taught me.

Chapter 15

I'm a Tar Heel born,
I'm a Tar Heel bred,
And when I die
I'm a Tar Heel dead.

I can still hear Baby Harper singing. Sometimes he would sing a hymn. More often, he was singing his version of the blues. The words were worried in his mouth, and then cracked open like melon seeds and made so generous that his whole life story could fit inside each syllable. You should hear what the humble "Tar" could hold within it. He taught me the words to this song but never taught me what "Tar Heel" meant. So at the age of seven, I thought that the lyrics were about a woman wearing some kind of high-heeled shoes. In school I would learn that the song was the unofficial anthem of the state of North Carolina, and that "Tar Heels" was the nickname for the farmers who supplemented their subsistence income by boiling down pine sap to make tar. I also learned that the song was a rousing, thigh-slapping manifesto of statehood and loyalty and specifically of the reputation of these farmers for standing their ground on the battlefields during the Civil War. Baby Harper's rendition was all about fate.

After a week's worth of failed fairy tales—stories that made my eyelids flutter open and not shut—my father tried telling me stories that belonged only to him. Thomas told me of an island off the coast of a different world. On this island, there stood a city whose buildings were made of glass. He told me that at the heart of this city was a forest with trees, ponds and a lake, swans and horses, and even a small castle. He told me that the streets of the city were filled with bright yellow cars that you hopped in and out of at will and that would take you wherever you wanted to go. In this city, there were sidewalks overflowing with people from the whole world over who wanted so much to be *there*. He told me of its neighborhoods, with names like Greenwich Village and Harlem and Chinatown. At the nucleus of these stories was my father, and spinning around him was the city of New York. Long before I would see them in photographs or in real life, my father had given me the white crown lights of the Chrysler Building and the shining needle of the Empire State. His words triggered incomings after incomings, but I was enthralled, finally enchanted by what he was saying to me. His stories rarely had a plot, no character development to speak of—no one evil or good or beautiful or wicked—and the stories rarely had an ending or any kind of a resolution. My father's stories were mostly descriptions of people, places, and things. Impressionistic and episodic, they would often begin with a statement of fact, which nonetheless seemed improbable and fantastical to me then. *In the city of New York, the trains run underground.* My father would then pinpoint a specific memory and offer it to me like a perfectly preserved butterfly so that I could examine the miracle of its wings. *Early one morning on the IRT—the train line that ran underneath the west side of the island—I saw an old woman sitting with a wicker basket by her feet. She reached down and took out of the basket a china teapot and a cup, and she asked the young man sitting next to her if he wanted some tea.* From the very beginning, I had the feeling that my father and the young man in his stories were one and the same. *The young man thought about it for a quick second and then he said yes. She poured him a cup. She handed it to the young man, and he took a sip and said, "Thank you very much." Of course, no liquid of any kind had come from the pot.*

I was fascinated by these stories because he, the storyteller, was fascinated by them too. Sometimes Thomas would pause for what seemed like a long time trying to find just the right words. At least that was what I thought he was doing. I don't know why he stopped telling these stories to me. Maybe he ran out of them. But by the end of our first summer together, my father no longer came to my room at bedtime to lull me, if not to sleep, then to a faraway place, where he was Prince Charming, by the sheer fact that he was there.

Of course, I had an easier time falling asleep after the stories stopped. But I missed them. Missing the storyteller was worse. I made up another game to pass the time between darkness and sleep. I would imagine myself with the young man on the IRT, with him on the sidewalk, both of us staring up at the Empire State Building, with him in a taxi as it navigated us through the streets of a city built of glass. I saw us there clear as day.

Maybe this was why I wasn't surprised when I saw the photographs. I was surprised by their existence, certainly, but not of the scenes that they depicted. I experienced instead an odd and impossible feeling, as if I were reliving them. Young Thomas, handsome and fresh-faced (by that I mean that he was lit up from within), standing by the Bethesda Fountain in Central Park, beside him a young woman whom I didn't know but whom I recognized. Young Thomas, smiling and his hair disheveled, as if he had been running against the wind, sitting on the cascade of steps in front of Columbia's Low Library, next to him the same familiar woman's face and body. Young Thomas—this time alone—in his law school graduation gown, a hand resting on the marble and granite base of *Alma Mater,* her outsize, sculpted feet barely visible at the top edge of the photograph. There were only twelve of them, these black-and-white images of another Thomas. They came to me tucked inside of a large envelope that was probably once white but had since ivoried.

In a box, marked HANDLE WITH CARE, my great-uncle Harper had also sent me four H.E.B.'s, though these were not numbered on the spines to indicate their place within the chronology of his life. When Leo saw me taking them out of the box, he asked who had sent me their old wedding albums. I had never thought of the H.E.B.'s in that way. In other words, I had never really seen them for what they were. All the H.E.B.'s were white and embossed with doves, and occasionally there were roses. I laughed out loud, thinking of how that must have been Baby Harper's idea of a joke all along.

Postmarked Boiling Springs, the box arrived in New York City in November of '97. Leo and I were still living in the brownstone in Chelsea. We were just beginning our discussion, which turned into a negotiation, about getting engaged. We had been dating for almost seven years and living together for two of those years. He was fully Dr. Leo by then, having just completed his residency in psychiatry. (Kelly had dubbed him *that* from the start of our relationship; her coupling of his professional title with his first name turned out to be a succinct and prescient characterization of his ego and his hubris.) Why therapy or analysis wasn't eventually stipulated as part of our medical prenuptial was a mystery to me. Maybe Dr. Leo thought he was fully capable of making all the necessary mental health assessments for himself. Maybe he thought that the "depression" that silenced me for days could be managed by a prescription or two. That our nights of sleep interrupted by my mumbled cries of "Fire!" would go away with medication as well. And of equal importance to Leo, that the awkwardness that I exhibited in front of his mother and father and older brother would dissipate the next time we gathered for Thanksgiving dinner, just the five of us seated around a table so large that when we spoke to one another we had to raise our voices, as if in anger, in order to be heard.

Leopold Thomas Benton—I may have fallen in love with him

for his middle name as well—came from a small family, which was part of his appeal. When I realized that his only brother was unmarried and probably would remain so, given his personality, I knew that there would be no nieces and nephews to scream my name aloud at every family gathering. The fact that both his father and mother were the only children within their families was an heirloom that I couldn't have foreseen but greatly cherished. This meant that Leo had no cousins with their attendant families milling around his parents' Beacon Hill home, the place where he was headed when we met on the New York–to–Boston train. Leo grew up in this four-story brick row house that had been in his family since it was built, in 1795, and whose front steps and cornflower-blue painted door were now photographed by straying members of tour groups, who swarmed the streets of Beacon Hill coveting American history, the Boston Brahmin edition. What I hadn't anticipated was that Leo's distinguished but sparse family tree meant that he would want to add to it, to make it fuller with new leaves.

Of my family, I had told Leo mostly about Baby Harper, because I loved saying his name aloud. Leo's eyes flashed brightly when he first learned of my great-uncle's nickname. Leo said that it was a clear example of how my family had sanctioned and prolonged the infantilization of my great-uncle. I looked at Leo and thought, You had to go to medical school to learn *this*? Of course it was, Dr. Leo. My grandmother Iris had to keep her younger brother a child because if he became a grown man she would have to see whom that man desired and that would have shamed her. Everyone in my family knew this, and none of us were doctors except for the juris doctorate kind. Leo never had a sense of humor when I joked with him about how there were in fact two doctors in our brownstone. Leo said that a doctor in law was like a mother-in-law. What he meant was that both didn't count for much.

Leo had heard about Baby Harper but had never met him in person because my great-uncle, after his first flight to New Haven, became a traveling man. Sometimes with Cecil but more often on his own, my great-uncle was seeing the world. The world he chose to see surprised me. I thought he would be like my grandfather Spartan and head to Europe for the Western-civilization highlights. Baby Harper went instead to South America. During my first year of law school, I received a postcard sent from Cartagena that said, "You got into Columbia and so did I! But they spell it a bit differently here." Baby Harper added that he had longed to see this part of the world ever since reading *One Hundred Years of Solitude.*

My great-uncle traveled the way that people used to travel. He would dress in a suit and tie for his airplane flights. I offered to send his fedora back to him so that he could complete his ensemble, but he wouldn't hear of it. He would stay for a month or longer in one city, taking his time to see what was in the guidebooks and what wasn't. Baby Harper never sent me an e-mail, which gave me the great privilege of opening up a physical mailbox and finding his handwriting floating on the other side of a sandy beach or behind the façade of a church. He claimed that he was too old to learn new languages, so instead he familiarized himself with the literature that had been translated into his own language. The librarian in him came out of retirement and steered him to the English translations of José Donoso's *The Obscene Bird of Night* before he flew off to Santiago, Chile; to Eduardo Galeano's *The Book of Embraces* prior to his two months in Montevideo, Uruguay; and to Clarice Lispector's *The Hour of the Star* before leaving for Rio de Janeiro, Brazil.

Baby Harper was sixty-six years old when he began his life as a traveler in late August of 1990. His subsequent journeys were scheduled from mid-January to the end of August. He preferred to be in Boiling Springs for the beautiful autumn days that North Carolina offered up to its inhabitants as a reward for surviving the summer. He also wanted to be home for the trifecta of American holidays: Thanksgiving, Christmas, and the New Year. Also, Cecil was unwilling to travel during that time of the year because the Home of Eternal Rest tended to be busiest during the holiday season. Apparently, the following was a classic quip among morticians—

people in the funereal business would never circulate a "joke"—that Cecil shared with Baby Harper: "If Thanksgiving doesn't seal the deal, Christmas will."

Baby Harper also stayed in Boiling Springs during the holidays to make sure that DeAnne wasn't alone. When she realized that their roles had reversed—he was in a committed relationship and she was the one on her own—she retreated into the blue and gray ranch house and refused the first of his many invitations to Thanksgiving dinner at the Greek Revival. "Cecil will be cooking" was how my great-uncle Harper came out to his niece in the autumn of 1987. It was a sentence so simple and complicated all at once. Words are like that, I thought, as his voice on the telephone informed me of DeAnne's reaction. My great-uncle was trying to make light of the situation, but I could tell that he was hurt by DeAnne's refusal. His voice had the same quality that it had had right after Iris had passed away. It sounded like he had pebbles in his mouth.

DeAnne didn't join Baby Harper and Cecil at their holiday table until Thanksgiving of 1990. I think her change of heart had to do with Baby Harper flying away earlier that same year, to my college graduation in May, then to Cartagena in August. DeAnne must have been as shocked as I was at Baby Harper's full embrace of air travel. Perhaps she was more shocked at being truly alone in Boiling Springs.

Did it feel like gravity was no longer the law of the land, DeAnne? How the forested hills and the cultivated fields no longer held you to them. Their history and memories were no longer yours, which made your body so light that you floated and drifted, which wasn't the same as flying and soaring. Did you want to hold on to someone's hand so that Boiling Springs would come back into view?

Baby Harper's description of their first Thanksgiving together made me wish that I had been there for him. Cecil had attempted a new recipe that called for deep-frying the turkey, which when done improperly made the twenty-pound bird shrivel up to the size of a roasted chicken. DeAnne didn't talk to Baby Harper or Cecil for most of the meal, except when Cecil brought out his usual spread of three kinds of pie: the traditional pumpkin, a pecan (a nod to his late mother's Texas roots), and his personal favorite, a lemon meringue. It was the lemon meringue that finally brought words out of DeAnne's mouth, and they weren't kind. According to Baby Harper, DeAnne was channeling Iris that day. As Cecil presented her with the third of her dessert options, DeAnne said, "Oh, my, I had no idea we were celebrating Easter today."

That did it.

Cecil placed the antique silver pie server, which Baby Harper had bought for him as a third-anniversary present, down on the table and calmly walked himself and his lemon meringue right out of the dining room of the Greek Revival. Cecil sat in the kitchen and ate the entire pie by himself while Baby Harper drove DeAnne home. She was only fifty-eight years old then, but her eyesight was that of a much older person. Her degenerative night blindness had made her dependent on Baby Harper that evening and, she knew, for many more evenings to come, which didn't help to lighten her mood.

In the car, there was silence.

Baby Harper walked DeAnne to the front door of the blue and gray ranch house. Before going inside she gave him a note, which he said looked as if it had been held tightly in her hand the whole day.

"I forgive you," DeAnne had written.

For what, Baby Harper wondered as he read those three words by the light above his rearview mirror. He could think of more than one thing that he had done in his life that would merit forgiveness in her eyes. He decided that it didn't matter. He told me on the telephone that the note was DeAnne's way of calling a truce. Baby Harper tore up the piece of paper and threw it confetti-like out of his car window as he drove home to the Greek Revival, where he would apologize long into the night and all through the weekend to Cecil.

In 1990, I, unlike DeAnne, had again declined my great-uncle's invitation to join him and Cecil for Thanksgiving. I told my great-uncle that I needed to stay in New York City to study, that if I didn't, my first year of law school might be my last, and that I would call him again soon to see how it all went. I had changed our routine from a call once a week to a call twice a week because seeing him in person in New Haven had told me something that his voice on the telephone hadn't—that Baby Harper was getting old.

I then caught a train to Boston because I didn't want to be in the dorms with the foreign students and the handful of American ones, the strangers and the estranged. I had made a reservation at the Lenox, a hotel in downtown Boston that had a grand lobby with promising historical details and tall arrangements of fresh flowers and autumnal leaves, but whose rooms, at least the ones that I could afford, looked as if the life had been beaten out of them. I cried when I opened the door of my hotel room. I was thinking about Kelly's most recent letter to me and about her addiction to making life-changing mistakes. "It's now a habit I can't kick," she wrote. I hadn't thought about my refusal to return to Boiling Springs as a habit, but it was. Like biting my fingernails or smoking a pack of cigarettes a day, the act of not returning home had an ameliorative effect on my psyche. It had begun with the idea, new and fizzy in my eighteen-year-old brain, that family was a choice and not fate. If that were true, then I chose not to have a family. Like Bartleby the Scrivener, I would prefer not to.

Four years of choosing "not to" had brought me to that hotel room with its faded floral bedspread and carpeting the color of cigarette ash. I pulled down the covers and climbed into bed. There, in the dark, I said this in lieu of a prayer:

I miss my great-uncle Harper and his chosen family, Cecil.
I miss Kelly, closer to me than a sister.

I miss my father. For every reason and every thing.
I even miss my grandmother Iris.

I added Iris because I, at the age of twenty-two, had just begun to understand how rare it was to have someone in my life who would never lie to me. DeAnne I didn't miss because I knew so little about her. There it was, the full listing of the members of my family, and they were all in Boiling Springs, two of them already beneath its soil by then.

In the moment before sleep, I thought about the young man who had kept on finding another thing to say to me until the train pulled into South Station, when he asked for my phone number before saying goodbye. "Leo*parsnip*," I said aloud to my hotel room. Then, as easy as taking another breath, I said it again.

The following November, I returned to Boston for the first of the seven Thanksgivings that I would spend with Leo and his family. We ate bland, hearty New England food together, and never did I see a deep-fried turkey or a lemon meringue pie on their table. I once made Leo livid by calling his mother "Goody Benton." Not to her face, of course, but still I had crossed some sort of invisible WASP line with him. I tried to make it up to him by saying complimentary things to his mother, about her homemade cranberry sauce and her silver gravy boat. I picked out that vessel for commendation because "Benton" tasted of gravy, not the under-salted, defatted turkey gravy that Goody Benton served every year, but the milk gravy thick with crumbled pork sausage that southerners poured over our biscuits. I kept this factoid to myself and focused my comments instead on the curve of the handle and the gleam of the silver. Leo told me afterward that the gravy boat was a "sauceboat" and that it had been made by Paul Revere. Goody Benton probably thought that I was coveting her family heirlooms.

I decided that none of it mattered to me. Leo's family was his and not mine. Mr. and Mrs. Benton—I wasn't sure that even Leo knew their first names—were unfailingly polite but never enthusiastic toward me. Their older son, Collin, was enthusiastic enough for all of them. Collin was an investment banker who had spent a couple of years working and living in Hong Kong. He thought that meant that he and I would have an instant rapport. We had nothing in common. He, nonetheless, liked to touch the small of my back when guiding me through the rooms of his parents' house. He always made sure to help me with my coat so that he could stand too close behind me. When we first met, Collin said that I reminded him of someone he used to date. After a couple of minutes in his company, I began to feel sorry for that unfortunate young woman.

In order to take Thanksgiving off as a long weekend every year, Leo the intern and then Leo the resident had to work on Christmas Eve and Day. Perhaps that was another reason I loved him. Leo's restrictive schedule provided me with a convenient and deflected excuse for not going back to Boiling Springs for the holidays. My own school and then work schedule, that of an associate trying to make partner in eight years, kept me in New York City for the rest of the calendar year.

Baby Harper never gave up, though. At the beginning of every November, he would send me a Hallmark card—overflowing cornucopias, dimpled pumpkins, nonchalant turkeys—inviting me to "fly South" for Thanksgiving. So in 1997, when the box with the H.E.B.'s and the photographs of young Thomas arrived, I thought that my great-uncle was just trying a new tactic. He, of course, also included a greeting card, which I read first. When I took it from its bright orange envelope, I could hear my great-uncle hiccupping. The card featured a pudgy, round-faced little Native American girl holding hands with a pudgy, round-faced little Pilgrim boy.

Inside the card was a sheet of lined notebook paper on which Baby Harper had written on both sides. His letter began with the fact that he had finalized his travel plans (and reading list) for the upcoming year. From mid-January to mid-February of 1998, he and Cecil would be going to Buenos Aires, Argentina (Manuel

Puig's *Kiss of the Spider Woman*), and then to Bogotá (Gabriel García Márquez's *Love in the Time of Cholera*), which would be a second trip to Colombia for my great-uncle and a first with Cecil. I knew that Baby Harper's main frustration with Cecil was his unwillingness to leave the Home of Eternal Rest in the hands of his assistant director and travel more often. The length of their planned trip and the two destinations must have been quite the coup for Baby Harper. In the next line of his letter, my great-uncle explained how the tug of wills had been won. He wrote, "I said to Cecil, 'Darling, your customers are already dead. What's the worst that could happen to them?' "

My great-uncle's use of "darling" jumped from the page, a frog becoming a prince. It made me think of Leo and how this word had never come from his pen or his mouth. I thought about reading the word aloud to myself. Then I thought it was better if I didn't.

"Cecil gets highly disturbed," my great-uncle continued, "when I insist on referring to his bread and butter as his 'customers.' CLIENTS, he'd correct me with all the indignity that he had suffered on their behalf. Then it dawned on me. Why have I been fighting with the dead when I should have been enlisting them as my allies? I let the topic drop until after dinner. Then, as we were sipping our decafs, I said to him, 'You've got to see the world *for them,* Cecil.' "

That did it, according to my great-uncle Harper.

That sentence freed Cecil, or rather gave him another mission in life. His Home of Eternal Rest was the funeral home of choice for Cleveland County because Cecil, a.k.a. Mister T, possessed a profound empathy for the dead. He understood that their needs were different now. That what their surviving relatives wanted for them wasn't what they would want for themselves. Those clients with very specific desires would write him a detailed letter and pay him in advance for their caskets, flowers, and burial plot so that the living couldn't interfere. Cecil knew the lockets that women wanted buried with them—around their necks but tucked discreetly underneath their dresses—because the lockets held the memories of men who weren't their husbands. He knew the creased photographs that men wanted placed inside their suit jackets, right-hand-side chest pockets, because that was where these faces—strangers to the rest of the families of the deceased—had long resided. Cecil knew of the flawed and stunted and secreted-away lives of his clients, and he knew that Baby Harper was on to something. These people would want to see a greater world than what they had known all their lives. He would see it for them.

Baby Harper ended his letter with a few lines about the contents of the box. "I've sent along some photographs," he wrote. "I think we should go through them together. (Your divan or mine, Vista Girl?) I want you to live with them first, though."

I spoke to my great-uncle Harper eight more times on the telephone. We never discussed the unnumbered H.E.B.'s or the photographs of young Thomas. Out of deference to my great-uncle, I was waiting for a time when we would both be in the same room again. I should have just said what was in my heart, which was, I love you more and more.

Chapter 16

For the lovesick and the lovelorn of Chapel Hill, George Moses had a remedy. For twenty-five cents, he would reveal it to them. First he would feel the coolness of their coins in the palm of his hand. He would close his eyes to intensify the sensation. Freedom would feel like this, he told himself. Then George Moses opened his eyes and asked, "Is the gentleman ready?" The young man nodded his head, his pen and paper in hand, waiting for the spell that would make his beloved's heart beat as fast as his. George Moses knew the beloved's first name, the color of her hair but rarely the color of her eyes. Love was fallen into from afar, back then. With what he was given, George Moses composed a poem. The letters of the beloved's name began each line:

Joy, like the morning, breaks from one divine—
Unveiling stream which cannot fail to shine.
Long have I strove to magnify her name
Imperial, floating on the breeze of fame.
Attracting beauty must delight afford. . . .

The young man's pen flew across the piece of paper. He asked George Moses to repeat the poem so that he could be certain that he had copied down every word. George Moses did as he was asked. After the second recitation, the young man stifled a sigh. Later that night, he transcribed George Moses's poem onto a piece of fine stationery, which would be discreetly delivered to the beloved. The young man marveled again at how the slave, who could neither read nor write, had captured the ecstatic rhythm of his heart. He wondered how the slave knew that her name came to him with the dawn. That when she entered his thoughts his body felt bathed in sunlight and immersed in rushing water all at once. That in those moments she enjoyed complete dominion over him, erasing from his memory all other smiling faces but her own. The young man, for a brief instance, felt jealousy. The slave *knew* his Julia. The thought came to him, then left him embarrassed by his own irrationality. The slave was a slave. He couldn't possibly know his Julia.

That night George Moses placed the coins into his master's palm. George Moses was allowed to keep only the five-cent piece. Tomorrow would bring him closer to his own beloved, George Moses thought. His work wasn't done, though. Before sleep came for him, he composed a poem for another young man's palpitations. Lucy was the cause. George Moses knew something that this young man didn't. It was the third poem this week that George Moses had been paid to compose for the same Lucy. George Moses wondered which one she would care for best, which one she would read to herself at night, blushing deeply from her forehead to her bosom, and which one would free her heart.

In February 1998, I picked up my phone and heard my secretary's voice saying, "Mrs. Hammerick*DrPepper* is on line one*breadand-butterpickles.*" I didn't hesitate because I must have known. As

DeAnne's voice began to tell me about the telephone call that she had just received at the blue and gray ranch house, my fingers instinctively found their way to my computer's keyboard. I clicked onto the CNN website, and there, in the terse wording of a developing news story, dateline February 16, 1998, was a plane crash over the coast of Colombia, all onboard feared dead.

"Linda*mint,* are you*cannedgreenbeans* there*applejuice*?" DeAnne asked.

I nodded my head.

"Linda*mint*?" she asked again.

"I'm still*sourcream* here*hardboiledegg,*" I said.

"There's*applejuice* no*grapejelly* body*cannedmushrooms,* Linda*mint.* What am I supposed*gingerale* to do*grits*?"

It took me a moment to understand what DeAnne was asking me. Her question was childlike and far from existential. After the passing of her husband and her mother, DeAnne knew what was required of her. The funeral arrangements gave her something concrete to do, even if in the case of Iris it only meant sitting by Baby Harper's side as he made all the necessary calls. But now Baby Harper had gone and flown and none of him had made it back to Boiling Springs. What's a funeral without a body or even a cup's worth of ashes, was what DeAnne was asking me. She would have asked Mister T this question, but he had flown too.

We still have each other, was what I was thinking. I didn't say it aloud because I wasn't sure whether it answered DeAnne's question and whether she would take it as a blessing or a curse. I wasn't sure how I understood it either. So, instead, I said to her that I would get on a plane tomorrow and we would figure it out together.

"Linda*mint,* no*grapejelly*!" DeAnne said, her voice raised. "Please*lemonjuice* don't take a plane*greenbellpepper.* For my sake*applepie,* drive*cannedbakedbeans* home*Pepsi.*"

"I'll try*coleslaw* to get ahold of Leo*parsnip.* Maybe he can come*applebutter* with me. I'll call*Doritoschips* you*cannedgreenbeans* right*Frenchfries* back*watermelon,*" I said.

"Please*lemonjuice* do*grits.*"

Click.

"Mom*chocolatemilk*?" I said aloud for the first time in years.

DeAnne and I had last spoken to each other eleven years ago. That fact was less remarkable to me than the fact that we just had a conversation and the reason for it.

I didn't want to call Leo at the hospital. I didn't want to have to say the words to him. I picked up the phone and called Kelly instead. I tried the number at the Greek Revival first. I knew that she was house-sitting for Baby Harper and Cecil. I hoped she would be there because I didn't know the phone number at her office or her apartment. She didn't have any of my numbers either. We hadn't thought about expediency. We hadn't imagined that one day we would need to hear each other's voice immediately, when even a letter, overnighted, would be too late. The phone rang five times, and then I heard her voice.

Dear friend, I thought.

I said the words to her. We sat there, 691 miles from each other, but as close as two human beings could hope to be. I heard her begin to cry, and I knew that meant I could begin too. I didn't have to say that I was coming home. She knew that I would, and in between sobs she asked, "When?"

"As soon*Tang* as I can," I replied. "DeAnne*cannedcranberrysauce* wants*saltedbutter* me to drive*cannedbakedbeans.* It'll take a couple-*friedokra* of days*hardboiledeggyolk.*"

"Leo*parsnip*?" Kelly asked.

"I haven't told him yet."

"You*cannedgreenbeans* should*instantblackcoffee.*"

"I will. Kelly*cannedpeaches*?"

"Yes."

"Baby*honey* Harper*celery* was in love*Nestea.*"

"Your great*cannedtomatosoup*-uncle*dates* was luckier than most."

"Amen*grapefruitjuice.*"

Silence.

"Kelly*cannedpeaches,*" I said, "I better go*boiledcarrots.* I'm at work*NillaWafer* still*sourcream.* I'll call you*cannedgreenbeans* as soon*Tang* as I know*grapejelly* more."

I hung up the phone and I waited.

How long—a minute, an hour, the rest of day—before I would call Leo with the news of my great-uncle's passing? What I was waiting for was the need to tell him. I sat at my desk until my secretary knocked on my door to ask if I wanted anything before she went home for the day. I sat there until the woman who came at night to empty the wastebaskets and vacuum the carpet knocked on the same door. I waved her in, wished her a good night, and headed out into the hallway. When I came back to my office, the message light was blinking on my phone. It was Leo. He had called from the hospital to ask when I was coming home tonight and whether I could stop by the drugstore and buy him some shampoo. The day-to-day enterprise of living together Leo and I did very well. We took care of each other, which I had thought was the same as saying we cared for each other. I called his cell phone.

"Linda*mint*?" Leo answered.

"It's me," I replied.

"Hi. I can't talk*cornchips* for long*grapeNehi.* I just needed a couple*friedokra* of things*tomato* from the store*brancereal*—"

"Baby*honey* Harper*celery* and Cecil*boiledshrimp* are dead*molasses.* Their*applejuice* plane*greenbellpepper* went down today*oatmeal.*"

"Oh, my God*walnut.*"

God had nothing to do with it, I thought.

"DeAnne*cannedcranberrysauce* wants*saltedbutter* us to drive*cannedbakedbeans* to Boiling*parsley* Springs*lemonJell-O,*" I said.

"When?"

"I want*saltedbutter* to leave tomorrow*breakfastsausage.*"

"Tomorrow*breakfastsausage*?"

"Yes. Come*applebutter* with me."

"Let me ask. But, Linda*mint,* I highly doubt*instantvanillapud-*

ding it. I'm scheduled every*Ritzcracker* day*hardboiledeggyolk* for the next week and a half*brownie.*"

"Right*Frenchfries.*"

"Linda*mint?*"

"Yes, Leo*parsnip.*"

"I'm sorry*glazeddoughnut* for your loss*fruitcake.*"

"Me too."

"I'll see you*cannedgreenbeans* tomorrow*breakfastsausage* morning*Hardee'scheeseburger.* We'll figure*collardgreens* it out*strawberryjam.* OK?"

"OK."

Leo was an attending psychiatrist at St. Vincent's Hospital by then. He no longer had to work the twenty-four-hour shifts that he did as a resident, but he was still obliged to cover an overnight shift at least several times a week. On those days, he usually got home from the hospital by 7:40 A.M. This gave us a half hour together before I left for the firm. We would sit at the kitchen table and trade bits of information about our lives. The state of the quart of milk in our fridge: sour, almost empty, we should try fat-free. The status of the dry cleaning: drop off, pick up, they lost two of your shirts. We would take out our calendars and find the next night when we would both be home for dinner and consider our options: order in, make a reservation somewhere, I'll buy some steaks. We rarely had a disagreement. This wasn't the same as we often agreed. Simply put, we had only a half hour, and a half hour wasn't long enough for a fight. These were the metes and bounds of our committed relationship. We should proceed to the next step, we thought. We had to consult our calendars first, though.

The morning after Baby Harper and Cecil's passing, I woke up with a pounding headache caused by the bottle of two-hundred-dollar Scotch that I had swallowed the night before in order to coax sleep. (Anyone who claims that expensive alcohol doesn't cause a hangover is someone who hasn't had enough of it to drink.) I opened my eyes, and the first words that came to me were "I'm sorry for your loss." How could Leo have said this to me? Goody Benton probably taught him that corseted, bloodless expression of condolence. If I married Leo, wouldn't I be Goody Benton too/II? For that brief moment when my mind drifted from Baby Harper to Leo, I felt a jolt of shame. My great-uncle had been dead for only a day, and I was already planning for a life without him.

Leo and I shared a duplex, the first and second floor of a brownstone on a tree-lined block of West Twenty-second Street. I had bought the place after my second year of practice. I was flush with money, and I needed a way to invest it. I had no school loans to pay off because my great-uncle had made sure that both my college and law school tuition were paid for in full. He said that the money came from one of my father's many life insurance policies. The Reasonable Man was a financially prepared man. Whenever I went to the ATM, I would look at the amount "available" and wonder whose bank account this was. I couldn't spend my salary, direct-deposited into my checking account like the proceeds of some secret lottery, fast enough. Perhaps this was why I loved the practice of law.

I had loved it first for a very different reason.

The law gave me an entirely new vocabulary, a language that non-lawyers derisively referred to as "legalese." Unlike the basic building blocks—the day-to-day words—that got me from the subway to the office and back, the words of my legal vocabulary, more often than not, triggered flavors that I had experienced after leaving Boiling Springs, flavors that I had chosen for myself, derived from foods that were never contained within the boxes and the cans of DeAnne's kitchen.

Subpoena*kiwifruit*.

Injunction*Camembert*.

Infringement*lobster*.

Jurisdiction*freshgreenbeans*.

Appellant*sourdoughbread*.

Arbitration*Guinness.*

Unconstitutional*asparagus.*

Exculpatory*Nutella.*

I could go on and on, and I did.

Every day I was paid an astonishing amount of money to shuffle these words around on paper and, better yet, to say them aloud. At my yearly reviews, the partners I worked for commented that they had never seen a young lawyer so visibly invigorated by her work. One of the many reasons I was on track to make partner, I thought.

There were, of course, the rare and disconcerting exceptions. Some legal words reached back to the Dark Ages of my childhood and to the stunted diet that informed my earlier words. "Mitigating," for example, brought with it the unmistakable taste of elementary school cafeteria pizzas: rectangles of frozen dough topped with a ketchup-like sauce, the hard crumbled meat of some unidentifiable animal, and grated "cheese" that didn't melt when heated but instead retained the pattern of a badly crocheted coverlet. I had actually looked forward to the days when these rectangles were on the lunch menu, slapped onto my tray by the lunch ladies in hairnets and comfortable shoes. Those pizzas (even the word itself was pure exuberance with the two *z*'s and the sound of satisfaction at the end . . . *ah*!) were evocative of some greater, more interesting locale, though how and where none of us at Boiling Springs Elementary circa 1975 were quite sure. We all knew what hamburgers and hot dogs were supposed to look and taste like, and we knew that the school cafeteria served us a second-rate version of these foods. Few of us students knew what a pizza was supposed to be. Kelly claimed that it was usually very big and round in shape, but both of these characteristics seemed highly improbable to me. By the time we were in middle school, a Pizza Inn had opened up along the feeder road to I-85. The Pizza Inn may or may not have been the first national chain of pizzerias to offer a weekly all-you-can-eat buffet. To the folks of the greater Boiling Springs–Shelby area, this was an idea that would expand their waistlines, if not their horizons. A Sizzler would later open next to the Pizza Inn (*feeder road* took on a new connotation), and it would offer the Holy Grail of all-you-can-eat buffets: steaks, baked potatoes, and, for the ladies, a salad bar complete with exotic fixings such as canned chickpeas and a tangle of slightly bruised alfalfa sprouts.

Along with "mitigating," these were some of the other legal words that also transported me back in time:

Egress*redvelvetcake.*

Perpetuity*bottledFrenchsaladdressing.*

Compensatory*boiledpeanuts.*

Probate*Reese'speanutbuttercup.*

Fiduciary*Cheerwine.*

Amortization*Oreocookie.*

I wanted, most of all, to say these words to my father. The lexicon of the law had allowed him to be part of a world much greater than Boiling Springs and Shelby, greater than Raleigh, than the state of North Carolina. These words, I knew, must have comforted him as well.

The smell of pancakes cooking and bacon burning rose through the air vents that led from the kitchen straight up to our bedroom. I took a deep breath and found coffee beginning to brew as well. Leo had called in a favor. The attending psychiatrist for the day shift had come in two hours early and covered for Leo that morning. In the Manhattan predawn, Leo had headed home. He stopped at the corner deli and bought a pint of blueberries, a lemon, maple syrup, and peppered bacon. When I came downstairs, I saw these items spread out on the kitchen counter. Over his jeans and white T-shirt, Leo had on an apron, which made him look like a progressive little boy playing house. He put a finger up to his lips and shushed me before I could say anything. He sat me down at the kitchen table and placed a plate in front of me. On the plate was a small robin's-egg-blue box.

Before I could object to his incredibly poor timing, Leo launched into a dizzying speech about how life, despite our best efforts, was impossible to plan for. How he had bought the ring three months ago and had been waiting to propose. How he had already arranged to take time off from the hospital—a full two weeks—so that we could celebrate at his parents' cabin in the Berkshires. In true WASP code, the "cabin" was a sprawling compound on 110 acres that included a five-bedroom main house, a converted barn for the grandchildren who had yet to materialize, a swimming "hole"—a lake the size of the Wollman skating rink in Central Park—and an apple orchard that required Mr. and Mrs. Benton to hire a local family to harvest it each fall.

Leo was more animated than usual, which accelerated his already rapid speech pattern. His words were running up against one another as they rushed to leave his mouth. He must have seen the look of confusion on my face and how my eyes kept on darting over to the coffeemaker. Leo poured me a cup and sat down beside me. He explained as slowly as he could that the vacation, which he had negotiated and bargained for and agreed to work the remaining year's worth of weekend shifts for, was to begin *two* weeks from now. Proposal, ring, acceptance, vacation, all was to happen *two* weeks from now, he repeated. The news yesterday about Baby Harper and Cecil's passing, and my request that we leave immediately for Boiling Springs had forced his hand.

Did he really say "forced" his hand, I remembered thinking.

Leo, sensing his momentum dissipating, his pancakes becoming cold pucks, the grease congealing white around the strips of bacon, picked up the pace of his proposal.

I said yes.

Leo opened the robin's-egg-blue box and placed the ring on my finger. It was a diamond solitaire, traditional, multicarat, and expensive. Of course, the ring was a perfect fit. Leo was a planner. He probably had measured my finger while I was asleep.

Leo kissed me. I closed my eyes and opened them up again. I

understood in that brief moment of darkness that the apron was very important to me. Leo seemed younger and more vulnerable in the apron. I needed to see him in it. I smiled. He smiled back at me.

Leo then requested three things of me. First, we would keep the timing, if not the destination, of his original plan. We would wait two weeks and drive to Boiling Springs. We could stay with DeAnne for all or some of the time, depending on how I felt, he said. Second, I would quit smoking. Third, I would get a full medical checkup before we officially announced our engagement.

Agreeing to the first stipulation was easier than the second and third.

It seemed suddenly absurd that I had intended to get in a car that day with Leo and head to North Carolina for some indeterminate amount of time. I hadn't told anyone at the firm that I was planning to be away. I had a conference call scheduled for later that afternoon. I had a meeting in Detroit the following week. Leo and I didn't even own a car. We would need to rent one, but by the time that I had remembered this detail the night before, I was too drunk to do anything about it. Also, in all honesty, the idea of seeing DeAnne in two weeks as opposed to two days wasn't that objectionable to me.

As for the rest of Leo's requests, I understood them for what they were. Leo had made me a conditional offer. If the conditions weren't met, the offer would be void.

When I arrived at the firm that morning, I telephoned Kelly first and told her that I wouldn't be back in Boiling Springs for another two weeks. I told her that my work schedule and Leo's were a tangled mess. I didn't tell her about Leo's proposal or whatever it was. She would have asked me the question that we have been carrying within us since we were little girls, waiting for the day when we could answer with an unqualified yes.

Are you in love, Linda?

No.

Will you marry him?

Yes.

Why?

Because the two questions are not one and the same.

Yes they are.

How would *you* know, Kelly?

It was at the edge of such a chasm that a friendship could meet its untimely end.

Then I telephoned DeAnne. I didn't hear the reprimand that I had expected or the word that I thought she would throw at me. "Selfish" had disappeared from her vocabulary. Her voice echoed on the line, as if she were sitting in the middle of an empty room, as if she were the empty room. DeAnne said that she would wait until I came back home before doing or deciding anything. She said that Baby Harper would have wanted it that way.

At 1:12 A.M. on February 16, 1998, American Airlines Flight 1520 from Bogotá's El Dorado Airport, en route to Charlotte's Douglas International, went down minutes after flying over the city of Santa Marta at the edge of the Caribbean Sea. According to the inhabitants of Santa Marta, some claiming that they had seen the moment in their sleep, Harper Evan Burch and Cecil Tobias Brandon and 262 other bodies transformed into birds. The flock, so large that it blocked out the moon, then flew headfirst into the sea. These inhabitants also reported hearing in their sleep a song that they would later identify as Patsy Cline's "You Belong to Me."

Fly the ocean in a silver plane,
See the jungle when it's wet with rain,
Just remember till you're home again,
You belong to me.

Cecil's last will and testament bequeathed his estate, with one small exception, to his "life companion," Harper Evan Burch, and if predeceased then to his nephew Clay Tobias Mitchell of Fayetteville, North Carolina. Clay, a thirty-seven-year-old middle school mathematics teacher, immediately quit his job and moved with his own life companion, Gregory Puckett Ames, to Shelby, where the two men saw to it that the Home of Eternal Rest would continue to meet all the needs of the county's dearly departed. The folks of the greater Boiling Springs–Shelby area were comforted by the fact that there was another Mister T to turn to during their time of loss. They welcomed Clay and Gregory to town with an outpouring of Bundt cakes and casseroles, and then they gave them the bodies of their dead to prepare for burial. Trust couldn't be delineated in a clearer way. These folks also found comfort in reminding one another that it was 1998. What they meant was that life around them had changed. Shelby had a Chinese "bistro" *and* a Thai restaurant, and Boiling Springs no longer had Gardner-Webb Baptist College but Gardner-Webb University, complete with out-of-state students and even some from overseas, mostly from small Third World countries where the Southern Baptist Convention International Mission Board was most active. Cleveland County was more cosmopolitan in other ways as well. The county was no longer dry. Beer and liquor were now available for purchase without ever having to cross the nearest state line. I had meant to ask Baby Harper whether that was the real reason Iris had driven to Spartanburg, South Carolina; whether her glass of Dr Pepper had hid a fifth of something stronger.

Cecil set forth in his will that his body was to be cremated and his ashes kept in a silver urn, which could be found on the mantelpiece in the master bedroom of the Greek Revival. He also wrote that under no circumstance should there be a funeral or memorial service. He'd already been to so many of them, I could almost hear my great-uncle explaining. Cecil long ago had set aside some money—the amount that the average person would spend on a casket, flowers, burial plot, and yearly upkeep of said plot—in a high-interest-bearing account, and he specified that upon his death the interest should be used to fund a yearly scholarship for "any young man or woman from Cleveland County who wanted to study the funerary customs of other countries; travel is most encouraged." At the time of his passing, the account was worth $1.2 million.

Kelly wrote in letter #1,297 that when Clay and Gregory came to the Greek Revival to pick up the silver urn, the three of them each did a shot of tequila in Cecil and my great-uncle's honor. They weren't sure what liquor Colombians drank, but tequila seemed to be in keeping with that part of the world, she wrote. When I read this, I thought about how much my best friend had changed. The Kelly of our youth would have known that Colombia's alcohol of choice was *aguardiente,* a sugar cane–based anisette, because she knew everything worth knowing in the world. The Kelly of our approaching thirties was an assistant financial-aid officer at Gardner-Webb and was distributing Southern Baptist scholarship money to the smaller, poorer, browner countries of the world that she knew nothing about.

My great-uncle Harper didn't leave a will. DeAnne was his closest living blood relative. She inherited all that he owned, including the Greek Revival. DeAnne asked Kelly to stay in the house until we could decide what to do with it and its contents: the mourning embroideries, the antique furniture, the one hundred H.E.B.'s, the shelves of books organized not by titles but by the thoughts and emotions that their pages evoked, the silver objects that my great-uncle gave to Cecil for their anniversaries, and the master bedroom that was unbeknownst to us the exuberant heart of the house. According to Kelly, even Clay and Gregory were surprised by its decor. She wrote that the three of them, after a couple more shots of tequila, decided that if Scarlett O'Hara and Carmen Miranda had been lesbian lovers and they had had a baby—via the turkey baster method—and that baby grew up to be an interior decorator, then he would have been responsible for the amalgam of tropical colors, rich velvets, and floppy-straw-bonnet motifs that they found inside Baby Harper and Cecil's bedroom.

"In other words, you mean that Baby Harper was the decorator," I wrote back. "Was anything painted Peony Red?" I asked Kelly in the postscript. I made her promise that she wouldn't touch a thing until I had a chance to see the room for myself. I was, in fact, more concerned about what DeAnne would do to the room.

Chapter 17

Shoot me through the heart. Transform and transfigure me. Allow me to feel beloved till my last breath. I prayed to you, Virginia Dare, because you too were an orphan. Jesus had a mother and a father and yet another Father. Jesus was lucky. You and He both came to a violent end, were resurrected, and live on now in stories. I found your story, with its inexplicable abandonment and unquestioned adoption, more moving. He lived till the age of thirty-three. How old were you, Virginia, when the arrows pierced your most vital organ? Legend left you lying on the forest floor, leaves and insects underneath your still-warm body. But there were the minutes right before death, unheralded and untold, when you had just fallen, your flesh half animal and half human. Your ears, still that of a doe, heard the footfalls of two men running toward you from opposite directions. Fear fluttered through your body before leaving through your parted lips, already those of a woman, as a barely audible O! Your arms, a stretch of alabaster skin, ended not in hands but in hooves. You used them, clumsy as they were, to touch the two arrows that extended from your chest, like the limbs of a vestigial twin. Pain, a sudden downpour, soaked every inch of your body, which was changing with each labored breath. You believed that this pain had nothing to do with your body, though. You believed that it had everything to do with longing and loneliness. One set of footsteps was coming near. The other had stopped, tangled up in old age and in vines. You glanced down, examining the state of your body, and thought of how you didn't want O! to see you this way. In between, inchoate. In your last moments of consciousness, you saw the faces of a young man and a young woman who looked so much like you that you shuddered, as if ghosts had emerged from your own body. You heard them saying in soft tones a version of your name. You thought "Mother" and "Father" in a language that you knew but had never said aloud. One of them commanded you to "stay." The woman and the man then disappeared. In their place, you saw the face of O! as he knelt down beside you and began to rock his body back and forth in the throes of regret and grief. You knew that his body would do this for many more days to come. The pain you felt increased, and you let out another quiet O! He thought you had said his name. In a way, you had. You closed your eyes—both were those of a woman, as was the whole of your body now. Your memories, though, remained a hybrid of animal and human. You faded away to a recollection that belonged to the former:

You are running through the forest. You smell sunlight, you taste the wind, you feel the buzzing of bees and echoing of bird songs, you see whiffs of honeysuckles and fresh pine sap in the air, you hear blood, salty and thick, rushing into your mouth.

My first instinct was right. The photo albums that my great-uncle had sent to me were an invitation. Leo looking over my shoulders wasn't how I had wanted to view their contents, so I had taken them to work with me. There, alone in my office, I got to know Harper Evan Burch. Within the covers of the four unnumbered

H.E.B.'s was the incomplete documentation of another life. My great-uncle looked beautiful in these photographs. In the most recent ones, he looked straight into the camera as if he knew this to be a fact. In total, the existence of these albums disproved my long-held beliefs that Baby Harper disliked being photographed, that until Cecil he was always alone when he wasn't with us, and that he was uncomfortable in his own skin. As it turned out, my great-uncle Harper was uncomfortable only in his day-to-day clothes.

As a young man—he looked to be around sixteen or seventeen in the earliest of these photographs—Baby Harper, wavy hair and pin-cushion lips, wore a light-colored suit, a button-down shirt, and a striped bow tie. I smiled when I saw him in such familiar attire, comforted by the fact that he had adopted his costume so early on. Baby Harper sat in a high-back chair, his legs crossed. On his feet was a pair of black high-heeled pumps, much too small for him. There was a visible bunching of flesh at the front of the shoes, and his bare heels hovered over the shiny back of theirs. His eyes were downcast, but his back was good-posture straight. The photographer had documented both the resolve of Baby Harper's upper body and the exuberance of his lower half, one pointy toe aimed toward the camera and the other one up toward the ceiling.

Baby Harper began with his feet because shoes were easy to slip in and out of, easy to find lying around the green-shuttered colonial that he shared then with Iris and Walter Wendell, and easy to kick underneath the bed if either of them walked into his bedroom without knocking. Perhaps for the same reasons, hats and gloves were the next items to appear in these photographs. The gloves Baby Harper was always careful to hold in one hand or lay over a knee, as their fabric would be sure to stretch and give him away.

The first time the camera saw Baby Harper in a dress, he hadn't discovered the importance of a bra or rather a well-stuffed one. The dress was probably Iris's, which meant that the back zipper must have been left undone, as his sister was only a slender size six back then. The front of the dress, darted and generously cupped, was on

Baby Harper's body both taut and caved in. His lips, a straight line, showed his disappointment. There were two more photographs of Baby Harper in this same dress. Both were unintentionally arty, almost abstract expressionistic close-ups of where the hem of the garment met his bare legs. The dark plane of fabric against the pale skin clearly showed one thing. Baby Harper had taken the important step of shaving his legs. My great-uncle kept them shaved for the remainder of his life, which was why we never saw him in a pair of shorts. He probably shaved the hair on his forearms as well, which meant that his preference for long-sleeved shirts wasn't a shroud of modesty but of necessity.

I wished I had been there for him. I wanted to be the one behind the camera. Turn your head to the left, lift your chin, sit up a bit straighter, relax your shoulders, fix the right strap of your dress, deep breath, and now smile. Whoever said these words to Baby Harper never allowed his own face to be photographed, as if that person knew that one day he would run for public office and would want to win. Of course, Wee Willie came to mind first. But whomever the photographer was he eventually departed, and no one was left in the room but Baby Harper. By the second album, I could see in his right hand a cable release, with its long thin cord snaking out of the frame, signaling the presence of a tripod, silent and unhelpful. I was jealous all the same.

As I leafed through the pages of these albums, Baby Harper transformed himself step by step into a woman, whose wardrobe borrowed less and less from Iris and more from sources who were closer to him in dress and shoe size. His suppliers were probably the revolving roster of nameless "girls" who cooked and cleaned under the watchful eyes and sharp tongue of my grandmother Iris. These cooks were, of course, not girls, but black women in their forties and fifties. Their dresses bordered on the matronly despite my great-uncle's efforts to add jaunty scarves and decorative brooches, and their shoes were sensibly heeled, made more for housework or churchgoing than for hosting a dinner party. Their wigs, however, became increasingly elaborate. Updos, cascading curls, Betty Boop bangs. My great-uncle, a natural blonde, was by then a raven-haired beauty.

When he switched from black-and-white to color film (I wondered who had developed all these photographs for my great-uncle and whether he had charged him extra to keep his secret), Baby Harper's makeup popped into the foreground. His use of eye shadows, monochromatic sweeps of pigment and glitter, reminded me of Kelly's and my early experimentation with Ocean Lite. His lips were thankfully never Flamingo Paradise, as he gravitated toward more vibrant hues, maraschino-cherry and candy-apple reds.

Like an artist, Baby Harper had his prolific periods and his fallow times. There seemed to have been many years during which he set his camera aside, no longer interested in the self-portrait. When he finally resumed, he did so as a woman who had discovered the transformative power of mail-order catalogs. His outfits, color-coordinated and secretarial, looked as if they were lifted right from the pages of the JCPenney catalogs that DeAnne had around the blue and gray ranch house in the mid-seventies, with their pages full of cowl-neck sweaters, A-line plaid skirts, and cork-soled wedges. Baby Harper, most likely in his fifties by then, also had a mane of honey-blond hair, layered with windblown curls. He looked like Farrah Fawcett's older sister. He was finally coming into his own, perched comfortably at the edge of his green velvet divan, blue eyes shining, cable release still caught in his right hand.

"If you are lucky, you are born not once but many times." My great-uncle wrote this on the front page of the last of the unmarked H.E.B.'s. The handwriting was his. The sentiment, I assumed, was his too, though I had never heard him say it. I decided that it was a prayer, one that for him had come true. Baby Harper was in love with Cecil. Baby Harper was engaged in foreign travel. Baby Harper had found a different South. The last album was devoted to all three. Cecil and Baby Harper sharing a park bench nestled in a garden of calla lilies. Cecil and Baby Harper sitting at a café table on a terrace overgrown with purple and red bougainvilleas. Cecil and Baby Harper standing in front of a sunset, fishing boats bobbing in the harbor behind them. They always held hands. They smiled into the camera, which adored them right back. The photographer was a stranger, a fellow traveler, or perhaps a native-born. Cecil had on what I assumed was the approved vacation-resort wear for funeral directors, a dark suit with a gray polo shirt. Baby Harper looked like an art history professor from a small liberal arts college east of the Mississippi. In his sixties, my great-uncle had graduated from blond tresses to a shoulder-grazing auburn bob. His dresses—black, dove gray, or beeswax ecru—were loose (to accommodate the weight that he had gained since being with Cecil) but tailored with architectural details. Flying buttress sleeves, quatrefoil buttons, dentil-molding hems. Baby Harper wore necklaces that were large and made a statement, mostly about which South American country he had traveled to most recently. Silver beads, birds and various animal totems rendered in clay and fired in blues and yellows, and bright, sturdy red seeds.

My great-uncle sent me beautiful postcards of his travels. From Cartagena, he sent me the Iglesia de San Pedro Claver. From Santiago, the Mercado Central. From Montevideo, the Palacio Taranco. From Rio de Janeiro, the wide-open arms of a modernist Jesus. I never thought it unusual that Baby Harper, the family photographer, never once sent me a photograph that he had taken, whether alone or with Cecil. My great-uncle had trained my expectations, crafted for me what was normal, and answered all the questions that I never thought to ask him with plausible assumptions and givens. Most important, once these expectations were in place, he tried never to disappoint me. That was his definition of love.

Baby Harper must have had doubt in his heart, though. He wanted me to live with these photographs first, he had written, as if his body could ever enter my home as a stranger and that we would grow more comfortable with each other only with time.

Maybe he meant just the photographs of young Thomas in New York, but even those faces and those bodies, my great-uncle should have known, would be familiar to me, as he had always been to me.

I'm coming home. I should have said this to my great-uncle Harper. I said it to DeAnne instead. It was a phone call that took place about six months later than she and I had expected. I hadn't told her about Leo's offer, my acceptance, and his rescission. I hadn't told her about my cancer and my surgery. I hadn't told her about being taken off the partnership track and shifted onto the "of counsel" one, the dumping ground for competent but undervalued senior attorneys. We think this is a better fit, the partnership committee had said to me. Their statement was vague but also to the point. The firm's generous medical leave policy apparently had its limits. Or more likely, none of them—lawyers hate to be confronted with their own mortality because they know that most of them are going to Hell—wanted to hear the word "cancer" even if the word "survivor" was attached to it. I was a risky investment, they must have thought. Nor had I told her that I had asked the firm for another leave of absence, this time a mental health one, indefinite and unpaid. In other words, during the months since Cecil's and my great-uncle's passing, things had gone back to normal between DeAnne and me.

I sent information that I wanted DeAnne to know via a conduit. Now that Baby Harper was gone, Kelly reluctantly took on that role for us. Kelly told DeAnne that I had been assigned to a case that was going to the U.S. Supreme Court and that the workload, while overwhelming and unrelenting, was helping me to deal with my great-uncle's death. Kelly must have gotten that story line from an episode of *Ally McBeal*. It was a ridiculous lie but one that was plausible enough for DeAnne, who didn't know—because I hadn't told her—that I was a trademark lawyer and that never in my five years of practice had I seen the inside of a courthouse.

Kelly, of course, knew everything. We had resumed our correspondence in earnest and, for me, out of necessity. Without the hourly cigarettes and the daily drinks, I was finding it a challenge again to manage the incomings. I wanted to hear Kelly's voice on the telephone, but I couldn't listen to it for very long. My relationship to the spoken word had regressed. I felt as I did in elementary and middle school. I retreated into the pages of books. I watched TV with the sound turned off. When I became lonely for the human voice, I found it in songs. I wrote long letters to my best friend. I wrote to her that I was coming home. Then I wrote that I was bringing Baby Harper and young Thomas back with me. I planned, among other things, to introduce them to DeAnne.

I hadn't been on a Greyhound bus since 1986, when Iris had her second heart attack. This time, Kelly had offered to fly up to New York City and drive with me back to Boiling Springs. I considered it, but I didn't want her to travel all that way only to turn back and head southward again. I thought that I could use the sixteen-hour-and-forty-five-minute bus ride to organize my thoughts. I wanted to prepare myself. I thought that I could be lawyerly about my return home. Approach Boiling Springs as if I were preparing for a meeting with a client or an adversary. Marshal the few facts that I had, formulate my theories, draft my probative questions. In my shoulder bag, I packed a legal pad on which I planned to jot down my notes. In my years of practicing law, I had learned that for non-lawyers, a legal pad was an intimidating item. Its size or rather its unusual length was part of the scare tactic. Its color was talismanic as well. Yellow connoting jaundice. Or perhaps aging. Or the slow passage of time. That was precisely what I wanted to do. Slow down time. Bus travel was the best way I knew how. The frequent stops, the waiting for all the passengers to collect themselves from bathroom stalls, from fast food lines, and from the sirenlike glows of vending machines. I wanted the inefficiencies of traveling en masse and cheaply, of road-tripping with people who collectively had more time than money.

The smells were the same, I thought, as I climbed aboard the bus at Port Authority. Once I settled into my seat and looked around me, I understood why. The passengers were the same. The teenagers who looked like runaways (because even in the August heat they had too many pieces of clothing on and none of the pieces were clean), the well-dressed elderly black women with shiny purses on their laps, the middle-aged white men with long hair, receding hairlines, and bellies pregnant with beer. The demographics of long-distance bus travel hadn't changed, except that there were now men from Central and South America, in their twenties, thirties, and forties, who looked uniformly exhausted, as if they knew that every state of the union would be the same for them: New York or North Carolina, apples or tobacco, produce fields or slaughterhouses. Their migration was a peculiar form of travel. Peculiar in that it was travel that took them nowhere. Wherever they landed, it was exactly the same. (Immigration was migration fueled by faith that *this* wasn't so.)

I waited for my body to adjust. Soon the artificial pine scent that came from the onboard restroom would permeate the rest of the bus, eventually masking the stale sweat (men with receding hairlines), the rose-scented hand lotion (elderly women with purses), and the musty cigarettes and pot smoke embedded in denim (teenagers). Somewhere in that mix was also the lime and leather of aftershaves (migrant laborers on their days off). I knew that soon my nose would no longer be able to pick out these scents, their individuality coalescing into one, which my nose would then assimilate and take no notice of for the next sixteen hours, like an eye adjusting to the dark. It would be the last forty-five minutes of the journey that would be the most difficult to tolerate. The bathroom would have been compromised by everyone on board, except for the most experienced riders, who knew how to time their intake of beverages to coincide with the scheduled stops. Then the shuffling of bodies waking from a cramped, light sleep would cause their individual scents to rise again and move up and down the aisle like anxious travelers.

Hand lotion and aftershave would be reapplied. Some kid in the back of the bus would steal a puff or two from a cigarette that he couldn't help but light up, though it was grounds for being thrown off the bus. No bus driver would give a shit with only forty-five minutes to go, the kid would think. He would be right. The bus driver would want to get to the destination even more than the passengers. He made this run three times a week. New York City to Gastonia (the closest Greyhound stop to Boiling Springs). Twenty hours and fifteen minutes, if there was a transfer, which there usually was. Or, the "express," which was the one I was on, could shave more than four hours off that time, but usually didn't because of the first rule of bus travel: Buses were always late. In light of all this, the bus driver would think, Who has time to throw some stupid kid off the bus? With only forty-five minutes to go, all the passengers would agree. With only forty-five minutes to go, I would pop another piece of gum into my mouth and fight the desire to join the kid with the cigarette at the back of the bus.

I had thought about making the drive home on my own, but eight years of living in New York City without a car had made me unsure of my driving skills, especially for such a long trip. Also, Dr. Holloway, my OB/GYN, had warned me that my body was more exhausted from the surgery than I would think. Dr. Holloway's waiting room played Gregorian chants and New Age music that mimicked whale songs. Instead of mints or hard candies, her receptionist's desk offered a large glass canister of granola, which her patients scooped into paper cups, which they then recycled. I thought her use of "exhausted" was therefore less medical and more self-helpish in nature. At my one-month follow-up, Dr. Holloway said that the removal of any vital organs, and the ovaries, she leaned in and whispered, were of course *very vital*—my ovaries can't hear you, doctor; they're already gone, I almost said aloud—resulted in a trauma that the body could recover from, but afterward the body would continue to grieve for what had been taken from it.

"Wow, your doctor sounds like she was high," Kelly wrote in letter #1,301. Kelly and I made a joke of Dr. Holloway's words, but I knew that we both were thinking about this idea of our bodies grieving. Kelly thought about the absence. I thought about the void. We both had just turned thirty, and we never had imagined our lives in quite *this* way. To be honest, we never had imagined anything about our thirties. What little girls would? Kelly had thought that by the end of high school she would be homecoming queen or at least one of the homecoming court. When she thought of college, it was only in *tableaux vivants* of sorority parties and UNC football games and boys who all looked like Wade. (He, like Jesus, remained our male archetype.) I imagined leaving Boiling Springs. After my father died, I imagined New Haven and New York City. I thought these cities would be like Heaven. I would see there all the people whom I had loved. I would see my father, who hadn't died but, like Wade's mom, had run away from home to find true love. I would see my great-uncle Harper because I would send him a first-class plane ticket and together we would set up house. I would see Kelly because she never lost her pregnancy weight and instead regained her beautiful, full-figured intelligence. Finally, I would see Wade. But this time, I would recognize the orange sherbet boy first because I would be the one who had changed completely. I used to think about Wade every day. All through college and in law school, I thought about him. Even after I met Leo, I thought about him. Now I thought about Wade only when I caught the cross-town bus or a Greyhound bus home.

On the other side of the tinted glass window, a green sign with GASTONIA in white letters came into view. The word was rippling in the midmorning heat. I couldn't remember whether Boiling Springs had its own exit sign off the highway, but it must have. It felt like the world routinely bypassed us, but I know that it really hadn't.

Jerry Lee Lewis and Fats Domino came to Boiling Springs. The Wright brothers and Virginia Dare came to Boiling Springs. Dill and Boo Radley came to Boiling Springs. South American magnolias and JCPenney catalogs came to Boiling Springs. New cars from Detroit and plastic hair barrettes from Taiwan came to Boiling Springs. Flamingo Paradise and Ocean Lite came to Boiling Springs. Ersatz pizzas and all-you-can-eat salad bars came to Boiling Springs. De facto segregation and dead-end jobs came to Boiling Springs. Queers, Jews, Chinks, Japs, and Gooks came to Boiling Springs. On the whole, it was like any other American city, only smaller and duller and with less crime.

Inside the bus, there was a collective sigh. For every passenger there was a different reason for his or her exhalation: lovelorn, forlorn, war-torn, relief, regret, remorse, resigned, steeled, staved, and staunched. All were released into the stale air, changing for a moment its chemistry, making its odors detectable again to those bodies, like mine, who had adapted and grown used to them. As a group, we might never arrive, but we would get there. The sign on the highway made it seem real, I thought.

I looked down at the legal pad on my lap. There was yesterday's date, August 3, 1998, on the first page, followed by a lot of writing, and only two questions at the end. I read them again. I asked myself, Is that all I want to know from DeAnne? I answered, Yes, that is all I want to know.

Chapter 18

On May 25, 1910, the Bishop Milton Wright flew. "Higher, Orville, higher!" he ordered his youngest son in an excited voice that made the bishop an eight-year-old boy again and not the eighty-two-year-old man that he was. Orville already had taken them 350 feet in the air. Together, father and son flew for seven minutes. Below them, the bishop's elder son, Wilbur, stood at the edge of Huffman Prairie, among the grazing cows that had been pushed to one side of the pasture for the occasion. Ohio has too many cows, Wilbur thought. Maybe this was why he and Orville *had* to invent their flying machine. It was their antidote to a life among these lumbering beasts, heavy with milk and steaks. Ohio always made Wilbur feel this way. Dayton, especially, made Wilbur morose. Kitty Hawk, North Carolina, had made him immortal. Le Mans, France, had made him beloved. Why must a man travel so far from his home to feel these ways? Wilbur wanted to know. The cows offered him no insight.

"God could have heard him. He was screaming so loudly!" Orville told Wilbur afterward. Orville was still breathless. Their father was already on his way home for a much needed nap. Wilbur nodded his head because he had nothing that he wanted to say aloud. We didn't even flip a coin, Wilbur thought. I'm the elder son. Why didn't he trust *me*? Wilbur wanted to know. Orville stood there smiling broadly, sunlight filtering through his dark hair. Wilbur resented his younger brother for this too. Wilbur's own full head of hair was by then only a memory. The tips of Orville's mustache were still perfectly waxed, Wilbur also noted. Dashing bastard, Wilbur thought, and was then remorseful. Wilbur patted his little brother on the back, and together they walked away from their flying machine.

Of the two brothers, Wilbur was the first to die. He was forty-five years old, and death came to him in the form of typhoid fever. He had traveled to Boston and brought it back with him to Dayton. Boston, Massachusetts, would make him mortal. He suffered all the known symptoms: fatigue, muscle aches, and diarrhea. As Wilbur lay on his deathbed, he could feel every inch of his body as if he had been scrubbed raw with a bath brush. The few hairs that he had left on his head he felt acutely as well, as if someone had just inserted them one by one into his scalp with a needle and thread. For once, he was glad to be balding. He sincerely hoped that Orville would be spared such pain.

Edith was by his side, the Sarthe River far below them. So was everyone else in the town of Le Mans and in all of France, or so it seemed. Edith smiled at him and clutched on to his right thigh even tighter than before. Her husband would never know, she thought. He was in Le Mans looking up at them. I'm making you famous, Wilbur heard himself saying to Edith. He knew that this wasn't a fanciful boast. He wasn't a prideful man. He was stating a fact. Edith Berg, as he had claimed, would be written into the history books as the first American woman to be a passenger on a flying machine. Edith took her eyes off the ground and looked again into Wilbur's startling blues. She was thinking about making another kind of flight with him. His voice sounded so strong, confident, and convinced. That was when Wilbur knew that he had been hallucinating. The fever was taking him away.

By the age of fourteen, I had figured out that I was neither a Chink nor a Jap. In my ninth grade history book, I read the following sentence: "Nguyen Van Thieu was the president of South Vietnam from September 3, 1967, to April 21, 1975." For a split second, I thought the president's name was a typographical error, perhaps a missing vowel or an extra consonant tucked into a Dutch name. Then I recognized it as "the unpronounceable part" of my name (that was what Kelly called it). I had never seen "Nguyen" printed in a book before. So while it belonged to me, I didn't recognize it. My full name had been carefully written at the top of my report cards from the second through the eighth grade in the perfect flowing penmanship of my teachers, so I had known from the start that "Linh-Dao Nguyen" was a part of me as much as the "Hammerick" was.

In the other four paragraphs about Vietnam in my history book, I learned that the war was still in progress in 1968, the year of my birth, and that it ended for the Vietnamese in 1975, the year of my second birth at the blue and gray ranch house. I filed these facts away. They were connected to me, but I wasn't connected to them. This pattern would repeat itself as I learned more about Vietnam. Ho Chi Minh, Hanoi, the Tet Offensive, the fall of Saigon. I filed these facts away too. All that I learned about Vietnam had to do with war and death and dying. At the time, I had no body, which meant that I was impervious and had no use for such information. If I were my great-uncle Harper, I would have named the file "Not Applicable."

What I wanted to know about myself I never read in a book in high school, college, or law school. I saw it on television. Three years ago, in 1995, I saw myself, or rather my doppelgänger. He was a British man in his late thirties with thinning blond hair. I had just turned on the television and was about to turn off the sound, but I didn't because of this man's speech pattern. He was fighting with his words. Some were jumping out too quickly and he was trying to impede their progress. Others were reluctant to emerge, and he had to spit them out with deliberate force. As I listened to him, I realized that his speech pattern was in fact no pattern at all. The only things rhythmic about him were his eyes. He blinked them in rapid succession as he paused, stalled, recoiled, and unspooled his words. I lit a cigarette, inhaled, and turned up the volume.

"*Mr. Roland, would you say that living with synesthesia has been disruptive to your to day-to-day life?*" the interviewer asked, her own cadence broadcast-smooth.

"*Would you say that living with your sense of smell or your eyesight has been disruptive to your day-to-day life?*" Mr. Roland asked the interviewer, in lieu of a response.

The camera cut to the interviewer's face as she attempted to process what Mr. Roland had just posed to her. Hoping to make her case in another way, she then asked, "*Can you describe for me the tastes that you experienced as you said those words?*"

"*Certainly. Mashed peas, dried apples, wine gum, weak tea, butter unsalted, Walkers crisps. . . .*" Mr. Roland replied.

What I was experiencing at that moment wasn't an out-of-body experience. It was an in-another-body experience. Everything but this man and me faded into darkness. He and I were at the two ends of a brightly lit tunnel. We were point A and point B. The tunnel was the most direct, straight-line route between the two points. I had never experienced recognition in this pure, undiluted form. It was a mirroring. It was a fact. It was a cord pulled taut between us. Most of all, it was no longer a secret.

I don't remember getting up, but I must have. I do remember kneeling in front of the TV. I touched the image of Mr. Roland's face as his words jumped, swerved, coalesced, attacked, and revealed. As the interview continued, he became more comfortable with the interviewer, and his facial tics and rapid blinking lessened. He masked what he couldn't control by taking long sips from a glass of water (or perhaps the clear liquid was gin). He also turned his head slightly and coughed into his left hand, which provided him with a second or two of privacy. It soon became clear to Mr. Roland and to me that the interviewer wanted him to perform for the camera. After each question-and-answer exchange, the interviewer would ask him for the tastes of her words and then his. Mr. Roland was oddly obliging, much more so than I would have been in his position. I soon realized that his pool of experiential flavors, in other words his actual food intake, was very British and that he didn't venture far from home for his gastronomical needs. "Curry fries" was the most unusual taste that this piano tuner from Manchester listed. The word "employment" triggered it, he told the interviewer. I said "employment" aloud and tasted olives from a can, which meant I tasted more can than olives. I felt more than a tinge of envy.

The interview, which appeared to be taking place inside of Mr. Roland's kitchen, segued to an MRI scan of Mr. Roland's brain, followed by a series of tables and graphs that documented the blood flow to different areas of his brain as he was experiencing a "state of synesthesia." The voiceover, a deep male voice more smug than authoritative, defined synesthesia as a neurological condition that caused the involuntary mixing of the senses.

What a poor choice of words, I thought, and one that Mr. Roland surely must have objected to as well. Is your hearing or your eyesight involuntary? They are automatic and, if you're lucky, always present.

Mr. Roland—not his real name in order to protect his privacy, according to the voiceover—suffered from auditory-gustatory synesthesia. (Suffered? Mr. Roland and I both have dropped dead and are now rolling over in our respective graves. We *suffered* your insult, sir!) The voiceover went on to list other forms of synesthesia—

each combination more fantastical than the next, each combination a couplet (and sometimes even a triplet) to the ingenuity of the human brain.

The voiceover promised a baker in Terre Haute, Indiana, who saw colors when he heard music, every note bringing with it a vivid shade on the color spectrum. There was a flutist in Hamburg, Germany, who experienced flavors as shapes and textures. Her favorite was white asparagus, which was a pleasing hexagonal form with smooth bumps all over its surface. There was a writer in Tuscaloosa, Alabama, who saw all her words in colors because each letter of the alphabet appeared to her in a different hue. According to the voiceover, the name of the writer's hometown, with its preponderance of vowels, which were jewel tones of reds and oranges and pinks, was her favorite word. The Tuscaloosan wrote instruction booklets for a manufacturer of toasters, blenders, food processors, and other small home appliances. Even the voiceover, insensitive as he was, found this fact worthy of further exploration.

The interviewer appeared again on screen, this time walking up to the front door of a suburban house, a minivan parked in the driveway of its attached two-car garage. It could have been anywhere in America. The camera was peering over the interviewer's back as a woman in her mid-forties opened the door and asked the interviewer to come inside. I knew that this had to be the home of the Tuscaloosan. The interior of the house—every visible item within it—was white. The sudden disappearance of colors was disorienting. I thought my television was losing its reception. I thought that the voices of the interviewer and the Tuscaloosan had become quieter and suddenly more difficult to hear, as if they were in the midst of a snowstorm. I even turned up the volume on my television set to compensate for the misperceived muffling. The effect was so jarring and complete because both the Tuscaloosan and the interviewer were dressed in white from head to toe. The former was in a white sundress and the latter in a white pantsuit. The interviewer had dressed according to the request of the Tuscaloosan, who found great comfort in and was therefore very protective of the sanctuary that she had created inside of her own home. The written word was visually stimulating enough, the Tuscaloosan told the interviewer. Of course, not all the letters were pleasing to her—the letter *w* was the color of a rusted car fender and *o* was a ring of green phlegm—but she was always "emotionally stirred by them," as the Tuscaloosan put it. So much so that she often found it overwhelming after a long day of writing and editing at the office to take in the colors of her surrounding world as well. The Tuscaloosan likened it to a butcher who goes home and finds a big piece of steak, a pork loin, and a chicken for dinner every night.

"*The butcher loves what he sells but would rather have tofu on most nights,*" the Tuscaloosan said, smiling shyly at the interviewer.

"*Ms. Cordell, given your chromatolexic synesthesia, the fact that you became a writer seems to me a natural fit. But may I ask why instruction booklets?*" the interviewer asked.

"*You mean why am I not a poet or something more interesting?*" Ms. Cordell shot back, as if she had heard this objection to her chosen genre too many times before.

"*Well, yes. You said earlier that you were emotionally stirred by words. Why not channel that into writing that is more, well, creative?*"

My patience for the interviewer was growing thin. Because the Tuscaloosan's relationship to the written word is different from yours, I wanted to shout at the television set.

"*Because my relationship to the written word is different,*" replied Ms. Cordell. "*I'm moved by letters and words in the way that you may be moved by the colors of a sunset or a field of wildflowers or the inside of a slaughterhouse.*"

Ms. Cordell, almost as obligingly and patiently as Mr. Roland had, explained that sometimes a letter would dominate a word, causing the other letters around them to cower and become dim. The *u* in "instructions," for example. Because of its location right in the middle of the word, its neon-pink glow was the star of the show. The letters in "techniques," however, were more of an ensemble production. The new-grass green of the *t* gave way to the lemon-pie-filling *e* followed by *c*, with its black Labrador sheen.

Ms. Cordell then abruptly stopped her description of the cooperative spirit of "techniques." She must have seen the look in the interviewer's eyes, which I could clearly see too, because the camera was documenting it. I saw there a mixture of fascination and disbelief and pity. I know it was the pity that made Ms. Cordell silent.

Forget about the interviewer. Better yet, pity her. She has only five senses. Go on, Ms. Cordell, tell me what the word *techniques* does to you. It makes me taste cheesecake, graham cracker crust and everything, I wanted to tell her. I lit another cigarette and took a couple of long drags instead.

"*Words are more than little definitions on a page for me. If I wrote a 'beautiful' sentence or a line of a poem, it would be beautiful only to me,*" Ms. Cordell said, after a long pause during which she had closed her eyes and shaken her head from side to side.

I was back in the tunnel of light, and Ms. Cordell was point C.

"*I write this sentence in every booklet: 'Always follow these safety precautions when using this appliance.' I never tire of the sentence because it shimmers with golden light throughout. Do you see what I mean?*"

The interviewer couldn't see what Ms. Cordell meant. Nor could I. Not really. But the difference was that I believed her. The interviewer didn't.

Black-and-white photographs of Ms. Cordell as a young girl were now fading in and out of the screen, as her voice recounted how she had first tried to tell her mother about her world. She was six years old, and her mother slapped her so hard that she fell backward, hitting her head on the linoleum floor. The bump on the back of her head, so tender that it forced her to sleep on her stomach for a week, taught her to keep the colors to herself from then on.

If Leo had walked into our living room at that moment, he would have had me committed. He had just moved into the brownstone, and we were then in the only honeymoon period that we would ever share. On those mornings when he was already up and at the hospital, he left a note on his pillow so I would wake up to a "good morning" from him. During my long days at the firm, he called and left messages with my secretary, requesting that Ms. Hammerick "call her doctor for an appointment." Every day, he brought home small potted plants to fill our windowsills with green growing things. (I made him stop when I learned that they were from the bedsides of patients who had passed away.) Even at this apex of his love for me, Leo would have put me away.

I was on my knees in front of the television, and not only my hands but my face was also pressed against the screen. I was no longer as interested in seeing the images as becoming one with the images. I wanted to give the six-year-old girl who would grow up to be Ms. Cordell—not her real name also to protect her privacy—a hug and tell her about Mr. Roland and me. I knew that the information about our existence would have comforted that little girl in Tuscaloosa because it would have comforted the one in Boiling Springs. I would have written to her that "Tuscaloosa" tasted of candied sweet potatoes, the kind that we southerners served at Thanksgiving, complete with a topping of marshmallows and crushed pineapples. I would have asked her for the colors of the letters *l*, *i*, *n*, *d*, and *a*. She would have written back, her words dipped in proprietary ink, indelible to her, made visible to me.

I stood up and stepped back from the television in order to light my third cigarette in a row. The incomings were returning, and I wanted to experience Ms. Cordell's world and not mine for as long as possible. The photographs of her as a young girl had given way to old home movies. She was in a long dress with a corsage around her wrist, and beside her was a woman who, given the resemblance, must have been her mother. They both had the same pixie nose that seemed out of place in their otherwise serious, angular faces. The voiceover returned to say that synesthesia was hereditary and could be passed along via either the maternal or the paternal side of the family. The condition, according to the voiceover, was most often found in women. There was the sound of a key turning a lock.

Leo was home. I turned off the television and went into the bathroom to put out my cigarette. I was ashamed of both acts.

When Leo moved in, I had agreed to no longer smoke inside of the brownstone. He said smoking would kill me and that the smoke would get into the upholstery of the Knoll split-rail love seat, which had moved into the brownstone along with Leo. (He called it "the Knoll," as in "please don't put your feet on the Knoll!")

The moment I heard Leo at the door I knew that I didn't want him to see Ms. Cordell or Mr. Roland. I didn't want him to diagnose them as delusional or schizophrenic. Nor did I want to see that look of fascination, disbelief, and pity in Leo's eyes. I wanted to continue to love him.

Very early on in our relationship I knew why Leo had fallen in love with me. His reasons were so simple and devastating that I immediately forgot them. I willed myself never to think about them again. For almost eight years, I didn't. But when he told me that he was moving out along with the Knoll and all the other pedigreed pieces of furniture that he had brought with him, I suffered a total recall. He loved me because he loved hearing the sound of his own voice. Or as he had put it at the end of our first date, I was a "reallyl*popcorn* good*cannedpineapple* listener*Americancheese*." That was the simple reason. The devastating reason was that I was rare, probably one of a kind. My southern accent, my Vietnamese face, my Boiling Springs, my Baby Harper, my Yale, my Columbia, my Dolly Parton, my unfettered appreciation for his subpar lovemaking and limited vocabulary of seduction, my love of the Law, my baton twirling, my dance moves, my childhood intimacy with Jesus. Leo had never met anyone else like me. The connoisseur in him found that difficult to resist. Leo was also a perfectionist and, in the end, that part of him opined that I was too flawed to keep. When Leo moved out, the only thing that I didn't regret was my instinctive reaction *not* to share my synesthesia with him. I had withheld and it felt good.

After Leo went to bed that night, I locked myself in the bathroom, turned on the fan, and said "synesthesia" aloud. I tasted capers, which made me follow with "thing," the word that made me taste tomatoes, because the two flavors complemented each other and because I could. I thought about Mr. Roland in Manchester. I wanted to know whether he played this game when no one else was around. Whether he preferred sweets to sours, and what words were most bitter in his mouth. Most of all, I wondered whether he had ever thought about traveling beyond the northwest of England and exploring, perhaps, the sun-drenched coasts of the Mediterranean and the flavors that flourished there. It would do him good, I thought. I said good night to Ms. Cordell and imagined that the dictionary was her favorite book. I thought about the flutist from Hamburg and whether the rest of the program had featured an interview with her or whether she alone had refused to share her world with the grasping-at-straws interviewer and the assume-the-worst voiceover. I thought about this flutist's definitions of "touch" and how they differed from mine. I fell asleep sitting on the floor of the bathroom, my back resting against the tub, thinking about the baker from Terre Haute and whether his record collection was organized spectroscopically.

I knew that I had watched a program on PBS because there had been no commercials. Also, the interviewer, while not particularly astute, didn't have much makeup on and had flyaway hair. In my office the following morning, I checked the TV schedule and found the name of the program. I did some research and found an address to which I wrote away for a transcript and a tape of the show. I had them sent to the firm's address. When they arrived, I read through the transcript and found that I had missed the first third and the last third of the program. The transcript began with the scientific theories on the causes of synesthesia, which were many and which I skimmed. I wasn't interested in the theories. I was interested in the effects. I wanted to know about the flutist and the baker. I knew that Leo would have been horrified by my lack of scientific curiosity, but the theories, the scans, the tables, and the graphs made me feel like a lab rat. Or worse, a person with an incurable disease.

The transcript revealed that the flutist from Hamburg—identified as Mrs. Ostorp but also not her real name; her two daughters had objected to its use, fearing it would violate their privacy—had passed away before an interview with her could take place. Mrs. Ostorp left behind a diary that she had kept since she was fifteen years old. It wasn't a daily diary but more of a compendium to which she would add an entry whenever she encountered a new flavor. Some entries were stunning in their simplicity. A ripe plum was a five-spoked wheel, not polished smooth but worn by use. Some were many pages, with the entry for "labskaus"—a hash of corned beef, potatoes, onions, beets, and salted herrings topped with a fried egg, a gherkin, and pickled herring—at an astounding fourteen and a half pages long. The transcript stated that while Mrs. Ostorp had one of the rarest, or rather the least documented, of the fifty-four known forms of synesthesia, her case would always remain a question mark because she never agreed to a cerebral blood-flow test, which would have documented the changes in her brain metabolism during a state of synesthesia. In other words, there was no proof of Mrs. Ostorp's world except for her words, which couldn't be relied upon. Insufficient. Unreliable. Refutable.

No wonder her daughters didn't want their mother's real name used in the program, I thought. Who would want a liar, a fabulist, a crackpot for a mother? The next time someone tells me the sky is blue or the soup is too salty or the upholstery is nubby or the music is too loud, I'll ask for a cerebral blood-flow test and the resulting tables and graphs. Otherwise, I'll shrug my shoulders and say, "Prove it."

The Terre Haute baker must have thought the same thing because he agreed to an interview but not to scans or tests. According to the transcript, he introduced himself to the interviewer as "Cornelius Henry Harrison, but my friends call me Corny."

I imagined that he looked straight into the camera when he said this, because a man who admitted that his nickname was "Corny" had nothing to hide, I thought.

"Mr. Harrison," the interviewer began, " 'color hearing,' as it's sometimes known, is the form of chromesthesia that you claim to possess. It's one of the most common forms of synesthesia—"

"Common, huh? I'm sorry to disappoint you, but that was how God made me," the baker said, interrupting the interviewer.

"I'm far from disappointed, Mr. Harrison. I'm quite honored to meet someone with your condition. My favorite composer, Olivier Messiaen, also had color hearing. If I may, I'd like to read to you a quote of his and see—well, I don't mean see—but rather to get your reaction."

The interviewer was finally becoming self-conscious of her language. The uncomplicated verb *see* was tripping her up, becoming thick and multilayered and cumbersome, holding on to meanings that weren't her own but that she had to acknowledge were there anyway.

"I don't know who that guy is, but go right ahead," Corny replied.

"Messiaen was a French composer known for compositions that were deeply influenced by his Catholic faith, by Eastern mysticism, and by his synesthesia. According to him, what he saw were, and I quote, 'musician colors, not to be confused with painter's colors. They're colors that go with music. If you tried to reproduce these colors on canvas it may produce something horrible. They're not made for that. . . . What I'm saying is strange but it's true.' "

"Strange but true. That pretty much sums it up," Corny said.

The rest of the interview proceeded in a similar manner. A kind of verbal sparring was occurring between them. The interviewer was ultimately unsuccessful in her efforts to elicit from Corny anything but a matter-of-fact response to what she called his "gift." She ended by asking Corny why he became a baker.

"Because that was what the army taught me to do," Corny replied.

God and the army made him that way, I thought. Case closed, lady!

"But, Mr. Harrison, did you never consider a career in music or, perhaps, as a visual artist?" the interviewer persisted.

"I have a high school diploma. Guys like me, we don't consider careers. We get a job," Corny said.

You're asking him the wrong questions. Ask about the sound of granulated sugar being poured into a stainless-steel bowl, the whirring motor of an electric mixer, or his fist punching down bread dough. A flat, B minor, or C sharp? Or did he prefer music made by others when he worked? If yes, then ask what songs and colors moved this man to make the lightest cakes, the chewiest cookies, breads with tender crusts?

The interviewer's career-counseling advice, ignored and shrugged aside by the Tuscaloosan and Corny, were validated at the end of the program, in a closing segment about famous "synesthetes" who were all writers, composers, or painters. There was Vladimir Nabokov, who, like Ms. Cordell, saw the letters of the alphabet in colors. Nabokov, fluent in Russian, English, and French, made a distinction between the long English *a* and the French *a*. The English one had "the tint of weathered wood" while the French was "polished ebony." The transcript was silent about Nabokov's synesthetic relationship to the letters of the Cyrillic alphabet. Nabokov wrote both in Russian and in English, but the latter was defined as a "foreign" language to him because it wasn't his mother tongue. But what if English was more familiar or felt more like home to Nabokov for reasons that his readers have never considered?

I, fluent in only one language, tasted foreign words only when they sounded to me like a word in English. *Beau,* the French word for "handsome," for example, shared the same incoming as the English word *bow* (as in a decorative knot made of ribbons, not what you would do in front a king). Both words brought to my mouth the taste of MoonPies, one of the better-tasting store-bought delights of my childhood.

I turned the transcript's page and read about Nabokov's "alder-leaf *f*, the unripe-apple of *p*, and pistachio *t*." I longed to see them. I vowed to reread *Lolita*, keeping in mind that every time Nabokov wrote her name it ended with a dollop of pistachio green and a starless night.

There was the painter Wassily Kandinsky, who, like Corny, saw colors when he heard music. But unlike the no-nonsense baker from Terre Haute, the opposite was also true for Kandinsky. When the painter saw colors, he heard musical notes and sounds. Kandinsky, an avid cellist, claimed that the cello was the musical instrument that produced for him the deepest blues.

There was Alexander Scriabin, yet another composer, whom Corny would have no qualms admitting that he had never heard of. I, on the other hand, felt a distinct sense of embarrassment and loss that I had never heard of Scriabin, as if I had failed to meet a member of my own family, an uncle who lived just over the state line or a half brother I should have recognized because we have the same eyes and nose. According to the transcript, the program featured a recording of Scriabin's composition *Prometheus: The Poem of Fire,* as the credits rolled.

I have read and reread the transcript of the program, which was entitled "Synesthesia: Sense Something Different?" (Even PBS couldn't resist the easy puns that littered the landscape of this topic.) I preferred reading the transcript to watching the tape of the program, because with the transcript I could forget about the interviewer's facial expressions and the voiceover's irritating tones and concentrate instead on the specific and intimate worlds that were evoked by each of the synesthetes. I have looked to the transcript for an alternative family tree. I have e-mailed the program's producers asking for the real names and addresses of the piano tuner from Manchester, the instruction-booklet writer from Tuscaloosa, the baker from Terre Haute, and even the two surviving daughters of the flutist from Hamburg. I explained to the producers that I too had synesthesia. My implied message was that privacy surely couldn't be an issue among *us.* I received an e-mail back that stated that the producers would forward my name and contact information to the subjects of the program, thanked me for watching, and would I consider making a contribution to my local PBS station. None of the individuals who were profiled in the program have contacted me. So much for that tunnel of light. It should have been no surprise to me that recognition, like so many other things in life, was subjective. I told myself it was good enough to know that these people existed. I was disappointed all the same.

I have been more successful in getting to know the famous and deceased synesthetes profiled in the program. I have used the transcript as a road map for further research on the lives that they lived. I read Nabokov's memoir, *Speak, Memory,* and pieced together the beginning of *Lolita.* According to Nabokov, the two *l*'s were "noodle-limp" white, and the *o* was an "ivory-backed hand mirror." As for the *i,* Nabokov uncharacteristically left it as a vague member of the family of "yellows." I saw Kandinsky's paintings with names like *Opposing Chords, Funeral March,* and *Fugue* and searched them for the cello's plaintive notes. In *Fugue,* they were in the upper-right-hand corner of the canvas, two fillips of intense blue, perhaps the very notes that Kandinsky described as "calling man towards the infinite." I heard performances of Messiaen's *Quartet for the End of Time,* a chamber piece for clarinet, cello, violin, and piano. Though the composer specified that the *Quartet*'s second movement had "blue-orange chords," followed by "blue and mauve, gold and green, and violet-red, with an overriding quality of steely grey," these colors remained invisible to me. But what I heard made my heart feel as if there was another heart inside of it, a world within a world. Finally, I read about Scriabin's *clavier à lumières,* an instrument that he invented for *Prometheus.* The clavier featured a color-coded keyboard and was played like a piano. Though when the keys were pressed, no musical notes came from the instrument. The clavier instead produced a projection of colored lights. I had a recurring dream that I was in the audience at Carnegie Hall in 1915 when the clavier successfully premiered. I had another dream that during this New York performance of *Prometheus* I was by the composer's bedside as he lay dying in Moscow. Around him were his friends and family who had gathered for an intimate performance of the same composition, complete with a child-size clavier. Scriabin, I dreamed, died hearing *and* seeing.

Chapter 19

WHEN BABY HARPER WAS TWENTY-SEVEN YEARS OLD, THERE WAS a great snowstorm that covered most of the American South. It was remembered as a region-wide state of emergency by the adults of Boiling Springs and treasured as a pageant of fairy-tale-like scenes by their children, who woke up to a world covered in marshmallow fluff and rock candy crystals. These children thought of the witch's house in "Hansel and Gretel," except that they felt not a modicum of fear. Because, unlike those abandoned siblings, these children awoke to find their fathers at home on a weekday and their mothers making hot cocoa. Best of all, they awoke to the prospect of not having to go to school that day and for days to come. So many of their dreams had come true all at once.

Baby Harper, still more boy than man, braved the cold and stumbled through the streets of Boiling Springs marveling at the buildings and houses and how they looked like cakes covered in seven-minute frosting and coconut flakes. When he saw that every branch of every tree was encased in ice, he thought of Cinderella's toes and how they were visible through her perfect-fit glass slippers. Boiling Springs was shut down for days, not a car moving on any of the snow-covered streets. There were only children running and screaming and laughing. It was January 29, but these children all thought of it as another Christmas Day, when their world, wrapped in a thick blanket of white, was a gift.

For the next five days, Baby Harper went out every morning before these children awoke, and he took photographs of the transformed Boiling Springs. He later entered one of his photographs into the Shelby *Star*'s "Blizzard Contest." Entitled *Ice Debutantes,* the black-and-white image was of a grove of trees with their branches so weighed down by snow and ice that they appeared to be gracefully bowing. His photograph lost to one of a snowman in a top hat, which was entitled *Snowman in a Top Hat.* During the longest, hottest days of August, Baby Harper would always show me the photographs that he had taken of the blizzard of 1951. It was my great-uncle's way of practicing mind over body.

The Greyhound bus pulled into Gastonia's Union bus station on August 4, 1998, an hour and twenty-five minutes late. The bus's tinted windows couldn't hide the fact that it was almost noon outside, and the rooftops of the cars, sitting unprotected in the station's parking lot, were radiating waves of heat. The moment I stepped off the bus, I saw Kelly. She was sitting inside her car, its motor idling. The windows were rolled up, and I could see from the movements of her bangs that the air-conditioning was turned up to high. She waved. I waved back and motioned for her to stay. I remembered how she hated the heat, how it gave her rashes in the folds of her stomach and along her inner thighs. She popped open the trunk as I approached the car, and I placed my suitcase inside. The last photograph of herself that Kelly had sent to me was from her college graduation from Gardner-Webb. That was seven years ago, and that was the mental image that I had of her: long blond hair parted to the left, her body a perfect size six, her mother beaming proudly (thinking that the worst was over). The woman waiting for me in the car wasn't the Kelly in that photograph, but the grown-up version of the fat girl who was my dearest friend. Kelly leaned over and gave me a hug. I held on to her for longer than she probably expected, but she didn't pull away. Kelly had omitted from her letters that she had gained back all of her pre–high school weight. Her hair was also no longer bleached and was again the warm strawberry-blond shade that I had combed my fingers through and braided when we were ten, when love was nothing we ever thought of falling into but was something we felt all around us, like the temperature of the air, whenever we were together.

"I can't believe you*cannedgreenbeans* recognized*RCCola* me," Kelly said, her voice muffled against the side of my neck.

"You*cannedgreenbeans* look great*cannedtomatosoup*," I said, letting her out of my embrace.

"My mom*chocolatemilk* hates*NutterButtercookie* it," Kelly said, as she looked into the rearview mirror before backing her car out of its parking space. What she meant was that her mother hated her, again.

"That's all right*Frenchfries* 'cause I hate*NutterButtercookie* your mom*chocolatemilk*," I said.

Kelly let out a quick, sharp laugh. That was what we used to say to each other in the face of maternal neglect and stagnant unpopularity, as if one of us hating back was a force field that could negate and reverse the sting. Sometimes hating back worked and sometimes it didn't. That afternoon, the incantation from our youth lifted Kelly's mood, and she looked over at me and smiled before asking, "Where to first*Pepto-Bismol*, Linda*mint* Hammerick*Dr-Pepper*?"

"I was thinking of Bridges*creamcheeseDanish* for lunch*unripebanana*," I replied. "But what*grahamcracker* time*cottagecheese* do*grits* you*cannedgreenbeans* have to head*corndog* back*watermelon* to work*NillaWafer*?"

"I don't," Kelly said. "I took the day*hardboiledeggyolk* off in your honor*boiledcabbage.* Also, I'd no*grapejelly* idea*Swisscheese* when your bus would*candiedapple* actually*strawberryyogurt* get here*hard-boiledegg.* Don't you*cannedgreenbeans* want*saltedbutter* to stop*cannedcorn* by your mom's*chocolatemilk* place*roastturkey* first*Pepto-Bismol*?"

"I told her I was on a later*pimentocheese* bus. So I'm not due*grits* in till tonight*banana,*" I said.

"Linda*mint,* I know*grapejelly* she's been really*popcorn* looking for*Triscuit*ward to your visit," Kelly said. "She called me twice*spaghettisauce* last*blackpepper* night*banana* to remind*deviledegg* me to pick*M&M's* you*cannedgreenbeans* up*FrootLoopscereal.* You*cannedgreenbeans* know*grapejelly* she can't drive*cannedbakedbeans* at night*banana* now, right*Frenchfries*?"

"That's why I told her I would*candiedapple* be arriving at night*banana.* I didn't want*saltedbutter* her pick*M&M's*ing me up*FrootLoopscereal.*"

"Wow."

"What*grahamcracker*?"

"You*cannedgreenbeans* haven't changed," Kelly said, swallowing a small somersaulting sound.

"Kelly*cannedpeaches*? Did you*cannedgreenbeans* just hiccup*meatloaf*?" I asked.

Kelly didn't tell me until I had placed my order for a pulled pork sandwich, coleslaw, fries, extra sauce, and Cheerwine that she had been a vegetarian for the past four years. There were three items on the Bridges menu that a vegetarian could eat: hushpuppies and the aforementioned slaw and fries. Kelly ordered all three and a diet 7UP. I asked her in jest whether she had become an atheist too. Renouncing pork was the equivalent of renouncing God in our part of the country. She laughed that off, and we ate the rest of our lunch in silence. I was eating too quickly to talk, making loud, appreciative noises that prompted the two elderly men in the booth in front of us to turn around and stare. Kelly was silent because she knew that I had quit smoking, which meant that the incomings were unmitigated and that I would appreciate a break from talking. After my last bite, I wiped sauce from the corners of my mouth, and Kelly asked me whether I wanted to stop by the liquor store before heading over to Baby Harper's.

"I haven't had a drink*EskimoPie* since the surgery*bottledItalian-dressing*," I said.

"You*cannedgreenbeans* don't mind*apple* if I drink*EskimoPie*, do*grits* you*cannedgreenbeans*?" Kelly asked.

"You*cannedgreenbeans* didn't mind*apple* that I ate pork*Tabcola* in front*grapejuice* of you*cannedgreenbeans*, did you*cannedgreenbeans*?" I replied.

We drove to the liquor store, and Kelly came back to the car with a bottle of tequila, a bottle of gin, and two bottles of bourbon. They were having a sale, she told me, as she placed the bag on the backseat. My best friend was an overweight, thrifty, vegetarian lush, I thought. Kelly had failed to mention these developments in her letters to me. I expected that there would be other revelations as well.

The twenty-minute drive from Shelby to Boiling Springs felt eternal, which was different from feeling like an eternity. Eternal was the feeling that the journey was ongoing and would continue whether you were along for the ride or not, that there was no hurry to reach your destination because your destination would patiently await you. The occupants in a car heading toward the ocean often experienced this feeling, which coincided with the moment when the salt air reached their nostrils. They knew then that the ocean was there but not yet in sight. Their anticipation would relax into inevitability, and their journey would become for them the reason for the drive. The ocean, they knew, could wait. Boiling Springs could wait as well. Kelly may have missed a turn or two, taking us in a wide loop around Shelby, along roads that were bordered on either side by fields of sweet potatoes, their heart-shaped leaves levitating low to the ground. The speed at which we were traveling may have slowed, tractors passing our car on the two-lane roads. We began to shiver in the car's circulated air, which hovered at sixty-eight degrees, while outside the black-tarred roads softened under the August sun. Kelly was behind the wheel, and I was riding shotgun. The moment seemed eternal and familiar, but it wasn't. Because by the time that Kelly had gotten her driver's license, our friendship in high school was strictly that of two pen pals. We were no longer by each other's side, in each other's physical company. Kelly and I were now reenacting these lost summers of our teens, the summers that we would have driven on these same roads, the car radio blasting, as opposed to the silence that we found ourselves in now.

"Kelly*cannedpeaches*?" I asked.

"Yes, Ms. Hammerick*DrPepper*," Kelly replied, a smile on her face.

"Why didn't you*cannedgreenbeans* come*applebutter* to my grand*potatosalad*mother's funeral?" I asked.

The question came from a place so deep within me that I hadn't anticipated its formation. I was taken by surprise, but Kelly wasn't. She kept on driving, hands at ten and two. Her response came slowly but fully formed, as if she had been thinking about it for a long time.

When my grandmother had her third heart attack in February of '87, Kelly was already back in Boiling Springs and enrolled at Gardner-Webb. During that week in between Iris's passing and her funeral, when we were all waiting for magnolias in the freezing cold, I didn't see or hear from Kelly. At Iris's funeral, I saw Kelly's mother, Beth Anne, and her father, Carson junior, but I didn't see her. I returned to New Haven, and after several months of not writing I sent Kelly a letter with the newspaper clipping of me smoking in front of Sterling Memorial Library. I never brought up my best friend's absence, nor did she.

Kelly made the correct turns now. The kudzu-covered trees and telephone polls were becoming a blur. We were finally heading with intention and speed into Boiling Springs. By the time that we pulled into the driveway of the Greek Revival, Kelly told me that she had been ashamed.

"Ashamed*cannedchickennoodlesoup*? Of what*grahamcracker*?" I asked. "You*cannedgreenbeans* mean*raisin* of Luke*greenbeancasserole*?"

"No*grapejelly*," Kelly replied, shaking her head. "Luke*greenbeancasserole* says hi*greenLifesavers*, by the way*cannedpears*—"

"You*cannedgreenbeans* two have been in touch*cannedvegetablesoup*?" I blurted out, interrupting her.

"I was go*boiledcarrots*ing to tell*brownsugar* you*cannedgreenbeans* but—" Kelly began.

"Jesus*friedchicken*, Kelly*cannedpeaches*!" I said, interrupting her again. "What*grahamcracker* the hell have you*cannedgreenbeans* told me? What fuck*limesherbet*ing else hasn't been in your letters?"

"Don't get angry*jellydoughnut* with me, Linda*mint*. You*cannedgreenbeans* know*grapejelly* that when your grand*potatosalad*mother passed away*cannedpears*, every*Ritzcracker*thing*tomato* was already*orangejuice* so different*Listerine* for me. Are you*cannedgreenbeans* ready*orangejuice* to go*boiledcarrots* in now?" Kelly asked.

"No*grapejelly*," I replied.

"All right*Frenchfries*," Kelly said. "It's cooler in here*hardboiledegg* than in the house*freshpeaches* any*rice*way*cannedpears*. I can't believe your great*cannedtomatosoup*-uncle*dates* never*bubblegum* installed any*rice* air-con—"

"Tell*brownsugar* me why you*cannedgreenbeans* were ashamed*cannedchickennoodlesoup*, Kelly*cannedpeaches*. I just don't understand*eggnoodles*," I said.

"Linda*mint*, you*cannedgreenbeans* may have for*Triscuit*gotten this, but you*cannedgreenbeans* had gone off to Yale*avocado*. I was stuck at Gardner-Webb*cannedfruitcocktail*. Do you*cannedgreenbeans* remember*butterpecanicecream* what*grahamcracker* we used to call it? The Intellectual*BLT* Pimple*honeydewmelon* of the Carolinas*cannedpeas*," Kelly replied.

"We did not!"

"We did, Linda*mint*."

"Jesus*friedchicken*—"

"Yeah, well, I'm pretty*grilledcheesesandwich* sure*cannedtuna* Jesus*friedchicken* would*candiedapple* call it that too," Kelly said, followed by a familiar sound, a spastic little intake of air.

This time I knew. Baby Harper was there, welcoming me home, mind over body.

We stepped inside the Greek Revival and were met by the smells of witch hazel, burned coffee, and lemon Pledge in the air. Or more likely, these smells were in the upholstery and the curtains. Baby Harper had lived in this house since he was thirty years old. Back then, young men of his age had wives and children and a mortgage. But before moving to the Greek Revival, Baby Harper was living in the green-shuttered colonial, the house where he had been born. His sister, Iris, and his brother-in-law, Walter Wendell, weren't really sad to see him go, seeing how he was just going down the street from them. His niece, DeAnne, probably counted the days, on her fingers and toes, till his departure. When Baby Harper moved into the Greek Revival, he had his cameras, his photo albums, his books, his records, his record player, his clothes, his wigs, and a set of pots and pans that Iris had given him for his thirtieth birthday. He lived in the Greek Revival without furniture until he acquired the pieces one by one with the help of the classified ads in the Shelby *Star*. The first piece of furniture that he purchased was a divan, which doubled as his bed for a while. The divan was covered in a faded peach-colored damask, which Baby Harper said looked like the color of sadness itself. He replaced the damask with a rich green velvet and began to build a life around it. He was living alone or as a "confirmed bachelor," as men like him were known back then. He told himself that he wasn't afraid of such words. He put Bill Haley's "Rock Around the Clock" on the record player, and he danced until sweat rolled down the side of his face. That was in 1954, when he had no idea what the rest of his life would have in store for him.

"Do*grits* you*cannedgreenbeans* want*saltedbutter* to see it?" Kelly asked, her body already headed upstairs toward Baby Harper and Cecil's bedroom.

Ever since Kelly wrote to me about it, I had wanted to see Cecil and Baby Harper's bedroom with my own eyes. When I was growing up, I never thought to see it. Why would I? It was only where my great-uncle slept at night. I didn't know that his bedroom was an Easter egg, a Fabergé egg, the yolk of an egg, the surprise center of this dear man.

"Has DeAnne*cannedcranberrysauce* seen it?" I asked.

"No*grapejelly*."

"Really*popcorn*?"

"Really*popcorn*. She comes*applebutter* over here*hardboiledegg* every*Ritzcracker* week, but only for a cup*macaroniandcheese* of coffee and to bring me a casserole*poundcake*—"

"Really*popcorn*?" I asked, amused by Kelly's weekly exposure to the curse of my childhood.

"Really*popcorn*."

"I'm so sorry*glazeddoughnut*, Kelly*cannedpeaches*," I said, laughing out loud.

"Me too," she replied. "I keep*Hardee'shamburger* tell*brownsugar*ing your mom*chocolatemilk* that I'm a vegetarian*garlic*, but she keeps*Hardee'shamburger* on bringing over this stuff*pigsinablanket* that tastes like beef."

"Beefy macaroni*lemonmeringuepie*?" I asked.

"Oh, my God*walnut*, yes! Beefy macaroni*lemonmeringuepie*."

We were both laughing so hard by now that Kelly was making snorting noises and I was tearing up.

As so many of my letters to Kelly had been devoted to the terrible things that DeAnne did to food in our kitchen, Kelly had done everything that she could to avoid DeAnne's cooking. Our sleepovers at the blue and gray ranch house always began after the dinner hour. Our sleepovers at the Powells' red brick house, on the other hand, always began precisely at the dinner hour. For all of her shortcomings as a mother, Beth Anne Powell was very respectable in the kitchen, as was evident by the size of her husband and her daughter (before the age of fourteen). Because the food at their dinner table didn't repulse or bore them, the Powells had the habit of lingering over their evening meals. The Powells ate a lot, and they ate it slowly. They weren't messy, crumbs-falling-from-their-mouths kind of people. Most of the time, like my family, they didn't talk. There was only a steady chewing, and sometimes Carson junior would let out what sounded a lot like a moan. He was a man who enjoyed what was happening in his mouth. When I first ate dinner over at the Powells', I was embarrassed for Kelly's father for these noises that came rolling out of his mouth whenever he would open it up to fork in more food. Then I understood that these noises meant that he was happy.

"Your mom*chocolatemilk* thinks that she's imposing*pepperoni* by having me stay here*hardboiledegg*," Kelly continued. "I've told her that the rent on my place*roastturkey* is cheap*apricotnectar*, and the rent here*hardboiledegg* is, you know*grapejelly*, free*ChipsAhoy!cookie*. But she keeps*Hardee'shamburger* on bringing over the casseroles*poundcake* any*riceway**cannedpears*. To thank me, I think. And, like I've said, she usually has some coffee and then she goes. She really*popcorn* hasn't shown any*rice* interest in seeing the rest*Twinkie* of the house*freshpeaches*."

Curiosity has never been a strong suit of DeAnne's, I thought, and then decided not to say it aloud. Because making fun of DeAnne's cooking was one thing, but making fun of her intellect seemed to me suddenly cruel.

Standing there in the entryway of my great-uncle's house, a

staircase away from his and Cecil's bedroom, I had another revelation. Their bedroom was a bedroom, just a part of their day-to-day life together. It was a museum now. It could wait.

"Kelly*cannedpeaches,* could you*cannedgreenbeans* drive*cannedbakedbeans* me home*Pepsi* now?" I asked.

Chapter 20

George Moses was already known in Chapel Hill for his poems when Professor Ma'am, as George Moses called her, taught him how to read and write. She thought it only right that someone teach the alphabet to the slave-poet so that he could write his poems down for himself. She began their lessons with the Bible, but it soon became clear to her that George Moses already knew the Book of Genesis by heart. She turned next to the secular Genesis of America: the Declaration of Independence. George Moses thought that this document had a lot of good ideas in it. Professor Ma'am explained to him that the ideas were, in fact, the ideals of their country. George Moses thought Professor Ma'am was addled or perhaps just a wishful thinker. That night, though, George Moses cried himself to sleep, thinking about the beautiful words that Professor Ma'am had read to him. At their next lesson, she showed George Moses a book about the history of this Declaration. She read, pointing to each word so that he could follow along, about the signers of the Declaration and about its first public reading in the city of Philadelphia on July 8, 1776, when a great bell had rung out beforehand. George Moses didn't know it, but he would see this bell for himself.

One day Professor Ma'am showed George Moses a publication entitled *Liberty*. Its frontispiece featured an illustration of the bell, which had by then become a symbol for another kind of freedom. George Moses said those three words aloud and recognized in them the beginning of a poem. Professor Ma'am then announced to the slave-poet that she, along with like-minded folks in Chapel Hill, were going to buy him his freedom and send him to a free state to live. They would do it by publishing his poems in a book, the proceeds of which surely would be enough to satisfy his master's asking price. George Moses kept silent as his benefactress detailed the plan that, if successful, would separate him from everyone whom he had ever loved. His mother. His brother. His sisters. George Moses's heart was heavy with grief and desire.

George Moses's book, *The Hope of Liberty*, was published and sold. When all the funds were collected, the amount wasn't enough for George Moses's master. James Horton wasn't a greedy man. He was a spiteful man. Spite, George Moses should have known, was worth more to those who possessed it than any amount of money. Professor Ma'am, who didn't know such things about the world, cried when she told the slave-poet that his master had refused to sell him even though the governor of North Carolina himself had spoken on George Moses's behalf. George Moses thought that this was the end of the story, that he would die as he had lived, a slave in the slave state of North Carolina.

War changed everything.

Fates fell on the battlefield. Masters became men again. Property became men and women and children again too.

George Moses, a sixty-nine-year-old poet, packed what he had, which was a couple of books and a wool suit for the colder clime, and headed for Philadelphia, where the Liberty Bell had rung for him at last. He waved goodbye to his loved ones in Chapel Hill and said, "Come and visit me!"

And they did.

I met DeAnne Whatley Hammerick for the first time when she was sixty-six years old. I knocked on the front door of the house where I grew up, and she answered it. She had lived there all along, and now she lived there all alone. She had had ash-blond hair, so it was difficult for me to tell, especially in the strong light of the afternoon sun, that her hair had turned completely white. She wore it short, which made her look a bit like the British actress Judi Dench. She had on a pink and white gingham shirt, a pair of khaki pants, and white slip-on tennis shoes. From head to toe, she appeared to be what she was, an upper-middle-class white woman, comfortable and at home.

You're here early, Linda! Come on in. You're letting all the cold air out. That was what DeAnne would have said to me.

You're here early, Linda! Come on in. We're letting all the cold air out. That was what the woman who answered the door of the blue and gray ranch house said to me.

The first difference was in the pronoun used. "We" never existed between DeAnne and me. She avoided it as assiduously as she avoided the word "mom." She called me "Linda," and "you"; once, when I was fifteen and had just dyed all my clothes black, she called me "your daughter." My father slowly said these two words back to her to remind her that she had signed the adoption papers as well. The second difference was the intonation. DeAnne's would have been surprised followed by accusatory. This woman's tone was surprised followed by a touch of humor. The third difference was in her eyes. DeAnne's were blue glass. This woman's eyes were like Iris's in the years before she passed away, fog rolling over a lake. The fourth difference was that DeAnne would have smelled of cigarettes. This woman had the scent of someone familiar to me. It was witch hazel. My great-uncle was here too, I thought.

I pulled my suitcase into the hallway. The table with the three spindly legs was still there, on it a stack of incoming mail awaiting attention. To my left was the dining room table, where our family had so suddenly stopped eating our dinners together, and the sideboard, where the store-bought cakes and pies had sat in their paper boxes. To my right was the living room couch, where Baby Harper and Iris had sat when we first met, and the easy chair, where my father had watched the evening news. The curtains, the carpeting, the paint on the walls, the bones and skins of the house were all the same. It was possible that I had missed this house more than the one occupant who remained. I knew the house better.

DeAnne Whatley Hammerick and I got to know each other the same way that any two strangers who meet in a foreign city would have. We asked each other questions and we answered them. We did so slowly and methodically and with a sense of purpose because we understood, without having to say so, that when we parted company we wouldn't see each other again for a very long time.

We began in front of the TV. I played for DeAnne Whatley Hammerick the tape of the PBS program about synesthesia. I asked her to pay special attention to Mr. Roland. I knew that we had to begin there in order to set the pacing of our conversations to come. Otherwise, how would she understand the hourly breaks that I would need or the days of silence that would interrupt us and sequester me inside my bedroom?

Long after I had gone to bed that night, DeAnne Whatley Hammerick stayed up. I found her asleep the next morning in the easy chair. I made some coffee for us, and then I woke her. She said that she had watched the program four times. I nodded my head to acknowledge that fact. I had no idea what that fact would mean for us. Then she asked me whether it hurt. I explained again to her that I didn't experience shapes and textures the way that Mrs. Ostorp did. DeAnne Whatley Hammerick shook her head and said that wasn't what she was asking me. What she wanted to know was how much did it hurt me not to be believed.

DeAnne Whatley Hammerick told me that when she was a young girl she tried to tell her mother about these little pieces of paper with writing on them that she found in her bed. Every morning, she would find a new one. Every morning, she would try to show it to Iris, but by the time that she got her young mother's attention the note would have disintegrated into a ball of pulp. Iris then would scold her for being unkempt and scrub her tiny hands clean of their bits of paper and ink stains.

We sat at the kitchen table staring into our cups of coffee. Outside, Boiling Springs was about to earn its name, as it did on most August days. We felt the heat and the humidity pushing themselves into the house, past the windows and the doors, as strong and blustery as any winter storm. We felt lucky to be inside. We looked forward to September, when the outside temperature and the inside one would begin to switch places. We would embrace the warm air then and beckon it to our sides, pushing the cold drafts out into the open.

This was how we began all our mornings together. I would wake up first and make us a pot of coffee. DeAnne Whatley Hammerick would join me in the kitchen and make us a breakfast that involved no cooking. Bowls of milk and cereal, tubs of yogurt, halves of a grapefruit. Then we would begin to talk. At first, her words were tentative and shy. She tried to use the fewest possible words to convey her thoughts. She was conscious of how she had only partial control over their effect on me. She was self-aware and self-editing almost to the point of silence.

I reminded her that I had lived with my condition for as long as I could remember, and what that meant was I knew when to say when. (It was like knowing when to close my eyes at the scariest moments in a movie or when to walk away from the all-you-can-eat buffet.) I tried to assuage her concerns by sharing with her words with incomings that I adored and craved. I told her "mom" tasted of chocolate milk. DeAnne, when she had heard this fact, had told me to hush my mouth. DeAnne Whatley Hammerick looked at me and asked low-fat or whole.

We missed Baby Harper. He was our next topic of discussion. She said that she had started using witch hazel as a toner on her face every morning so that the scent of him would be in the house still. I told her I thought it was a good idea, and I started doing the same, which made his presence seem even stronger in the recirculated air of the air-conditioned house. We knew that we wanted to give him a memorial service and that he wouldn't mind that it was many months late. I told her about his filing system and about the folder labeled "The End," which we would need to consult to make the arrangements. Of course, we would use the Cecil T. Brandon Home of Eternal Rest. The new owners, Clay and Gregory, when they first moved to Shelby, had stopped by the blue and gray ranch house to pay their respects. Clay looked exactly like a younger version of his uncle Cecil, so much so that DeAnne Whatley Hammerick said that she screamed when she opened the front door. Gregory ran toward their car, which was parked on the street in front of the house. Clay just stood there, calm as clover, because this had happened to him before. Folks in the greater Boiling Springs–Shelby area were so taken by the family resemblance that some even joked that Mister T didn't pass away—he just went to South America and came back with a facelift. DeAnne Whatley Hammerick let out a quick, sharp laugh after she told me this. Kelly at the age of thirteen and smart girls everywhere would have recognized this woman as one of their own. DeAnne wouldn't have found that joke the least bit amusing. For a second, I wasn't sure that I found the joke amusing either. Then I laughed out loud.

Baby Harper had asked for no fresh flowers, so we compromised and filled the smaller of the two chapels at the Home of Eternal Rest with potted plants, mostly bromeliads, in honor of Baby Harper's favorite southern continent, the point of origin of these sturdy but florid tropical plants. Clay said that he could donate them afterward to a retirement home nearby and that none of the plants would go to waste. We all thought that Baby Harper would have approved of the compromise.

When Clay and I first met, over a home-cooked meal at the Craftsman bungalow that he shared with Gregory, he said that I looked like the childhood photographs that they had seen of me.

"We liked you best with your long hair and we're glad to see you wearing it that way again," Gregory added, as he poured me another glass of wine.

Gregory and Clay must have known that I was wearing a wig now, but they were polite southern gentlemen who, if they wanted to (and they did), could compliment a sow covered in mud.

After my surgery, my body had undergone what my OB/GYN called an "abrupt" menopause, which brought with it a host of unpleasant, to say the least (which *is* my forte, after all), symptoms, including partial hair loss. Kelly, of course, hadn't said a word to me about my wig. Just like I hadn't said a word to her about her weight gain. She, though, had known to expect the mane of long black hair because I had written to her when I decided to buy it. I told her that my own hair was becoming so thin that it was just easier this way. One less thing to think about in the morning, I wrote. "Asian women," I added, "are the main providers of the raw products needed for high-quality human hair wigs anyway!" What I meant was that I could be related to my wig.

As for DeAnne Whatley Hammerick, she must have known too, but like so many of the things between us, I was waiting for her to bring it up first, and she was probably waiting for me to do the same.

I took another sip of wine and politely asked Gregory if he had any Scotch in the house. I wasn't supposed to drink alcohol with the anti-anxiety medication that I was taking, but that night I had to. I wanted to be able to converse for as long as possible with Clay and Gregory, these two men who seemed to me to be sent from

God. Gregory, in fact, looked a bit like Jesus with a beer belly and a mullet. So much so, that I had blushed when he had answered the door of the bungalow.

I had missed out on seeing my great-uncle's life with Cecil. I knew that in front of me that night were two different men, but still one of them was a gay southern funeral director. I figured *this* was as close as I was going to get at a second chance. By the end of the evening in their company, I understood that it was better than a second chance. What I was seeing in Clay and Gregory was a caring, functioning relationship, not just the ghost of one.

Clay and Gregory had invited DeAnne Whatley Hammerick to dinner that night as well. She had telephoned them right away when we received their handwritten invitation, complete with a proposed menu, in the mail. She said that while she did love Gregory's grilled trout, she would have to decline this time. Linda, however, is very pleased to accept, she said on my behalf. I think it's best that you young folks get to know one another without me underfoot, she explained to me after she hung up the phone.

We did get to know one another, and as it turned out, Clay and Gregory already had had a head start.

After Gregory's compliment, sweet but a bit too revealing, Clay quickly chimed in that they had seen childhood photos of me in my great-uncle's albums. "I hope you're not offended that we looked through them. We were just trying to get to know Uncle Cecil and Harper better," Clay explained.

"We didn't see any photos of Harper but we saw a lot of you," Gregory added.

"We always meant," Clay resumed, "to spend more time with my uncle and Harper, but you know how life gets. Too busy, too tired, too late. Those two invited us to Thanksgiving dinner I don't even know how many times."

There was a long pause, as if Clay was trying to remember exactly why they, like me, had never made it to the table at the Greek Revival.

"Fayetteville is so close, and we still somehow managed to, excuse my French, fuck it up," Gregory finally said, finishing the thought for Clay.

We all drank more wine and I had some Scotch. We traded stories of our misspent youths in North Carolina. I vowed to eat at their home as often as possible in the time that I had left in Boiling Springs. As promised, on the menu that night was grilled trout served with a fresh spinach salad, which was wilted right before serving with a warm bacon vinaigrette. When there was nothing remaining on the table that we could consume, Clay went into the kitchen and returned with a lemon meringue pie and an antique silver server. The three of us knew exactly what was going on. We were trying to get to know one another *and* the ghosts of Cecil and Baby Harper at the same time. We wished that we had all met under different circumstances.

Sometime after midnight, when the outside world was all hush and stars, I said goodbye to Clay and Gregory. I promised them that I would stop by the next day with some photo albums of my great-uncle Harper and Cecil that they hadn't yet seen.

The caterer from Asheville arrived early in the morning to set up in the Home of Eternal Rest's kitchen. DeAnne Whatley Hammerick thought it best to have the memorial service and the lunch in one place, as the people who had known Baby Harper were getting on in years and would appreciate the "one-stop mourning." Another quick, sharp laugh from this woman who had inherited Iris's sense of humor, but it was less like battery acid and more like a splash of cider vinegar.

We arrived an hour ahead of time to have coffee with Clay and Gregory. They wanted to respect Cecil's wishes about not having a funeral or memorial service, but we all agreed that Cecil was a part of Baby Harper's life. Therefore, Cecil wouldn't mind if his photograph was displayed at the front table alongside the few photographs that we had of Baby Harper when he was a boy. Clay and I had discussed whether or not to include a photograph from their travels together in South America. We decided that those images were private, which we told each other was different from saying that they were secret. I admitted to Clay that I hadn't shown them to DeAnne Whatley Hammerick yet. Clay said that he didn't think that was necessary. We *all* have a right to a private life, Linda. Not everything has to be shared or shared right away, Clay told me.

We had mailed out thirty-five invitations and placed a notice in the Shelby *Star.* A hundred and twenty-seven people attended the memorial service for Harper Evan Burch. Clay opened up the sliding walls between the two chapels, and we were able to accommodate them all. Kelly pulled me aside, and we went into the kitchen, where she handed me a flask. It was full of vodka. Then she gave me a breath mint. Kelly was prepared; she was a Boy Scout of a drunk. I was grateful that one of us was ready. I took a swig and a mint, and then asked the caterer if they could supplement what they had made with orders of barbecue from Bridges. Phone calls were quickly made, cars were dispatched for the pickup, extra plates and cutlery were set out, more tea was brewed, sweetened, and iced, and bottles of Cheerwine and Dr Pepper added to the refrigerator.

The memorial service itself was brief. DeAnne Whatley Hammerick spoke. Then I spoke. We tried not to say the cliché things that were said in honor of the dead. We didn't succeed. We said we loved him. We said we missed him. We said we knew that he was enjoying his time now in Heaven. Then we handed out the lyrics to Patsy Cline's "He Called Me Baby," and we all sang a rousing tribute to him.

Now each night, in dreams, just like a song
I still hear baby, baby
Still hear baby, baby
Still hear baby, baby, all night long.

We drew out the last word, fitting inside the last *o* everything that we weren't eloquent enough to say about Harper Evan Burch. Then we ate.

We had been able to smell Bridges's vinegary sauce, its sharp notes tickling our noses, as we sat in the chapel. We knew what was awaiting us, and we knew that it would be good. The food that the caterer had prepared for the estimated thirty-five guests was served as the appetizers: dainty pimento-cheese sandwiches—made not with white sandwich bread but with a brioche loaf, which started a wave of "Oh, my!" and "Oh, dear!" among those of my great-uncle's generation who weren't quite sure that they approved of the substitution but eagerly ate the sandwiches anyway, bite-size buttermilk biscuits with thin slivers of baked ham, little tureens of summer squash casserole. I had ordered that dish for Kelly, the lone vegetarian in a sea of pork eaters. It was also a veiled reference to our childhood nemesis Sally Campbell, who, beautiful as she might have been and still may be, would always be to us a member of the humble squash family.

Later that night, we the remaining family gathered at the Greek Revival, and we danced.

DeAnne Whatley Hammerick sat on the green velvet divan. At first, she blushed at the sight of two men dancing. Then she tapped her stocking feet. The pitchers of mint julep that Gregory made for us had encouraged her to take off her shoes. I complimented her on the bright red nail polish on her toes, adding that I had never seen them painted before. I could have added that I had never seen her drinking alcohol before either, but I thought that would make her self-conscious and forestall further metamorphosis. She leaned in and whisper-yelled that BABY HARPER had worn this very shade ON HIS TOES. Something about that divan always encouraged confessions and revelations, I thought. Or perhaps it was the julep. Either way, we raised our glasses, hers full of julep and mine full of sweet tea, both garnished with sprigs of mint from the garden. She pointed to the leaves and asked me what I was doing in her drink. Kelly, who was sitting next to me, let out a single hiccup.

DeAnne Whatley Hammerick and I looked at each other and we thought the same thing. Baby Harper had decided to stay in the Greek Revival for a little while longer.

At the memorial service, Kelly had two of my great-uncle's cameras hanging around her neck. When she lifted a camera up to her face, she was secure in the knowledge that it would hide her as sure as a veil. She spent the afternoon discreetly photographing all of the attendees, men and women I had never seen before but who all had known Baby Harper well enough to miss his presence on earth.

DeAnne Whatley Hammerick and I asked Kelly to live in the Greek Revival for as long she would like. Cecil, who had shared the house with Baby Harper beginning in 1987, never gave up having a house of his own, which was the Craftsman bungalow that Clay had inherited as part of his uncle's estate. This explained why I hadn't seen much evidence of Cecil around the Greek Revival. The decor was all Baby Harper. Like his uncle, Clay wasn't really a Greek Revival sort of man. Clay seemed lost in the grandly proportioned rooms and around green velvet. So while Clay and Gregory had a firm claim, morally if not legally, to half of the Greek Revival, they had no interest in it. I could tell that they doted on Kelly and would rather see her ensconced there as well. The four of us danced that night to a stack of 45's, the needle skipping their worn grooves. DeAnne Whatley Hammerick curled up on the divan and slept, snoring softly.

What would Iris have thought, I wondered. Here was her sixty-six-year-old daughter, drunk and shoeless and sleeping in the living room. Here was her thirty-year-old granddaughter, hair flying, sweat dripping down, dancing up a summer rainstorm with her fat best friend and two gay men.

My grandmother Iris was named for the *Iris prismatica*, a flower more commonly known as the slender blue flag. From the moment of her birth, her eyes had reminded her mother and father of this flower's dazzling hue. The problem, which neither of her parents had anticipated, was that the name also meant that she had only one eye. Iris was a Cyclops for the rest of her life. She saw not the world but only her narrowed worldview, which in the end diminished us all. Iris, may God forgive me for thinking this, but I'm glad that you are no longer with us.

Chapter 21

From the Greek *syn*, meaning "together," and *aisthesis*, meaning "perception," the word "synesthesia" was the scientific name for my condition and the key to a mystery. I was happy to have the key, but it didn't roll off my tongue. I couldn't use the word "synesthesia" to explain my very specific relationship to the world in the same way that someone else would use "achromatopsia" to refer to his or her color blindness or "amusia" to communicate his or her inability to recognize or process music. Perhaps I just needed to live longer with the word. I have been synesthetic for many more years than I have known a name for it. Maybe it was this asymmetry in years that explained why I felt that the word couldn't possibly hold enough within it the entire body of my experiences. Perhaps it was also my discomfort with the easy language of labels and names. Was I not proof that they were often inaccurate, insufficient, or incapable of full disclosure?

A mystery could be an unknown set of facts or a known set of facts that had been kept secret. Often the holder of a secret would claim that he or she was protecting something or someone more valuable than the set of facts itself. Often this claim wasn't the full truth, which wasn't the same as a lie. We kept secrets to protect, but the ones most shielded—from shame, from judgment, from the slap in the face—were ourselves. We were selfish in our secret-keeping and rarely altruistic. We acted out of instinct and survival, and only when we felt safest would we let our set of facts be known.

Kelly and I wrote long letters to each other. We hand-delivered them now because we wanted to see each other as much as possible while I was back in Boiling Springs. During the week, I would meet Kelly for lunch at her office at Gardner-Webb. Sometimes I would borrow DeAnne Whatley Hammerick's car and sometimes DWH—that was what Kelly and I called her in our letters now—would drop me off on her way to run an errand or visit with her coterie of friends.

These friends were the women who had been the first to marry and to have children, and they had watched as DWH was the first among them to become a widow. At first they felt sorry for DWH. Then they envied her. Some now had lost their husbands too, but in other ways. A younger woman or a weak heart, surprisingly, wasn't the most common reason. Golf, fishing, and televised sports more often accounted for the absences and the abandonments. After a lifetime of competing with one another via the accomplishments of their husbands, these women one by one found themselves without these men. They looked to DWH for guidance on what to do next. They joined her at her weekly water aerobics class at the Gardner-Webb gymnasium. They liked how the water's resistance felt against their skin. Like a caress, they thought. They laughed when DWH insisted that their skin wasn't wrinkled, only puckered from being in the water too long. They read the same novels that DWH did, and then they gathered in one another's homes and watched the film adaptations, which most of them preferred. They cut their hair short like a boy's and asked themselves why they hadn't done it sooner. Their exposed napes thrilled them, like teenage girls baring flat, toned midriffs. Beth Anne, Kelly's mom, was one of these women. She had lost her husband to the law firm of Fletcher Burch or, rather, to its latest incarnation. After my father passed away, her husband, Carson junior, had taken over as the firm's managing partner. In 1993, he merged the firm with a larger one based in Raleigh, which had 120 lawyers statewide. Gone were the days of Carson junior arriving home at 5:30 P.M. for dinner and never working on Saturdays. At first, Beth Anne turned to Pastor Reynold for guidance. He suggested that she consider missionary work. Spreading the Gospel of Jesus Christ to sub-Saharan Africa would "recharge your batteries," he told her. Beth Anne telephoned DWH for a second opinion. DWH told her that she shouldn't replace an absent man with a dead one, even if the dead one were the Son of God.

"Are you sure *my* mom said that to your mom?" I wrote to Kelly in letter #1,308.

Kelly assured me that all of this had taken place.

Beth Anne had taken DWH's advice and stayed in Boiling Springs.

According to Kelly, Beth Anne lost her husband and her svelte daughter at around the same time. "By the end of 1993, I had re-fatted," Kelly wrote in letter #1,309. Kelly, who had been born with the same body type as her father, had wide hips and sturdy thighs and a barrel chest. Kelly calculated that she was exercising for more than 70 percent of her waking hours in order to keep herself at an acceptable size six. She gave up her gym membership and was very soon thereafter an unacceptable size sixteen again. In letter #1,310, I suggested a compromise, "Exercise for 20 percent of your waking hours and be a size twelve." But in all honesty, I loved Kelly re-fatted.

Over the past weeks, as we ate our lunches together, mostly in silence, with our letters to each other in our purses waiting to be read, we decided that Kelly needed a new job and a new wardrobe.

In a reversal of our roles, I took the lead and informed Kelly that Baby Harper could be her resource for both. We would begin with the inside of Baby Harper and Cecil's bedroom, I told her. We made plans to meet at the Greek Revival after she got off from work that day.

As Kelly had described it, the interior of Baby Harper and Cecil's bedroom was a jaw-dropping example of high camp. My great-uncle's adoration of *Gone With the Wind*, so chastely expressed downstairs in the deep green velvet of the divan, was up here in full ruffled-parasol bloom. The love that he felt for the other South was expressed in his use of tropical colors, which weren't exuberant but drunken. The walls were painted Peony Red and trimmed with Mango Tango. The ceiling was a splash of Pineapple Punch. Kelly and I both had the funny feeling that right before we opened the door to their bedroom there had been movement inside.

I headed over to a large walk-in closet, more of a small dressing room, and found inside exactly what I was hoping to find: a trove of exquisitely tailored dresses that were understated and modern and architectural and completely out of place in their present surroundings. Kelly, nonplussed by Baby Harper's postmortem confession, asked if I knew who his seamstress was. Kelly admired the tiny, even stitches and the touches of embroidery—mostly simple geometric shapes that resembled Mackintosh roses, which had been too small and subtle for me to see in the photographs. We agreed that we both had seen the rose design before but we couldn't remember where. Kelly tried on all the dresses, and I told her that she looked like a very chic museum curator, because she did. (I left out the part about how museum curators by definition had to find a new profession once their dress size exceeded a four, there being something about the art world that demanded, at least in their women, the nonexistence of body fat.)

It took another couple of days for us to locate where we first had seen the stylized roses that were embroidered on Baby Harper's dresses, usually just one or two right at the hem. We were over at Clay and Gregory's for dinner, and we spotted the same design at each corner of their tablecloth. Clay said that the table linens had been sewn by his uncle Cecil. Kelly and I looked at each other and knew that the funeral director had a postmortem secret or two of his own. Cecil Tobias Brandon, a.k.a. Mister T, was a discerning designer and sewer of plus-size women's clothing who had found his muse right here in the greater Boiling Springs–Shelby area.

As Gregory served us slices of end-of-the-season peach pie, I proposed that the Home of Eternal Rest should again provide its clients with a bereavement photographer. Clay agreed wholeheartedly but said that it had been a difficult position to fill. He had placed an ad in the Shelby *Star* but had gotten calls mostly from wedding photographers who wanted to make a bit of extra money. These photographers didn't seem to understand that the sensibility required was entirely different, Clay said.

I showed him the photographs that Kelly had taken at Baby Harper's memorial. She had shot both in color and in black-and-white film, which explained the two cameras around her neck that day. In these images, there was the person being photographed, and in their eyes there was an evocation of whom they were mourning. The only word that I could find to describe Kelly's photographs was "elegiac." Clay said that *that* was precisely right, and no other word was needed. Kelly got the job.

It was the third week of September, and our dinner tonight was to celebrate the last official day of summer. There was always something about those long hot days that encouraged us, whispered in our ears, to become someone new.

After Kelly and I said good night to Clay and Gregory, we decided that we didn't want to go home. The night was temperate and full of stars. She had a full tank of gas. I had twenty dollars in my wallet. We felt like we could go someplace and be somewhere. We decided that we would go to Shelby and sit on one of the benches in the courthouse square. We wanted to see the courthouse glow in the dark. We wanted to hear the leaves of the water oak trees rustle. We hoped that we wouldn't get arrested for loitering. We were pretty sure we weren't drunk.

Kelly parked the car on Main Street, and we walked out onto a movie set. The streets around the courthouse, which long ago had been turned into a museum, were empty. The cupola, domes, and columns struck fear into no one now except visiting schoolchildren, who were less fearful and more bored by what they found inside. The other three streets that made up the courthouse square, Lafayette, Washington, and Warren, were named for Revolutionary War heroes. The statue in front of the former courthouse, however, was erected in honor of the "Confederate Heroes of Cleveland County." The young man with the rifle in his hand looked out now at a red and gold sign for a Thai restaurant across the street, which, like the other restaurants and shops lining the streets of Shelby, was closed for the night. Kelly and I sat on a bench near the base of the statue, and we stared up at his tight britches, his rifle, and his hat. We were both thinking of another young man from these parts, whom we hadn't spoken of or written about in years.

Thanks to Kelly's recent letters, I was caught up on the news and the whereabouts of many of the members of the BSHS class of '86 and assorted others. Some of them had gone to Gardner-Webb with Kelly, some had attended other in-state schools or found work nearby, and the rest had disappeared into the vastness of the United States and reinvented themselves. What Kelly shared with me had offered little by way of surprises. "Homecoming Queen Sally Campbell lives in Shelby and is married to a doctor," Kelly wrote. "They have twins, and she is pregnant with her third. One of the three Kens is now an assistant principal at BSHS. Another of the Kens died in the Persian Gulf War." Chris Johnson, the third of the Kens, was one of the ones who had slipped away. Kelly had no information about him so I offered to fill in his biography for her. I sent this to Kelly:

"Chris Johnson, former BSHS student body president, attended Duke University, where he became the president of his fraternity. He majored in pre-law but during his junior year enrolled, on a dare, in an Introduction to Women's Studies course. He then switched his major, wrote a thesis entitled 'The Myth of the Southern Belle: A Construction and Reconstruction of Gender Differences and Accompanying Privileges,' graduated with honors, and will become the first openly gay professor to receive tenure at a small but prestigious liberal arts college in Georgia."

Kelly wrote back and demanded more. "What about the *other* Chris Johnson?" she asked. "He was in the class of '85, but surely Ms. Hammerick, the newly appointed Class Secretary, knows of his fate too," Kelly joked.

I sent her this:

"After graduation, Chris Johnson, a.k.a. the black Chris Johnson, arrived in Philadelphia with three hundred dollars in his pocket and his cousin's address. He found his cousin living in an apartment with one window and two folding chairs. For the privilege of sharing it, Chris would have to hand over his three hundred dollars. 'For the whole year?' Chris asked. 'No, for the month,' his cousin answered. Chris used his money to buy a bus ticket across country instead. He ended up in Bellevue, Washington, where he was hired in the mailroom of a company that made personal computers. A year later, the company went public and soon thereafter every one of their employees, including Chris, became millionaires."

Kelly wrote back that she was glad to know that stoner Chris was rich and most likely experiencing periods of happiness. She wanted to know about the other two stoners, the girl and the guy who dressed and looked like each other.

I sent her this:

"Susan Taylor put herself through night school and became a registered nurse. Tommy Miller joined the army and was given an honorable discharge. He is now an insurance executive. The high school sweethearts, who have both recently quit smoking, are now married and living in a two-bedroom condominium in Richmond, Virginia."

In letter #1,313, Kelly asked me if that was true. "That one didn't seem like a joke," she wrote.

"I have no idea what has happened to Susan and Tommy," I wrote back. "I just wanted for them a comfortable life unmarked by chronic unemployment, unwanted pregnancy, domestic violence, prolonged drug use, or the indignity of having to pump gas or clean house for a former homecoming queen."

"Sally wasn't as bad as all that," Kelly wrote. "You just never got to know her, Linda."

I let that topic drop. Kelly was right and wrong. I never knew Sally or the three Kens. Kelly, likewise, never knew Chris, Susan, or Tommy. BSHS was like a one-room schoolhouse. How we managed to avoid one another was an example of the highly choreographed dance that still kept us apart, a mystery to one another.

Of course, I knew it was significant that Kelly hadn't included Wade in her BSHS Who's Who. I waited patiently, reading about people whom I hadn't thought about since graduation and would never think about again. I waited, with less and less patience, making up the lives of those about whom Kelly had no information to keep myself amused and to pass the time. I waited till Kelly's silence finally confirmed what we had long known.

On a park bench in the first hours of the first day of fall, Kelly reached for my hand. We are going to get arrested for sure, I thought. Open displays of same-gender, transracial affection was certainly a misdemeanor of some kind. Kelly laughed, quick and sharp, when I said this to her. She took out of her purse a photograph and placed it on my lap. She also took from her purse a tiny flashlight, which she shone on the image: Luke, thirteen years old, tall and lanky, with a mop of disheveled hair, blond like his father's was when he had spent his days in the sun.

"He's such a beautiful*cherrycoughsyrup* boy, Kelly*cannedpeaches,*" I said, touching the photograph lightly with my fingertips.

"I told you*cannedgreenbeans* he looks just like his father," Kelly said, smiling.

"Has Wade*orangesherbet* met him?"

"No*grapejelly,* I haven't been in touch*cannedvegetablesoup* with Wade*orangesherbet* since he graduated from college."

"Really*popcorn*?" I asked.

"Really*popcorn.*" Kelly replied.

"Where did Wade*orangesherbet* graduate from?"

"I thought you*cannedgreenbeans* knew*peanutbutter.* He went to UNC at Chapel Hill*driedapricot* for a year. Then he transferred to Cooper*ambrosiasalad* Union in New*peanutbutter* York City. You*cannedgreenbeans* know*grapejelly,* it's free*ChipsAhoy!cookie* tuition there*applejuice* and all, so his father couldn't stop*cannedcorn* him. I'd no*grapejelly* idea*Swisscheese* Wade*orangesherbet* was interested*sloppyJoe* in art. Did you*cannedgreenbeans*—"

"Yes," I said, interrupting her.

If this were a movie, then this would be the moment with the sounds of crickets chirping.

"I'm sorry*glazeddoughnut,* Linda*mint,*" Kelly said.

"For*Triscuit* what*grahamcracker*?" I asked. What I meant was for which thing was she most sorry. Sleeping with Wade or for not telling me about it until now.

More crickets. Cue leaves rubbing themselves against the starlit dome of the sky.

"I didn't tell*brownsugar* you*cannedgreenbeans,*" Kelly continued, "because I never*bubblegum* told Wade*orangesherbet.* He knew*peanutbutter* that I was pregnant. I just never*bubblegum* told him that he was the father."

"Why the fuck*limesherbet* not?" I asked.

"Because—I'm sorry*glazeddoughnut* about this too—he didn't mean*raisin* that much to me. We were together only once. You*cannedgreenbeans* know*grapejelly,* what*grahamcracker* I mean*raisin*?"

"No*grapejelly*."

Crickets, leaves, the wings of bats disturbing the air above our heads as they flew from water oak tree to water oak tree.

"I think it's time*cottagecheese* to go*boiledcarrots,*" I said.

"No*grapejelly,*" Kelly replied.

"What*grahamcracker*?"

"I said no*grapejelly*. We're go*boiledcarrots*ing to sit here*hard-boiledegg* until you*cannedgreenbeans* for*Triscuit*give me, Linda*mint*."

"Well, you*cannedgreenbeans* better make yourself comfortable then."

Crickets, leaves, bat wings, and the sounds of our breaths going in and out of our bodies.

"Did you*cannedgreenbeans* know*grapejelly* about Wade*orange-sherbet* and me?" I asked finally.

"Yes," Kelly replied.

We sat on the park bench until the stars faded, until the birds began their songs, until cars began making their way slowly up and down the streets, their drivers still drowsy, rubbing sleep from their eyes. Kelly fell asleep with her head on my shoulder. I sat there, my eyes on the statue of the soldier, my ears full of the steady breathing of my best friend. I knew that she wasn't the cause for what I was feeling. Wade, the orange sherbet boy, had traveled to the city of our dreams. He had left this place and its people behind. So had I, I thought. The truth was that I believed that it was this place and its people who had kept the orange sherbet boy and me apart. That if Wade and I had grown up elsewhere, we would have become high school sweethearts, gone to the prom together, broken up during our first year away at different colleges, found each other again after graduation, and moved in together, living happily for at least some time. The truth was that the locus of our failure lay elsewhere. Our geography was only partially to blame.

Chapter 22

All families were an invention. Some families were machines. Some were gardens, full of topiaries or overgrown with milkweeds. Others were Trojan horses or other inspired works of art. Sinister or a thing of beauty, we often couldn't tell because we were too close to them to see. We created them with our bodies or with our will. We had children because they could be had. Biological or adopted, they were helpless and had little to say in how they would fit into the larger body. All children learned to adapt and thrive, or they died. Their first lessons of survival were learned within the home. Some children never grew up. Some hid within their own skin. Some shone like the sun or glowed cool like the moon. We added to our selves—we built our machines, tended to our gardens, created our objets d'art—because we desired, above all things, to outlive our bodies. We knew that when we died, our families—if no one else—would remember our faces and repeat our names. In that way, we lived on. But we failed to acknowledge our selfish desires. We spouted grandiose assessments of what we had done. *We gave you life,* we said to our children. *We saved your life,* we said to the children of other people whom we took into our homes.

Both statements were true. Both statements were the beginning of the story and not the story itself.

On the last night of summer, DWH had stayed home to host a dinner party of her own. She had her women over and they had me on their minds. I had been in Boiling Springs for almost two months by now, and DWH and I still hadn't gotten to the heart of the matter. Together, the women would come up with a plan.

On my first day of law school, a professor, all white hair and dark bow tie and pinstripes, had stood at the lectern of an arena-like classroom and declared that the Law was a spiderweb. He meant that there was no easy and obvious starting point. Everything about the Law was interconnected, interdependent, interwoven. I had thought of the professor's words every morning as DWH and I had inched closer to the center of our web with a question and then retreated again to its edge with a response.

I had asked DWH what it was like for her when Thomas passed away. Her response was an example of our progress and non-progress. She began by reminding me that they had been married for almost twenty-five years. She missed waking up to the sounds of him getting dressed in the morning. She missed the smell of his shaving cream in the bathroom. She missed the half a piece of toast that he left uneaten every morning. She missed the sound of his car door purposefully opening and closing, the bookends to her day. She missed seeing him at the head of the dinner table. She missed the easy chair with his newspapers neatly arranged at its feet. She missed hearing him snoring beside her in the middle of the night. DWH paused, took a deep breath, and confessed that after a couple of months of feeling this way she realized that it wasn't the same as missing *him.* I sat at the kitchen table, coffee cup in hand, on my plate a grapefruit half, emptied of its pulp, and I was speechless. DWH had become her mother's daughter. DWH had inherited the mantle of family truth teller. To claim that I wasn't unnerved by it would be a lie.

DWH and the women decided that if it was too difficult for her to begin at the beginning then she should begin at the end. The elegant symmetry of their reasoning took them by surprise. They celebrated by helping themselves to seconds of the homemade desserts that they had brought to the potluck dinner. They looked up to DWH, but none of them were foolish enough to allow her to cook for them. They feasted on spoonfuls of banana pudding, made with a meringue topping because it was for a party, after all. They sliced another wedge of lemon icebox pie, a summertime favorite because who wanted to turn on the oven at this time of the year? They were grateful, though, that Beth Anne had made the effort to bake, as her red velvet cake melted in their mouths and disappeared in the instant after DWH had thoughtfully set aside a slice for me to have for breakfast.

When Kelly dropped me off at the blue and gray ranch house, the sun had already risen. DWH was already in the kitchen with coffee brewed and waiting. The wedge of cake, sheathed in its tight plastic wrap, beckoned. I sat down and gave thanks for women like Beth Anne, who practiced the endangered art of baking (one day "baked from scratch" may sound as archaic and faraway as "alchemy"). I ate the cream cheese frosting first, and then as I tucked into the garnet sponge of the cake, DWH asked me whether Baby Harper had sent me the photographs. I concentrated on the moist crumb of the cake. I thought about how its flavors—butter, cocoa, and vanilla—had no relationship to its flamboyant color. Red was a decoy, a red herring, and with each bite there was a disconnect between expectation and reality. That was the main source of the cake's charm.

"Linda*mint,* did you*cannedgreenbeans* hear*hardboiledegg* me?" DWH asked.

I nodded my head.

"I'd asked Baby*honey* Harper*celery* to send them to you*canned-greenbeans*," she continued.

My heart was in my ears. Its beats were almost drowning out DWH's voice.

"Thomas*orangeNehi* loved*Nestea* her. I know*grapejelly* he did. That's why you*cannedgreenbeans* came to be with us," DWH began.

The story of my life, according to DeAnne Whatley Hammerick, began in the fall of 1955, thirteen years before I was born. Young Thomas, twenty-three years old, was in his third and last year of Columbia Law when he met a young woman named Mai-Dao. She was twenty years old and a senior at Barnard. She was a rare bird in his eyes. Young Thomas told her that he was from the South. She told him that she was from the South too. He, unlike many Americans at the time, knew that her country had been partitioned into North and South just the year before. Well, I would have never known; you don't have even a trace of a southern accent, he replied in his leisurely drawl. Then, he fell in love right there on the steps of Low Memorial Library, while the corridor of trees, which led from the street into the wide plaza before them, turned colors. He fell in love, even though Mai-Dao had told him that she was engaged to a young man back home. The school year ended, and she returned to her hometown and young Thomas to his. Before she left New York City, she gave him the photographs of their time together. What she couldn't say to him was that she couldn't keep the photographs. These things, if kept, were always found. They traded their mailing addresses, and he, like a teenage girl, promised to write. He did. He wrote to her many times after he returned home to Charlotte, once after he moved to Shelby, and one more time in 1960, on the day that he moved into the blue and gray ranch house in Boiling Springs with his new bride. Mai-Dao, like a teenage boy, didn't reply.

Over the years, as the name of Mai-Dao's country became a

household word even in Boiling Springs, Thomas couldn't see the news of her country's civil war, the deployment of U.S. troops there, and the body bags that returned without thinking of her. In 1968, the year that she gave birth to me, though he didn't know that back then, he thought of her as he watched her hometown—it was the southern capitol, so he thought that it would keep her safe—exploding on his television set. He hoped that she was far away from there. He imagined her back in New York City. He tried to imagine how her world had changed. He tried not to think about her, a married woman, as he was a married man.

On April 30, 1975, Thomas and DeAnne sat riveted in front of their television set as Dan Rather announced that Saigon was "now under Communist control." DeAnne remembered her husband closing his eyes and keeping them shut as he listened to the reporter announcing that Saigon had been renamed Ho Chi Minh City.

The letters addressed to Thomas began arriving at the blue and gray ranch house soon after. They were postmarked Chapel Hill, so DeAnne wouldn't have paid much attention to them, except for the foreign name in the return address.

Then came the telephone call on the night of July 5. It was 11:30 P.M., and DeAnne and Thomas were already side by side in bed. Thomas hung up the receiver and ran out of the house, still in his pajamas. DeAnne heard her husband's car door slam shut. When she heard his car door open, it was 4 P.M. the following day. She went to the front door of the blue and gray ranch house, and I was asleep in his arms.

Thomas had to tell DeAnne the story of my birth mother's life, or what he knew of it. That was DeAnne's precondition for agreeing to my adoption. DWH, the truth teller now, told me that she, in fact, didn't feel like she had a choice. Thomas had already made up his mind. She might as well get the whole story in the process, DeAnne thought. She also thought that it would be better (for her) if she made the decision then and there to believe that what her husband, Thomas, was telling her was true.

DeAnne asked to see the photographs. Then she asked to see the letters. She told Thomas that he had to throw everything away. He promised her that he would. He didn't. After he passed away, she found the photographs in his office. The letters she didn't find there. DWH said that when Thomas showed the letters to her she couldn't bring herself to read them. The handwriting was all curves and delicate loops, and all she could imagine was the body of the woman who wrote the words. DeAnne made Thomas read the letters aloud to her. So as I slept in the guest bedroom of their house, Thomas and DeAnne sat at the kitchen table and talked for the remainder of the day.

Mai-Dao wrote her first letter to Thomas on May 1, 1975, one day after the fall of Saigon. Mai-Dao had been in Chapel Hill for almost a year already. Her husband, Khanh, an assistant professor of economics at the University of Saigon, was a postdoctoral fellow at UNC, and after much bribing and string-pulling back in Saigon, she and their six-year-old daughter had been able to join Khanh in September of '74. Mai-Dao took with her to Chapel Hill the last letter that Thomas had sent to her in Saigon. Since the first day of her arrival in his home state, she had been taking mental notes of what she liked about his South, so that she could share them with him. Then she reread his letter, dated December 10, 1960—*he'd written to her on our wedding day, Linda*—and the letter reminded Mai-Dao that she knew nothing about his life in the fourteen years since then. Thomas must be a very different man now, Mai-Dao thought. So she set aside the idea of writing to him and tried as best as she could to settle into her new temporary home, a trailer that Khanh had rented for them in order to make the most of his small monthly stipend. She thought it was a storage shed when they first drove up to it. The interior was the size and width of a corridor in the three-story villa that her father had given to them as a wedding present back in Saigon. Khanh reminded her of how lucky they were to be here and not there.

That became her mantra in the months to come: lucky to be here and not there. She enrolled her daughter in the first grade and was amazed at how quickly a young child could pick up a new language, like it was just a shiny new toy. Mai-Dao audited classes in the art history department of UNC and thought often about traveling up to New York City and seeing the Metropolitan Museum of Art again and, of course, her beloved Central Park. Khanh told her that there was no money for such a pleasure trip. She looked at her husband, amazed at how the young man who had shown up for their dates in a chauffeured car had changed. She couldn't have imagined that he would become so serious and practical, with worry lines cut deep into his forehead. Lucky to be here and not there, she reminded herself. She went to the library and checked out a cookbook—the first one she had ever read—and fed her husband and daughter American-style meals, which the cookbook author, Betty Crocker, assured her were both economical and nutritious. Mai-Dao wasn't a very good cook, so every once in a while she and her daughter would go to the supermarket and indulge in the American snack foods and sodas that she had missed so dearly when she was in Saigon. "Thomas, did you know that there is a soda in Vietnam that tastes exactly like Dr Pepper?" Mai-Dao asked, in the first of her eight letters to him. *I don't know why, Linda, but that always stuck in my head. Maybe because of your grandma. You know how she drank that stuff like water.*

On April 30, 1975, Mai-Dao and Khanh and their young daughter had sat in their rented trailer home in front of a small TV set, one of the few things they owned outright here, and had watched in disbelief as "there" disappeared. Mai-Dao started to cry when she saw the word YESTERDAY appear at the bottom of the tiny screen, the white text superimposed over the footage of the evacuation of Saigon. Khanh whispered in her ear that she shouldn't cry in front of their daughter. Mai-Dao stopped, though she knew that it wouldn't change a thing. Her father was a general in the army. Khanh's father was one as well. When Dan Rather reported that South Vietnamese servicemen and their families were among the seventy thousand South Vietnamese who had made it safely to Thailand, Khanh turned to his wife and said that they would hear something from their families soon.

How? she wondered. Who would have had the forethought in the chaos of an evacuation to write down the address of a son and daughter who were lucky enough to be in a city called Chapel Hill? Even its name sounded distant and safe, Mai-Dao thought.

Over the next day or two, while her husband went to his office at the university to make the necessary telephone calls, listing their names with the International Red Cross, and trying to reach his distant relatives in Paris, Mai-Dao tried to keep herself from thinking about her mother being shoved and pushed into a helicopter or into a boat—*if* my mother was lucky, Mai-Dao reminded herself—by cleaning the trailer home, washing every item of clothing that the three of them owned at the Laundromat, and writing a long, belated letter to Thomas. "I'm here with my husband and my daughter" was how Mai-Dao began her letter. *Thomas choked up when he read those words to me, Linda. I could have told him to stop reading, but I didn't.*

DWH had been speaking very slowly, pausing in between words, stopping in midsentence. The incomings, given such a cadence, were acute and more assertive than usual, as if the tastes triggered by the words literally had more time to sink in. I had to excuse myself from the kitchen table. I went into the living room and telephoned Kelly at the Greek Revival. I asked her to bring over a bottle of whatever she had. It wasn't even noon, but Kelly, in true form, didn't ask why, didn't sound a bit surprised, and came by the blue and gray ranch house in less than fifteen minutes with a bottle of bourbon, two-thirds full. Kelly came to the back door of the house, said good morning to DWH through the screen door, handed me the bottle thoughtfully hidden inside of a fancy shopping bag underneath a layer of tissue paper, and was on her way again after she had squeezed my hands so hard that my fingers almost went white.

I poured for myself a juice glass full of bourbon and asked DWH if she wanted one as well. I couldn't remember at that moment whether I had explained to DWH about the ameliorative effects of alcohol. We had discussed cigarettes and their effects on my condition during our morning talks, but I wasn't sure whether the topic of alcohol or sex had reached the breakfast table yet. It didn't matter, because DWH answered yes. *You know, your grandma loved to mix that stuff with her Dr Pepper.*

Iris's truth serum of choice, I thought.

Thomas, according to DWH, admitted that he immediately wrote back to Mai-Dao. He glossed over the contents of his letter, except to say that he had included his telephone number and had asked Mai-Dao to call him. She never did, but she did send a second letter to him at the blue and gray ranch house. *Your grandma told me that meant that he'd never been unfaithful to me before. A cheating man would've known to give his office number and mailing address, your grandma said.* Mai-Dao wrote that there was still no news about her or her husband's families. For once in her life she didn't mind so much that she was an only child. Her husband, Khanh, was unable to sleep or eat, worrying about his five younger brothers and their wives and children. In the middle of the night, Khanh would be in his office on campus trying to telephone them, one number after the other. Their lines had all been cut. How soon after the end of a war does the telephone service resume, Mai-Dao wondered. How about mail delivery? She didn't know these answers, but she wrote to her mother and father every day just in case they were there waiting to receive word from her. Mai-Dao thought often about her favorite building in Saigon, the Central Post Office, and she wondered if it had survived the last days of the war in one piece.

Mai-Dao wrote to Thomas that she felt guilty that she was worrying about a building, even if it was one designed by Gustave Eiffel, when the people who had gathered there were now so scattered and unaccounted for. She felt so guilty that she wouldn't dream of sharing these thoughts with her husband. Her daughter was too young, of course, to understand. Mai-Dao wrote that she was grateful that she had Thomas for a friend.

Thomas responded to Mai-Dao's second letter, asking her if he could come to Chapel Hill to see her. *I knew he didn't want to admit that to me, but he had to. That's how much he wanted you, Linda.*

Mai-Dao sent back a third letter, this one short and unequivocal. She wrote that a face-to-face visit wasn't a good idea right now. Maybe when things were more settled. Still not a word from my family or Khanh's, Mai-Dao added. Thomas swore to DeAnne that he never drove the 191 miles from Boiling Springs to Chapel Hill, until he received the telephone call summoning him there. He continued to write to Mai-Dao, though.

In her fourth letter to Thomas, Mai-Dao thanked him for his generous offer, but she thought that she and Khanh would be able to manage. *Thomas admitted that he had offered to send her money, Linda. He said he would have told me, if he had.* Mai-Dao wrote that she had found a part-time job at the main library on the UNC campus and was working during the hours when her daughter was at her summer school. The job kept her from thinking, which was what she wanted right now. The extra money was helping out too. Mai-Dao asked Thomas if his wife worked outside the house. *I knew he hadn't brought me up once in his letters. She had to.* Mai-Dao wanted to know because she was surprised at how much her husband had objected to the idea. Khanh had never been that sort of a man, not a dinosaur by any means. Khanh was caring, thoughtful, and one of the most intelligent men she had ever met. *It must have hurt Thomas to read that—the first time to himself and then again to me.* Still no word from our families, Mai-Dao wrote. Every night Mai-Dao dreamed that she was aboard an airplane that was about to land at the Saigon airport. The plane circled low over the southern capital, so low that she could see the red roof of the Opera House and the twin spires of the Basilica, the wide boulevards, and the cramped alleyways. Every night, she realized too late that it was a nightmare because the plane she was on would never land.

Thomas thought it was time that he became more involved. It was already the beginning of June. A month had passed since the fall of Saigon, and Mai-Dao and her husband still had no news about their families. Thomas wrote to Mai-Dao and offered another type of assistance, one that he knew she couldn't turn down. He asked for the names of her mother and father and of the immediate members of Khanh's family as well. Thomas wrote to Mai-Dao that he would contact a family friend who was a congressman. This man could make the right phone calls, Thomas assured Mai-Dao. *Willie Hoyle had just been elected to his first term, Linda. I know it's hard to imagine, but back then we thought that Willie could really get things done.*

Mai-Dao's fifth letter arrived soon after, and it was only a couple of lines long. Thomas knew that he had overstepped again. Mai-Dao wrote that Khanh thanked Thomas for the offer of assistance, but Khanh felt that this was a family matter. If Thomas would be so kind as to send them the name of the congressman, Khanh would contact the gentleman directly to inquire about what resources he and his office could extend to them. Thomas knew from the formal tone of the letter that Mai-Dao wrote the letter but that Khanh was either looking over her shoulders or dictating it. Thomas confessed to DeAnne that he had wanted to go to Chapel Hill right then and there and talk man-to-man with Khanh, to talk some sense into him.

Reasonable Man–to–Reasonable Man, I thought.

Before Thomas could write back, Mai-Dao's sixth letter arrived at the blue and gray ranch house. It was five pages long. This one was really from her, Thomas knew. She apologized for her previous letter. She confirmed that Khanh had asked her to write it, and she blamed its content on Khanh's lack of sleep. Her husband was becoming irritable and somewhat irrational, she wrote. He had been threatening to buy a plane ticket to go to Thailand to search for their families. Mai-Dao had to remind Khanh that he held a passport issued by the Republic of Vietnam, a country more commonly known as South Vietnam and one that no longer existed under either name. If Khanh, now a citizen of nowhere, left the United States, he might never be able to return.

Lucky to be here and not there, I thought.

Khanh, a man who rarely raised his voice in anger, yelled at Mai-Dao that night. He didn't need to be reminded of the obvious, he screamed at her. But he did, Mai-Dao insisted in her letter to Thomas. She wrote that she had brought up Thomas's offer to contact a congressman in the hopes of calming Khanh down. Her failure to anticipate Khanh's reaction she blamed on her own lack of sleep. Otherwise, she would have known, would have kept Thomas's offer to herself for another day, and sat there silently by her husband's side instead. Khanh demanded to know how she knew Thomas Hammerick, and how long the two of them had been keeping in touch. Khanh assumed the worst, that he had been cuckolded from the first day of their marriage, and that there had been other men. Mai-Dao sat there, stunned. When she became engaged, her mother had warned her that no man wanted to know about a woman's past. Her mother told her that it was best to pretend that you have been reborn, an innocent baby in his arms. Her mother, Mai-Dao wrote to Thomas, was always right. *You might want to take another sip, Linda. Just bring the bottle to the table.* Mai-Dao wrote that the worst part of the argument was that their daughter, Linh-Dao, was in the trailer and had heard everything that Khanh had said. The girl from birth had been a quiet child, so quiet that sometimes they would forget that she was in the room. Mai-Dao asked Thomas if he had any children of his own. *All those letters, Linda, and he hadn't told her anything about our marriage.*

Thomas saw that this sixth letter from Chapel Hill had a different return address. Mai-Dao had used her work address at the UNC library. He wrote back to her there. Thomas told DeAnne that he expressed his regret for the misunderstanding that had taken place between Mai-Dao and her husband. Thomas, however, reminded Mai-Dao that she didn't need her husband's permission to proceed. With or without Khanh's approval and cooperation, Thomas could still approach the congressman for assistance. Thomas urged her to send him a list of names immediately, but if she really wanted Khanh to make the call, enclosed was Congressman Hoyle's phone number and mailing address.

Thomas waited two and a half weeks before he received his seventh letter from Mai-Dao. Her letter wasn't what he had hoped for. There was no list of names. There was no "Thomas, I will call you soon." There was no "Thomas, I will see you in Chapel Hill." There was only news about Khanh's family. His youngest brother, Trac, and his wife were among the refugees who had made it to Thailand. There was still no news of the whereabouts of Khanh's four other brothers and their families. Trac had made contact with their second cousin in Paris, who had telephoned Khanh.

According to their second cousin, Trac and Khanh's father had shot himself in the early-morning hours of April 29. Their mother had refused to leave her husband's body alone and unburied when Trac came for them. Khanh received the news of his father's death with a kind of stoicism that surprised Mai-Dao. Khanh immediately concluded that it was better that way. A proud man like his father couldn't have survived a subjugated life, he told her.

What about your mother, Mai-Dao wanted to ask Khanh. Mai-Dao confided in Thomas that she felt that suicide was a cowardly act. Her father-in-law had deserted the woman who had been by his side for the past thirty years, who had borne him six sons, and whom he knew would be tethered to his body until the end of her days.

The news that Khanh didn't take as well was Trac's desire to emigrate to France instead of joining him in the United States. According to their second cousin, Trac felt that the United States had abandoned and betrayed South Vietnam. How could I live *there,* Trac had asked their kinsman. Khanh lost his temper when he repeated to Mai-Dao this part of the long-distance conversation. France colonized and humiliated us for eighty years, Khanh yelled at Mai-Dao. Had Trac forgotten *that*? Trac should have just stayed *there,* if he was so stupid and proud.

Or he should have just shot himself like your father, Mai-Dao thought and kept to herself. She wrote it in her seventh letter to Thomas, though. She also wrote that it made her feel guilty to do so, to send and receive personal letters at her place of work, hiding away more and more parts of herself. This wasn't how she had ever imagined her life to be.

Thomas, as was his habit by then, wrote back to Mai-Dao immediately. He didn't receive her eighth and last letter to him until July 7. Thomas wasn't the first person to read the letter. DeAnne was. *It was now my business too, Linda.*

On July 6, as the sun was beginning to set, DeAnne had agreed to my adoption. DeAnne told Thomas that her second precondition was that they would never speak about my birth parents again. *Otherwise how could I learn to love you, Linda?*

DWH remembered the letter shaking in her hands. DeAnne saw again the handwriting that seemed to her so alive with another woman's body and movement. The letter was only half a page long but full of sadness. Mai-Dao wrote that Khanh had found the letters that Thomas had sent to her and again had accused her of adultery. Khanh said that if it weren't for their daughter, he would leave her. Mai-Dao thanked Thomas for his kindness and his friendship, and she apologized for all the years in Saigon in which she had ignored his letters. She wanted him to know that she had kept all of his letters back then as well. Mai-Dao then asked Thomas not to write to her again. She would be in touch again in the near future, she promised. Mai-Dao's letter was postmarked July 3, 1975.

The bottle of bourbon was bone dry. The afternoon was almost gone. The late-afternoon sunlight was making every growing thing in the backyard look as if it were lit from within. All the windows in the blue and gray ranch house were wide open, letting in the sounds of birds and lawn mowers and the occasional passing car. The temperature inside and outside was the same, a rare equilibrium that we registered as the feeling of being comfortable in our own skin. DeAnne Whatley Hammerick and I were still the same. We didn't break into two or three or four pieces. Our limbs were all accounted for. Our internal organs were pumping and filtering. We were a bit light-headed, but that was just the bourbon talking. DWH and I, finally, had begun the complicated process of doing something that most people, especially a mother and a daughter, could never seem to do. We were forgiving each other for who we were, for how we came into this world, for how we changed or didn't change it for each other.

The story of my birth parents' final days in Chapel Hill was what my grandmother Iris, the secret bourbon drinker, had thought would break me in two. On her deathbed, my grandmother thought of these two people whom she had never met but who had changed her family, reinvented it in a way that she couldn't have foreseen.

DWH had skipped past the story of Khanh and Mai-Dao's death because she had no idea what really took place. I was the one who was there, the only one who had survived. But to bear witness I had to remember. What took place inside that trailer home in the days and hours and minutes before the fire on the night of July 5, 1975, was lost to me. Whoever carried me out, his or her face was blank to me. Whoever stayed inside, by force or by choice, became strangers to me. The years of my life with them, the life before *this* life, had been erased or, rather, my memories of them had been erased by my benevolent brain. The last word that this man or this woman had said to me was the only thing that remained, as a taste of bitter in my mouth. A fire had made everything else about them disappear.

This was what Thomas told his wife:

The firemen had found me on the gravel driveway of the adjacent trailer home. I was in a nightgown. I was wrapped in a sheet. I appeared to be sound asleep while a fire ate its way through the narrow corridor that I had called home. Tucked inside the pocket of my nightgown were my passport and the first letter that Thomas had sent to Mai-Dao in Chapel Hill, the one with the phone number of the blue and gray ranch house, which she had never dialed. A Chapel Hill police officer telephoned Thomas instead.

Thomas claimed me. He told the police and the social worker that night that he was related to Mai-Dao by marriage. That his cousin, who had died in the war—*that was the only part of the story that Thomas told that was true, Linda; his cousin Brett Hammerick died in the battle of Khe Sanh*—had been married to Mai-Dao's sister in Saigon. That no one on the American side of the family knew of their marriage. That the Vietnamese side of the family was all in Saigon, unaccounted for and unreachable. Thomas told DeAnne that it had been instinctual. He didn't mean the instinct to lie. He meant the desire to bring me home. A child needed a father and a mother, he said to DeAnne.

As Thomas recounted his sudden dash toward fatherhood, DeAnne sat at their kitchen table and thought about what he had told her years ago when they were still dating. Not all men have to become fathers, Thomas had assured her. They wouldn't need to have children in order to be a family, he had agreed with her. *I never thought I would hear a man say these things to me, Linda.* Though I had assumed otherwise, DeAnne had known from the time that she was in her early twenties that she didn't want to have children. *I didn't want to become another Iris, Linda.* Her mother, Iris, had told her that no man would think that was natural. DeAnne thought that meant that she would be alone for the rest of her life. But then she met Thomas, and he had made her believe that her fate would be different. Thomas, in a way, had kept his promise to her.

DWH told me that she was completely unprepared for motherhood. She was glad that I was such a quiet child. She admitted that during the first few years of my life at the blue and gray ranch house she sometimes would pretend that I wasn't there. She would close her eyes and imagine that everything had stayed exactly the same. This became more difficult to do as I grew older. *Thomas loved you so much, Linda.* What DWH meant was that as I grew older I began to look more and more like the young Vietnamese woman whom her husband had loved. As the years passed, the second precondition to my adoption—that they would never speak about my birth father or mother again—did little to alleviate this fact. Thomas and DeAnne didn't have to mention my birth mother's name. When I was in the house, Mai-Dao was in the house. As the years passed, though, the second precondition was what Thomas and DeAnne clung to. One silence had led to another, and eventually the silences became the life preservers dotting the dangerous ocean between them. In this way, Thomas and DeAnne survived.

DWH said that she had turned to Iris for comfort, though she knew that there would be little there but truth.

And you also turned to Bobby. This thought didn't keep me from reaching over the kitchen table and holding on to DWH's hands. I was understanding for the first time how lonely DeAnne must have felt in the blue and gray ranch house, even when Thomas and I had been around.

Iris told DeAnne that to have a child was to enter into a contract. The judge's wife explained to her daughter the basic concepts of contract law: promise, obligation, and duty. Iris, the truth teller, said that love wasn't required. In a pinch, "like" would do.

Thomas turned to Baby Harper. He entrusted my great-uncle with Mai-Dao's letters. DWH told me that after my great-uncle passed away she had found them in the bureau in his bedroom. *I've a set of extra keys to his house. Your great-uncle was always sweet on Thomas. We always keep the secrets of those we love.* DWH said that the letters were waiting for me now on the hallway table.

Of course, I had wondered how DeAnne Whatley Hammerick could have remembered in such plaintive details the contents of all those long-ago letters. I had thought, in between our sips of bourbon, that she could be making this all up. I decided that it didn't matter. At least it was a story, I thought. We all need a story of where we came from and how we got here. Otherwise, how could we ever put down our tender roots and stay.

ACKNOWLEDGMENTS

I am indebted to the following for the gift of a beautiful space and a vibrant community in which to write: Ledig House International Writers Residency, the MacDowell Colony, Santa Maddalena Foundation, Bogliasco Foundation's Liguria Study Center for the Arts and Humanities, Ucross Foundation, Hall Farm Center for Arts and Education, Lannan Foundation, and Hedgebrook. This book would not have been possible without the generosity of Bard College, New York Public Library Young Lions, PEN/Robert Bingham Fellowship, and Princeton University's Hodder Fellowship.

Here's to the early believers and chance takers: Elaine Koster, Janet Silver, and Martin Hielscher. I am grateful to have you on my side.

Here's to the intrepid first readers and volunteer fact-checkers: Barbara Tran, David Eng, Trac Vu, Quang Bao, Benjamin Anastas, Dora Wang, Deborah Ottenheimer, and Kristin Brenneman Eno. I owe you a dinner. Please don't come collecting all at once.

Here's to the team at Random House: Kate Medina, Sally Marvin, Jynne Martin, Avideh Bashirrad, Lindsey Schwoeri, Amy Edelman, and Vincent La Scala. Thanks for giving this book a home.

Most of all, I am grateful to Damijan Saccio. I would be lost without you.

Bitter in the Mouth

Monique Truong

A Reader's Guide

HOW A MOCKINGBIRD GAVE BIRTH TO A LITTLE CANARY

"An' they chased him 'n' never could catch him 'cause they didn't know what he looked like, an' Atticus, when they finally saw him . . . he was real nice. . . ."

His hands were under my chin, pulling up the cover, tucking it around me.

"Most people are, Scout, when you finally see them."

The epigraph for *Bitter in the Mouth* is an exchange between Scout and her father, Atticus Finch, which appears on the last page of the closing chapter of Harper Lee's *To Kill a Mockingbird.* For Scout, "him" is a reference to a character in *The Gray Ghost,* a favorite book of hers and her brother, Jem, which Atticus is reading to ease her into sleep. For us, "him" is also Boo Radley, the sequestered subject of the Finch siblings' childhood curiosities and fears who had emerged to save them from the very real evils that inhabit their town. "Him," in addition, could be a myriad of characters in *To Kill a Mockingbird* who are occluded by hearsay, lies, illness, poverty, racial prejudice, or plain old ignorance. The blinders are so many, and Scout is just beginning to recognize them as the novel ends.

When I first read *To Kill a Mockingbird,* I was eleven years old, a little older than Scout and not as old as Jem. I don't think I read the book for a school assignment. I was a voracious reader and probably picked it out on my own from the library. My family was living in Centerville, Ohio, by then. I can still remember my father boasting to my mother that our new, solidly middle-class neighborhood was once home to Erma Bombeck *and* Phil Donahue. What my father meant was, Look how far we've come! And we really had.

In 1975 my family had come to the United States as refugees from the Vietnam War, and now there we were, four years later, sharing the same sight lines of detached houses with their well-tended lawns bordered by impatiens and yew shrubs that the media elites had had of the Midwest before they made it big and moved elsewhere. Never mind. My father still had a point.

Centerville, Ohio, was a world away from Boiling Springs, North Carolina, the first place in the United States we had called home.

On the pages of *To Kill a Mockingbird*, I must have noted the similarities between Scout's hometown of Maycomb, Alabama, circa 1935, and Boiling Springs, North Carolina, circa 1975. The azaleas, the screened porches, the respect afforded to the baker of a really good layer cake, among all the other details, must have sounded just right to me. The leafy oak trees and the courthouse square must have reminded me of the same at the heart of nearby Shelby. I must have found in Atticus's words and actions a primer for understanding why the children of my small Southern town had taunted me for the color of my skin. Before I came to the United States, I didn't even know that my skin had a color, and I could have never imagined that the color would be "yellow."

I write "must have" because I'm not certain of what I actually took away from the complex, multi-themed *To Kill a Mockingbird* after my first read of it. Except for this: I remember reading in my bedroom and experiencing the uncanny feeling that if I pulled the curtains back from the windows I would see the streets of Maycomb. Of course, I now can say that Harper Lee's writing—

so clear, precise, and pointed—had "transported" me into Scout's milieu, but at the age of eleven I just knew that the feeling was akin to magic, and that a book had cast the spell.

I've read *To Kill a Mockingbird* many times since, and each time I find something new, something that thrills me as a reader and a writer. I'm uncomfortable describing it as a "coming of age" novel, because to me it's so much more. Unless "coming of age" means, in fact, a heartbreaking indictment of the flawed world that adults have created for their children to inherit. The genre probably does mean that, and perhaps that's why these narratives that we read in our youth mean so much to us and stay with us for the rest of our lives like the truest of friends.

When I decided to set *Bitter in the Mouth* in the American south, I immediately turned to *To Kill a Mockingbird* for inspiration. I also read Truman Capote's first novel, *Other Voices, Other Rooms.* It's a perfect companion read with Lee's novel, as Capote and Lee were friends from childhood and he was the real-life inspiration for the character Dill, the impish instigator who brightened the long summers for Scout and Jem.

As I re-read, I was reminded of how Scout is an absolute credit to her nickname. She's smart, outspoken, independent, and brave. She's everything that a girl should be in 1935, 1975, 2011, and beyond. Lee's characterization of Scout made me think about how many of us girls begin our youth this way, and how these interior traits—so delicate because they are just forming—get clumsily and cruelly chipped away. How the focus of attention is then too quickly directed toward the outside of our bodies. I began to think about my characters, Linda Hammerick and Kelly Powell, as coming from the same bright, sturdy stock as Scout, and that these three girls would have been fast friends.

I re-read, I also underlined this sentence from the first chapter of *To Kill a Mockingbird*: "There were other ways of making people into ghosts." The statement is attributed to Atticus. It's his response to Jem's heated speculation that Boo Radley must be kept inside of his house with chains or other forms of intimidation. I hadn't remembered ever reading that sentence before. That's one of the pleasures of re-reading for me. The text of a well-written book remains very much alive, offering up different parts of itself, or perhaps I, very much alive and changing, am newly receptive to passages that have previously been eclipsed.

Boo Radley is Lee's most evocative creation. He has his counterparts in most, if not all, Southern Gothic novels. Boo Radley belongs to a long line of shrouded, hidden, secreted away, or for some other reason "unseen" characters who are the embodiments of the anxieties, fears, and violations of the norms of the family, the community, and the greater world around them. In Capote's *Other Voices, Other Rooms,* for instance, the figure in the shadows is the feminine alter persona of Uncle Randolph.

While re-reading *Mockingbird,* I began to think more about what it means to set a novel in the American South, and how I could contribute to a genre that has already given readers so many of the defining narratives of the region. By the time I reached the last page of it, and the passage that would become the epigraph for my own novel, I was asking myself this question: What if the narrator, Linda, was the family secret? How would she "reveal" herself to the readers, and how would that unmasking change how her story is ultimately understood? In short, who do we see when we "finally see" her?

The closing exchange between Scout and Atticus sparkled anew for me for another reason as well. In my mind, "him" was Boo Radley and the other characters in *To Kill a Mockingbird.* I had forgotten until I re-read the passage that Scout was actually referring to a character in *The Gray Ghost.* I did a bit of quick research and found that it was a real book, part of the once popular Seckatary Hawkins series of children books written by Robert F. Schulkers.

That Harper Lee is one cheeky writer. Her main character learns an important, indelible life lesson from a book on the last page of her own book. What elegant symmetry! Why hadn't I seen it before? What an apt way to affirm the inherent power of reading and reading young.

Monique Truong
January 2011

QUESTIONS AND TOPICS FOR DISCUSSION

1. *Bitter in the Mouth* is a novel that invites us to consider what it means to be a family. How are families defined and constructed within its pages?

2. Linda Hammerick begins her story with her great-uncle Harper because she believes that "a family narrative should begin with love." How does her great uncle, AKA Baby Harper, help her to understand what it means to be loved? Pg. 142, 132, 121, 157, 185

3. Linda's "secret sense," auditory-gustatory synesthesia, causes her to taste words. How does her unusual relationship with "the word" shape Linda's personality and life? What other characters in the novel have a unique relationship to "the word"?

4. According to Linda, "We keep secrets to protect, but the ones most shielded—from shame, from judgment, from the slap in the face—are ourselves. We are selfish in our secret keeping and rarely altruistic. We act out of instinct and survival and only when we feel safest will we let our set of facts be known." Consider the secrets that are kept in the novel and by whom. Do these instances prove Linda's assertion or disprove it?

5. Linda's grandmother Iris is the "family truth teller." What are the examples of Iris telling us the truth in the first half of the novel? Did you understand them to be "truths," or were they, in a way, hidden in plain sight?

6. Linda Hammerick and Kelly Powell have been best friends since the age of seven. What did they have in common that brought them together?

7. "Fat is not fate." This is one of the ways that Linda distinguishes herself from her best friend, Kelly. What is fate, then? What are the examples of fate in *Bitter in the Mouth*?

8. Author Monique Truong states that "while my first novel, *The Book of Salt,* features an unreliable narrator, *Bitter in the Mouth* is a novel that plays with the idea of the unreliable reader." She goes on to say that "the first half of *Bitter* is constructed as an invitation to the reader to fill in the blanks." What do you think Truong means by this? What were the blanks in Linda's story, and how did you fill them in? Did you fill in the blanks based on the stories that Linda tells about her immediate family, your own life experiences, or perhaps on what you know about the author of the novel?

9. In the second half of the novel, Linda reveals a significant part of her life story to us. Did the revelation of this fact change the way that you understand her and her story? Did you go back and re-read the first half of the novel? If yes, what did you see that you did not see upon the first reading?

10. Consider your first impression of Linda. Although her synesthesia is a rare neurological condition, were there still ways in which you found yourself relating to her sense (pun intended) of being different and disconnected from her family and from the other children in Boiling Springs?

11. What if the author had switched the order of how she told you Linda's story? In other words, what if "Revelation" came before "Confession," and you were presented with the opportunity to identify and to relate to Linda based on her external difference first, as opposed to her internal difference. Consider how your own identification with Linda would have been different. Would it have been lessened or heightened or unaffected?

12. Linda tells us that her first memory was a word that triggered a bitter taste. What word do you think it was and who spoke it? What are the clues that lead you to the word?

13. Is Linda Hammerick a Southerner? Is *Bitter in the Mouth* a Southern novel? Why or why not?

PHOTO: © MARION ETTLINGER

MONIQUE TRUONG was born in Saigon and currently lives in New York City. Her first novel, *The Book of Salt*, was a *New York Times* Notable Book. It won the New York Public Library Young Lions Fiction Award, the 2003 Bard Fiction Prize, the Stonewall Book Award–Barbara Gittings Literature Award, and the Seventh Annual Asian American Literary Award, and was a finalist for the Lambda Literary Award and Britain's Guardian First Book Award. She is the recipient of the PEN/Robert Bingham Fellowship, Princeton's Hodder Fellowship, and a 2010 Guggenheim Fellowship.

About the Type

This book was set in Caslon, a typeface first designed in 1722 by William Caslon. Its widespread use by most English printers in the early eighteenth century soon supplanted the Dutch typefaces that had formerly prevailed. The roman is considered a "workhorse" typeface due to its pleasant, open appearance, while the italic is exceedingly decorative.